Ancient Echoes

Revised Edition

Ancient Echoes

Series Book 1

Barbara Monahan

AuthorHouse™ LLC
1663 Liberty Drive
Bloomington, IN 47403
www.authorhouse.com
Phone: 1-800-839-8640

Published by AuthorHouse 07/30/2013

ISBN: 978-1-4634-7433-1 (sc)
ISBN: 978-1-4634-7434-8 (e)

Library of Congress Control Number: 2011915081

This book is printed on acid-free paper.

ANCIENT ECHOES SERIES, BOOK ONE

Samantha screamed for her life as she ran from the wolf, its glowing red eyes filled with hatred as it chased her in a relentless battle for her very soul. Long white fangs gleamed in the moonlight, as it snarled its intent. Razor sharp nails reached out to her, trying to rip the flesh from her body again and again.

She tore the branches from her face as she raced through the thick green foliage, the demonic creature hot on her trail, snapping and snarling as it chased her over the rough terrain.Even the vines that slithered along the slippery rock were like evil tendrils taking on a life of their own, trying to wrap themselves around her ankles as she ran. Her lungs were burning, about to burst. She looked up through the thick foliage blocking her view. The wind howled as it blew across the barren fields, reminding her that evil was all around her. She was just out of reach of the crumbling castle. Just a few more seconds, and she'd be safe.

She could go no further, her body spent, searing waves of agony overtaking her small aching frame. Then she saw him, standing on the step of the castle, surrounded by an aura of complete control and power. Strange blue eyes stared at her, through to her very soul. She was safe, every battered ounce of her body knew it.

Extending his left palm toward the creature, he uttered an ancient word, his voice filled with authority. Instantly, pure white hot energy shot from his hand toward the creature, destroying it immediately. As if it never existed, the demon dissipated into thin air, leaving only a thin trace of black smoke and rancid smell. She reach out to him in desperation, her final hope, then all went black.

CHAPTER ONE

Boston U.S.A.
Present day

Samantha still vividly remembers that ominous morning late in July when the doorbell rang. A letter was being delivered to her, one which needed her signature. Looking back, it still seems unreal, finding that she alone had been named sole heiress of a long forgotten crumbling castle in northern Scotland.

Someone had left her an incredible fortune, but for some unknown reason wished to remain anonymous. The only hitch was that she alone was to use the extravagant sum, and only on renovations of a specific castle in the Highlands of Scotland, now in total disrepair. The Will stipulated that she come to Scotland alone, with no accompanying family members or friends.

Rosestone Castle, which had been initially constructed sometime in the late first century, was now nothing more than a forgotten rock pile, sitting high atop a large plateau overlooking the North Sea. The castle was located on a considerable stretch of much sought after real estate in northern Scotland. It hadn't even made it to the tourist's list of castles for the curious sightseer.

Samantha and her family also found it strange that it stood for the most part unnoticed, for over 500 years. Absolutely no one had taken any interest in it, or the land it was on, for centuries. It was as if it never even existed.

Bordering on the northeast coast of Scotland, its view of the North Sea was breathtaking. For centuries, this desolate area of ancient rocks had been left untouched, its true owners remaining a mystery throughout the ages, to the present day. Now, a big international company was intent on purchasing the considerable piece of property. The plans were to clear the remains of the castle, and develop a multimillion dollar business on the site.

But someone of considerable means refused to let that happen. This unknown person remained determined to thwart those plans by legally blocking the sale of the castle and its land, with the sudden appearance of an Irrevocable Trust. It specified that all land and the castle itself were to become the sole property of a Ms. Samantha McKinley who currently resided in Boston.

Sounds great, right? If she had only known where this journey would eventually lead her, she might have had second thoughts on accepting it. But for some reason, Samantha was drawn to it. Deep in her soul she knew there was no backing out, no rescinding due to cold feet. But why?

At first, Sam totally dismissed any ideas of attempting to renovate a structure that old, it was almost a total impossibility. Gradually though, after several discussions with her father, older brothers and several lawyers, the idea began to grow on her. Who knows? It could be well worth her trouble in the end.

Then there was that continual ache in her heart, for something or someone. It was a feeling she couldn't shake, and one she would not discuss with her family.

Finally, with the approval of family and close friends, she decided it may be worth it after all. A nice B&B in Scotland sounded like a lucrative financial move. Tourists from around the world flock to that type of thing, and the place it was situated seemed perfect. A lovely castle, with a breathtaking view of the sea. What could be better? After all, someone had left her a huge sum! Still, it baffled Sam why they wouldn't divulge a name.

In the end, she packed up, bid her family and friends good bye, and flew to Edinburgh. There, she began literally the fight for her very soul. This is her story . . .

CHAPTER TWO

The long flight to Scotland was uneventful, even quite comfortable. Sam had plenty of time to ponder the seemingly enormous task that she alone had strangely inherited. How in the world does a simple twenty two year old woman from Boston go about the seemingly impossible task of reconstructing a 1st century castle? Alone, no less! But Sam was filled with steely determination, and bent on finishing the task.

She believed she could start a profitable business from the historically correct renovation of the castle, then return home to Boston. The problem was, no one knew what the castle originally looked like. There were no drawings or rough renditions of Rosestone. No vague sketches, or descriptions in some long forgotten book. It was a total enigma. Still, Sam's resolve was firm. Backed with more than enough money, she would succeed at making it work.

The seven hour trip was finally over, as the giant 747 began its graceful descent to the landing strip. Sam peered out the plane's rain covered window, as the tires firmly hit the tarmac and the big bird came to an eventual stop at Edinburgh's International Airport.

As the passengers awaited clearance to leave the aircraft, she watched the pouring rain from her window. Another thing to get used to, she smiled.

After exiting the plane, she fought her way through the crowd, following the other passengers down to the lower level where she would continue to the baggage claim, and finally to customs. Easily spotting her two bright red suitcases, she engaged in a brief battle with fellow passengers, and was finally able to retrieve them from the crowded conveyer belt. Following the crowd, she headed to customs, and the usual drama there. Luckily, the contents of her two suitcases remained somewhat intact after the thorough inspection.

Finally finished, Sam hurried to the exit to continue the fight for a taxi. As she left the customs area, she spotted the large red sign instructing all passengers to please proceed to the taxi pick up point, located on the right side of the airport. Following directions, she soon found herself engulfed in a crowd of taxi drivers awaiting prospective customers. They stood just outside the exit door, hopefully catching some of the weary, travel worn passengers who needed a ride to their next destination.

"Taxi, miss?" She turned to find a handsome young driver smiling at her. He was attractive and somewhere in his early twenties. She grinned at the smooth Scottish brogue.

"Yes, thanks," she said, as he carelessly tossed her two suitcases into the trunk. Whatever possessed her parents to buy her red designer luggage she thought, as he slammed the trunk closed.

Sam had decided to travel light this trip, bringing only two pieces with her. She would make a point of buying whatever she needed later. After all, money was no problem now. The mere thought of someone leaving her that much was simply ridiculous.

Then she spotted the nearby sign, 'We offer fixed fares for most journeys.' She wondered if that included traveling to the Highlands for a first glimpse of her castle.

The rain continued, splashing over her thin white blouse, making it uncomfortably transparent. Looking down, she was mortified to find that the blouse was now totally drenched, and everything under it very visible.

"Thanks a lot," she managed, positioning her shoulder bag across her chest.

The cabbie just grinned. "Where to?" he asked, as he held the passenger door open for her. He quickly jumped into the driver's seat and pulled onto the busy exit lane, which brought heavy traffic away from the International Airport.

"I'll be staying in a hotel here in Edinburgh for business, but I'd like to see the ruins of Rosestone Castle first," she told him politely, as he passed several large airport vans and buses.

It was almost noon in Edinburgh, and the traffic was moving along slowly due to several International flights which recently landed. Sam was beginning to feel the famous jet lag, but the thought of seeing Rosestone for the first time had her adrenalin pumping.

He gave her a puzzled look. "Rosestone?" he asked, stopping at a red light.

"Yes, the castle ruins. I believe it's situated somewhere near Aberdeen."

"You realize miss that those ruins are at least two to three hours from the outskirts of Edinburgh. Do you mean Edinburgh Castle? That's much closer," he politely informed her, thinking this American didn't know one castle from another.

It was true, most vacationers were just happy to experience a castle, any castle. Most didn't know the different names, locations, or even cared about their history.

She shot him an irritated look.

"Ok then, Rosestone it is lass." He was just as happy, the fare was what he worked for.

"I guess you already know that it's now just a crumbling ruin? Not much to see up there, just some rocks and maybe a few walls if you're lucky," he told her, attempting some pleasant conversation to help settle her ruffled feathers.

American women, he smiled to himself.

Sam sat quietly for the beginning of the trip. She was definitely feeling tired, but kept alert taking in the different houses, shops and landscapes along the way. *I'll sleep later*, she thought to herself, engrossed in the lovely Scottish landscape and scenery.

Luckily, the heavy rain had finally subsided, and the sun was slowly emerging from behind thick, grey clouds. Sam kept busy by studying the scenery. It was all so different from her native Boston. Finally, she began to yawn. The long drive, plus the overnight flight had finally caught up with her.

She was suddenly famished, her stomach beginning to growl after the small meal they gave her on the overnight flight. Luckily, she remembered to buy something at the snack bar in the airport. She quickly searched her purse for the two honey granola bars she'd purchased there.

"It's quite old and literally falling apart by now," the driver told her, attempting some pleasant conversation as he maneuvered his taxi up uneven terrain. "Been like that for decades. No one really knows much about it, at least no one I know."

At one point they had a breathtaking view of the North Sea.

"That's worth the ride itself," she sighed, gazing out at the deep blue water.

"Would you like me to pull over, so you can get a better look?" He wondered why the view was so special to her.

"Sure, that'll be great," she said, putting her window down to enjoy the magnificent seascape. "Such a romantic view."

A sudden thought flashed through her mind. She should be admiring this with someone very special, other than the young cabbie who obviously couldn't care less about the view. But who? He pulled his cab to the side of the narrow dirt lane and parked it.

"Must have been so wonderful for those who lived in the castle ages ago," she sighed, lost in time.

The young man turned to face her. "I remember long ago, there was an old superstition about the sea and that particular castle."

"Really?" she said, perking up immediately. She hungered for any piece of information she could get. "Tell me about it."

"Well, I was just a lad when my grandparents told us stories about strange lights coming from the sea on certain holidays. I never understood what they meant. Seems that it happened mostly on Beltane and Samhain."

Sam laughed. "I guess they told you that kind of garbage to make sure you'd behave."

"No," he fired back at her. "They actually believed that stuff. There were many who reported seeing very strange things up there at night. We were threatened with a good thrashing by granddad if we ever went up there."

She could tell he was dead serious. "Well, what did you do?"

"You know how kids are, always doubting what their elders say. I went up to the grounds one night with a buddy, and we swore we'd never go again, night or any other time for that matter."

Sam gave him a look of concern. "Why, what happened?"

"We watched the sea for a while," he continued. "It was a new moon. Anyway, suddenly we thought we saw someone come out of the waves. This guy was stark naked. I couldn't get a very good look at him from where we were hiding. I swear, he changed into a black cat right in front of us. Shape shifter, isn't that what they call it today? We ran like hell back home. Never did tell anyone since that day."

He turned to look Sam in the eye. "I'll never return there, ever."

An uncomfortable silence followed. Neither had a thing to say. Finally, after several lengthy minutes, Sam spoke up. "Do you mind if I get out and take a short walk around, just for a few seconds?"

He wasn't surprised that she was starting to feel a bit cramped, especially after the long flight. "There's a small clearing coming up in about five minutes," he told her. "It's safe to park there, and the view is great."

"Good," she said, rubbing her legs. "I'm beginning to feel like a sardine."

In a matter of minutes he pulled off the road, onto a clearing. Two other cars were also parked there, probably for the same reason. She gave the others a friendly smile. Americans, she thought, watching the women as they snapped photos of the sea. Their husbands, all in shorts, formed small groups to chat.

A sudden feeling of loneliness filled her heart. She missed her family already, wishing they were there to share the breathtaking scene with her. Slowly, other cars and vans pulled in, as the passengers climbed out to walk around and stretch their legs.

"Go ahead, enjoy yourself," the young driver told her, as he pulled out his cell phone. "Whenever you're ready, just give a shout," he smiled, dialing a number on the phone.

"Thanks," she said, opening the door and stepping outside. This is heaven, she thought. She walked around to stretch her legs, nodding and smiling at the other tourists. The scenery was fantastic, a clear unobstructed view of the sea.

Sam's anxiety to finally get a glimpse of her castle grew. She wondered what it looked like now. The letter failed to give her a good description, there were no pictures and her thoughts ran wild. Would there be *anything* left? After several minutes of stretching and breathing the clear ocean air, she climbed back in and they took off again.

"Guess you're anxious to see the ruins," he smiled. "Is there a special reason why you picked this one? Scotland is littered with castles, many in much better shape than Rosestone. No one has that kind of money needed to buy the land," he continued, eyeing her suspiciously. "They've even advertised it on one of those fancy real estate websites here in Scotland. You know, the type a billionaire would use. Asking a king's ransom, so I've been told. Don't know why anyone would want to spend so much on a stupid pile of rocks."

Sam took that personally. She had to struggle with the urge to hit the innocent driver for the crude, ignorant remark. Why did it bother her? After all, it really wasn't much of a site by now. Her reaction baffled her for the remainder of the trip.

Soon they were able to see the rocky plateau where the castle was supposedly located. It too, was a breathtaking sight. Just the place where you'd expect to find a castle.

About twenty minutes later, and after several sharp turns and deep uneven potholes, they finally reached the long narrow road which led up to the crumbling stone ruin. The road was obviously very old, and the only one around. It had been cut from the side of the mountain. A small stone bridge connected the castle grounds to the mainland. Sam imagined how many people had traveled across that bridge during its glory days.

"You know, there are many rumors about this old place," he told her.

"Really? What kind of rumors?" Her curiosity was beginning to get the better of her, and she was anxious to learn all she could.

The driver paused several seconds, as if debating what to say. "Well," he began, "first of all, there are those who say it's haunted."

Sam turned in shock. "Haunted? Why would people say that? It's just an ancient pile of rocks by now. Why would anything want to bother haunting it?"

"Don't really know lass. Others say there's some kind of portal, or doorway somewhere on the castle grounds, which leads to other times and dimensions. It's been very much talked about because of that, even had a piece about it in the local newspaper last year. They called a team of International Astrophysicists up to the grounds to see what they thought."

"Well?" she asked anxiously, "what did they say?"

"They couldn't seem to agree upon an answer. The only thing they did agree on was that there was definitely something strange going on here. Mentioned something about ley lines, or some foolish thing. Others say they've even seen sudden flashes of bright light coming from somewhere on the castle grounds. Seems to have quite a reputation."

He stopped suddenly, feeling guilty about telling her so much. After all, tourists from everywhere were a valuable asset to Scotland.

"Sorry lass, I shouldn't be telling you stuff like that, seeing you seem to have such an interest in it."

Sam was on a roll now, wanting to hear it all. "Portals?" she muttered to herself. Suddenly every word of that Celtic History course she took at Boston University came to life in her mind. She remembered reading about ancient places, and portals to other dimensions and times. Cold chills began to make their way up her spine. Don't be ridiculous, she told herself. Every castle has a ghost story.

"Don't let it bother you, lass. You know how these old places are, always have their share of rumors, and ghost stories. Personally, I don't believe a word, especially the one about the knight. That one's really too much!"

That was it. "What knight?" she asked impatiently. "What are you talking about?" Sam's mind was on overdrive now, and she began to wonder if he was just making this all up, for her sake.

He paused and looked at her for a few long seconds. "Do you scare easily, lass?"

"No," she huffed indignantly, refusing to give him the upper hand.

"Good. Some people, you know tourists and the like, have said they've seen a medieval knight up here, but he vanishes into thin air as soon as they see him."

"What?" Such garbage, she thought. Some people would believe almost anything they were told. Did he take every American for a fool? Perhaps she should suggest he visit

New York City, then he'd have a real reason to be afraid, she grinned.

"It's true," he continued. "It's rumored that he's protecting the old place. Nobody knows what he's supposed to be protecting it from. Can you believe that? Kind of sad I think."

Sam wasn't buying it. "I can't believe all this nonsense," she snapped. "Protecting it from what? Why in the world would anybody want to protect a bunch of rocks? That's just ridiculous." The last thing she needed was tales of apparitions where she was supposed to renovate.

"I don't know," he said, looking out to sea. "Those who understand and study this kind of thing say it has to do with certain holidays, the evening, and the summer and winter solstices. Sorry, but I was never one to get into that kind of stuff," he grinned. "Too interested in cars and women."

She watched as he casually checked her left hand for a wedding ring. When he found none, he continued. "Isn't it a wee bit dangerous for a lass to be traveling from America alone?"

Sam stared over at him, knowing what he was getting at. The sudden impulse to tell this guy she *wasn't* alone hit her like a brick wall. But she was, and he knew it.

"I'm meeting friends that live near the castle ruins," she shot back, hoping he would drop the subject.

"Anyone special?" he persisted with a devilish grin.

"Yeah," she told him firmly. "My fiancée. He's from that area, and I'll be staying with him for a while." There, it was out. Maybe he'll shut up now, she hoped.

Instantly, the image of a gorgeous blond man flashed through her mind. Her heart skipped a beat at his beauty and form, and she almost wanted to cry. Just as quickly, the fleeting image was gone, leaving Samantha alone and aching for his company. Pulling herself together, she turned to once again look at the sea. It brought her peace, even if just for the moment.

Samantha McKinley was a petite redhead, with deep green eyes that sparkled when she was excited. Her hair hung loosely past her shoulders, an eye catching mix of different tones of red. Her father always told her it came from the Scottish side of the family. She had a bubbly personality, and made friends everywhere. She also had a very dangerous sense of curiosity, and a short leash when angered.

Having had more than her share of dates back in Boston, she still hadn't found the one guy who could match up to her strict requirements for a man. She spent most of her time at the university library, with her head buried in books, studying. It helped to keep her mind off the fact that she still hadn't found her soul mate. Someday, she pondered glumly, I'll find Mr. Right.

"Would you mind pulling around to the other side, and let me out for a few moment, I'd like to walk around a little, and get a better look at the place while I'm here."

"Sure," he said pleasantly, never understanding why tourists would pay so much to fly to Scotland and see a pile of ancient rocks. "Take your time. I'm in no hurry." If she wanted to spend all day at these ruins, it was okay with him he thought, yawning. Her money.

As she climbed out of the taxi, and turned to get her purse, she caught him giving her the once over. Men, she huffed disgustedly. They're all the same, no matter where you go. What I wouldn't give to find a *real* man.

The minute Sam put her feet on the castle grounds, the sky darkened for a moment, and a strange wind swept over them. The unnerving feeling that something dark and menacing was watching her, following her every move, gave her the chills. There's definitely something strange about this old place, she thought. It was as if something sinister was waiting for her to come, and step foot on this soil.

"That was odd," she noted, looking back at the cabbie who was now gabbing away on his phone. He stopped to glance up at the sky, clearly noting the wind and dark cloud, but shrugged his shoulders and continued with his conversation.

"A lot of help he is," she huffed sarcastically. She began to walk around the castle alone, getting some idea of the work cut out for her.

It was true, the castle was in bad disrepair. Nothing had been done to it in centuries. Just a few outside walls remained, with some stone formations left inside. Sadly most of them were crumbling, or totally missing, with a few turrets amazingly still in place.

The top tower had been destroyed, and the back of the building mysteriously missing, almost as if it had been blown off somehow. It was partially covered with thickly overgrown weeds and vines.

She surveyed the entire ruin, somehow feeling a tinge of sadness and possession. Its crumbling, broken walls, empty windows and deserted gardens seemed to call to her very soul. So lonely and forgotten. So mysterious.

Sam turned to look at the sea situated directly in front of the castle. Its crashing, foam covered waves seemed to greet her, to welcome her, in a crazy way.

"It's so beautiful," she whispered, gazing at the castle's lovely silhouette against the blue of the sea. For a split second, she thought she saw people looking out the gaping holes which were once windows! She jumped back with fright, blinking several times and rubbing her travel weary eyes. No one. Not a single soul was there except her and the taxi driver, still in his cab and still on the phone.

Again, she strained her neck, looking up at the castle through bright sunlight. At least ten people, dressed in 17th century garb, stood there looking back at her.

"Insane!" she thought, once again rubbing her eyes. She dared to glance up once more, but they were gone. Was she truly losing it?

"I must be really sleep deprived," she muttered. Not one person was there. Sam wanted to run back to the taxi and tell him to bring her back to the airport. Then her stubborn nature kicked in.

They were right. She fought to pull herself together. It's certainly a mess, she thought dismally. Taking a few more steps, she found herself face to face with another more intact section of wall. A few still well defined window holes remained, and Sam's mind thought back to who would have gazed out those windows, and what they would have seen. There wasn't a bit of graffiti to be seen, which seemed amazing to her, coming from Boston. Perhaps the knight was protecting that too, she thought sarcastically.

I can definitely see why no one would choose to take this place on. It would probably take a fortune and a complete city of workers to renovate it correctly. That is, if anyone ever knew what it looked like in the first place.

Again, Sam thought of the extravagant sum she'd inherited. But where did it come from?

CHAPTER THREE

Samantha felt it, as she walked closer to the castle ruins. The unnerving feeling that she was being watched filled her brain, sending all her red flags up. That's crazy, she thought, examining the beautiful red sandstone from which the castle was built. Time had certainly taken its toll on the poor place, yet she felt something especially endearing about this particular site.

Most of the northern wall was still amazingly intact. A large empty space now existed where the front gate and door must have been. Tangled overgrown foliage and thick brush grew up the sides of the wall remnants. The remainder of the surrounding land was covered with thorny bushes and creeping vines, knotted together in an unsightly mess. So much work here, she thought, taking in all that would need to be done to bring this pile of rocks up to a modern attraction for tourists.

All at once she stopped dead in her tracts, again aware of the same eerie feeling. There was no doubt she was being watched, but by whom? She turned around, surveying the immediate area, but saw nothing. There was no one there but her. What's wrong with me? It must be the old jet lag theory that they always talk about. She tried to catch up on her sleep during the overnight flight, but apparently it wasn't enough.

Squaring her shoulders, and reminding herself why she was there in the first place, Sam continued her slow walk through the thorny brush and slippery, uneven ground.

As she eventually circled around to what had once been the courtyard, she began to notice a strange humming vibration which seemed to surround the entire grounds. Searching for a possible cause, she could find no source for the low humming noise. No power lines, or large power plants visible anywhere. It wasn't loud, just a soft constant vibration, which seemed to be slightly stronger at different locations of the castle grounds.

Her mind raced for an answer. There was no one there except her and the driver, waiting back at the front entrance. He was probably still on his phone. Yet something was definitely wrong here. She sensed an evil presence, which seemed to steal the warmth from the sun itself. Chills covered her back and neck.

Heavy feelings of nausea suddenly hit. Her face grew red hot, her legs weak and shaking. Samantha tried desperately to summon all of her strength, but it was no use. Her legs gave way, causing her to plummet down onto the wet stony terrain below. Landing face down in the mud, her terror took full control.

"Oh God, what's wrong with me?" The taxi was around the corner and out of sight. She tried to scream, but was unable to make a noise. She felt a stinging pain close to her left ear, as something warm trickled down her face. When she touched the area with her hand, she was shocked to find fresh blood. She had cut her face on something during the fall.

"Are you alright, lass?" a voice asked. His soft, sexy brogue seemed to both calm and excite her. Looking up, she got her first glimpse of what was behind that brogue.

Tall, golden blonde, extremely handsome, and very strong. She should have been scared, but his smile was so warm it drew her in and instantly relaxed her. Before she could answer, he bent down, taking her hand and quickly pulled her up from the wet ground. His touch warm and comforting.

Sam stared into the most amazing deep blue eyes she had ever seen. His gaze was almost hypnotic, and she sensed he could see through to her very soul. He was so different from other men.

"You've hurt yourself," he said with genuine concern. "Permit me to clean the blood from your face."

Before she knew it, he pulled a spotless white handkerchief from his snug jeans pocket and began to gently dap at the cut on the side of her face. The nearness of his body filled her mind with thoughts she'd never think of. Suddenly there was no pain, as if it had never happened.

As he returned the handkerchief to his pocket, she saw a beautiful tattoo on the palm of his left hand, the symbol of a blazing sun. Strange, she thought. What an odd spot for a tattoo, one could hardly see it.

"It's just a small cut, should heal soon," he smiled, as he caught her staring down at his hand.

Who was this strange, sexy man, and why did he seem so excited to see her? It was as if he had been waiting, as if he knew she would eventually come. But why? Sam pushed the question to the back of her mind for the moment, and concentrated on what he said.

"Let me introduce myself. My name is Kieron, and I'm glad I was here to assist you. I often come to relax and meditate . . . you know, get away from this crazy world."

Samantha was truly dumbfounded. Was she dreaming? She had never met such an attractive man. She judged him to be about thirty, yet there was a timeless air about him. Something very familiar about him beckoned her closer, if she dare.

"I'm Samantha, but all my friends call me Sam," she stuttered, unable to tear her eyes away from that body. "Thanks for helping me. I don't have a clue what happened, just suddenly got sick. It's really embarrassing."

"There is no need for embarrassment," he told her softly. "Are you feeling better now?" His sincerity was unquestionable. Refreshing, she thought.

"I think so. Thanks again, Kieron," She tried to adjust, her muddy blouse. She realized she'd torn it somehow when she hit the stony ground.

"Aye lass," he smiled radiantly, "Kieron MacClaire."

He searched her face for several seconds, as though expecting some reaction to the name. "I didn't see you here, thought I was alone."

Sam couldn't help but stare, and couldn't explain her sudden attraction to him. Never had she felt that strong an attraction toward another human being.

He wore faded blue jeans, boots and a pure white linen shirt that looked like it came straight from the 17th century. He was a bit taller than most men she'd met, probably around six foot six. The sense of pure energy and strength coming from him was undeniable.

His hair was the purest golden blonde, and reminded her of sunlight itself. It hung down almost to his trim waist, tied back in a queue. His eyes were a very strange and unique color blue, and seemed as if they knew each and every thought she had, which thoroughly embarrassed her. She had never seen such beautiful eyes. He was every woman's fantasy, she sighed longingly, but most definitely belonged to someone else.

Sam gazed up into that rugged face and temptingly full, sensuous lips. There was no doubt he had a trail of women following him everywhere. His girlfriends were probably all beauties, she assumed sadly. But what was a gorgeous hunk like him doing in this rock pile all alone? There had to be a reason.

"I was probably deep in thought on the far side of the castle," he told Sam softly, as his eyes hungrily took in her petite, perfect figure. "I often go there to escape everyday misery."

She couldn't imagine someone with his looks being alone anywhere. She began looking around for another woman, but it seemed fate destined them to meet alone.

Sam had never considered herself a heartbreaker, yet there he was, starring at her as if she were the most beautiful woman in the universe . . . almost as if he had been waiting for her. He was so different from any other man on planet earth. Something very old, yet modern at the same time. He was timeless.

Sure, she thought sarcastically. He probably just left the last woman, and was awaiting the next, when I barged in. Men with those looks could pick and choose. The thought was depressing, and she forced it from her mind. Probably has a wife and babies at home. That was enough to cool her heated blood. She checked his left hand for a ring, and was relieved to find none.

"Are you sure you're not injured?" he asked in earnest.

"I'm okay," she smiled, trying to keep her eyes off that body. "I'd like to ask you a few questions, if you have the time. Perhaps you could fill me in on any history about this place?"

"Time?" He chuckled softly, as if enjoying a private joke. "Lass I have plenty of that. I'd be more than happy to answer your questions. Would you mind if I walk along with you? Such a lovely young lass shouldn't be alone up here."

Again, Sam bristled with the feeling of being watched by something sinister. "Thanks," she told him, as they began to walk. "I'd love the company. Not many people seem to be interested in this old place."

He looked at her for a long moment, as if wanting to say something. "Aren't you interested, Sam?" he asked softly. "Haven't you come all the way from Boston just to see it? To touch these old walls, and stand on her soil?"

Whew, she thought, that was deep. How did he know she was from Boston?

"How did you know where I'm from?"

He looked down at her, his smile filled with seduction. "A lucky guess? Perhaps the Boston accent."

"I guess that does kind of give it away," she blushed.

"Nonsense," he smiled, taking her hand. "I find it delightful. It would seem we have no control over where fate throws us in this life." He turned and gave her a strange look.

What was he talking about? Deciding to put it out of her mind for now, they continued the walk. For some reason, she knew she should heed his warning. Figuring this would be the only time she'd ever see him, she decided to enjoy the encounter while she could.

"So tell me Sam, what were your thoughts when you first saw this castle?"

"Well," she began, "I never saw a real castle. I

Guess I was expecting something a little more . . ." she trailed off, unable to find the right words.

"Together?" he asked, bordering on a laugh.

"Yeah, kind of."

He smiled that strange smile that told her there was more to Kieron MacClaire, a lot more.

Sam had quickly forgotten about the poor taxi driver, patiently waiting out front.

"Hey lady, will you be much longer?" he yelled, as he turned the corner to find her. It had been at least an hour since she left the taxi, and started her walk.

Kieron turned immediately, and stared at the young man. "You may leave now," he told him with subtle authority. "I'll bring the lass safely home, that is, if it's alright with her." He turned and smiled down at Sam.

"Ah, well sure," she told him, stumbling for the correct words. "That would be fine, I suppose."

"It's no problem at all. I have to drive back to Edinburgh tonight myself. I'll drop you off at your hotel."

How did he know where she would be staying? She couldn't help but notice the shiny new black sports car, parked at the far end of the road. Nice, she thought.

Not knowing why, Sam instinctively trusted this man, a stranger whom she had only just met. She knew it was certainly not the right thing to do, and definitely not something she was accustomed to doing.

The driver instantly obeyed. Walking back to his taxi, he pulled her two suitcases from the trunk, and stood them on the side of the muddy dirt road.

"Sorry," Sam said, groping through her purse. "I'm afraid you'll have to take dollars," she apologized. "Haven't had time to change them yet."

"Allow me," Kieron interceded. "It's the least I can do for such a lovely American lass," he smiled, placing a stack of bills in the cabbie's outstretched hand. "I'm happy you've bothered to come check on her safety."

The driver gave him a peculiar look, then realized how much Kieron had given him. He was almost about to return some. Almost.

"Keep the change," Kieron said automatically, putting his hands in his pockets.

Sam once again began to blush. She was experiencing true chivalry for the very first time.

The cab driver didn't seem to care which currency he received. "Thanks," he said, stuffing the wad of cash into his shirt pocket. "Have a nice vacation here in Scotland, and stay away from those knights!" he laughed, climbing back in his taxi.

"Foolish child," she heard Kieron murmur, as they watched the young man fly down the narrow dirt road, radio blaring and tires kicking up dirt and pebbles.

"Thanks for saving me," she said, "I guess I really looked stupid."

"Absolutely not," he said softly. "It was my pleasure. I'm sure you've had more than this to worry about during the last few days. Please don't give it another thought," he told her with that soft, reassuring voice.

He offered her his arm, as they started walking down the rocky trail that was probably once a lovely flower covered path. The sound of crashing waves below the high cliffs filled the air.

"I love the sounds of the sea," she sighed, breathing in the fresh sea air which surrounded the area.

He looked at her with the strangest smile. One that told her there was much more to this castle that she would love.

Again, her attention was drawn toward the constant vibrations which seemed to come from the castle itself.

"What's causing that noise?" she asked, looking around the area.

He completely ignored her question. "It's a magical and wonderful place here Sam, don't you agree? There are many things that don't meet the eye, but are of great importance. In due time, I will explain it all to you. Hopefully some things won't need an explanation."

She found his statement a complete enigma, but thought it best not to push the issue for now.

Kieron was like a walking archive of information about Rosestone. His great knowledge of the ancient ruin was amazing, quickly answering her every question, sparing no details. He could accurately point out vital facts which would have been of life threatening importance back then.

"May I?" he asked, as he placed his arm protectively around her shoulder. Sam was stunned, not expecting such a bold move so soon. She savored the feeling of safety it brought.

"I guess you're probably like this with all your women," she joked.

He grew very serious. "No Sam, you're wrong. My wife died many years ago. It was a terrible blow to me, I loved her more than life itself. It's been a very long time since I've felt this connection to any woman. I feel I've known you for quite a long time."

Yeah right, she laughed to herself. The appropriate come on line, with a Scottish touch.

He looked at her as if she should know something. She found herself totally thrown off guard by his comment.

"You mean there's no long line of women, just waiting their turn?" she asked, half-jokingly.

Kieron remained serious. "No other women. I chose to remain single, and not get involved until I've met that certain woman I've been waiting for, then I will look no further."

Sam was speechless. How romantic, and unlike the men of her modern world. So polite, yet so much more, she thought. Devastatingly handsome, but also warm and caring. Not your everyday ego maniac, lurking at the gym. But was he telling her the truth?

"And you?"

"No," she sighed, feeling that there should be. "I guess I'm more of the bookish type, spending too much time at the university library. Men aren't drawn to the scholarly type."

"Scholarly type?" he repeated softly, with the trace of a smile. "That type of woman holds special beauty, Sam. It tells a man much about the precious gift he possesses. A true woman is well versed in important things in life, for example her family and heritage. Her love and devotion to her family are what's really important."

"The men of my country are more like idiots," she snapped. "They only appreciate what they can get out of a relationship." Her deep sarcasm was quite evident.

He looked directly into her eyes for what seemed like an eternity. In some uncanny way, again she felt he was trying to tell her something.

"I hope you won't judge me on those standards," he said with an amused smile. What world did he come from?

"You sound like one of those charming knights of old, who would fight any dragon for his lady's hand."

He looked at her with such honesty, it took her breath.

"I would. I would fight worse than a mere dragon," he told her, eyes filled with unknown meaning.

Just then, she caught the gleam of a silver handle from what appeared to be a knife, tucked snugly into the back of his thick leather belt. It suddenly became quite clear to her, she should be afraid. He automatically sensed her fear.

"Don't let the dirk scare you, lass. It's solely for your protection."

How did he know? What did he mean *my protection?* Protection from what? She was starting to wish she hadn't sent that crazy young cabbie away so soon. Then she remembered, it was *Kieron's* idea.

A sudden fear came over her. Good going Sam, all alone in the middle of an ancient rock pile, with a man twice your size and a knife, or whatever he called it, under his belt. Sounds like the makings of a perfect day.

"So tell me Sam," he continued as they walked along the uneven rugged terrain, "why exactly are you up here by yourself?"

Again she began to doubt her sanity, telling the taxi to leave them up there totally alone. She must be nuts. She hesitated, not knowing if she could trust him with that information. She was tempted to lie, but sensed he would see right through it.

"Well," she began, "I seem to have had the misfortune of inheriting this old pile of rocks."

There, it was out. She waited for some crazy reaction like everyone else, but he just looked over at her from under thick golden lashes.

"Misfortune?" he said quietly. "I don't believe you'll think of it as a misfortune for long. Speaking quite frankly Sam, you'll be perfect here. It'll just take time lass, and that you'll have plenty of." Again, he smiled to himself as if enjoying a private joke.

Oh great, up here in the middle of a large rock pile with a gorgeous serial killer. I've had better days. The worst part is now she'd admitted there was no one waiting for her, anywhere.

"But you must be careful, watchful for the dangers within."

Here he goes again, she thought. A real nut case, spitting out all these prophetic phrases that make no sense. Just my luck. This whole thing was beginning to freak her out. Who was this guy, anyway?

"What do you mean? What dangers?" she demanded. She wanted to find out whatever she could about the castle, then politely ask him to drive her back to Edinburgh.

CHAPTER FOUR

Kieron took her hand and led her to the remains of what once was a beautiful white stone bench. Its graceful rounded edges now jagged and broken off into a pile on the ground below.

"Sit with me a moment, Sam," he told her as he wiped the old bench clean with his hand. She sat down next to him, as he pulled her close to his strong body, and began to fill her in on things pertaining to the castle.

He told her some facts from Rosestone's history, and gave her a quick glimpse of the people who had lived there in time gone by. Just listening to him describe the past and its people, seemed like he lived there with them himself, it was so realistic. But how did he know all this?

He named them all, not forgetting one, and was able to describe what each one had done there. He made her laugh at some of the stories he told, and filled her eyes with tears of sadness at others.

"How do you know all this?" she asked. "You must live in history books all day!"

"You could say it's a hobby of mine," he smiled. "I thoroughly enjoy ancient Celtic history and its people, and sometimes teach a course at the University in Edinburg. It's been my life's passion, up to now," he said, giving her a strange look. Again, her heart jumped when she looked in his eyes.

"I've been watching this castle for a very long time, more than some would believe. It holds a special place in my heart," he said lovingly, as he looked over to the crumbling walls behind them.

"Would you like to know the legend behind Rosestone?" he asked. "It's very old, and I guarantee you won't find it in any modern day history books," he laughed cynically.

"Absolutely!" she nodded, eager to learn whatever she could about her newly acquired inheritance. Looking off into the barren fields, he began the long forgotten story of Rosestone Castle.

"Legend says the castle was initially constructed sometime before the 1300's, by the MacClaire Clan, a proud Celtic people from unknown origin. In its initial years, Rosestone was attacked by a wandering group of Vikings."

"Vikings! This is getting more interesting by the minute."

"Aye lass. The original Vikings were a proud seafaring group which raided coastal regions, plundering and laying claim to all they found. These Norsemen were highly skilled fighters, quite capable of killing and conquering any group of able bodied men who happened to oppose them."

He looked at her quickly, as if anticipating a response.

"But there was one fierce group who were a deviation from the others, more malicious than the rest. They were even opposed and rebuked by their brother Vikings, for their malicious behavior. They say these renegades were the result of evil ancient spirits, mating with humans, producing a new race of hybrid immortals. They were referred to as The Devil's Vikings, or the Dark Vikings by the people of that time. Of course, this is all just myth and legend, according to modern day scholars." She sensed his definite sarcasm.

"Should I continue?" he asked hesitantly.

"Please do. I find it all very interesting."

"They possessed powers far superior to their brother Vikings, and could be defeated by only one group of warriors."

"Who?"

"The Keepers of the Light, a band of immortal angels, who were sworn to defend this world from abominations such as these. They were the only ones who were able to eliminate them for good. These hybrids paid homage to Merlin, the famed sorcerer, who himself is a dark powerful spirit. By doing his will, they gained high ranking and prestige in his realm of dark magick."

"Some say they were simply a product of fiction, and never existed. That is to be debated," he smiled mockingly.

Kieron paused, as if gathering strength to say what was next. He turned toward the west wall of the castle. "In the 1700's two brothers, Duncan and Angus MacClaire inhabited this great domain. Both were druids, well versed in ancient ways. They were honest and noble lords, even though their linage is questionable to the people of modern day Scotland. They knew of these lost souls, and worked effortlessly day and night, to protect their castle and keep it free from their tyranny."

Sam clung to his every word, lost in this ancient Celtic legend.

"There came a point in history, when they seemed to disappear, but in actuality they merely left this dimension, and went to another."

"But why would they want this particular castle?"
"Jealousy," he said.

He looked over at her. "Do you like science, lass?"

"Sure," she told him, wondering where all this was going. "It was one of my favorite courses in college."

"Good. There are many who believe this castle was constructed on ley lines. Do you know what they are?"

Sam was silent for a brief moment, as if trying to remember. "Sort of, I remember hearing about them back in Boston, once or twice. Something about the earth's magnetic fields, right?"

Kieron smiled his approval. "Correct. Ley lines are areas of the earth's electromagnetic energy. These lines are scattered across the earth's surface, and meet at certain points. Where they meet, the magnetic energy is the strongest. Some say it's a magical force which runs through the earth. Legend says the ancient ones had the ability to harness and use this energy to cross over to other parallel worlds or dimensions."

Pure garbage, she thought. She tried her best to hold in a laugh.Was he crazy? Did he actually *believe* all this crap he was telling her? Such a shame, he was way too handsome to be a nut case.

"So, what's that got to do with this castle?"

"Remember that strange humming you noticed when you first stepped foot on these grounds? That's the direct result of the strong energy deep beneath this castle. It's a direct portal to another dimension."

Sure, she grinned, *and I'm Cleopatra.*

By now, Samantha didn't know what to believe. To think she'd been entrusted with something which had so much mysterious history to it. Either that, or this guy was flat out crazy. This old rock pile was slowly turning into something she couldn't quite grasp, and it was beginning to scare her.

Kieron continued. "Something terrible took place here around the early 17th century, a cataclysm that almost brought about the decline of this beautiful castle. It was said it had to do with twin sons, and a terrible fight which came close to eliminating everything in the castle."

"What in the world where they fighting about," she asked innocently.

He smiled. "It was very complicated," he said, "but it seems that one of them was supposedly possessed."

"Possessed! God that must have been awful for the people who lived there." Half of her wanted to tell him he was just plain crazy, the other was terrified it may be true.

His voice suddenly filled with deep sadness. "Aye lass, it was indeed terrible for all."

"So what did you mean about watching out for dangers?"

Kieron got up from the bench, reaching for her hand as they began a slow walk through a thickly overgrown pathway, leading to the rear of the ruins.

"Sam, many here in Scotland believe these grounds have been cursed," he said, as he stared out over the rolling barren fields. "They won't come right out and say such things, but many hold that belief."

Sam followed his gaze. There was nothing but weeds and a thick overgrowth of crawling vines. She noted the quick change in his demeanor. He was trying his best to hide a deep anger.

"All this land was once plentiful," he told her, extending his arm out toward the fields. "Once beautifully covered by magnificent gardens second to nowhere else in this world." He stopped suddenly, as if being unwillingly pulled back to reality.

"The oldest MacClaire brother, Duncan, had two beautiful daughters. Both inherited his druid abilities, and both were ravishing beauties. It's been said their mother was from another time, somewhere in their future."

"What!" she cut in quickly. "That's totally ridiculous! Now you're talking time travel?"

He smiled and continued. "You don't believe in time travel lass? It's a topic that science is still trying to figure out, yet it's been used for centuries."

Samantha shook her head. "You'd have to prove that one to me. I don't believe that it's at all possible. We haven't progressed that far."

"Be very careful what you wish for," he grinned, then continued with his story.

"Their father loved both his daughters immensely and fought to protect them from the many evils lurking in the outside world. Wise beyond their years, they were his delight."

"That's amazing."

"Ah, but there's more," he cautioned. "The older of the two daughters fell in love with one of these dark ones, a sorcerer who had mysteriously shown up at Rosestone. No one knew who he was, or from where he came. She was quickly drawn to this handsome stranger, despite her father's firm request to stay away. Her attraction to him blinded her to his true nature, and what he really was."

"Who was he?"

Kieron smiled briefly, avoiding her question. "Duncan was wary of the stranger, and was able to see through his guise. He saw him for who and what he really was, and forbid him to ever step foot on his land again. But he knew the evil would not disappear forever, and would eventually show up sometime in the future."

"Before leaving, the stranger invoked an ancient curse on both Rosestone and the two daughters. His lover, the older sister, died mysteriously only one month later. Her parents were heartbroken with grief."

Sam watched as his handsome face seemed to fill with pain, as if somehow experiencing these difficult emotions here and now.

"In fear for her life, Duncan sent his younger daughter away from the castle, under the strong protection of a trusted friend, who was a powerful knight. If she were to return to Rosestone, she too would also die."

Again, Sam was mystified. "How in the world did they fight such a thing?"

Kieron smiled, "It's said the original founder of the castle, Dermott MacClaire, had been in possession of a brilliant opal amulet, which emitted powerful deadly rays. He kept this amulet on himself at all times, for the liquefied sunlight which it held brought instant destruction to these dark beings. They'd do anything to avoid its supernatural powers."

"What was the stranger's name?" she asked, treating the entire thing as some ridiculous myth which people had handed down through the ages.

"Merlin, or Ambrosius, as some know him, the darkest of sorcerers. He alone wields power over those who are unfortunate enough to be kept hostage in his evil realm.

Of course this legend isn't found in our history books, it's something passed down by oral repetition, one generation to the next. Modern day scholars rebuke the legend as impossible and ridiculous," he scoffed.

"What happened to the other daughter?" Samasked quickly. "Did she ever return home?"

"No Sam," he said sadly. "She never returned to Rosestone. She was forbidden by her loving father, who feared for her life. She was loved and well cared for by the powerful knight. They eventually married, to her father's great joy. He loved her enormously," he said quietly, sending Sam another piercing look.

"The Legend says she's waiting until she can once again return home and find this ancient amulet. It's the only way to break the curse placed on this magnificent castle centuries ago. Only then, will she be allowed to return to her home."

Sam sat silently for several seconds, mulling over what she just heard. "What a terribly sad story. I've never heard that before. No one's ever told me a thing about this old pile of rocks. I don't even know who sent me all that money!" she burst out in frustration.

She suddenly realized what she'd just told him. Great, now he knows I'm not only alone, but have money also. Good going. She began to slowly walk away.

"Wait, there's more Sam," he said hesitantly, "but I doubt you'd want to hear it now. It'll soon be dark, and I can see how tired you are. Perhaps I should take you back to the hotel for the remainder of the day. I can easily see you in the morning, that is, if you agree."

She loved the sound of his deep, sexy brogue. Yes, she did want to see him again, many times, in fact.

Those mysterious eyes held a definite sadness this time. "I don't wish to frighten you lass. You've only just arrived here."

"I don't scare easily, if that's what you're afraid of," she snapped. "Go ahead and finish it, it won't bother me at all. Anyway, it's nothing more than an old fairy tale, at the most."

"Fae?" he said raising a golden brown. "I don't think we should drag them into this at the moment. They cause enough problems on their own."

She gave him a strange look, then stood and folded her arms. Hungry and irritated, she was having a difficult time trying to be nice. She was not easily intimidated, and not about to be scared off by some crazy tale this strange man told her, even if he was the sexiest man she'd ever laid eyes on.

They walked along, side by side, neither saying a word. What had she gotten herself into? Hours from Edinburgh, in the middle of nowhere.

Kieron sensed her anxiety. "Alright Sam," he agreed with a great deal of hesitation. "I'll tell you the rest if you insist, although I guarantee you won't be happy with me when I finish."

She nodded in agreement, happy to finally get it over with. The sooner she got safely back to her hotel room in Edinburg, the better!

"Fine, let's hear it."

He continued with his story. "That, unfortunately, was not the worst of it."

"What else could possibly be worse?" she quipped. For sure he was mentally imbalanced somehow. Figures, I finally find Mr. Right and he's totally off the wall. The Scotts are famous for handing down these kind of legends. Just look at Loch Ness.

She wished she'd brought her cell phone with her when she left the U.S., like her father had suggested. Instead, she opted to buy one when she settled in Edinburgh. Now, she was totally dependent on Kieron for transportation back to the city. Bad move. She tried to fight back the fear that was slowly engulfing her.

He acted as if he were on the verge of telling her something she would regret forever. His expression was one of sadness. He took her hands in his and kissed them reverently, lovingly. Somehow in her heart, she knew that whatever was coming next would be bad. Sam braced for the worst.

"Ok, I said I want to know the whole thing, remember?"

He lifted his head and stared into her eyes. She felt spellbound, unable to think on her own, somehow held in place by his strange hold over her. Then he proceeded to tell Samantha McKinley the words which would forever change her life.

"It's you Sam, you're the daughter who finally returned home."

CHAPTER FIVE

Sam jumped up from the bench, speechless and scared. Her heart was pounding madly. He's crazy, she thought. There's no way out. This is where my life ends, at some long abandoned rock pile in Scotland. She said nothing for the longest time, her brain unable to function coherently. She felt as if she had been slammed into a brick wall.

She backed away from him.What did he say? Surely it wasn't what she heard. "You *are* crazy," she told him. "I've heard enough of this crap! I want to go to the hotel, now!"

She tried to run from him, but her legs were too weak, and she began to fall. Kieron was at her side in a flash, catching her and gently cradling her in his embrace. He began to cover her face with soft, gentle kisses.

"No Sam. I'm not crazy, just desperately trying to protect you," he whispered soothingly.

"From what?" she railed, half sobbing. "You?"

Hot tears of fear and frustration rolled down her face.

Head bent low, he softly kissed away each one. "Relax Sam," he whispered. "I'll never hurt you. I know you hate me at this moment, and I don't blame you one bit," he told her, gently brushing long strands of red hair from her eyes.

"I can understand what the effect of hearing that must be like, just try to calm yourself for a second, okay?"

He rocked her in his arms, the feeling calming her and easing the shock. She began to feel better, safe and sheltered from whatever evil lurked at this strange place.

He looked down into her green eyes. "Please trust me on this Sam. Try to understand the seriousness of what I'm saying. I know you think I'm crazy for telling you all this, but every word I say is the truth. There is a curse on these grounds, a very dark ancient power wants you dead. "Yes Sam, *dead!*"

"Ok, I'm sorry," he said, releasing her suddenly. "I never meant to hurt you, just protect you. I'm not a killer, or maniac, as you think."

She was shocked. "You can read my mind?"

Kieron let out a deep sigh. "Only when it's necessary. I considered this one of those times. Please forgive me, I needed to make certain you understand. Think what you may of me, but I am telling you the truth."

"Ok," she agreed, finally relaxed since he obviously had no intention of hurting her. "You've made your point. I heard the story. Sorry if I don't believe a word of it."

"That's fair enough for now. Are you still upset with me?" he asked, mischief dancing in those blue eyes.

"I guess not. Perhaps you could make it up to me somehow." What was wrong with her?

He immediately shot her a smile dripping with pure seduction. "I could definitely do that, lass," he whispered low, "in many different ways."

"She turned bright scarlet, and tried to clear her mind. It seems she had a hard time trying to form any logical thoughts with him so close. She glanced at his magnificent body, what woman would pass on that!

Kieron lowered his head and slowly kissed her. It was a gentle, innocent kiss at first, filled with apology for having scared her. But it soon escalated into something much deeper, filled with passion and sexual need. She clung to him, as if her life depended on him. Her emotions were tumbling out of control, and she craved one thing, Kieron MacClaire.

As his lips pressed against hers, she felt herself lose all control of space and time. Strange scenes filled her mind. She saw faces of people she never met, and the breathtaking inside of a gorgeous castle. She realized she was no longer in the 21st century, but somewhere else, with people she'd never seen before . . . or did she? Various scenes played out before her. She walked with Kieron through lush, colorful gardens. Glancing up behind her, she saw the image of the most beautiful castle imaginable. Then in a second, it was gone, and she was back at the ruins wrapped securely in his arms.

A tinge of sadness filled her as she realized she was still in the 21st century, in the middle of an ancient rock pile. She pulled back, looking up at him in confusion. What had just happened? What she saw in return was the love she'd always hoped to find, complete and eternal. She gasped at its intensity.

It was now late in the day. They'd spent most of it touring the ruins, and talking about its past. Sam was finally convinced he wasn't some crazed serial killer, just a very strange, sexy man, who she just happened to meet. Simply a brief encounter, that's all, yet never before had anything felt so right.

The sun was beginning its slow descent in the sky. She had enjoyed most of the day with him, and knew it was coming to an end shortly.

"There's one more thing I want to show you before I drive you back to town."

He led her to the far side of the castle where the remains of a large terrace stood. There, built into the thick red sandstone wall, was a circular stained glass window. It spanned at least twenty feet in diameter, and was made from spectacular stained glass, which formed a unique pattern, one which Sam had never seen in any other structure.

An ornate pattern of concentric circles or spheres, the outer circle the largest, until it ended with a magnificent round crimson stone in the center. Throughout the circle, the twelve signs of the zodiac had been etched. A true astrological masterpiece.

"What do you think?" he asked. "It's an ancient design, used by the original Celts long ago when they first settled in Scotland."

The beautiful glass sparkled with the last rays of the setting sun. Each section seemed to come alive in a spectacular show of vibrant color.

Samantha looked up in amazement. "It's breathtaking!" she said, staring at the rainbow of colors. "But how has it managed to survive all these centuries? There's not even one crack in it. That's impossible."

Kieron paused for a moment, as if choosing his words carefully. "It's being protected," he told her, watching her reaction."

"Protected? Protected by what? That glass doesn't have one crack in it. What could keep it intact throughout all those centuries?"

He gave her a cautious look, she saw the challenge in his mysterious eyes. "Do you believe in magick?"

"Of course not," she snapped. "There's no such thing."

He grinned, his eyes twinkling with ancient knowledge.

"Are you sure, Sam?"

Kieron turned to study the ancient wonder, totally ignoring her question. "It's called an astral sphere. Some say it's a portal to another dimension, or cosmic doorway. s It's long been believed that some of the darkest spirits have escaped a life of imprisonment by slipping through this portal undetected."

"Dark spirits? What are you talking about?" she asked, never taking her eyes from the glass.

"They're the dark souls I spoke of, trapped in another dimension, from evil deeds done in ancient times. Once here on our plane, they're free and undisturbed by anyone to perform their ghastly deeds on the human race. Horrid acts, born from severe jealousy or unfounded hatred for some reason. They can disguise themselves as anyone or thing. This is what is stalking you in your nightmares Sam, but they are real, and there is only one way to kill them, and by only a select few."

"How did you know about my nightmares?" Sam still wasn't convinced. "What has all that got to do with this castle?"

He smiled, admiring her courage. "They've been sent here by Merlin, to finish a curse which was started centuries ago. Do you want me to continue?" he asked, hoping not to scare her away before he could finish.

Sam squared her shoulders. "Why not? I might as well listen to the whole thing. After all, I've inherited it, it's mine for good or bad."

He nodded his head and continued. "The evil ones do their stalking and prey on the innocent during the dark hours of the night. It's then, when this world is devoid of the supernatural strength which comes from the rays of the sun, they attack. The magnitude of power in the sun's rays is the only thing that will kill these hopeless creatures."

At that exact moment, the sun slipped down into the horizon, leaving the landscape suddenly cold, dark and lifeless. A sudden chilling wind swept the grounds, as Kieron pulled her closer, protecting her from something. The wind picked up, sky itself, seemed to grow darker over where they stood. He watched it cautiously.

In an unexpected flash of movement, he grabbed her, pulling her body down to the cold ground beneath them, using himself as a human shield to protect her.

Samantha screamed in anger ready to punch him, when she caught the first glimpse of the demon. A huge black wolf with fiery red eyes, lunged at her from behind the castle's east wall. Its body was covered with thick black fur, and she could see the sharp white fangs as it snarled at her with deadly intent. Sam screamed in sheer terror as the creature leaped into the evening night, headed straight for them. The demon from her nightmares, alive and about to kill her.

CHAPTER SIX

Before she even realized it, Kieron outstretched his left arm toward the creature. He spoke a strange word, and instantly a brilliant beam of golden light shot from his palm.

The beast immediately burst into flames, black ashes falling to the muddy ground beneath. Sam was riddled with terror. She hadn't believed him, she was a fool. The creature was real, and there was no doubt it was after her. She broke down in uncontrolled weeping, and wanted to go home . . . she'd seen enough.

Kieron held her tightly, a virtual fortress from any evil. His warm kisses covered her face. He gently lifted her chin so she was staring into his eyes. "Shh lass, don't be afraid, it's gone now. I won't let anything harm you, ever."

His hands slowly caressed her back, as he chanted strange words and phrases which seemed to calm her. She felt her body instantly relax, filled with a soothing peace.

"What the hell was that thing?" she managed to get out, "and how did you do that? I mean, kill it?"

He took her hand and helped her to her feet. Kieron couldn't help but smile at her expression. "It's called a Craegen, a demon from another, dark dimension. The word is from a long vanished civilization. There are many demons here, hiding about the castle's grounds. They've been sent by the master sorcerer himself, Merlin. He's the dark wizard Duncan MacClaire himself banished centuries ago. I had hoped to get you away from here before the sun set and darkness moves in, it's the only time they dare roam."

"Craegen," she repeated slowly, as if trying to make some sense of it.

Kieron smiled as she covered her nose from the nauseating smell that still lingered in the air. Several moments passed in silence, as she tried to absorb what had just happened, with Kieron monitoring her every expression.

After several minutes, she looked up at him. His expression was calm and peaceful. Strange, she thought after what he'd just done. "You aren't from here either, are you."

"Would you hate me if I wasn't?"

"I'm not really sure of what to say. It's certainly a shock, but not as much as seeing that hideous thing. Then again, you did save my life."

Kieron began to laugh, "I certainly hope you don't put me in the same category as that. I'm from your earth, but long ago. I've been sent to protect the human race from the evil which is slowly overpowering it."

"Are there others like you?" she asked, studying the symbol of the sun on his left palm.

He smiled. "Aye lass, many others. We're called Keepers of the Light, ancient angels from the beginning of time, who've been sent here to fight dark spirits, and prevent them from overrunning this world. I know that might seem a little hard to believe right now, together with everything else."

Sam's brain was quickly going into overload. She hadn't eaten since her flight, and that was definitely not a lot. She needed to leave this place, eat something and sleep.

"You're an *angel*?" she said incredibly, looking up at his beautiful face. Could it be possible?

"Aye, as are all the other brother warriors in my order. Someday I'll explain everything to you," he whispered softly, caressing her cheek, "but you've just arrived here, and I doubt you're ready to hear it yet. You need to open your mind."

"Open my mind? Was he for real? After what she'd just seen? This guy was for sure some kind of lunatic.

She found herself again wrapped in his steely arms, his lips kissing her softly. But this time she didn't seem to mind, in fact, her mind told her it just might be what she needed.

"You don't act like an angel," she teased.

He looked down at her with a passion that took her breath away. "I'm also a man, lass," he said in his deep brogue which set her soul on fire, "and have all the desires and wants a man has."

That was it. Message received. Sam was in over her head, unable to free herself from this timeless angel, who was also a fierce warrior. He pulled away suddenly, as if sensing danger. She whimpered in unwillingness, as he released her from his strong embrace.

"Come Sam," he told her quickly, "we must leave this place now. Time is essential. I dare not keep you on these grounds another minute, the risk is too much. The sky is growing darker, and the threats grow stronger. Let me take you back to your hotel, so I'll know you'll be safe for the night."

Sam offered no complaint, and obediently followed his command. She was certainly not about to argue.

"If you're still in the mood, I'll explain more to you then," he told her. His decision to leave now held a certain unseen urgency about it.

"Will you promise to stay, and not leave me alone?"

He said nothing, but gave her a look that set her soul on fire. What would life be like, married to an angel? For some reason deep in her soul, she already knew the answer.

They drove back to Edinburgh, then on to the hotel where she'd made her reservation. The night was clear and breezy, the drizzle had finally stopped. She put her head back on the seat, resting her eyes from the long day, as Kieron drove down the slick main street.

As he drove, Sam sat silently admiring the car's interior. She took in the luscious coffee brown leather, and deep wood grain trims. Her eye was suddenly attracted to the object dangling from the rear view mirror. It was a piece of dark green marble artwork, hanging from a braided black silk cord. It had been painstakingly carved into an intricate design, and appeared to be quite old.

Kieron noticed her fascination. "Do you like it, lass?"

"It's lovely," she answered. "What is it? It must mean something very special."

"It's called a Triquetra, an ancient Celtic sign for eternity."

She touched the smooth marble with her fingers.

"Have you had it for a long time?" she asked, slowly rubbing her fingers across the lovely dark green surface. "It's so beautiful and different, like something from long ago."

"That it is. It was given to me quite a while ago by someone very special."

Sam tried hard not to ask the next question, but her female curiosity got the upper hand. "A woman?"

He smiled at her, eyes twinkling with a thousand answers, but said nothing. Then to her astonishment Kieron reached up, lifting the silk cord off the mirror, and handed to her. "Beautiful and timeless, just like you Sam," he told her smoothly. "Here, it's yours now."

She was shocked. “Oh no, I couldn’t just take this, it’s special I’m sure,” she said, gazing at the many swirling colors of green deep in the marble.

“Not as special as you. Promise me you’ll always remember what it means, okay?”

She nodded, and slipped the piece in her purse. “Eternity,” she whispered. Samantha McKinley was quickly falling in love with this strange, fearless angel from long ago.

“Hungry?” he asked as he pulled his car into the parking lot of McCord’s Bar and Restaurant, a popular local eating spot. He knew she hadn’t eaten since the flight, and wanted to be sure she did before finally crashing at her hotel.

He parked the car, and was immediately there to open her door and help her out. Wow, she thought, her sleep deprived brain barely functioning. This would never happen on any of her dates back in Boston. She’d be lucky if they even held the door open for her. What a refreshing change. He gave her another of those seductive smiles. I’ll most likely never see him after tonight, she thought despondently.

Kieron led her inside and up to the meticulously dressed head waiter. “Good evening, Kieron,” he said, to Sam’s surprise.

Kieron had obviously frequented the place enough to be known on a first name basis. Probably with a thousand different beauties, she told herself, as a trace of jealousy started to take hold. Sam never considered herself beautiful, and the sudden knowledge that Kieron was so well known was strangely disturbing. He squeezed her hand and pulled her close to him, as if sensing her fears. “There are none as lovely as you,” he whispered. She looked up in surprise, especially when he bent down and kissed her in front of everyone.

"Usual table, sir?" the waiter asked politely, as he grabbed a menu from the counter.

Kieron nodded, and they proceeded to a lovely corner table, with a window overlooking the front entrance. Sam stumbled along behind, as he pulled the chair out for her.

"I will remember this night forever," she said, taking in the lovely attention to detail that was thoughtfully put into the décor.

He turned to her. "Aye Sam, forever," he repeated with a haunting smile.

They settled in at the quiet romantic corner, Kieron occasionally glancing out the window to the parking lot directly outside.

"Are you expecting someone?"

"No, just like to see who or what's coming in," he replied casually. "Don't worry, it's been a habit of mine for many years. What would you like?" he asked, handing her a menu.

Sam was quickly going into fatigue overload, her hunger diminishing as she fought to stay alert.

"They're famous for their seafood," he smiled, watching her try to stifle a yawn.

"Oh, I don't know. How about whatever you're having." She wished this entire scenario could have happened after she'd settled in Edinburg for a few days, and wasn't so tired.

He ordered Scottish smoked salmon with a side dish of scallops sautéed in a luscious wine sauce, his favorite. Sam ordered the same. The attentive waiter took their orders, leaving them alone in the candlelight.

"Forgive me lass," Kieron told her, eyes glimmering. "I shouldn't have kept you up there so long. It was definitely selfish of me. Now you're overly tired, and it's my fault."

"Don't be silly," she smiled, feeling another yawn coming on, "I could have asked you to take me back to the hotel a lot earlier." The waiter set a bottle of Chablis on the table. Obviously, he was accustomed to Kieron's taste in beverages, too.

Kieron deftly uncorked the bottle, expertly pouring the first glass. "Allow me to sample it first," he said, bringing the glass to his lips

"Excellent." He carefully poured wine into the second glass, handing it to Sam. Kieron watched in amusement as she quickly downed it.

"Easy Sam," he grinned, "you're already over tired. Wait until our food comes. I don't want to have to carry you out of here."

She began to laugh, knowing he was right. The wine would only knock her out without eating first.

"Then what would you do?" she asked coyly, sending him a clear message. The alcohol was already starting to work.

He gave her a wicked smile, sending erotic chills down her body. It told her everything.

Hmm, she thought, might be the perfect ending to a long difficult day. The waiter arrived, bringing their dinner and ending a very dangerous conversation.

Kieron was all too aware that if he chose, he could have his way with her once they reached the hotel. But what he wanted from Samantha McKinley was much, much more.

"A toast," he smiled at the sleepy eyed Samantha. "To your first trip to Scotland, and most of, all your successful renovation of Rosestone Castle."

Sam touched the glass to his. "To Rosestone." She had absolutely no idea where that toast would eventually lead her.

The dinner was delicious, but inevitably Sam became too tired to finish, and between the fatigue and the alcohol, just sat there doodling with her fork.

"Sorry," she apologized, "guess I'm not as hungry as I thought."

"Quite understandable, you're just exhausted. It's my fault for keeping you up there so long. Perhaps a good night's sleep is what you really need right now."

He could easily think of a few other things that would keep her awake all night, but quickly dismissed the thought. He'd waited ages for her return to him, and would not ruin it to fulfill his own selfish needs.

He pushed his plate to the side and left money on the table to pay their bill, more than enough to cover the tip. It was one of his favorite places where he could relax, surrounded by good and trustworthy friends. The restaurant was run by a family he had befriended for many years, much more then he'd ever speak of.

"Oidhche mhath," he told his friend, wishing him a good night in Gaelic. The waiter smiled returning the same, then glanced curiously at Sam.

"Forgive me," Kieron said, turning to Sam. "This is Miss Samantha McKinley. She just arrived from America today, and is quite interested in the story behind Rosestone Castle. It seems we've spent too much of the day sightseeing up there."

Sam glanced down, noticing the symbol of the sun on the man's left hand. It was exactly like the one on Kieron's left palm. Strange, she thought, but said nothing. Her mind was slipping into sleep mode, and did not have energy for another incredible conversation. The waiter shot Kieron a cautious look, then spoke to him in pure Gaelic.

By now, Sam was having a hard time keeping her eyes open, and frankly couldn't care less what language they were speaking. She needed to get to the hotel, soon. She gave Kieron's sleeve a firm tug, which broke the seemingly serious conversation. "Sorry," she smiled shyly, "but I really need to get back."

Sensing her urgency, Kieron instantly put an end to their conversation. "Forgive me lass, we'll leave immediately." He wished his friend a final good night, then quickly left the restaurant.

After unlocking the car door, he helped Sam in. He secured her seatbelt, then left the parking lot, headed toward her hotel.

"Sorry Sam, Liam is a good friend of mine. Unfortunately, I haven't seen him much lately. His other duties frequently keep him away from home. We've been good friends for many years. I often come here with one of the professors who teaches over at the university, to have a fine dinner and talk about the old days. We're all very close friends."

Kieron and Liam's friendship went back several centuries, but no one knew except Liam's family, and a select few of Kieron's closest friends. They were brothers, Keepers of the Light. Some things were best left unmentioned. He glanced over at Sam, surprised to find she was still awake.

As he drove, he began to tell her a little about himself. He taught a course in Celtic Folk Lore and Mythology there at the university. Living in a small house near the campus made it easy for him to walk to his classes.

Sam listened as she fought sleep. She had been on an emotional roller coaster all day, and was quickly losing the battle.

Glancing over at her, he whispered, "Sleep Sam, and know that I love you." She instantly closed her eyes, drifting into a blissful deep sleep.

Twenty minutes later, Kieron pulled into the parking lot of the hotel where Sam was staying. He managed to conveniently find a spot near the front entrance. Protectively carrying the sleeping Samantha through the lobby, he stopped only to retrieve the key from the front desk. He completely ignored the curious looks from several others who were also checking in for the night.

With a wave of his hand the door unlocked, and he pushed it open with his foot. After placing the slumbering Samantha onto the bed, he removed her shoes, then pulled the soft down coverlet up around her shoulders.

Kieron stood next to the bed, gazing down at her beautiful innocence. He loved her dearly, but there was still many things left unexplained which could easily tear them apart. He pushed aside the urge to join her on the bed, and make love to her all night, he knew he had to wait. He would first prove himself to her, then win her heart.

He bent down, gently pushing her beautiful red hair from her eyes, and placed a kiss on her forehead. "Good night my love," he whispered softly. "May the angels watch over you until tomorrow."

After checking the windows and bathroom to make sure she was safe, he pulled out his car keys and silently left the room, carefully double checking the door after him. Kieron knew he had to leave her quickly, for if he lingered too long, he would never be able to resist what his heart yearned for. That would be a mistake and not how he wished for it to happen. She was much too special.

CHAPTER SEVEN

Sam had the best night's sleep in her life. No more nightmares. Refreshed and eager to begin her first entire day in Edinburgh, she faced the sad realization that she was alone. He didn't stay, as she'd asked. She was both sad, because she missed him, and furious, because she felt he played her for a fool.

God knows, he was a gorgeous man. She was very sure that somewhere there lurked several beautiful women, or even a significant other. Oh well, she sighed, that's what I get for being so gullible. He's probably way out of my league.

She dismissed the disturbing thought, and decided to shower and see the sights of Edinburg herself. After all, she hadn't traveled across the pond just to meet a man. Sam set her mind on what had to be done today. She wasn't going to mope about some crazy guy who she didn't even know. So what if he was the sexiest male she'd ever laid eyes on.

Sam stepped in the bathroom and gave a sigh of relief when she saw the large shower. A nice selection of fragrant body washes and shampoos sat in a wicker basket on the edge of the sink. She quickly peeled off her clothes, opened the glass shower door, and stepped inside. The hot water worked wonders on her aching muscles, and she soon began to relax. She reached for the lavender scent body wash, and poured the silky lotion in her hands, lathering up a bubbly foam. The rich soothing scent filled the air with its pleasant fragrance.

The hot steam worked wonders, slowly easing the aches from her explorations yesterday. It was really too much for her first day, she realized. She should have waited until she was more settled, before taking on the tedious taxi ride to see the castle. But then she probably wouldn't have met Kieron, or would she? There was something eerily familiar about the man, something which drew her to him like a powerful magnet. Well, it was certainly fun while it lasted, although she was now convinced she would never see him again. A shame, he was a once in a lifetime man, even with his crazy fantasies about that old castle. Then there was that wolf . . . *that* was definitely real.

She shivered as she played back the frightful scene in her mind, recalling how he'd saved her. What were the chances of a wolf attacking her on her first day at the castle?

She smiled as she recalled his seductive smile, and delicious brogue. An *angel.* Really, did he think she was crazy? Yet the shocking manner in which he killed that thing was enough to make the most hardened disbeliever change his mind.

Samantha decided to take a few extra moments in the shower, indulging herself in the soothing, delicious fragrance, and mentally preparing for the day. Who knows what today's agenda would bring? She would forget this man called Kieron, and get on with her reason for being in Scotland to begin with.

After shampooing and rinsing her hair, she turned to replace the shampoo bottle, and froze! The shower door was misted over with steam, but Sam was still able to make out a dark shadow, quickly fleeting across the bedroom wall! Someone was in her room. She held her breath, her brain unable to rationalize what it had seen.

It appeared to be the size of a small child, but was a blurred form and moved quicker than a human could move. Instantly, her thoughts shot back to yesterday, and the creature Kieron had killed. Her entire body was trembling, heart hammering in her chest.

"Hello?" she called out from the shower. "Is someone there?" There was absolutely no reply. Hands shaking, she dropped the bottle and managed to turn off the water.

Sam opened the glass door, and reached for the white bath towel, folded neatly next to the shower. She quickly wrapped it around her wet body, and tied it in a knot. Gingerly, she stepped out of the shower and to the edge of the bathroom. Terrified, she peeked around the corner. Nothing. With slow deliberate steps, she walked toward the door and checked the lock. It was still bolted soundly from within. Her heart began to pound and her throat grew tight.

She immediately noticed the smell of something burning. It wasn't cigarette smoke, but more like an electrical fire. She spun around, surveying the room. Then she saw the burnt areas on the carpet, almost like very strange footprints. What in the world? She bent down to touch the marks with her finger, only to learn they were scorching hot. Sam stood there for several moments, trying to understand what she was looking at. Her brain was on override. What happened in here?

Turning toward the closet, she got her first glimpse of the note. It was a folded piece of paper, lying on her pillow. At first she just stood there in shock, unable to believe what she saw. Her feet refused to move, and she was having difficulty focusing. Where had it come from? Had Kieron been in her room, and left it while she showered? Impossible, since the door was still soundly bolted from inside. She knew it wasn't there when she awoke.

Someone had definitely been in her room while she showered, but who? And what caused that strange shadow? The very thought was enough to make her want to book the next flight back to Boston.

Sam stood over the small note for several seconds, debating whether to open it. Who else knew where she was staying? She knew no one in Scotland except Kieron.

Summoning all her courage, she picked it up. Immediately she realized it had been written in some foreign language. Who would leave her a note that she couldn't read? It made no sense. Again, she thought of that mysterious shadow.

This whole place is starting to freak me out, she thought, again glancing toward the door. It was at that moment she remembered Kieron's warning . . . someone wanted her dead. Ridiculous! She had no enemies in Scotland, no friends either, for that matter. It occurred to her that maybe she should call her family. Her father would have good advice. Then again, she didn't want to disappoint them. She knew how proud of her they were for taking on a task like this, alone. Forget the call, she told herself. I'll figure this one out myself.

Sam promptly got dressed, slipping the strange note in her pocket. She was not going to let some prankster ruin her valuable time here. Someone from the university would surely be able to figure it out.

* * *

"Good Morning Ms. McKinley," the elderly gentleman at the hotel desk greeted her. "There is someone trying to contact you."

"Contact me?" She already figured sooner or later, she'd hear from the law firm which originally sent her that letter, back in Boston.

"Yes, he left his number," he informed her politely, handing Sam a piece of hotel stationary with a phone number scrawled on it. She took the paper, glanced at it quickly, then slipped it in her purse. Just as she'd expected. her lawyer was trying to contact her. He knew where she'd be staying, and wanted to set up an appointment to review her inheritance paperwork.

"Thanks a lot," she smiled, as she headed toward the lobby door.

With yesterday still clear in her mind, and still unnerved by this morning's experiences, Sam took a deep breath. She told herself she would not be frightened from her castle, by anyone. This was definitely a once in a lifetime event, and one she wouldn't miss out on. Gathering her wits, she left the hotel with a fresh mindset. This was going to be a new and rewarding day.

She confidently strolled out through the hotel double doors, and right into a hard body. "Kieron!" she stammered as he quickly caught her up in his strong arms.

"Sam, are you okay? I thought you saw me. Sorry lass."

She looked irritated, and wondered why he returned. The damage was already done. "What are *you* doing here?" she quipped with fire in her eyes. "I thought you had some kind of class to teach, at least that's what you told me."

"Ah," he smiled as she raged at him. "I can see that something has gotten under your skin. Actually, I wanted to stop over here to make sure you were alright. Your day yesterday was less than favorable."

Still looks as gorgeous as yesterday, she thought. What was it about this sexy man that scrambled every bit of logical thought she had? How in the world could any woman sit in a lecture hall and watch him for one hour without drooling all over herself, or worse, she thought as erotic chills flooded over her body. She wondered how many of the women in his classes sat fantasizing about him during his lectures. Probably all of them, she grinned. Could he be dating any of them, or worse, living with one?

She forced the thought from her mind. After all, once the B & B was finished, she would return to Boston and never see him again. Why should she care if he was even slightly attached, or if he hadn't spent last night with her?

Get over it McKinley, she told herself. You aren't here to find a husband. Let him do what he wants, why should you care?

"Where are you off to now?" he asked, with that sexy accent.

She looked up to find the same burning passion in those eyes. Focus, she told herself.

"I have to see an attorney. I'm sure it's about Rosestone, I've been expecting someone here to eventually contact me." She tried to concentrate on the subject at hand, and not the fact that he'd left her last night.

"May I see you tonight?" he asked smoothly. She glared up at him, with full intentions of telling him no. He was a waste of her time, just another womanizer, this time on the other side of the pond. Despite her firm resolve, she knew she was lost. She could feel her heart skip a beat at the thought. He certainly didn't need to say what was on his mind. But why get involved with a man who she really knew nothing about?

"I'm not sure," she said, trying to ignore her feelings. "I don't really know you that well."

There was something about that smile, something he knew and wasn't telling her. She debated it in her mind, but knew she would give in. "Well, maybe."

His smile was ferial, and told her she wouldn't be wasting her time.

Suddenly, her countenance changed. He could sense her fear. "Since you're here, could you please take a look at something for me?"

"Of course Sam, is there something wrong?" He took her arm, guiding her over to the coffee shop in the hotel's lobby. It was very busy at this time of the morning with people coming and going to their destinations.

They sat at a small table where Kieron ordered from a pretty waitress. She was young, probably a student and made no attempt to hide her attraction for Kieron. She smiled and flirted, rubbing her hand up against his arm, to no avail. He didn't waver once in eye contact with Sam.

Sam watched the scene play out with increasing irritation, until she realized he was paying absolutely no attention to the pretty girl. When she saw the waitress was no threat, she quickly returned to the matter of the note.

"What's wrong Sam," he asked, "you look like you're ready to burst into tears." He reached across the table for her hand.

Sam pulled the neatly folded paper from her pocket, handing it to him.

"What's this?"

"Something terrible happened this morning," she told him nervously. "I'm telling you because I have no one else."

His expression quickly turned grave. "What do you mean? Are you alright?"

She nodded, staring down at her coffee. "I was in the shower when I saw the shadow of something horrible streak across the bedroom wall." She could sense the anger stirring inside him.

"Did you see who it was?" he asked, trying to remain calm for her sake.

"No. I got out immediately, but there was no one there. The door was still locked, but Kieron, I'm telling you someone was in my room! They left that note on my pillow."

His eyes fill with anger, as he glanced down at the note. "It's Gaelic, but done in ancient script." After two seconds, he dropped the note and slammed his fist on the table.

Sam jumped at his sudden show of anger.

He finally calmed, as though he needed time to gather his emotions. "You're in grave danger," he told her, glancing around the room. "This is no joke. I should have never left you alone last night. I can only ask your forgiveness. It will never happen again, I swear to you."

For a split second, she thought she heard him murmur "forgive me Duncan." Duncan? Who was Duncan, and why was he asking his forgiveness? His face showed a sudden fierceness which took her breath, and terrified her. She could sense then and there that he was capable of some fierce destruction. Whatever that note said certainly pushed his buttons, she thought wryly.

"Danger?" she repeated, feeling like a puppet on a string. "Danger from *what?* Please read the note to me!" She was on the verge of tears. She'd reached her limit, her nerves ready to snap. Her emotional explosion caught the attention of several university students sitting at a nearby table.

"Relax, lass," Kieron whispered. "Are you sure you want me to read this? It will be quite upsetting."

"Yes," she pleaded with tearful eyes. "I need to know what the hell's going on here!"

"Very well," he said. He smoothed out the paper and in a low tone began to read the short note. "*You escaped me once Druidess, now you will pay.*"

Instantly Samantha dropped her coffee, spilling the steaming hot liquid down the front of her shirt. She didn't scream, just sat there totally speechless and genuinely terrified. She stared straight ahead with no reaction, as if in a trance.

Kieron jumped up and grabbed several napkins from a nearby empty table. He tried to quickly blot up the coffee, before she could be burned, yet she showed no emotion. Samantha was in shock.

"Come lass," he told her gently, throwing some bills ūon the table, and helped her up from the chair. "We're leaving. This is no place for you now."

Sam was finally able to focus as Kieron helped her stumble out the door to his car. As they left the hotel, a strange wind came from nowhere, the air chilled noticeably. Sam remembered the same situation when she first set foot on Rosestone's grounds. Again, she felt she was being watched.

"Where are you taking me?" she asked feebly, her brain still in a fog.

He didn't answer, but quickly surveyed the area. Once she was safely in and the door locked, he answered. "To a place where I know you'll be safe . . . my home."

"But what about my appointment?"

"It can wait until tomorrow Sam. You can use my phone to call and reschedule. I'm sure he'll be just as happy to see you tomorrow."

Kieron started the car and tore down the busy city street. She leaned her head back against the leather headrest and closed her eyes, her mind still in a state of shock. Who would write such a horrid thing, and what did they mean? It must be some kind of hoax, she tried to convince herself, but the look on Kieron's face told her otherwise.

This entire trip was fast becoming a horrible nightmare. Sam tried to relax, as he swiftly passed almost every car on the street. The entire time she kept reliving the word, "Druidess."

"What about your other women?" she asked hesitantly as he hit the remote to his small garage. She was sure there was a significant other lurking somewhere, and Sam didn't want to feel like the intruder. It was just too impossible that a sizzling hot hunk like Kieron MacClaire lived by himself, even if he did think he was an angel.

He quickly turned the engine off, then reached across to unbuckle her seat belt. His anger had temporally eased, and his eyes were once again a peaceful blue.

"Look at me Sam," he told her as pulled her across the seat until she was wrapped snuggly in his arms. It was more an order than a request. She immediately obeyed, she had no choice.

"Look in my eyes Sam, for I tell you only truth, and am incapable of a lie. There is no other but you, never once in all these lonely 500 years."

He kissed her with a new sense of urgency, his body pressed against hers, as if instinctively needing to make up for all the time they'd lost.

Kieron walked her through the lush green which lead up to his back door. His home was definitely masculine, with strange pictures of swords and shields on the walls. They walked down the hallway, and into his study, where she smiled at various pictures of angels, some engaged in fierce battles with ugly creatures.

"Have a seat," he smiled, motioning to the large sofa. "Would you like coffee? Unfortunately, you didn't get a chance to finish any at the hotel."

She looked around, wondering if they were the only ones in the house. "Sure, but I don't want to be a nuisance."

"Trust me Sam, you will never be a nuisance. I'd rather have you here with me, that way I know you're safe."

"What did they mean by druidess?" she asked nervously.

"I'll be right back," he smiled, "then we'll talk." He left the room, headed for the kitchen.

She noticed the pictures of the sun hanging on the gold tinted walls. They were all beautiful, each showing the brilliant rays at different times of the day. Morning sun, with the start of its glorious rays, mid-day with full fire and blazing glory, and the soft pinkish setting sun at the end of each day. It would appear they were quite important to him.

In a matter of seconds, Kieron returned carrying a small tray with two cups of coffee on it. He placed the tray on the table in front of her. "Careful," he warned, "it's pretty hot."

She carefully reached for the cup, sipping it slowly. "Delicious," she smiled. "Good looks and he makes great coffee too," she joked. "What else can a girl ask for?"

He suddenly grew serious, taking her hand in his. "For you Sam, I would do anything."

Again, she became momentarily dizzy, feeling herself blink out of this time, and be thrown into another. As always, Kieron was at her side, but now they were inside the beautiful castle. Somewhere in the distance two tiny babies cried. He turned to her with so much love in his eyes. "Thank you," he whispered, kissing the back of her hand. A maid was suddenly standing before her, holding out two tiny golden blond babies, each with Kieron's mysterious blue eyes. Sam's heart filled with joy, as she reached out for the babes. Instead, she found herself back in Kieron's study, almost spilling her coffee again.

"What just happened to me?" she asked, searching his eyes for an answer.

He gave her a knowing smile. "Perhaps a wee taste of the past, or future I should say future? Why don't you tell me what you saw?"

She nodded, but the wonderful experience quickly left her mind, much to her dismay. "It's gone," she said, looking up at him with sadness. "I can't remember anymore. I felt I was right her, but in another time. Kieron, you were there with me." Suddenly her head began to throb violently. She put the cup down and held her head in her hands, moaning.

He was at her side immediately, pulling her close. "Don't worry love, it'll pass soon. Perhaps you're trying too hard to recall what you experienced. Forget it for now, you can always tell me later." He raised his hand and touched her forehead. The pain vanished instantly. "You're much too beautiful for a headache."

She gave him a puzzled look, but said nothing. Sam relished the feeling of peace

She looked over at him. "Did you really mean that?"

"Mean what, lass?"

"What you told me in the car about being alone all that time."

"You mean when I said I never married again in all those lonely years?"

"Yeah," she smiled eagerly, "that part too."

"Absolutely. There was only one woman made for me, and I decided that no other would ever satisfy me but her."

She thought it impossible. Even if he were what he said, an angel, how could he have gone so long without a woman?

With his looks, they would be throwing themselves at his feet, she grinned. She knew she would be one of the first

"Yeah, that part" she giggled, as he began to kiss her throat. Thick golden stubble from his chin both tickled her delicate skin, and made her want to cry out for more . . . much more.

"Aye, lass, I meant every word of it." He lifted his head and looked into her innocent deep green eyes. His thoughts went back to years ago, centuries ago, when they laid on a thick fur rug in the solar of their castle. He remembered her sighs as she cried out passionately. Their lovemaking was as urgent then as it was now. His soul mate, eternal precious wife. He would kill for her, and now that his long, lonely wait was over, he would never let her go again, no matter what.

Samantha gave herself to him completely, craving him desperately, as if she had finally awaken from a long deep sleep. Her world now narrowed down to one thing . . . Kieron MacClaire, her own personal sexy angel.

The afternoon rays now streamed brightly through the windows, covering them both with its powerful healing rays. He loved this woman deeply, and would do anything to make her happy. Kieron spent the rest of the day pleasing her in a thousand different ways, making sure his soul mate was satisfied, and would never have cause to want another.

CHAPTER EIGHT

"Good morning," said the perky young receptionist at the front desk of Tiller & Wagner's Law Firm. It was a well-established law office, specializing in estate planning, among other related things. "My name is Brianna. May I help you with something?"

The front lobby was decorated with impeccable taste. White marble spanned the entire length of the long reception desk. The floor was cherry hardwood, with rich hues of rose and hints of red running through its rich grain. Walls were covered with a delicate shade of ivory wallpaper which resembled lace, and showcased various degrees and diplomas. One could easily see that they were very successful.

Samantha stepped over to the friendly receptionist.

"Hi, I'm Samantha McKinley and I was asked . . ."

"Oh Ms. McKinley!" the young woman burst out in excitement. "I was counting on getting a chance to meet you. You've been the talk of the office for weeks!"

She was a pretty girl, perhaps a few years older than Sam, with short, curly auburn hair and bright greenish blue eyes which twinkled with sheer excitement.

Sam looked at her strangely. There was something familiar about her, as if they had met before.

"Have you ever been to the U.S.?" she asked. Perhaps their paths crossed somewhere in Boston,

"Why no," Brianna told her in her perky, friendly way. "I never got the chance yet, but always wanted to. Why? Is there something wrong?"

"Oh no," Sam added, "absolutely not. It's just that you look so familiar, I thought that perhaps I've met you someplace else. Well, never mind, it's really not important." Still, a lingering trace of doubt remained. Pushing it aside for the moment, she continued on with her business at hand.

"We were all looking forward to meeting the young American who is going to restore Rosestone Castle," Brianna smiled. "It's sure in a sad state now."

Samantha felt her face grow red. She wasn't sure if it was from embarrassment, pride, or maybe a touch of irritation. She could feel the curious hot stares from the three waiting clients, sitting quietly behind her.

"Well, I can assure you that it's been quite a surprise to both me and my family," she informed her. "Certainly not something that anyone ever expected."

"I guess not," Brianna laughed. "Well, just have a seat. Mr. Tiller should be right out."

"Thanks," Sam said, as she turned and walked to a nearby chair, giving the curious clients a polite smile.

She selected a magazine from the nearby table, trying to ignore the curious looks she was getting. Maybe I've made a big mistake, she began to wonder.

The thought soon vanished as the senior member, Brad Tiller came out to introduce himself. He was a tall pleasant, middle aged man, with slightly balding grayish brown hair. Sam guessed he had been a very attractive man in his prime. He led her down the short hall and into his posh office.

"I'm very happy to finally meet you, Ms. McKinley," he said as he shook her hand. "I'd be lying if I told you we haven't all been anxious to meet the courageous young lady from America who agreed to take on this huge task." His smile seemed sincere.

"It's strange," Sam told him, as she sat next to his fine mahogany desk. "I don't know any relatives here in Scotland. I can't for the life of me figure out why this job was given to me." She looked around the office, admiring all the family pictures on the wall behind him.

"That is a bit odd," he agreed, tapping his pen on the desk. "Had anyone ever written, or called your family about this before you actually received notification from us?"

"No," she said with a heavy sigh. "It was a complete and total surprise. I went up to see it yesterday, right after my flight landed. It's in pretty bad disrepair."

"Yes, I've heard as much. I've really never had the opportunity to visit the site for myself, though I've been told by many that it's almost in total ruins. I also heard somewhere that there are many odd rumors about that particular site."

Sam ignored that last statement.

He sat silently for a few seconds, as if contemplating whether or not to mention something. She wondered what he was holding back.

"Well," he continued, organizing the final paperwork on his desk, "someone certainly had the money to restore it. Do you have any idea why they've chosen to remain anonymous?"

"Not a clue," she answered, shrugging her shoulders.

"None of us could figure it out. My father's side of the family originated here, but that was many generations ago, and unfortunately, we've all lost touch. Even still, we're very sure they didn't have that kind of money. It was a total shock, especially to him."

"I understand," he said pleasantly, replacing a paper clip. "Wonder why they were so insistent on giving the job to you? Oh, please don't get me wrong, Ms. McKinley. I'm very sure you are quite an intelligent and capable young woman, but quite honestly, not many young women of today would want to be saddled with a chore like that. I'm very sure there would be other things you'd rather do with that much money! I can say that with certainty, since my daughter is your age," he laughed.

Sam nodded in agreement. "You're right about that, but it seems I have no choice. The letter you sent me stipulates that the money be spent on Rosestone alone."

He leaned back in his brown leather chair. "Indeed, it's quite clear on that issue. It seems such a shame, but that's how the Trust reads. Whoever drew it up was very specific about what they wanted done, there's nothing we can do about it. It's been written quite explicitly, and with much care. Someone knew exactly what they were doing when they put this together. I do wish I could change it for you, but unfortunately . . . ," he trailed off suddenly, as if someone had suddenly redirected his mind.

Samantha finished signing various papers to legalize her inheritance, then was done. He gave her a list of phone numbers for construction companies, stone masons and the like, which she would be needing soon. She thanked him for his thoughtfulness. After a polite goodbye, and a sigh of relief, she turned and left his office.

As she passed the front desk, she decided to stop and chat with Brianna once again. She wanted to pick up one of their business cards, in case of future need.

Again, she experienced the feeling that she'd met her somewhere before, but where?

"How did it go?" Brianna asked, as she hung up after a lengthy phone conversation.

"Ok, I guess." Sam was finally starting to feel the weight of the enormous task. "I feel pretty overwhelmed with it all right now. Someone left me more than enough money, but chose to remain strictly anonymous. It's pretty creepy. I can't for the life of me figure out why? It's all so confusing. No one knows who the person was, even Mr. Tiller. He agrees with me that it's a shame I can't just spend it my way, instead of on a pile of useless rocks," she said bitterly.

"Who in the world would want to have that castle rebuilt? And worse still, remain anonymous?" Brianna added. "I just don't get it, it makes no sense at all."

Sam nodded. "I guess it'll take me awhile to get used to the whole thing. I don't even know who to thank. Pretty bad, huh?"

Brianna took her hand, and gave her a reassuring smile. "That's not your fault. For some reason, they just didn't want you to know. You may find out someday down the line. It'll all work out, you'll see. It's a very big undertaking. I would just love to go up there with you someday to see it."

The sudden thought that Brianna had every right to see the castle flashed through her mind.

"I'd be glad to talk if you should ever find you need a friend," she offered kindly.

"Thanks," Sam said, "I'd really like that. I could sure use a shoulder to cry on now and then. At times, I find myself wanting to jump on the first plane back to Boston."

Brianna gave her a cheerful smile. "Oh please don't do that, Sam. There are many times I need a good friend too," she confided.

"Here's my home number," she told Sam, quickly scribbling it on a piece of stationary.

"Thanks. Unfortunately I don't have a phone yet. I've temporarily moved in with a friend I just met." She was desperately hoping Brianna wasn't going to ask about her living quarters.

"Friend?" Brianna asked inquisitively, eyes looking up from the number she was writing. "You already moved in with someone? How did you meet her?"

Sam could feel her cheeks begin to burn. "It's a him," she said, avoiding eye contact.

"Really?" Brianna grinned. "Who's the lucky man? Do I know him?"

She certainly hoped not. She could easily imagine the entire law firm lost in wicked gossip.

"He's a professor at the university. It's just a temporary situation for the moment, just to help me out," she said, desperate to change the subject.

"Of course," Brianna smiled knowingly. "Maybe I know this professor. What does he teach? What's his name? There aren't many single men left on campus these days," she laughed.

Oh here we go, Samantha thought mournfully. Soon the entire office will be talking about the little American whore who inherited Rosestone. I don't have enough trouble on my plate already. She just wanted to leave.

"He teaches a course in Celtic Mythology and Folklore," she replied, desperately hoping to avoid his name. "I happened to meet him up at the ruins yesterday. It was a chance meeting, that's all."

Sam was embarrassed, she knew her face was on fire. How did that look, moving in with a total stranger, on only the second day after you've arrived. She wanted to die from sheer mortification.

"His name is Kieron," she told her. "Sorry that's all he told me. It wasn't something I planned," she said, wanting desperately to leave the room, and drop the entire subject as quickly as possible. "It just kind of happened. He's doing me a big favor."

There, it's out, she thought. You're not getting any more information out of me.

"Kieron?" Brianna said, deep in thought, as if trying to piece a puzzle together.

"Is something wrong?" Sam asked, noting her strange expression.

Brianna sat down, looked toward the window, then back at Sam. "You must be mistaken, Sam," she said slowly. "The current professor for that course is Thomas Naughton. He's taught it for almost ten years now. It's one of the courses that I'm currently taking. Professor Kieron MacClaire taught it before he did. He died mysteriously about eleven years ago. Something's wrong. He must be someone else, perhaps impersonating him?"

Samantha was quickly becoming overwhelmed. What was happening? The whole world was falling apart and no one could see it!

Kieron, dead? Of course he wasn't. She should know after spending an entire afternoon of passionate lovemaking with him. No, Kieron MacClaire was very much alive.

Sam began to question her sanity. Was Kieron lying to her? Was he some kind of imposter? What about the class he never went to yesterday. When she had questioned him about it, he told her he was currently on leave from his position there. Sounded legit.

"I am incapable of a lie," she remembered him telling her.

So who was he? Tonight, she would demand the truth.

"Hey Sam!" Brianna yelled as Samantha dashed out the door, trying to flee the situation. "I sure didn't mean to upset you, please forgive me." She ran down the busy street to catch up with her.

"Oh, please don't worry about it," Sam smiled, as she stopped to cross the busy avenue. "I intend to get some answers from him tonight. It's time he levels with me."

"Hey, I get off early today, in about thirty minutes. Can you wait? I just thought of something that might help solve your problem."

Sam glanced at her watch. "I guess I could. Kieron said he would pick me up at three. It's only noon now. He gave me time to do some shopping," she said, glancing across the street at the many enticing boutiques. "What's the idea?" she asked, hoping it wasn't something else to cause her more embarrassment.

"Well," Brianna continued slowly, "I was just thinking about your problem. I still know one or two of the older professors pretty well, and I thought they may be able to help us with this Kieron guy. If he's really teaching there, they should definitely know."

"Sounds great," Sam grinned. "I'm dying to see what they come up with."

CHAPTER NINE

"Professor McInnis!" Brianna yelled out down the long busy university corridor. She had known the senior professor for many years, since her birth. He was always at her parent's house, she smiled. Seemed like he was part of the family, as she looked back. He'd been a very close friend of her father's. She remembered him always affectionately calling him his "brother", and how the two would seal themselves up in his library for hours, talking about "the old days." He now walked with a limp, and used a cane to steady himself. Time had taken a toll on the good professor.

"Brianna!" he called out in delight, as he gave her a big hug. "How are you, lass? Haven't seen you around lately. Is that bunch of blood thirsty lawyers keeping you busy?"

"Kind of," she smiled, turning to Sam. "I want you to meet my friend, Samantha McKinley. She just flew in from the U.S."

"Hello Professor McInnis," Sam smiled politely. "I'm very happy to meet you."

Niall McInnis had been a senior professor at the university for several years now. Although he was up in age, probably in his late sixties, she always thought he was the best professor there.

His classes on Ancient Celtic History were spell binding, capturing each student's complete attention. He was also one of the very few professors at the university who could brag of his students having a 100% attendance rate, with every class. Students flocked from all parts of Europe to hear him lecture. He held each one spellbound with his vast knowledge.

"You've come quite a way to see our lovely Scotland. Brianna was a student of mine for a few years, that is until those sharks kidnapped her," he grinned. "How can I be of assistance to you lovely ladies?"

He shifted the heavy pile of books to his other arm, as if in pain. "Sorry," he smiled. "My arthritis acts up every now and again. No fun getting old."

"We're here to pick your brain about someone who you might have known. His name is Kieron MacClaire. That's all we know about him."

The professor suddenly stopped where he was, looking out the window for a few seconds. It was as though he hadn't heard a word they said, or else didn't want to acknowledge it.

"Oh, Kieron . . . yes, may he rest in peace. He was a good friend, and an excellent professor. Really knew his stuff, and we all miss him dearly. What can I tell you about him?"

"What happened to him?" Sam blurted out. "I need to know what happened."

He shot her a grave look of concern. "Are you family, lass?" he asked, noting her agitation on the subject.

"No," she told him anxiously, "I met a man at Rosestone yesterday. He told me his name was Kieron MacClaire, and that he taught a class here."

"Rosestone?" the professor asked, looking up from his bifocals in obvious interest. "Now that's something I haven't heard of in quite a while. Are you interested in such lore, lass?" he asked, studying her over his thick gold frames.

Brianna was quick to explain the entire situation. The professor listened attentively, scrutinizing Samantha as if trying to sense information.

"Sad to say, we don't really know what became of Kieron," he told them. "A fine young man. Police just told the university that he had a . . . sudden accident. Very strange for such a brawny young lad, I always thought." They followed him as he limped down the hall to his office.

"Now that you mention it, I believe the last picture we have of Kieron was taken up at Rosestone. Strange, isn't it? He always loved to hang around that place, said it calmed his nerves. Acted like he was expecting someone. Anyway, it was taken on a field trip we took, uh, just before he died, if I'm not mistaken. Would you care to see it Sam?"

Her heart was pounding. A picture! This would be the ultimate proof.

"Absolutely!"

He limped over to the wall, dropping the heavy pile of books on his desk. "Ouch," he yelled, rubbing his left shoulder. "Those books were getting heavy. I'm not a strapping young lad anymore, but then you fine young ladies would never notice that, right?" he laughed, again giving Sam a curious look.

The two girls smiled up at him. "Such a sweet and loving old man," Brianna whispered quietly, while his back was turned. "I love him dearly."

The old professor heard every word, grinning to himself. He took down a picture of two men, which hung above an honorary diploma above his desk.

"I always put a date on things," he joked as he flipped the picture over. "You know, failing memory. Oh yes, here we are. Kieron MacClaire, taken at Rosestone, June 21st of 2000."

"Isn't that the Summer Solstice?" Brianna asked.

"Aye lass that it is. Picked a strange day to have an accident, if I do say so. Glad to see you remembered some of that class," he joked.

"Ah, Kieron," he continued, "He certainly was one to turn the lass's heads. A widower, you know. Never remarried. No one could understand it, I mean with him being so young and handsome."

"Here you go, my dear," he said, handing Sam the old photo. "I think it's a rather good one."

Sam sucked in a loud breath and grabbed Brianna's arm. "My God!" she gasped, "this can't be possible!" She looked carefully at the aging photo. It was Kieron, the very same man she slept with last night. He hadn't aged one day!

"Is there something amiss, lass?" the old professor asked her as she fell into a nearby chair.

"You say he died shortly after this was taken?" Brianna asked.

"Why yes, just a few days afterward, is there a particular problem I may help you with?" he offered as he noticed Sam's odd reaction to the picture.

"What do you think now, Sam?" Brianna asked.

To her amazement, Sam was silently crying, tears rolling down her pale cheeks.

"There, there lass," the professor said, patting her hand and offering his handkerchief. That's when she caught a glimpse of the small tattoo on the inside of his left hand.

A tattoo of the sun, exactly like Kieron's and on the same hand. She felt her face flush, but said nothing. There was more to this kindly professor than met the eye.

"I'm so sorry," he smiled at the two. "I guess this photo brings back old memories. They can sometimes be difficult to handle.

Samantha lifted her head from her hands, wiped her eyes and told him, "I live with him."

He was speechless and obviously a little confused.

Many minutes of silence passed before Brianna spoke up. "Can you please help us? I can think of no other to turn to."

He was becoming clearly annoyed. "Is this some kind of joke you young ones decided to play?" he asked briskly. "I'll have you know my time is very valuable. Brianna, what's this all about, anyway?" he huffed, as he sat to rub his knee. He was clearly in pain.

"This person you speak of is definitely not on our faculty now. Let me see if I can find anything about Kieron that may be of help," he told them, going through a drawer of old files. His fingers stiffly shuffled through papers of the past, now slowly fading with age, then stopped.

"Here we are," he said, pulling out an old folder. "Some of Kieron's hobbies. I can't seem to throw them out," he laughed as he read down the faded list.

"Let me see. He loved all things Celtic, you know. He was able to read the stars, an art that is long dead, and was a fantastic teacher. Could make one feel they were right there when he lectured. An expert swordsman, I must say. Seemed like he was born with a claymore in hand. Was a real tease with the ladies," he laughed, "but was very much in love with his wife, missed her terribly when she passed away. I was hoping he'd find a nice Scottish girl," then stopped abruptly, glancing over at Sam.

"Well, you know how the fates are," he laughed, trying to get out of an awkward position.

"Aye, here it is. The Legend of Rosestone Castle, it was his favorite. Sorry, but I'm not at all familiar with it. I do remember that he often spoke of it. Also spent a lot of time up there on the castle grounds, meditating, he used to say."

Sam turned to Brianna, letting out a sigh of frustration.

"Well lasses, hope I've been of some help," he told them as he carefully replaced the old files. "Sam, I suggest you get to the bottom of who that young man really is. Women can't be too cautious these days," he winked.

"I'd walk you fine ladies to the front of the campus, but I have a bad knee which is becoming worse by the minute," he said with a wince, reaching for his cane. "Probably should call that doctor again, although I recently saw him last Tuesday," he muttered to himself.

Poor old professor, Brianna thought. It hurt her to watch him grow old. He had always been there to protect and comfort her, especially since her parent's fatal car crash. He was the proverbial shoulder to cry on, and like another member of her family.

"That's okay," she smiled, "we know our way out. Hope you're feeling better soon!" she called out as they left his office.

She was a beautiful young woman, full of life, and he was worried about her.

Glancing at her watch, Sam realized it was much later than she thought.

"Let's hurry," she said, picking up her pace and trying to push through the crowd of bustling students who were now quite anxious to leave the busy campus.

"What? You really think he'll leave you here?" Brianna joked. "Come on Sam, that guy isn't going home without you, tonight or any other night. Lucky you! Does he have a brother?" They laughed as the two hurried down the busy university steps.

From nowhere, a huge black dog sprang out from the crowd, heading directly toward them. Large red eyes and sharp white fangs, it charged straight at them with deadly determination. People in the crowd started screaming, running from the fearful creature.

"My God!" Brianna yelled seeing the terror unfolding in front of them. "Look out Sam, it's headed straight for us!"

Sam froze, paralyzed with fear, eyes glued on the dog. Its malevolent eyes locked onto her.

"Why?" was her last rational thought.

Kieron was suddenly there, protectively standing in front of them, waiting. The dog slowed as it grew close, then came to a dead stop. Its demonic red eyes fixed on him. The two stood there for close to a minute, locked in a mental battle, man and dog, ... or where they?

Sam and Brianna clung desperately to each other, as Kieron stared down the black beast. Suddenly it let out a loud whimper, turned and ran off, to the crowd's amazement.

Brianna turned, just in time to catch a glimpse of the professor *running* down the university steps, without a cane. One minute he was watching them intently, the next he was gone. That's odd, she thought, remembering what he told them about his bad leg. It was as though he knew what was going to happen.

Kieron immediately led the two girls into his waiting car, as if nothing had occurred, trying to avoid any further attention. He helped them into the back seat, then slipped in the driver's seat, locking the doors.

Once inside the safety of the car, Brianna whispered a soft "thank you." She was still in shock from what could have been a very bad scene.

Sam sat speechless, recalling what had happen just a few days ago on the castle grounds. She realized she was slowly becoming a target.

"What was that thing, and why us?" Brianna finally managed to ask, as they drove back to the law firm where her car was parked.

Kieron quickly turned the car around, and drove through a back alley. "It's called the Cu Sith," he said, glancing in the rear mirror at Samantha. "Brianna, you need not fear, the beast was after Samantha."

Kieron pulled his car to the curb, letting the shaken Brianna out. He watched intently as she opened her car door, climbing into safety, then drove off.

Starting the engine, he backed out of the narrow lane, and headed for home, with Sam sitting silently in the back seat. "I will not lecture you lass, I know how scared you are right now," he said softly, as he maneuvered through the busy city traffic.

"The Cu Sith was sent by Ambrosius. The hound brings a message of death, Samantha. In our legends, it will show itself to those who will die in a fortnight. Do you understand yet why I want you to go nowhere without me?" he asked sternly, again watching her intently in the rear view mirror.

Sam nodded her head, but said nothing. She simply retreated into her own thoughts, and stared out at the passing sights of Edinburgh. Heart heavy with fear and regret, Samantha McKinley now contemplated going back to Boston.

CHAPTER TEN

Sam was slowly recovering from the day's excitement, and had kept strangely to herself. Kieron decided that it would be a good time to talk to her. He brought her back to his study, hoping to discuss things without upsetting her too much.

His ancient collection of books were stored in a large wooden bookcase, as tall as the ceiling, and as wide as the room. He kept a vast array of manuscripts, and books of every type, some leather bound and appeared very old and fragile.

"Well, what do you think?"

"What's in them?" she asked, taking in the large collection.

"There are many ancient volumes from ages ago. They're priceless Sam, and could never be replaced, that is in this century. Many of them house information on various languages which no longer exist. Others are filled with knowledge of the many universes. Many speak of the Fae, who allegedly inhabited your castle hundreds of years ago."

He looked at her closely, trying to find a trace of recognition. "Close your eyes and relax. Tell me, does any of that sound vaguely familiar to you?"

"No, not really. I've studied it in some of my classes, but never believed any of it was real."

Kieron sighed, then gave her an understanding smile. Her mind was still not acceptable to what he needed her to know. It would take time, he realized, and much patience. He knew the importance of not rushing the human mind into acceptance, it would happen in its own time, especially when such a large time lapse was involved.

He picked up his cup and settled on the settee next to her. Hopefully, some gentle probing might help to unlock the ancient memories which her mind refused to give up.

"Your father and I were very close. I did not share his bloodline, but was honored with his name, and treated like a brother in his magnificent castle.

He repositioned himself so he was more comfortable pulling Sam close. "Thousands of years ago, I was born an angel. As I perfected myself and grew in wisdom, I realized that my calling was different from many of the others."

He glanced over at her lovingly. "I, along with thousands of others, chose to join a band of angels whose job it is to defend this world from the dark ones which hunt down and kill the human race. We are the Keepers of the Light," he continued, "an order of immortal ancient warrior angels, who've refused the temptation of the dark side, and have taken an oath to defend humanity."

Sam was mesmerized, yet unsure.

"You've already witnessed one such example at Rosestone," he continued. "They're dark renegade spirits, who were once part of a noble Viking nation, but have pledged their souls to something evil, to gain wealth and a higher rank in a dark realm. Having been once led astray by his lies, they remain forever his captives."

"He has complete control over their black souls, and turns them loose on this world to do his bidding. They can no longer separate right from wrong, but instead are driven by a terrible thirst for vengeance."

Sam was spellbound, asking no questions, but taking in each word.

"There are many such as myself here on earth, but your race is for the most part oblivious of them," he smiled gently. "We are in every walk of life, but do not tell the world who we are. Niall McInnis from the university is another like myself . . . a Keeper of the Light."

Sam stared up at him in astonishment. "That sweet old professor? Like you? He doesn't look like he could harm a fly." She smothered the urge to laugh at the very thought of the kind old grey haired man with deep lines of wisdom fighting a demon, but the look in Kieron's eyes was chilling.

"It's wise that you heed my words lass, for you may someday have need of such a friend. Niall, for now, has made the choice to do what he loves most, teaching young people in your world. His old age is but a guise, so as not to attract attention to him when he teaches. Make no mistake Sam, he is quite capable of destroying the most powerful of demons. I personally, have seen the direct extent of his destruction."

Again he flashed Sam a chilling look, which told her this clearly was no joke. "We've been warrior brothers since the beginning of time."

Sam just sat there, trying to make some kind of sense from what she'd just heard.

"I saw the tattoo on his palm," she offered, reaching for Kieron's left hand.

"It's not a tattoo, but a birthmark. A sign of status in my world. All who are part of this band of brothers also bear this sign," he told her proudly, as she traced the beautiful marking on his palm. It seemed to glisten when the sunlight touched it.

"Then why does he say he doesn't know what happened to you, and that you're dead?"

Kieron smiled down at her innocence. Her soul was as pure as the whitest light, one that he would proudly guard and cherish forever.

"We are warrior brothers," he smiled. "He will cover for me whenever necessary. Don't you have groups like that in the U.S.? I believe I've heard of one in particular which has roots here in Scotland. That's all you need to know about the dear professor at this time. Just remember that he's fearless, and quite powerful."

The realization hit her. "It was you who sent me all that money, wasn't it?"

"Aye," he laughed as he kissed her neck. "It was from me. I knew you would be needing it."

"It sure came in handy. No one could figure who in the family had so much money."

Sam started to giggle, and he looked at her curiously.

"I should have told them it was from an angel," she smiled, snuggling up against his broad chest.

"Aye, you should have," he said, redirecting her train of thought to other things. "I love only you Sam, and will never hurt you in any way."

She kissed him with abandon, savoring his taste, and the safe feeling of perfect security she found there in his arms.

They finally fell asleep, several hours later. Wrapped in each other's arms, soul mates from the beginning of time.

* * *

After several weeks of constant construction, the castle started showing the first signs of a beautiful 17th century estate. Stone masons were hard at work, erecting perfect walls appropriate for the era. Sam added many of her own feminine ideas, and Kieron incorporated his personal touch. Together with all the other experts in their fields, Rosestone was once again slowly capturing its long lost grandeur of yesteryear.

Samantha had made good on her promise of never going up to the grounds without him. She hardly ever left his side, but did find herself yearning for some down time to be alone at the castle that she was beginning to love, and now think of as home.

Kieron was going to be gone for most of the day, something about a meeting with Niall McInnis. She knew better than to push him about particulars.

He told her it was of great importance, and frankly, she welcomed a day of solitude. He had given her a choice of either going with him to research books all day, or staying at home, to do as she pleased. It wasn't a difficult choice.

There were many things she needed to catch up on, Boston being at the top. Kieron had been encouraging her to talk with her family, as if it were the utmost of importance. Sam promised she'd stay put, call her family, do a little reading in his library, and catch up on needed sleep. She did none.

"I'll be gone for probably most of the day," he told her. "My cell is always in my pocket, please call immediately if you need something Sam. Please promise me you'll do this."

"I will," she smiled.

He pulled her into his arms and lifted her chin in his hand. "Sam, you know it's really important, promise me you won't leave this house for any reason. As long as you are inside, you can't be harmed."

"Ok" she sighed, "I promise."

He gave her a long kiss goodbye, then grabbed his keys from the nearby table and turned to leave. She felt safe in his home, knowing it was well protected against any evil.

She stood at the door, as he walked outside and disappeared into the garage. Such a fantastic man. His heart was overflowing with compassion and love for only her. She wondered what she had ever done to win such a prize. She would all too soon discover that answer.

Sam had every intention of obeying Kieron's wish, but as the day passed, boredom began to set in. She remembered Brianna's request to bring her up to the ruins one day when she was free. She could hear Kieron's bellowing now, before he even found out. But what could possibly happen, she thought, as she dialed Briana's office number. Somehow, Sam had lost her cell number, and wondered if they would mind giving it to her. When another woman answered the phone, Sam was told that Brianna was off for the day, and would not give out any personal information.

Oh well, she thought, looking out the window. There were still many hours of daylight left. What harm would it be to catch a taxi by herself, and see how things were progressing? She would be home in a few hours, and Kieron would never know the difference. He wasn't due home until later that evening.

Sam pulled out her wallet, paying the driver as the taxi left the castle grounds. It was around noon on a Friday, and most of the workers were quitting early, due to the week end. She smiled and bid them each good day as they hurried to gather their things and go home after a hard week's work.

Beginning her walk slowly, she surveyed the grounds carefully, taking in all of the recent changes. The walls were now five stories tall, and some of the windows had already been installed. She looked at the large gaping hole where the front door to the B & B would be, remembering the beautiful oak door Kieron had just ordered. The cost was ridiculous, but he said he'd have only the finest. He seemed to love this castle as much as she did.

Traveling on to the rear, she came upon an area which probably had once been a stable. It was now just a thickly overgrown tangled mess. Any remnants of a structure were covered by trailing weeds and thistle. Perhaps this is where a blacksmith had once worked? Every castle had to have a smithy, she smiled, as she imagined a tall, handsome kilted man working away at his trade. After discussing it previously with Kieron, they'd agreed it would be a great idea. They both loved horses, although she was far from proficient at riding. It would fit in well with the atmosphere of the 17th century.

A score of gardeners from the local nursery were packing up after a busy day. Their work was superb, and they'd been more than eager to comply with Kieron's exact specifications. The entire estate was beginning to shape up beautifully. It was just the beginning, but with time, it would be worth it after all. The business half of her thought it was turning out to be a perfect B & B, the other half cried out "home."

The sky was clear, with still enough time before she needed to call for a taxi. As she strolled closer to the castle walls, she was once again aware of that strange humming vibration. She soon began to get those strange feelings again, telling her something was very wrong. She was being watched, she sensed it with every nerve in her body. The dire warning that Kieron made remained fresh in her mind. She was a fool to try this alone. She'd never learn.

Fingers planted firmly on her bottle of mace, she continued her walk. Perhaps it was just a lone worker, packing up and getting ready to go home.

Rape was always in the back of her mind, as she clutched the bottle of mace in her hand. This time she would not be scared away. Now the legal heiress, she had every right to be there.

The vibrations were beginning to make her feel queasy. They seemed strongest at the north wall. For now, she avoided that part, and remembered not to dawdle too long.

As she continued her walk, she came upon the area which was reportedly once the chapel. Most of it was missing, as if blown away. What ever happened there?

Three workers were walking past, finishing up after a long day. Dying of curiosity, she decided to ask them.

"Sorry Ms. McKinley, but there is little known about that section of the castle. They say it was a chapel, but what happened there is still unknown," one of the young men explained.

"Aye," the other added, "There was a large explosion of some type. Must have been very powerful to have brought down the walls and roof. Was supposed to have been a real beauty, from what the history books say. I believe it was in the early 1700's when it was blown up in some unknown way. No one ever really knew how or why."

They bid her a good afternoon and quickly left. Sam stood there staring at the gaping hole where there was once a lovely chapel. There was something strange about that spot, something that almost bordered on terror, but she couldn't figure out what. She stood there looking at it for several minutes. Finally, she shook her head and continued.

She hesitantly stepped closer to the crumbling walls, wondering what could have caused such devastation in a chapel. Usually, that was the last place an enemy would attack, when a castle was under siege. More chills, and a definite feeling of evil seemed to permeate the area. She turned and quickly left.

It's almost terrifying, she told herself as she walked on through the rubble. Her head was beginning to throb, as she reminded herself to watch the time. Shrugging her shoulders, she decided to mention it to Kieron tonight, but then remembered she wasn't supposed to be here in the first place.

Deciding to put it in the back of her mind for a later time, Sam turned and headed inside the remains of the great hall, to see what changes had taken place there.

This was an area which would have been somehow attached to the castle itself, via a hallway of some sort. She immediately noticed that the vibrations were even louder there. Had the workers heard this, too? They must have, she told herself. Yet no one had mentioned it to her.

Suddenly, she heard a noise behind her. She spun around, only to find no one. The feeling of being watched was nearly paralyzing.

"Who's there?" she called out, thinking one of the workers had forgotten something. Again the noise. She was ready to bolt, then stopped dead.

"Samantha," a male voice said. "Samantha . . . take heed." A definite warning which sent her into full blown terror. "Who are you? Show yourself, now."

No one.

She forced her feet to take a step, only to trip over the edge of something embedded in the moss and dirt on the ground. Lying at her feet, was the tip of a silver blade. It seemed to call to her. She pulled the dirt covered dagger from the ground where it had been embedded for centuries, and wiped it off with the hem of her shirt.

It was beautiful, a silver dagger with a sparkling blue sapphire on the hilt. Stepping into the afternoon sun for a better look, she pulled some Kleenex from her purse, and wiped it clean.

"Duncan MacClaire" had been beautifully engraved next to the regally shaped hilt. Duncan MacClaire? Why was his dagger here, buried for centuries, and why did she find it? It was amazing it wasn't taken by any of the workers. Somehow, she knew it was for her alone. Could all this nonsense possibly have a single grain of truth to it?

Sam was quickly becoming tired and overcome with the emotions that suddenly flooded throughout her. Enough, she thought, slipping the gleaming dagger into her shoulder bag, and snapping it closed. "It's mine now." Somehow it gave her a boost of confidence.

She began the walk back to the castle's entrance, thinking about what it would look like when it was finished. It would definitely help if she could just find a picture of what the castle had looked like originally.

Sam's heart broke for her home and family, back in Boston. What were they doing now? It had been weeks since she'd left, and with her busy schedule, she hadn't called as much as she should. Feeling guilt ridden, she continued her lonely exploration of what had once been the stronghold of a happy, flourishing clan.

She stopped short, as she turned the corner in what must have led into a different part of the great hall. She heard voices, more like echoes. Not just one, but several this time. She quickly followed the voices who were laughing and deep in conversation. She wasn't alone.

Filled with new determination, and a good dose of questionable courage, she straightened her shoulders and told herself this was now her castle. But where were the voices coming from? There was absolutely no one around, and no cars or bikes parked anywhere in sight. There had to be some completely logical reason.

Her memory shot back to Kieron, explaining how Rosestone was built on crossing ley lines. Sam had to admit, she had never heard of them before. He told her how they harnessed the metaphysical energy in the earth, causing the constant vibration she felt.

"Where the lines cross, the energy is the strongest," he'd explained.

She followed the strange feeling, wanting to see where it would lead. As she walked toward the north wall, the muffled echoes grew stronger. She finally ended up outside the castle walls, next to the terrace housing the beautiful astral sphere. Impossible! She could almost hear the voices clearly now, except there was no one there.

Her mind went back to the people she'd seen on the castle walls when she first arrived. Who were they? Is that what she was hearing? Was this some type of portal, like the young taxi driver explained? Was she actually hearing ancient echoes from people of another time? Sam found that thought both frightening and wildly exhilarating, and found herself wanting to talk to them.

How wonderful it must have been to live here with your family, she thought sadly. Without giving it a thought, she unsnapped her bag, and pulled out the dirk. For some reason, she wanted to see it, touch it with her fingers. It comforted her, in some crazy way.

I must be in bad shape, she thought miserably, getting comfort from a centuries old silver blade, which may have killed and maimed who knows how many?

Sitting down on a large rock, she laid it across her lap, bent her head and cried. She was emotionally exhausted, and could take no more. Oceans of tears ran down her face, onto the gleaming steel. She cried for herself, and the sense of family she lost by coming to Scotland. She was a failure, and wanted to go back home. Let someone else take this on, she thought, tears streaming down her face. It's too much for me. Why me anyway?

As she sobbed, she once again heard the male voice, but this time it was very close, in fact, it was directly in front of her. Her head snapped up from her private pity party, to see a very handsome, well-built man who eerily reminded her of Kieron.

This man was tall and muscular, with thick brawny biceps, and a beautifully handsome face. His eyes were a lovely deep ocean blue, and his long dark brown hair was sprinkled with the slightest touch of gray, and pulled to the back of his head. He appeared to be in his forties, and wore strange clothes, as if from another time. The dead giveaway was a long sword, which he wore strapped to his back in a leather scabbard. Sam should have been absolutely terrified, but somehow wasn't. He smiled down at her with a tender expression.

"Why do you weep so, lass? Is aught amiss? Are you in pain?" he asked with genuine concern. His accent was slightly different from Kieron's.

Sam stared up at this ruggedly handsome man for several seconds. "Who are you, why are you here?"

He dismounted, stepping over to her. Bending down on one knee, he took her trembling hand in his. Sam knew she should be afraid, knew she should get up and run for her life. Was he a demon in disguise?

Then she remembered Kieron's warning, that there were many types of demons who crossed over, and were able to assume different shapes. For some reason she didn't fear him, but wanted to stay close. His countenance was warm and comforting, and any fear she had was quickly fading.

"Do not fash child, you are in no danger. I'm your father, Duncan MacClaire," he smiled. His eyes were beautiful, and conveyed a love and gentleness she had experienced only by Kieron.

Shock spread across her face. "I'm either hallucinating or dreaming," she said.

"Neither," he smiled tenderly. She felt a strange closeness to this large warrior. She could tell just by looking at his size and obvious strength that he was skillful, able to kill in a second if needed.

Before Sam realized what she was doing, she leaped up from the bench, and threw her arms around his neck starting a new crying streak.

"Shh lass," he whispered, holding her gently. "It will all be clear to you very soon. Your mother and I have missed you sorely. We are awaiting your return to us. Where has your husband gotten to, and why you are here alone?" he asked, obviously very concerned.

Duncan sat down on the bench, and pulled her down next to him. "I fear you are confused now, but do not fash over it. Kieron will lead you safely back home to us. You must be obedient, child. What he tells you is solely for your own safety."

"There are many dangers lurking here, the old one wants you dead. Remember, Ambrosius has cursed you to never return home again, but I will not allow it. For now, you must stay near your husband at all times, he is strong enough to protect you."

Sam looked up, realizing that daylight was almost gone. If Kieron was already home, she was in big trouble.

"Why are you here, and when will I see you again?" she asked, looking up into his loving face.

"I felt your sadness, your tears touched my blade. It's yours now. Keep it close to you, for one day soon you'll need it. It's very special, and to be used by only you, and for only one reason. You'll understand soon, lass. Be brave, remember my words."

As Duncan wiped the tears from her face, a sudden whirling noise filled the air. Before she realized what was happening, a large howling form materialized from the stones in the lower wall. This demon was larger than the one she had seen previously, and had a somewhat human form. It stood about five feet tall, and was grey in color. Dark soulless eyes filled with torment and anguish locked onto her.

Duncan was instantly on his feet, unsheathing the long claymore. As the demon sprang for Samantha, he swung the deadly sword in an arc, then brought it down, slicing the creature's head from its foul body. Sam watched in horror as it rolled down the steep cliff, into the sea.

He dropped the sword and grabbed Samantha. "Are you alright?"

"I'm okay," she stammered as she looked down at the grisly sight. Duncan swiftly kicked the decaying creature across the road and into the thick glen.

"Thank God you were here," she said, holding on to him with an iron grip. "Where did it come from?"

He cautiously scanned the grounds. "My senses tell me there are many in hiding here, around and under the large stone and rocks of this hallowed place."

Sam looked toward the castle. It was truly a picture of beauty and grace, with the sun almost gone, shooting rays of crimson and gold into the darkening sky.

"They await the hours of gloaming. The sun burns their dark cursed soul, so they remain captives of the night. They are sent by the sorcerer himself. He will not cease until the curse he spelled on you centuries ago comes to fruition, but I will not allow it to happen. That's why I sent you away with Kieron. He will always protect you, but you must heed his words."

Sam nodded obediently.

He looked down at her tenderly. "Now, you must leave this place, before more attacks begin."

"I will," she told him, fumbling through her bag until she found the cell phone Kieron bought her. "I don't have a car. I'll need to call a taxi so I can get home."

Duncan smiled in amusement, "Nay lass, you have no need of this phone, nor the taxi. Just close your eyes and think of home and I will deliver you there, to safety."

She looked up into his loving face. "Will I ever see you again?" The words tugged heavily at her heart.

"Soon love, we will all be together again soon. Are you ready to leave?" he asked, nervously searching the immediate grounds.

Sam nodded. "Yes," she whispered as she hugged him tightly.

"Oidhche mhath, good night. Know that you're always in my heart," he whispered, planting a gentle kiss on her forehead.

"Oidhche mhath," she whispered back, and closed her eyes.

Sam suddenly found herself standing in the middle of Kieron's library. Her head was spinning, and she fell into one of the soft cushioned chairs. She sat there, stunned, recalling what had just happened. She missed Duncan already, cherishing the feeling of safety she experienced being near to him. She remembered his words . . . *We will all be together again soon.*

Kieron had not yet returned. Should she tell him? Would he be upset that she had broken her promise? I'll have to deal with that when the time comes, she told herself, as she closed her eyes and fell into a deep, troubled sleep.

* * *

She was caught up in another vivid nightmare, running down a dark lonely road. A powerful evil chased her. It grew closer with every passing second. She desperately cried out for Kieron, as she raced through the lonely deserted field, but he didn't come. He was no longer there for her. Her heart was filled with pain and despair, as she realized it was over, he would no longer be there to save her from her demons.

It serves me right, she thought mournfully as she caught herself from tripping over the thick weeds and creeping vines. I will die like this, because I didn't listen to him, now he's gone.

Just then she tripped, her foot snagged in a thick patch of weeds. She fell to the ground, and braced herself against the impending attack. Kieron was gone for good, and Samantha McKinley had nothing more to live for. She closed her eyes tightly, braced herself and prepared to die . . .

CHAPTER ELEVEN

Niall McInnis opened the door to his tiny house, his sleek black cat Luthias, watching from high on a ledge above the front door. It was a place especially made for the cat, a place where he was secure and could easily pounce down on anyone fool enough to enter when they're not invited.

Luthias was also a shape shifter, an ancient species which has become almost extinct in modern times. He was a very close friend of Niall McInnis. He'd saved Niall from an unsuspected demonic attack, but in doing so, was cursed to spend the rest of his days as a shifter, changing into the form of a sleek black cat at will. Niall was forever indebted to him, and vowed to be his friend and protector forever.

It was a small house near the outskirts of Edinburgh, which Niall had once shared with his wife. They had been married fifty years, before she finally lost her battle with breast cancer, leaving him a grieving and lonely man.

Unfortunately, there were no children to help lighten his life. Niall took solace in his job, teaching students about the second love of his life, Ancient Celtic History.

He and Kieron were brothers in a very ancient band of immortal warriors, the Keepers of the Light. A select group of angels, gifted with a pure heart and soul, they voluntarily vowed to protect the world from darkness and evil.

Now, dark spirits were after a certain young American woman, Samantha McKinley. A personal vendetta originating centuries ago, and one which Niall McInnis pledged his unconditional help to his brother warrior, Kieron.

Something was wrong. Who was this American? Why was she so interested in Kieron? He knew Kieron better than himself, and he also knew she must be someone of extreme importance, since she claimed to be living with him. It didn't make sense.

Kieron was not a man to be easily swayed by women. In fact, over the past decades, Niall couldn't remember a single time when the mighty warrior had been smitten by a lovely face, or enticing lush figure. He was always ready to tease a young lass with that wicked, drop dead sexy grin of his, but that was where it stopped. No, Kieron MacClaire had remained a widower since the death of his lovely wife, centuries ago.

Niall had always hoped he would eventually find someone that he could be happy with, but the idea was a futile one. Kieron's pure soul was eternally bound to that of his wife's, Duncan MacClaire's youngest daughter. Their souls were now bound together in marriage for all eternity. Neither one would want nor long for another, it was just impossible. He would have none but her. The many centuries had been lonely ones for Kieron.

Luthias, Niall's cat, greeted them at the door, rubbing up against the old man's leg.

"Aye Luthias," he smiled, as he bent done to scratch the cat's head, "I've missed you too."

Kieron smiled in amusement as the sleek, black cat pranced closely behind them into the kitchen.

"Oh, so it's dinner you're after?" Niall grinned, tearing open a new pack of cat treats, and pouring the contents into his bowl.

"There, that should keep you happy for a while."

The cat quickly set into devouring the treats.

The two men walked to Niall's library, where Kieron explained the situation to his old friend. He told him about Samantha, and how his first meeting with her happened.

Niall hugged his friend in happiness. "Did you know it was her at first sight?" he asked, eyes misting with joy for his brother.

"Aye, her soul spoke to me. It was glowing with a golden ethereal light," he told him, smiling at the memory of Sam's face.

"I am overjoyed for you, brother. It's not often souls meet again, especially in this realm."

"I knew she would return to me, I just needed to wait," he told Niall as he sat in a plush brown leather chair.

"Aye, and wait you did. How long has it been now?"

Kieron shrugged his shoulders as he gazed out the window into the night. "Since that grievous day she was taken from me in death, five hundred years ago." Several seconds passed, filled with a tangible sadness.

Niall got up from his seat. "Well, let us waste no more time on things of sadness." He opened his liquor cabinet, and reached inside for a bottle of fifty year old Glenfiddich Whiskey, Kieron's favorite. He poured the whiskey into two fine crystal glasses, handing one to Kieron.

"Ah, you never forget my old friend," Kieron chuckled as he brought the glass to his nose, inhaling the rich aroma.

"We need to find that amulet," he said, sipping the expensive whiskey.

He turned to face Niall. "As you know, the sorcerer's power is great. He'll stop at nothing to kill her."

"That much is true," Niall agreed, glancing over at his vast collection of ancient manuscripts. "I was hoping you might still have something in one of your books, referencing it. I've researched quite extensively throughout my collection, but could find nothing. I seem to remember that somewhere there is information on it."

"It would be quite old," Niall answered as he rose and crossed the room. He stepped over to an old wooden desk, and spoke three strange sounding words from a now dead language. Instantly, there was a soft 'click', and the two bottom drawers in the desk popped opened.

"Always best to be safe," he grinned, as Kieron smiled approvingly. The bottom drawer held a sparkling clear case with two thick books bound in dark brown leather.

"Kept in a perfect vacuum all these centuries. I see you thought of everything," Kieron joked, as he picked up the case, placing it carefully on his lap.

Again, Niall uttered a single word and the box instantly opened. A soft "whish" was heard, as Kieron lifted the lid, after centuries of being locked away.

"These are the most ancient of all my collection, going back to several decades before the initial construction of the castle," Niall explained.

"The texts are in ancient Gaelic. As you well know, it vanished years ago, when Gaelic became more modified for the human race. The pages are worn with age. I've had to spell them several times to prevent their disintegration."

Kieron reverently opened the book, gingerly turning its faded pages. "It's magnificent!" he whispered, caught up in a history that modern society has no knowledge of. "Records of events and happenings since the beginning of time."

He gently turned the thin, parched pages, delighted to read about the ancient ones, once again.

"There is much about the ancient Vikings," Kieron noted, reading about the decision on the part of the Norse God Odin to construct a castle in northern Scotland. The requirements were that it must be constructed on strong ley lines, to secure a good electromagnetic pull for the portal, facilitating travel to and from other realms to ours. Second, it must be near a body of salt water, since that is one of the necessary properties for time travel."

"Aye," Niall noted, "It would seem the perfect place for any info on Rosestone, since many of the first known Vikings had much to say about the construction of the castle."

"It states," Kieron continued to read, "the large sandstone blocks used in its construction were made from a special material, which gathered electromagnetic energy from deep within the earth."

"One of the earliest time portals," Niall grinned. "Other forms developed later in time."

They researched into the night, both on the web and also in the remaining two priceless volumes of the professor's private collection.

The two gathered several significant manuscripts and papers, with help from Luthias, who also was able to read the most ancient of scripts. He was brilliant, and in his prior life had spent many a day and night in the Royal Scriptorium in Alexandria. There, he busied himself translating languages which were now dead, for Queen Cleopatra herself. It was reported that he served as both her confidant, and lover. Tales of his legendary sexual prowess found its way to Rome, and Caesar himself.

Together Luthias, Niall and Kieron began the long, dire task of finding anything pertinent to Rosestone and the lost amulet which was needed to break the curse. It was a long painstaking job, and Kieron's mid drifted back to Samantha, and what she was doing.

Sam had promised not to leave the house, so Kieron hadn't worried for her safety while he was gone. His home was heavily spelled against the very strongest of evils. He was absolutely sure she would be safe in his absence. Unfortunately there was one realm Kieron had forgotten, that of the mind.

* * *

Sam's nightmare continued. She screamed in terror as the demon caught her, shaking her violently with its razor sharp talons and tearing her delicate skin. Hitting and kicking with all her strength, she attempted to get the putrid smelling creature off her wounded body. "Kieron! Kieron help me!" she screamed out into the night, but Kieron was gone.

* * *

Several hours had passed as Kieron, Niall and Luthias sat researching information on this very necessary long forgotten amulet. Kieron was deeply engrossed in one particular book, when Luthias looked up in alarm. "Your woman is in danger," he said, green eyes flashing angrily.

"Sam!" Kieron yelled out, jumping up from the chair and heading toward the door.

Niall turned to Luthias. "Thank you my old friend," as he put the book down, and followed Kieron out the front door.

As they tore down the front porch steps, and into the calm starry night, a VW careened down the street and came to a screeching halt in the driveway. A very distressed young woman jumped out from the car.

"Professor McInnis! Wait please, it's me, Brianna!" she pleaded, trying to stop them before they made it to Kieron's car.

The professor stopped dead, noting how emotional she was, and wondering why on earth she was at his house at that late hour.

"Brianna, what's wrong? What is it lass?" he asked as he glanced at Kieron who grew more agitated by the second.

"It's Sam, I'm worried something's happened to her.

They told me she called my office number this afternoon, saying she wanted me to go up to the castle with her. I didn't get the message until I got home this evening. I know that it's late, but I have this terrible feeling that something's happened to her."

Kieron grabbed her by the arm. "Did you just tell me that Samantha went to the castle by herself?" he roared, holding her arm so tightly it began to throb.

"Yes, sometime this afternoon. I'm sorry Kieron," she apologized, trying to pull her arm free from his steely hold. "I know you didn't want her up there alone, I just figured you'd be with her. I've been trying to contact her, but she doesn't answer her cell."

Kieron yelled out a string of obscenities in Gaelic as he flew to his car, the professor hobbling along with Brianna behind him. Brianna managed to make it into the backseat, as Kieron tore away from the curb, tires squealing on the macadam.

In a matter of seconds, Kieron's car came to a screeching halt in front of his house. The lights in the library were on, giving him some hope that she was inside.

They ran in the house, Kieron tearing down the hall toward the library, and the professor trailing behind him reminding himself to limp.

"Sam!" Kieron roared, but there was no reply. He tore into the library, finding Samantha curled up in a fetal position on the carpet in the corner of the room. Totally incoherent, eyes fixed and dilated, she just stared into thin air with an expression of pure terror.

"What happened to her?" Brianna gasped, seeing her condition.

Kieron dropped to the floor, carefully scooping her up in his arms.

"Careful Kieron," Niall warned, "We don't know what injuries she's suffered."

Kieron nodded, as he carried her down the hall to the bedroom, and placed her gently on the bed. Her skin was flushed, but otherwise unmarked.

"Sam, my love," he whispered as he pushed strands of damp red hair from her eyes. "Can you hear me?" She was motionless, showing no sign that she was aware they were there.

Brianna began to cry frantically. "It's all my fault," she sobbed, staring down at the motionless form laying helplessly on the bed.

Niall pulled her close, trying to stop her tears. "Don't be ridiculous, lass. How could it be your fault? You didn't speak with her today."

"But if I had, maybe this wouldn't have happened," she sobbed.

"Check her pulse, I think she's in shock," Niall offered, as he pulled a clean white handkerchief from his pocket, and offered it to Brianna.

Kieron checked it immediately. "It's pretty weak."

He checked her from head to toe for any injuries, luckily there were none.

"What could have happened to her?" Brianna asked nervously, biting her nails and trying desperately to stop her tears.

"Something must have happened at the castle, but how did she get back? I doubt any taxi would have brought her home in this condition," he noted, rubbing his jaw as he did when trying to figure something out.

Kieron's expression was troubled. "Perhaps she returned by some other means."

Niall understood exactly, and desperately hoped he was wrong. "Since there are no physical marks on her, we must surmise the damage is purely psychological. For that, she must rest until her mind is ready to let go of the experience, whatever it was," he explained.

Kieron nodded, then thanked the professor and Brianna for their help. It was now almost two in the morning, and Sam needed rest and quiet.

He threw the professor his car keys. "Take Brianna back to her car," he told him, "and see that she gets home safely. I will be back sometime tomorrow to pick up my car. Samantha will need much rest. If there's any worsening in her condition, I'll take her to the University Hospital for further care. I'll call you later, and update you on her condition."

He politely thanked a sniffling Brianna for letting him know what happened. "Don't cry, I have no intentions of losing her," he joked, as he gave her a big hug. "She'll be fine," he said, but his eyes did little to hide his anger and concern.

Kieron flipped the lights on in the dark hallway. "I agree with you, she just needs a lot of rest, and I intend to be at her side every second until she wakes. I trust you can see yourselves out."

"Of course," Niall smiled. "Let me know later. I'll be waiting to hear from you."

Kieron promised he would.

"Come lass," Niall said, gently taking Brianna's arm. "I'll bring you safely home."

"Thank you, old friend," Kieron said, putting his hand on the professor's frail, slumping shoulders. "It seems you're always there to help me."

The old man smiled, eyes twinkling, "And I always will be," he said as they turned and left the room.

* * *

Sam moaned off and on during the remainder of the night. She neither opened her eyes, nor made any sign that she knew Kieron was with her. He carefully removed her clothes, bathed her unresponsive body with cool water, and dressed her in a new nightgown for more comfort. It was to have been a surprise, he thought glumly. Afterward, he took another washcloth, ran it under cool water and placed it on her damp forehead.

As the early hours of morning slowly rolled by, Kieron kept a faithful watch. Suddenly at seven a.m., she began to thrash back and forth, desperately yelling out his name.

"Sam, wake up. Wake up, your dreaming. Look at me Sam," he said calmly, not wanting to frighten her any further. She thrashed back and forth, as if fighting for her very life. Finally, she laid back on the pillow and opened her eyes.

"Kieron," she whispered, her face glowing with peace. "You're really here. I thought you left me."

He bent down, gently holding her trembling body. "Aye love, I am here, forever." He kissed her cheek, and Sam once again fell into a deep sleep, this one filled with peace. Her angel had come for her.

Despite her many protests, Kieron was taking no chances. He made her stay in bed for the remainder of the day.

"I know you're angry with me," she said timidly, as he entered the bedroom carrying a serving tray with hot lunch on it.

The morning sky was overcast, thick ominous clouds moving in from the west. A cool breeze blew the curtains open, filling the room with the lovely scent of roses from the neighbor's garden.

Carefully placing the silver tray on the bedside table, he sat down on the bed next to her. His eyes locked with hers, telling her that he could never in a thousand eternities be angry with her.

"Sam," he said caressing her cheek, "you must know by now how much you mean to me. My life without you, has been void and lonely. Now that you're with me again, I treasure each and every minute, and will do nothing to put you in danger. Can you understand that?"

He pulled her close, and closed his arms around her body. He was so heartbreakingly honest and sincere, she felt like a fool for the pain she'd caused him. After all was said and done, he wasn't mad at all, just worried sick. She was a stubborn fool for disobeying him and her father. Then and there, she vowed never to cause either pain again.

He picked up half of the roast beef sandwich he made, and tried encouraging her to eat. Afraid of disappointing him, Samantha tried taking a small bite, but was too exhausted.

"Is there something wrong, love? Perhaps some warm soup would be better right now," he suggested. To his dismay, she couldn't handle that either.

"I'm sorry, it was very sweet of you to do this, she smiled weakly, "but I just can't eat." She was filled with guilt at all the efforts he made to make her comfortable.

. "Don't worry, perhaps later. It's probably too early, and I mustn't force things," he added with an understanding smile.

What a once in a lifetime man, she thought. How had she been so lucky? Placing the tray back on the bedside table, he again sat down next to her.

"Sam, can you tell me what happened at the castle?" he asked gently. "I promise I won't be mad, nor will I yell. I can definitely understand if you don't want to talk about it just yet, but I would like to know sometime. It's very important."

Always so kind and thoughtful toward her, how could she be so selfish to put her feelings first? After all, this was her fault in the first place. Look at what she'd put them through, just to have her own way.

"Of course," she told him, feeling terrible. "I would do anything to take away this guilty feeling."

Kieron couldn't resist. He looked at her with mischief in his eyes. "I'll make a list of requests," he smiled wickedly.

She threw a pillow at him, but he only laughed, blowing her a kiss. Sam ended up telling him everything, including the meeting she had with her father.

"Duncan came to you?" he asked in amazement. "What did he say?"

Sam's face turned red with embarrassment. She fumbled for a few seconds, fiddling with the edge of the bed sheet.

Finally Kieron could take no more. "Out with it lass. I haven't seen him in many years now, what did he tell you?"

She looked down at the floor, not able to meet his eye.

"He said I should obey you."

Kieron burst out laughing. It was so genuine, she had never seen him laugh that hard before. He was always so solemn and serious.

"Kieron, it's not that funny," she pleaded, watching him roar.

"Oh, it is lass. It seems the powerful Lord MacClaire doesn't remember his lovely daughter that well. I can't imagine you obeying anyone, no less a man," he roared.

"Well," she said timidly, feeling her face grow hot with embarrassment, "you did ask."

He could sense her regret, and began planting kisses on her face and neck. "It's okay Sam, I was only joking with you. It's just that he doesn't realize the brave modern woman you've become."

Before she knew it, his mouth was on hers, and she no longer cared about anything else.

CHAPTER TWELVE

The day passed quickly. Evening rolled in, darkness covered the earth, and a heavy rain pelted down leaving Sam in a state of high agitation. Kieron had planned on taking her out for dinner, but she was still feeling skittish about leaving the house. Instead, they settled for pizza, salad and wine.

"That's even better," he told her, with one of his gorgeous smiles. "I don't have to worry about you freaking out on me in a restaurant. Would you mind terribly if I asked the professor over this evening?" he asked. "He was terribly worried about you, Sam."

Again she felt guilty. "Of course not," she sighed. "Guess I ruined his evening too, didn't I? Could we ask Brianna too?"

"Absolutely, after all, she was the one who tipped me off."

She looked up into those incredible eyes. "I feel like a spoiled brat who caused trouble for the entire family trying to have her own way."

He reached out and pulled her against him, enclosing her in his arms. Samantha sighed as she savored the strength and uncompromised love for her in those strong arms, the arms of a mighty angel warrior, her husband.

That evening, Niall brought Luthias along with him, tucked safely under his arm. He jumped down to the floor, as they entered the house.

Brianna laughed in amusement as she watched the curious cat check out the kitchen, looking up on the counter at the pizza boxes.

"You know pizza doesn't agree with you, Luthias," Niall said sternly. "Remember the last time you sampled some? You were up all night with a terrible stomach ache."

The cat gave him an understanding look, then took off around the corner for parts unknown.

Sam laughed. "It's as though he really understands what you tell him."

"Every word," Niall grinned. "He knows he shouldn't eat spicy food. He's much more comfortable with a bowl of fresh milk, and a good book."

Kieron just shrugged his shoulders and grinned.

The four of them had a pleasant evening together, enjoying pizza, wine and listening to Kieron and Niall's outlandish stories of things that happened in their past. Somehow, it seemed quite natural to Sam, having Niall and Brianna there in their company, although she didn't know why.

Niall turned to Kieron. "I just happened to find a very old manuscript with a very interesting piece in it about Rosestone," he informed him. "It was pushed far behind the others, guess I'd forgotten about it," he said, as he sipped on red wine. "There is a very good rendition of how it looked, when it was still standing. Would you care to see it, Sam?"

"Of course!" She almost flew from the chair to get her hands on it. Sam carefully opened the old leather bound book to the page he had marked.

"Careful," Kieron warned her, "that book is priceless."

"Oh, it's so beautiful!" she squealed. "So realistic, simply breathtaking!" She spun around, automatically showing the picture to Brianna.

"Wow, what a beautiful place to live," she said longingly.

Kieron looked over at Niall and grinned with satisfaction. "I'm glad you found it," he told the old man, as he continued to watch the two women with fascination.

"Well Sam, what do you think?" Kieron asked, but there was no answer. She was totally mesmerized by what she saw.

"Sam?" Kieron said again.

"Sorry. I just never dreamed it would look so beautiful. I can't get it out of my mind, it looks so, so . . . ," she trailed off as if somewhere else.

"So what?" he asked with a smile.

"So much like home," she whispered, finally shedding the tears she'd been fighting to hold back.

Brianna got up from her chair to hold Sam's hand. "You'll see it again, Sam. Once the renovations are finished."

A sudden picture flashed into Sam's mind, then left just as fast. It was one of Brianna, dressed in a 17th century wedding gown, standing with a handsome warrior, in Rosestone's lush gardens. It came and left so quickly, it actually made her dizzy.

"Are you alright?" Brianna asked.

"I'm fine. I just get these strange thoughts every now and then. Can't figure out where they come from," she said, wiping her tears with a paper napkin.

Niall looked over at Kieron with a knowing smile.

"It's okay Sam," Kieron said soothingly. "It's okay to cry because it *is* home. A home you were sent away from for your own good, by a loving family who missed you terribly. What you're feeling is nothing less than inherent memories.

What else did Duncan tell you?" he asked, as he massaged her shoulders gently.

She lifted her head to him and whispered, "He told me he loved me, and I was always in his heart." Then after a few seconds, "I miss him Kieron. Was he a good man?"

"Aye lass," Niall was quick to answer. "A very good and noble man, one of the finest. He was loved by all at his castle."

She looked up at him with a confused expression. She was afraid to ask him, afraid of what the answer might be. Finally summoning up the courage, she asked. "Did you know him too, professor?" not understanding how it could be possible.

A bright smiled spread over the old man's face. "Aye Samantha, I knew your father well," he grinned. "A wonderful man. I drank many an ale there in the great hall with him, Luthias, Angus, and of course Kieron."

Kieron was also laughing and nodding his head in agreement. "Ah Niall, those were good days, long passed."

"For the moment, brother," the old man said meaningfully.

Brianna shot Sam a frown. She was clearly irritated by something, but said nothing.

Sam was silent, as several strange feelings and visions flooded her mind, then quickly left. It was almost as though she was dreaming, yet remained wide awake.

"Angus?" she finally asked.

"Your father's brother. Also a fine man, but a bit stern if I remember, aye Kieron?"

"That he was," Kieron replied, with a nostalgic smile, "but only with the hired men. He was a teddy bear with his family, especially his nieces. He and his wife Morna had no children of their own."

"And my mother?" she asked hesitantly.

"Your mother, Kathleen, was beloved by all. She wasn't from their time either," the professor was quick to point out. "They say she inadvertently traveled back in time from the early 1990's. Something about an enchanted crystal that she found while vacationing on the ruins at Rosestone. When she met your father, it was a love match from heaven. She never wanted to return," Niall laughed heartily.

"True," Kieron added. "I doubt that Duncan would have ever let her go, even if she wanted to. He loved her so," he said softly, shooting a meaningful glance at Samantha.

She understood what he meant. How rare to find a love like theirs, in any century.

Sam was now growing homesick for a family she never knew. She wanted to go home. Home to a castle filled with a large, loving family . . . home to Kieron.

Sam temporarily excused herself to freshen up, after her tearful experience at the kitchen table. Walking to the hall, she spotted Luthias, sitting in the corner near a dish of milk which Kieron had laid out for him. She smiled comically at the cat, who refused to leave until the milk was gone. As she turned her back to continue down the hall, she had the strangest feeling someone was watching her.

She abruptly stopped, and spun around. There, where the cat had been sitting, stood a tall muscular man with bright green eyes that shone like emeralds, and hid a multitude of secrets. Long black hair hung down past his shoulders to his rock hard abdomen. His white shirt hung open in the front, until it disappeared beneath the waist of his snug leather pants. He stood there, arms folded, leaning against the doorframe, smiling at her. On his broad chest was a tattoo of a cat's head. Black leather pants hung low on his hips, and an emerald encrusted dagger tucked snugly under his wide leather belt. He was every woman's fantasy, barefoot and totally relaxed. Sam couldn't miss the huge bulge in the front of his pants, assuring her that this big kitty was more than ready to play. He said nothing, just looked at her with a smile dripping with seduction. A scorching hot fantasy in real time, more than ready for action.

She blinked several times, but he was gone, and the cat stared back at her as if she were crazy. After a second, it ignored her, and finished drinking his milk.

"Whew!" she said as she tried to regain her senses, once again heading down the hall. "How'd I miss *him*?" She fully intended to tell Kieron about it, then something very erotic hit her. They'd just think I'm a mental case anyway, as they probably already do. No, she smiled wickedly, I'll just keep this fantasy to myself, life at home might not be so terrible after all!

Brianna was proving to be the perfect friend, more like family, she thought. Always offering her help, or perhaps giving some needed advice. Sam was beginning to realize that she would never return to Boston, at least not permanently. Although she missed her family terribly, a new and different feeling was starting to grow, one which would eventually change her life in a way she could have never dreamed.

* * *

"Do you think your hulking boyfriend would mind if we went to lunch someday? Please!" Brianna complained during a frequent visit to Kieron's house.

She was there for the afternoon, a girl's day out, but inside instead. She longed to spend an afternoon just with Sam, for some good old fashioned girl talk. Since Sam's unfortunate event, Kieron had been glued to her hip.

The two sat in the kitchen, talking and enjoying some homemade ice cream that Sam had made, while Kieron sat close by in the study, reading one of Niall's ancient books.

"I would just love to," Sam told her, licking chocolate ice cream off her lips, "but you know how he is."

"Like a mother," Brianna said, rolling her eyes. "What could be wrong in just having a girl's day out? We would be in a busy restaurant, I can't see any danger in that," she argued.

"I'll fly it past him tonight and see what he says," Sam promised. "I know how he feels, but truth be told, I am starting to feel a little smothered."

"A little!" Brianna said, throwing up her hands, "I guess he's the first thing you see in the morning, and the last thing before you go to sleep!"

"Yeah, and that can be pretty nice at times, too," Sam kidded with a sheepish smile.

"I know," Brianna sighed, her loneliness was evident. "I just wish he had a brother."

"Well, apparently he did," Sam told her, "two, Angus and Duncan, although they weren't blood brothers. The MacClaires sort of adopted him into their Clan, guess they were very close."

Brianna threw her a troubled look. She wanted to say something, but stopped short.

"What?" Sam asked, looking at the strange expression on her face. "Come on girl, you can tell me."

Several seconds passed. Finally, Brianna looked her straight in the eye. "Sam, I hope you don't take this the wrong way, but I really don't know how else to put it. Do you really buy all this stuff he's telling you about time travel? I mean, really? Even the old professor seems to be all wrapped up in this stuff."

"I can't believe the two of them telling you all that crap the other night. He has that poor old man sounding like he's delusional. Just stop and listen to some of the stuff he's feeding you . . . time travel, families in the early seventeenth century. What's next? I'm starting to think you're getting way too wrapped up in it."

"You know I would never pry, or hurt your feelings on purpose," she continued, "but don't you think this whole thing is going too far?" She was dead serious.

Sam took a deep breath, looking out the kitchen window. "Brianna, if someone were to have asked me that question one month ago, I would tell them that unequivocally, beyond a doubt, there is no such thing as time travel. But, after what I've seen, and what both Kieron and Niall told me, well, yes, I do believe it."

Brianna looked at her, not wishing to push the subject any further. They were the best of friends, and she had no intentions of letting this or anything else ruin that relationship. Case closed.

"Do you know what I'd love to do Sam?" she asked, eyes glittering with excitement. "I'd love to go up and see that castle someday, just you and me. What do you say?"

Several seconds of silence passed. "Brianna, you know . . ."

Brianna quickly cut her off. "I know, I know, he would never allow it. But just for a few minutes, just you and me. What could happen?" she asked naively.

"A lot," Sam shot back sharply. "Believe me girl, you don't want to be there when the sun sets, not good. Those creatures are for real, and they mean business. Anyway, I swore to Kieron that I'd never do it again. I mean to keep that promise, Brianna. He is too good to me, and I won't break his heart, hope you can understand."

"Sure Sam," she said as she hugged her friend. "I do get it, really. I know how much you believe in him. He's a wonderful man, and quite sexy too, I might add. Lucky you!" she laughed.

"Best friends, then?" Sam asked with a grin.

"Forever," Brianna answered with a haunting smile.

"Aye, Brianna, forever."

CHAPTER THIRTEEN

"Absolutely not!" Kieron yelled with a voice that could bring down the house. "Sam, we've been through all this before."

Sam hung her head, "I know, I know. It's just that we'd like to go out for lunch or something, just us girls. I knew you wouldn't understand. Please don't be mad."

Kieron pulled her into his arms. "Sorry Sam, I didn't mean to yell like that, it wasn't fair to you. Will you forgive me?"

"You know I will," she whispered softly against his cheek. She knew when he looked at her like that, it meant only one thing. One thing that she would never deny him. She couldn't if she tried.

The next morning proved to be a busy one. Kieron never failed to provide different and interesting ways to keep Sam busy, as he managed to keep her close to him, and out of danger.

Sam was busy making coffee in Kieron's quaint country kitchen. They had both slept in, and it was now late in the morning.

"Smells good," Kieron told her. He opened the cabinet, pulling out two new mugs they recently bought at a small shop near the edge of town. He started taking her out on frequent shopping sprees to get her mind off staying home, telling her she could redecorate the kitchen into something she preferred, a more feminine theme.

Sam loved the idea, and quickly redecorated his small manly, no frills kitchen into a soft lilac feminine retreat. He offered no complaints about the color, and was delighted to see her happy. He would have pulled down the heavens for her, if she asked him.

She stepped over to him, handing him the hot mug with two hands. He took the mug, gently kissing her cheek. God, she thought, he looks gorgeous, even after a rough night.

As he took the mug, he pulled out a small velvet box from his jeans pocket, handing it to Sam. She looked down at the box with surprise.

"Go on," he urged, giving her a radiant smile, "Open it, it's for you."

Her eyes began to sparkle and her smile was radiant.

"For me?" she repeated, eyeing the mysterious little black box.

"I've been wanting to give it to you for some time now, but there always seems to be something else to do at the time. This is your time, Sam."

With trembling hands, she reached over and took it. The black velvet was soft and smooth against her fingers.

"Go ahead," he urged her in a soft voice, "open it."

Sam slowly lifted the top of the box. She was instantly met with a bright flash of blue light, almost blinding her to the object sitting inside. It was a ring. A majestic deep blue stone the size of a nickel, mounted on a band of sparkling yellow gold. Not just any blue stone, but something very special. This one gave off a strange glow of its own. It sparkled different shades of blue, and a light from deep within. She was thoroughly captivated by its beauty.

"My God Kieron, it's beautiful!" she whispered. "I could never accept such a thing of beauty. It must have cost you a fortune."

"Nonsense, put it on, it's yours," he smiled, taking the jewel from its velvet casing, and slipping it on the ring finger of her left hand.

The moment the stone touched her skin, she experienced a wave of dizziness, and was temporarily whisked into a different time and space. They stood together, hand in hand inside a circle of giant stones, each stone with a different color jewel embedded in the front of it.

Sam wore a silken shift of cobalt blue, and Kieron was dressed in the formal garments of his order. Niall was at his side, standing slightly behind them. They stood in front of a very tall man with long flowing white hair, and a shift of gold. His beautiful blue eyes glowed brightly, and he spoke strange sounding words to them from a long scroll, which seemed to shimmer on its own in the dazzling sunlight.

Sam looked up and saw angels! Swirling angelic creatures clothed in long white robes, gracefully flew through the sky, filling it with a chorus of majestic voices. They sang in unison as the strange man continued his reading. It was the most beautiful scene she'd ever seen. The ring was on her left hand.

In a flash, she was back in Kieron's kitchen, staring at the magnificent stone. "What just happened to me?" she asked, as she steadied herself with his arm.

"Don't worry, it was just a memory brought back by the ring. One of our wedding day, very long ago."

She paused for a moment. "Wedding day?"

"Yes, the day you freely pledged your love to me in front of our friends and family. The gem's not from this world, it's a priceless jewel."

It was a perfect fit. She looked up at him with a thousand questions. "Where did you get it?" she asked, as he brought her hand to his lips and reverently kissed the ring.

"It's always been yours, Sam. I've saved it throughout the many lonely centuries, waiting. Things are again as they once were. You are mine."

She smiled, remembering the enchanting vision of her wedding day. Simply perfect, she smiled happily.

* * *

That morning was overcast, with the promise of rain. Sunny days were a rare thing in Scotland, she heard folks say. As she stepped toward the table, her eye caught the morning newspaper still lying on the walkway.

"I'll get it, be right back," she smiled, as she placed her coffee mug on the table and opened the screen door. In two steps, Sam was outside, already feeling a few drops of rain on her face.

Kieron was refilling the coffee pot, with his back to the door.

She stepped down, onto the brick walkway and small front yard where the paper had landed, admiring the unusual variety of exotic flowers flourishing in the neighbor's garden. They always kept it landscaped to perfection, and she envied their green thumb.

Suddenly, without warning, a black silken hood was slipped over her head, and she was grabbed from behind by someone with incredible strength.

"Don't scream," a male voice with a strange accent threatened, as he tightened the silk cord around her neck.

Sam coughed and began to gag, having a hard time getting air.

He roughly pulled the jewel ring from her hand, throwing it to the ground. "You won't be needing that anymore," he sneered in contempt.

She knew her life depended on the next minute, Kieron needed to see her. She fought her best to stall for time, hoping his possessive nature would realize she was gone too long.

As a last resort, she decided to scream for her life, but it was too late. The powerful stranger dealt her a hard blow to her head, rendering her unconscious, and shoved her limp body into the back seat of the waiting car.

Samantha awoke in a dusty, dark room filled with stale cigarette smoke, and just a trickle of light filtering through torn black curtains. She was now free from the oppressive hood, but her head throbbed painfully from the blow, and she felt something sticky on her face. Where was she?

She suddenly realized she was bound both hand and foot, sitting on the cold hard floor. The taste of dried blood caked the side of her mouth, nauseating her. Who had kidnapped her, and where had they come from so quickly? She remembered going to get the paper, a hood being slipped over her head, hit from behind, then all went black.

Where was Kieron? Surely he heard her scream, why hadn't he saved her? Then the terrifying thought hit her, had they gotten inside the house too? Was Kieron hurt? She couldn't bear the thought and forced herself to focus on something else, something positive.

Survival, she must survive. She had too much to live for, as she felt a new trickle of blood run down her cheek and into the corner of her mouth. She spit the blood on the floor, the action making her head throb ten times worse.

Sam began to struggle and kick at the ties around her feet, when suddenly the old wooden door flew open. A tall man dressed in a black trench coat, stalked over to where she sat. He was very attractive, with long dark shoulder length hair. His trench coat opened slightly as he walked, showing Sam a very well defined body. But this man's eyes were blacker than night itself, completely void of any emotion. Terror filled her as she sensed he was one of Kieron's enemies, perhaps even . . . ." No, she refused to let her mind go there.

"So you're awake," he said with a cruel cold smile. His accent was a mixture of Scottish and something else, something very old.

Sam said nothing. She was in no position to start a fight with this man, whoever he was.

"I see you're bleeding," he said in an icy, matter of fact tone, gloating down at her bruised and bleeding face. "It's a shame to shed that precious MacClaire blood for nothing," he said sarcastically, as he crouched down closer to her.

MacClaire blood? What was he talking about?

"Your father would be most distressed to see you now," he taunted. "Perhaps we could strike a bargain, aye? After all, you always were his favorite."

Sam stared up at him through throbbing pain and a constant trickle of blood, struggling to focus. There was something vaguely familiar about him, she had seen his face before.

"What are you talking about? Why am I here?" she demanded. He smiled again, and it was then she suddenly remembered where she had seen him, *in her nightmares!* He chased her in her terrible nightmares, back in Boston.

"It's you!" she gasped.

"Aye lass," he smirked. "I am able to reach into many realms, even your dreams. I take it as a complement that you remember."

"Well it's no compliment, I assure you. Where are you from?" she demanded, half afraid she already knew the answer.

He avoided her question completely.

"I'm pleased to see that Kieron has educated you. I always wanted a bride with more than just good looks," he laughed mockingly.

"Bride!" she gasped. "Who the hell are you!" she yelled, this time bordering on hysterics.

"Sweeting, I am Merlin, darkest and most powerful of all sorcerers, come to finally claim my bride."

"No!" she snapped defiantly. "Where have you come from, and what the hell do you want from me? I never did anything to you!"

"Aye, but you have. You've taken the one thing I desire most, and was to be mine from the beginning of time." He looked down at her with envious, dark eyes.

"What?" she demanded, growing irritated with his stupid banter.

"Rosestone Castle," he said, in a cold arrogant tone.

Sam was speechless. It's all true, she realized as she remembered Kieron's repeated warnings. She felt her blood chill at the sudden reality of the situation.

Merlin's laugh ripped the very breath from her lungs. "I come from long ago, and from the present. Time is no hindrance to me, for I have full control of it. I travel through it at will." Black eyes danced with a mysterious power.

"What do you want with me?" she asked again, fighting to remain calm. Again, that smile told her she was in deep trouble.

"Long ago, my dearest, you and I had an encounter at your father's castle. I wished only for employment there, a simple request, so I might fill my pouch with coin. Lord MacClaire was a fool, by refusing me, he created a curse which has haunted these grounds ever since. I wanted your sister, since she was the weakest and most vulnerable. Again he refused me, using his powers to banish me from ever returning."

He paused several seconds, as if reliving the memories in his mind.

"Unfortunately for your father, she died quite mysteriously soon after I left," he gloated proudly, dark malevolent eyes filled with evil satisfaction.

"You killed her, you bastard!" Sam raged. "Liar! Don't lie to me, saying you came innocently to fill your pouch. You came to steal what wasn't yours to begin with. Not then, and definitely not now! Never, sorcerer. Every person in that castle knew what you wanted. You fooled no one, even the maids! You came to take it from the MacClaires, its rightful owners, but you were no match for my father, fool."

The sudden realization of what she just blurted out shocked her. How could she have known all this?

A large ebony cat suddenly leaped down from some unknown point, landing at Merlin's feet. It looked up at the sorcerer with strange iridescent green eyes, hissing wildly. Merlin tried to kick it, but the sleek feline proved to agile for the ageless wizard. Before he could act, the cat sprang up onto his back, digging his sharp claws through his cloak and into Merlin's skin. He shrieked, twisting and jumping, trying desperately to throw the cat from his back, but the feline hung on tenaciously, claws dug firmly into his skin.

Sam was tempted to laugh at the ridiculous sight. It was quite obvious that he was no match for the energetic feline. Then, as mysteriously as he appeared, the cat was gone! Vanished into thin air.

He glared down at Sam, who tried her best to keep a straight face. "Your feeble attempts to stop me are futile. I see that perhaps someone has enlightened you as to the end of the story. Could it have possibly been your angelic lover, Kieron?" he sneered in contempt.

Sam was enraged, "Don't tangle with him if you're smart, you'll never win," she mocked.

"Matters naught, beloved," he smiled. "Kieron will soon be, as your generation puts it . . . out of the picture."

Sam's heart filled with anguish at the thought. Courage, she told herself. Don't listen to his lies. You must be brave, he will come.

At the mention of Kieron's name, the sorcerer began to pace nervously, as if suddenly aware of immense powers. A small feather, white as snow, suddenly drifted to the floor, landing directly in front of him. He jumped back in shock, terrified. His gaze searched the room, as if sensing a hidden threat. Finally, convinced there was no one else in the room but the two of them, he began to relax.

"Let us get back to the bargaining, shall we?" he scowled nervously. "I will let you leave here, and return home under one condition."

"What condition?" she demanded.

"Such defiance, my love. I can see why Kieron wanted you so badly. It's quite unfortunate that he will never see you again."

Sam bit her lip and tried her best to hold back the tears. She would be strong to the end, as Kieron and her father would want.

"You'll sign a contract here and now, vowing to marry me, and be bound to me for all eternity."

The air she breathed seemed to choke her, and she was filled with dread.

"You see, it isn't that bad now, is it?" he grinned, lustfully taking in her enticing figure. Sam was immediately nauseated, and wanted to vomit. She used every ounce of concentration not to.

"After you do that, I'll set you free for the length of two weeks. In that time, you may put your business in order, and bid any friends and family goodbye. In exactly two weeks from this hour, I will return for you, no matter where you are. Do not be foolish and run my love, I will find you."

Sam began to think feverously. That wasn't bad at all. A lot could be done in two weeks. She would find Kieron and he would save her. She knew Kieron would kill him, he had told her his powers were much greater than Merlin's. Deep in her soul she believed him. "*I cannot lie*," he told her. She'd sign this stupid contract, and go home. Everything would be alright.

"Ok," she said without hesitation. "Let's do it."

He smiled victoriously, using his dagger to cut her hands free. She hoped he couldn't read her mind.

"One more thing, beloved," he told her. "You will sign in your own blood."

Now she started to get scared. What was he going to do?

A piece of parchment paper with everything written down instantly materialized in the air before them.

"What are you going to do to me?" she asked nervously, eying the blade.

He stepped closer to her, dagger in hand. Samantha held her breath, heart pounding fiercely. She could feel herself shaking.

"Don't worry," he smirked, "a small prick on the palm will suffice."

With that he grabbed her right hand and effortlessly drew the shining dirk across her tender skin. The cold blade stung as it cut her delicate skin.

She didn't say a word, but remained staunch through the entire ordeal. Kieron would be proud, she kept thinking. He flipped his hand, and a quill pen instantly materialized from nowhere. He dipped it into her fresh blood, then extended the paper and pen to her.

"Sign it now," he ordered, "and know that it's irrevocable."

Sam signed the paper without hesitation, all the time thinking that she would gladly die before she'd ever let this happen. With that, he cut her feet free, opened the door, and let her go. She tore out the back door of the empty warehouse, and never looked back.

Her two week countdown had begun.

CHAPTER FOURTEEN

Kieron roared with rage! He dropped his coffee mug when he heard her scream, and raced to the door, but was too late. The car was now out of sight. He yelled out a thunderous oath, as he looked down on the pavement where the newspaper still lay untouched, and saw her blood on the cold brick walkway.

Then he spotted the ring, laying in the grass where it was thrown. Someone had known what it was, and decided to discard it. He snatched up the ring in a fit of rage, putting it safely in his pocket. Only one person fit the bill, and Kieron swore he would find him.

At that moment, Kieron MacClaire became the savage immortal warrior which earned him a fierce reputation throughout the centuries. More than just an unstoppable warrior, he was a mighty angelic being, bent on revenge. He screamed an unearthly sound of rage and revenge which should have woke the dead. Anger flickered dangerously in his eyes, his mind now set on murder.

This had apparently been planned long ago, he realized, as his angelic blood boiled. He should have never let her go for that paper, but then, who would have thought the dark one would come so near to his home, with all the wards and spells that had been placed on and around it. It seems the sorcerer had become more cunning through the centuries.

"It doesn't end here," Kieron spit. "This time, you won't suffer just banishment, but death. Your dark soul will burn for eternity," he vowed. He would find her, no matter what. He only hoped that she would remain brave for whatever she had to face.

"*Watch over her, Duncan*," he whispered prayerfully. "I will find her, I swear."

In a matter of seconds, Kieron had Niall on the phone. "He grows more arrogant throughout the centuries!" Niall yelled. "Oh course I'll be at your side, brother. I'll wait here for you."

"I'm on my way," Kieron answered as he dashed to his car.

When Niall hung up, he reverted to something he hadn't used in literally ages. He headed to the basement, and the private room where he kept his most prized possessions. No one knew it was there, even his wife when she was alive, because they couldn't see it. It had been spelled so efficiently, it was undetectable to the human eye. No limp, or feeble gestures this time. This called for effective, successful tools, there could be no margin of error.

There in the corner of the room, placed safely on a shelf, sat a bowl covered by a cloth of spun gold. With a fixed smile on his wrinkled face, he pulled off the cloth, and once again admired its beauty. It was magnificent and timeless, fashioned from pure gold, the edges etched with various runes. Touching its smooth surface with his palm, the bowl mysteriously heated up and glowed like the sun itself. His scrying bowl, not used in centuries.

"Your time is up," he said eagerly, as he filled the bowl with water, and waited for his brother warrior to join him in the ancient ritual of scrying.

Just at that moment, Luthias ran into the room, pacing back and forth nervously. "What is it, old friend?" Niall asked, noticing the cat's agitation.

He instantly shifted into a warrior. "He has her."

"Who?" Niall asked.

"The sorcerer. He's holding her captive in a large warehouse, not far from here. I sensed his presence, and the woman's fear."

"Warehouse?"

"A large structure behind a barren field. I went there, the woman is being held hostage by the ageless one. I didn't kill him, for I sense that Kieron desires that prize," he grinned, eyes gleaming with the thrill of the hunt

"Thank you, Luthias," Niall smiled. "This information is priceless."

Kieron arrived in a matter of minutes, pure rage covering his handsome face.

"He found them," Niall said, as he tore through the front door.

"Where?" Anger seemed to radiate from his entire body.

Luthias stepped over to him "They're in a building behind the soccer field."

Kieron thought for a brief second. "I know exactly where they are. Will you come with us?"

"Of course," the sexy shifter replied. "It would be my pleasure."

The three ran out of the house, and into Kieron's car.

"I readied the scrying bowl," Niall informed him, as he started the car engine.

"Good, if we can't find them this way, we'll resort to the old fashioned one."

Luthias sat in the back seat. "Sam is unharmed. I didn't kill him, I knew you alone would want that pleasure."

"You're dead right," Kieron smiled. "That's all I need to know. Thank you Luthias. I won't forget this."

He turned the corner, and came to the old abandoned warehouse, adjacent to a soccer field. A team of teen age boys were in the middle of a game.

"This is the place," Luthias said, looking out the back window.

Suddenly they saw her, standing bewildered and confused at the curb. Kieron rolled down the window. "Sam!" he yelled, desperately trying to get her attention.

Niall looked closer. "What has he done to her?" he raged. "Her face is covered in blood!"

"Aye, but she is strong, and still alive," Kieron added. "Don't worry my friend, he'll pay throughout eternity this time. Why is she free?"

"Perhaps he's temporarily satisfied with something he got for the moment," Niall said hesitantly, preparing himself for Kieron's wrath. Kieron turned to face him, fire burning in his eyes.

"Easy Kieron," he said, "I didn't mean sexually. He might have gotten some information from Sam, something he needed to know. It looks like she put up quite a fight. It's time we put an end to this abomination."

Samantha was unnerved and frightened, but otherwise unharmed. She had managed to keep up the false bravado long enough to get out alive. Her left hand still bled from his blade, and her head throbbed with a headache from hell. Still, she was alive. She comforted herself with the thought that it could have gone worse, much worse. But where on earth was she now?

Luckily, it was still daylight, but soon the clouds and dark skies would roll in. She began to look around to try and get some bearings with her surroundings, but it was futile. She hadn't been in Scotland long enough to be familiar with anything, except her hotel, Rosestone and Kieron's house.

Kieron. The thought of him pierced her very heart. Where was he now? Was he dead? If she found that was the case, she knew deep in her heart she'd never go on. How could she without her brave warrior at her side? She had managed to stay strong, and not cry through the entire terrifying experience, but the thought of losing him was too much to bear. Finally, the tears rolled down her face, mixed with dry blood from the blow. Sam didn't care anymore. She had to find her hero.

From nowhere, a black car tore down the street headed straight for her. She panicked, trying to summon up the strength needed to run. Exhausted, all she could do was wait to see who was in the car. Then, the thought hit her. Kieron? Her heart soared at the thought. Could he have possibly discovered where she was?

The car stopped with a screeching halt, and Kieron jumped out, followed by Niall. His handsome face was filled with relief, but the traces of stress were evident.

"Sam!" he yelled as he grabbed her, pulling her into the safety of his arms. He held her as if there were no tomorrow.

"Sam baby, please forgive me. This was my fault," he said holding her head close to his heart. She could still sense his rage, deep within, as he gently brushed the dried blood from her face. "What did he do to you?"

She could sense the anger building in him like a mega volcano about to erupt. It was undeniable. She tried to conceal the cut on her palm caused by the dirk, but it was useless. He saw her wince as she tried to close her hand.

He took her hand in his. "What's this?" he roared when he saw the bleeding skin. "Sam, I must know the truth, what are you trying to hide from me?"

"He had her hands and feet bound with cord," Luthias said, suddenly appearing from the back of the car.

"Luthias!" she yelled, running to him. She threw her arms around his neck, and hugged him. "I was hoping that was you. Thank you for saving me."

He was about to wrap his arms around her, then looked over at Kieron. "My pleasure," he purred seductively.

Kieron smiled at him, wrapping his arms around Samantha. "I'm forever grateful to you, Luthias. Because of you she's still alive and at my side. Tell me what I can do to repay you, and it's yours."

Luthias glanced over at Sam.

"She is not an option," he grinned.

Luthias knew better, but wasn't one to pass up a chance. "I'll think about it," he told him.

Niall came to his defense. "I'm sure he realizes that, but I guess you can't blame a man for trying."

Kieron glanced back at Luthias, who was now sitting in the back of the car. "He's a good man, trustworthy and honest. I'll remember this."

In this way, the shape shifter left a mark on Kieron's heart, and earned the title of one of his trusted "brothers".

Kieron threw the keys to the professor. "You drive back, Niall. I have a much more important job to do right now."

He carried Sam to the car, helping her into the back seat, then settled in next to her. He pulled her so close she was almost on his lap.

Luthias sat next to them, looking out the window for any trouble. He knew his time with Merlin wasn't over yet, and he was eagerly anticipating his next meeting. Luthias himself, was a deadly force to be reckoned with. Time was running out for the famed sorcerer.

Reaching deep into his pocket, Kieron pulled out the ring, and slid it back on her ring finger. "Perhaps I need to spell it once or twice, to prevent it from ever coming off again. What do you say, Niall?"

Niall just laughed. "Well, I think it's fair to say that would probably be the first time a maiden needed to have her ring spelled to stay on!"

Feeling safe and secure once again, Sam slept, snuggled up against his warm chest. Her hero had come for her.

Niall looked over his shoulder. "Are we ready?"

"Aye brother, that we are."

* * *

Sam waited until later that day to tell Kieron about the marriage contract. She hoped he would eventually settle down, at least for a while. She worried that since she had been forced to sign in blood, it would somehow be irrevocable.

His anger hit a new high. "So he lost once, but that's not enough, huh? Absolutely, without a doubt, not going to happen! I don't care what he told you Sam. He will be dealing with a force much more powerful than his. He can't win."

"But he said I have two weeks," she said fearfully.

"After that, he'll come for me."

"Good, let him come. I'll be more than happy to deal with him. I should have killed him for your father while I still could. Wasn't the death of one daughter enough? Now he wants the other, who has been openly pledged to me."

"Look at me Sam," he said, turning her toward him.

"You are mine. Period. Forever. No one else will ever have you. We were joined as one, and no one will separate us, ever. This I swear to you." He took her hand and kissed the ring that symbolized their unity. Bending his head, he whispered softly . . . "Is tu mo ghra," "I love you."

The next afternoon, Kieron got a call from the professor, asking if he and Sam could stop over. In his searching he found an old book that was hidden away for centuries, one he had forgotten about, and was more than anxious for Kieron to see it.

It was early that evening, when Kieron and Sam arrived at his house. Rain was beginning to come down hard. He hugged Sam close to him as they walked from the car down the pebbled path to his door. Kieron kept a keen eye out for trouble, knowing only too well that all wasn't always what it seemed. Danger, even death was always one step away.

Tonight, he not only had his blade tucked snugly under his belt, but his claidheamh mor strapped to his back. Sam hoped no one would see him with the claymore. It was large and heavy, and twice as deadly when used by a skilled swordsman.

Niall took one glance at the claymore and grinned. "I see you've brought a friend tonight."

The two men laughed and went inside, swapping tales of battle for several minutes. Sam shuddered to think of either one using that blade on someone, or something. They were quite skilled and capable, both having centuries of experience with the heavy sword. It would be a gruesome end.

Niall broke out his bottle of Glenfiddich, and poured them both a glass.

Luthias, came out from the back room, book in hand. He greeted the two, shooting Sam a seductive grin.

"He never gives up, does he?" Kieron laughed.

"She is a beautiful woman," he purred seductively.

"Sorry friend," Niall said, "she's permanently out of the question."

"I'll always be grateful to you, Luthias," Sam smiled. She stepped over to him, and gave him a hug.

"That's enough thanks," Kieron warned with a smile. His possessive streak was beginning to show.

Sam smiled, kissing his cheek, as Kieron pulled her away.

"Thanks again," she said warmly, as Luthias nodded in understanding. "I will always be there to protect you," he smiled.

They headed to his living room, where Niall filled Kieron's glass. He turned to Sam. "Would you care for a drink?"

She began to blush. "I don't know, I never drank Scotch before."

"Well then, you don't know what you're missing," Niall grinned.

Looking to Kieron for guidance, she asked, "What do you think? Should I try it?"

"Of course my love," he said with a wicked grin. "I was counting on you getting drunk tonight."

The professor roared with laughter.

"Really Kieron," Sam scolded him, "you shouldn't talk like that in front of the professor." That threw them both into a new fit of laughter, and Sam gave up, heading toward the sofa.

"Don't worry about the professor," Kieron joked, "he could teach me a lot when it comes to women, right Niall?"

He smiled over at the kindly old man with the twinkling intelligent eyes.

"You forget Sam, that he only chooses the guise of an old man. Behind that front, he's a strong young warrior who any woman would love to catch."

Sam smiled at the dangerous thought.

Finally giving up on any serious conversation between the two friends, she picked up her glass and took a sip. And another. Soon, she was laughing and blowing Kieron kisses across the room.

"Lord, I've created a monster."

"Aye, you have. It seems she won't be coherent much longer either," Niall laughed, watching Sam slowly close her eyes, her head falling back against the soft pillows of the sofa.

Kieron watched with a smile. "At least this time I know where she is."

He positioned the sleeping, Scotch inebriated Samantha across the sofa so she'd be more comfortable. Niall brought in a throw from the bedroom, and gently laid it over her.

"Beautiful woman," he told Kieron as he stared down at the sleeping Samantha.

"Yes, she is," he replied.

"I can see why he wants her so much," Niall continued. "A fine balance of beauty and brains. Be very careful Kieron, he's cunning."

Kieron sipped his scotch. "He'll have to go through me first. I never let her out of my sight anymore. I know it must be hard on her, but hopefully things will change soon."

Niall nodded. "That brings us to the subject at hand. I told you on the phone that I found an old tome. What I didn't tell you was it lists some very interesting things about the Rosestone curse."

Kieron look up suddenly. "Are you jesting?"

"You should know me better," he smiled. "Read it for yourself." He walked over to the desk, and opened a drawer. Inside was a leather bound book, which appeared to be very old.

"Where did you find it?" Kieron asked, as he carefully took it from the professor."

"In the study. Luthias suggested I go through the part of the collection still boxed up. I'd basically forgotten I even had it. You know, it's not every day a man needs this kind of information."

"Look at the page I've marked," he instructed.

Kieron sat down next to the slumbering Samantha. He gave her one final look to be sure she was alright, then turned his focus to the old book.

There it was, staring him in the face. Information and ancient facts on spells. Rosestone was on the top ten. Kieron began to read feverishly. Suddenly he stopped, glancing over at his friend.

"Have you read this?" he asked with concern. The seriousness in his voice was unmistakable.

"I'm afraid to say I have. I didn't know how you'd feel about the whole thing," Niall said, as he gulped down a healthy mouthful of whiskey.

"We must go back," Kieron said gravely. "We must return to the 17th century. The text is quite clear. It states the first founder of Rosestone, Dermott MacClaire had in his possession the sacred amulet of Avalon, which has been coveted by many, for its powerful properties."

"Only this amulet is capable of breaking the curse which was put on Rosestone Castle. It's said that it contains several drops of pure sunlight, which had been changed to liquid by an ancient Norse sun god. This alone, when shown to the person responsible for invoking the curse, will cause a sudden explosion of pure energy."

He put the book down carefully, and looked up at Niall. "We must bring Sam back to 1610."

Niall took a final mouthful and put his glass down. "If Dermott MacClaire allegedly had this amulet on him, God knows where it would be now. We'd have to do much research to locate where he was originally buried."

He stopped and looked over at Kieron. "We'll have to find his burial site, and hope it's been buried with him, and not looted."

"Aye," Kieron replied thoughtfully. "There are many secret places hidden under the foundations of Rosestone, where he may have been interred. We'll have to ask Duncan, to see if he may remember anything pertinent."

Niall paused for several seconds. "It won't be easy," he sighed, looking off in the distance. "If I remember correctly, the Hall of Records would be a good place to start. Perhaps we'll get lucky, and find it soon."

"And what of her father's dirk?" Kieron asked, trying to figure out how it fit into the big picture. "She found Duncan's silver dirk, hidden in muck and dirt on he castle grounds."

Niall nodded, staring at the book. "It would make sense. Seems he wants her to use his own dirk to complete the deed. Kind of a personal revenge," he smirked.

"Sounds like a perfect ending for the wondrous sorcerer. Killed by beauty herself," Kieron smiled proudly, glancing down at Sam who was now sound asleep.

Niall began to laugh. "And just how do you purpose to get her back to 1610? I doubt she'll agree with the idea."

Just the thought of bringing Sam back to the 17th century was too much, even for Kieron. She was a strong willed young woman, born into a modern society, and certainly not raised to do whatever her husband demanded. The thought alone made him laugh.

Niall agreed, it was a major obstacle.

"Well," Niall said after a moment's thought, "the Glenfiddich seemed to do a fairly good job. Perhaps it's the best way for her to travel." They both began to laugh at the idea.

"Yes, but what happens when she wakes?" Kieron asked gravely.

"Ah brother, that's another day."

CHAPTER FIFTEEN

Kieron carried her back from Niall's house, and put her to bed, where she slept soundly all night and into the late morning.

He passed the night debating how he would tell Sam, and sincerely doubted that taking her back drunk would be the solution. She would most likely hate him forever when she woke, and that he would never want. No, he decided it was best to be honest with her, and tell her the facts up front.

He poured a second cup of black coffee, sat down at the kitchen table, and proceeded to explain the entire situation, as calmly as possible. He spared no details, explaining what the professor had discovered.

"What!" she screeched, as Kieron covered his ears and tried to stop laughing.

"Are you crazy? There is no frigging way I'm going back to the 17th century! Forget it, definitely not going to happen." She stood defiantly, hands on hips and glared at him.

"Wait a minute Sam, let me explain first before you bring down the house. It's not like you'd be going alone. Niall and I would be at your side each moment. Plus Sam, you'd finally get to meet your family."

Silence.

That did it, his wild card worked. Sam paused in her tirade of emotion, and looked over at him, interest peaking.

"My father?" she said softly. "I would see him again?"

It seems she had taken an immediate liking to Duncan, which warmed Kieron's heart, and gave him hope.

"Yes, your father, mother, uncle and all the rest of that noble clan. I doubt you'd want to pass up an opportunity like that?" He looked at her hesitantly, hoping she'd agree.

She instantly calmed, mulling over the precious chance. "Yes, that would be nice," she said longingly.

"Remember though," he cautioned, "it won't be all fun, Sam. You must kill him, you alone. Do you understand? He *must* die."

A look of fierce determination swept over her. "Oh yes Kieron," she said with icy contempt, "I do understand, more than you know." She seemed to change, her demeanor becoming one of steely determination. The old Sam was gone, never to return. Now, Samantha was a changed woman, with one intention in mind . . . Merlin's destruction.

He relaxed and took another mouthful of coffee. Case closed.

Kieron gave her several minutes to renege, but it didn't happen. She would kill this evil which threatened to take away the joy in her life. She fully understood that she alone must put an end to it. Duncan would be at her side. She instinctively knew he wouldn't fail her.

"I'm ready Kieron," she told him, with a distant fire in her eyes.

The castle had come along nicely during the last several months. Stone masons were following the specifications for building the walls to Kieron's exact specifications. Windows had been chosen to reflect the time period, the front door was cut from he finest oak, a colorful stain glass window sat above it, with the MacClaire Coat of Arms. It showed the clan's colors of indigo and gold, as specified by Kieron. It would become a majestic sight.

The finest gardeners in Scotland had been summoned by Kieron. They were busy planting flower beds, and arranging lovely shrubbery designs in the once barren fields behind the castle. Kieron had asked to have the remainder of the back field covered with purple heather, his favorite.

Sam stood in front of the castle, admiring its gradual rebirth. It was already breathtaking, with its tall silhouette against the blue sea. She looked up to the sky. It was noon, and the sun was at its zenith.

As she stood wrapped in Kieron's strong embrace, Sam was almost able to forget the dark threat which hung over her. She turned to look up at his rugged, handsome face. "How long will we be gone?"

He caught the tinge of regret in her voice. "Just long enough to do what must be done. I know you'll miss this place, but this way you'll have the chance to see Rosestone as it *really* was, centuries ago. It's the chance of a lifetime, Sam."

"I know," she sighed, "guess I'm just kind of scared. What if something goes wrong?"

"Don't be afraid," he whispered, "it's been done before, many times. Even your mother Kathleen hesitantly fell back in time, to your father's great delight," he grinned.

"She must have been terrified," Sam said, trying to imagine going through that experience alone, and by mistake.

"Well, I suppose at first it was a bit strange," he agreed, "but Duncan stood on his head to make her happy. I daresay she wouldn't have left afterward if she could."

She smiled up at him. "Somehow I believe that, just knowing him for those few precious moments." He saw the tears in her eyes.

After doing a final stroll around the grounds, they headed back to where Kieron's car was parked.

"You know, I'd bet you'd like to go shopping for some new clothes," he said, pulling out from the dirt road. "I'm sure you're getting sick of living out of those two suitcases."

Sam was delighted. "Really? I do need new things, but so much has happened lately, well, I didn't want to bother you."

His eyes took on a definite twinkle. "I don't see it as a bother love, more as a challenge."

"Challenge?"

"Aye, it's like an endurance test. See how many hours I can sit, waiting for you to decide what you want."

Sam watched his body shake with laughter. She rolled her eyes, and raised her hand to give him a punch, but he caught her fist in midair, kissing it tenderly.

"I know of a few spots that I bet you'll love," he smiled. "Feel like checking them out?"

"Sure!" Her excitement was a very pleasant change from the suspense and drama of the last few days.

Kieron pulled up to a stylish boutique, one of the more famous for young women, and parked the car.

"Are you going to wait out here?" she wondered. "I may take a while, you know how women are with clothes."

He gave her an impish smile. "Absolutely not. I'm sure they'll be able to find a chair for me to sleep in for about five hours," he joked. "Remember, there's no way I'm leaving you alone. Perhaps you'd rather I buy out the entire store, and bring it all home, so I can help you with a personal fit?" he asked with a wicked grin.

"And I suppose you'd do just that."

"Of course, how many boutiques are there? We could do them all"

"Really Kieron," she said in a more serious tone. "You spoil me way too much. I don't deserve it."

He pulled her across the seat, and into his arms. "No lass, you deserve that and a whole lot more. Just say the word, and it's yours." The passion in his eyes told her everything.

"We'd better go now," she told him, as she opened the door and climbed out to the sidewalk. In a second, he was out of the car, holding the door for her.

"You really don't need to keep doing this. It's just not necessary."

"Aye, but it is. A man must do everything possible to show his soul mate how much he cares."

She stretched up to kiss his cheek, and he grabbed her firmly around the waist. "Would you be more interested in other activities, rather than shopping?" he grinned. She rolled her eyes and walked into the lovely boutique, with Kieron trailing behind.

He made himself comfortable in a cushioned chair outside the dressing room, keeping an eye on every person who entered the store. Patiently he waited, as she tried on everything from jeans to dresses. He had a definite preference for the halter top and shorts look. Several hours later, they stumbled wearily back to his car with enough shopping bags to fill his trunk, and then some.

"Whew, that was fun!" she grinned, collapsing into the front seat.

He threw her a seductive look. "You owe me."

"Ha!" she answered, "you'll have to wake me first."

"Oh lass, trust me, you will be very awake," he promised as he started the engine, and headed for home.

*   *   *

Brianna dropped by late the next morning to see how things were coming along after her kidnapping ordeal.

"God that must have been awful!" she said, staring at the pretty redhead who by now had recovered and was looking forward to her trip back in time.

Kieron sat at the kitchen table, pouring over some old texts the professor had dropped off. He smiled up at Brianna, greeting her with the customary, "Madainn mhath."

She smiled back at him, returning his greeting. Is he always this polite?" she asked.

"Always," Kieron smiled.

She looked over at Sam, as he politely pulled the chair out for her. "God, do I wish he had a brother," she sighed longingly.

Kieron glanced at Sam, as if to say something, but remained silent.

He turned toward Sam. "So, are you nervous about this trip back in time?"

Sam looked up from the huge stack of clothes purchased yesterday. "Actually I am, but I'm going to relish meeting everyone, especially seeing what the castle was like in its day of glory."

"Boy, just think of all those drop dead men you'll meet!"

Kieron's eyes quickly left his book. "She better not be looking at any men," he teased.

Sam touched his hand affectionately. "Don't be silly Kieron, how could any man compare to you?"

"I don't think such a thing is possible," he teased, "even back then." All three laughed for several seconds, then Brianna went on with her questions.

"So, when do you leave?" She still had a hard time understanding how he could pull off such a feat.

Kieron stared out the window for a few moments, thinking. "I believe it's best to do so in a few days."

Sam nodded in agreement. She had been given a two week notice, then her time was up. Merlin would come for her. Five days had already passed. She looked down at her quickly healing palm, images of that horrid day flashing through her mind.

"Sam, don't," Kieron whispered as he took her hand in his. Instantly the painful memory disappeared.

Brianna glanced over at Kieron who was still busy with his book. "Could I ask a favor?" she said timidly, drawing his attention from the thick book. He put it down on the kitchen table, and looked into her eyes. They were filled with a loneliness he understood all too well. Such a sweet girl, he thought sadly. How could he refuse her anything, she had been so good to Sam.

"Of course lass, you need to just name it," he replied kindly.

She looked straight at him. "Take me with you."

"Brianna!" Sam gasped, "Surely you're kidding."

"I'm not kidding. Look at me, twenty six and not a single decent man in sight. Men of this century are a joke, they only want one thing, and then they drop you for another. I would just love to meet a man from that time," she said longingly.

"Anyway, what do I have to lose? My parents are both dead, and I have no other family except two very old, dying grandparents in a nursing home. Who would even care?"

Kieron was touched, for he of all people knew the pain of loneliness. His heart broke for this young woman, but he knew the risks of time travel, and would not subject a soul to it unless there was a dire necessity.

Sam sat speechless. She didn't see that one coming. She too felt heartbreak for her dear friend, but never having experienced time travel, was left to accept Kieron's decision.

He looked down at the floor, wondering how to avoid breaking her heart any further. She was kind and gentle, and he could see the shining purity of her soul. He abhorred causing another pain at all costs, if not absolutely necessary.

"Brianna, I know how you feel, honestly, I do. But just think about it for a moment. You'd be living in the 17th century, where you know no one. Life for a lass was not always easy back then, certainly not filled with all the luxuries you have on hand today."

"You would meet a good man, of that I'm sure, for there are many decent men working at Rosestone. It wouldn't be the life you are familiar with here in modern day Scotland though."

"Right," Sam agreed. "I very much doubt I'd like living there for a long period of time. We're going for one reason only, and when that has been accomplished . . . ," she took a deep breath as if experiencing the moment now, "we are returning, right Kieron?" She looked to him for support and agreement.

"Aye love," he replied kissing the fading scar on her palm. "We will most certainly be returning to this time when our task has been completed."

"Well. I guess I can see your point," Brianna said staring down at her coffee cup. "I doubt I'd enjoy living back then, without all my necessities," she admitted.

"I can't even see my beloved Sam doing it for a second more than she needs too," he teased.

"You've got that right!" Sam added quickly. "I like this time, has everything a girl needs," she smiled, looking over at the huge stack of new clothes.

"Lucky girl," Brianna smiled.

Kieron's mood suddenly lightened. "Perhaps Brianna, just perhaps, I may bring a present back to you. Please don't hold me to it lass, for I don't exactly know how things will go for us, but I promise you I'll keep you in mind."

She was elated! "You'd do that for me? God Sam, no wonder you love him so much." She jumped up from her chair, and threw her arms around Kieron.

He just laughed and planted a quick kiss on her forehead. "You deserve it, lass."

Sam sat there with a huge smile, so proud of her handsome lover. So kind and thoughtful, always thinking of others. Her love for him grew more each passing day. She couldn't imagine her life without him, even if it meant not being able to return, but she'd never tell Brianna that.

* * *

The days continued to fly by, and time was quickly running out for Sam. She tried to keep busy doing all the necessary things, but was increasingly aware of the date.

She made it a point to call her family in Boston, telling them she was going on a vacation with a girlfriend, and would call when she returned. She dared not tell them the truth, knowing they would be on the first flight to Scotland, and bring her back to be committed!

Kieron stopped over at the construction site, and spoke with the workers. He instructed they were to stop all work on the site as of the following week, and he and the owner would be out of town for a while. He said they would be notified immediately on their return. Although they were all eager to finish the renovations, he sensed that most of the workers were happy to take a temporary reprieve.

As the final days drew near, Sam was getting more agitated and easily annoyed by the hour. "So, what happens when he learns we've gone?" she asked, fiddling with a bookmarker from one of Niall's books.

"He already knows, Sam. You can't fool this evil prince, he's been around for a long, long time. Merlin is no fool. If my hunch is correct, he will probably already be there waiting when we arrive."

"Time and space are no barrier to him. He's a spirit born from the union of a Druid and Goddess. His powers are far beyond those of mere mortal men, or any of the many sorcerers of old. He has retained complete control over the spirits which once inhabited this earth as Viking warriors. They will obey his every command, to gain a chance of freedom from his dark realm of tyranny."

Sam looked up with fear and fascination. "So, this is what I'm supposed to kill? Why me?"

"Because you are strong and fearless enough to pull it off, Sam. I have every faith in you, so does your father," he reminded her softly.

* * *

The night before they planned to leave, Sam invited Brianna over for the evening. Kieron still had a few things to finish, and Sam wanted to see Brianna one last time before she left. She had every faith that Kieron would bring her safely back when their task was completed, but she hated to say goodbye to her dear newly found friend.

It was already 8:00 p.m., and darkness again covered the old city as Niall's car pulled into the driveway.

"Hey Sam!" Brianna yelled out, as she jumped out from Niall's Land Rover. She had come to think of him as a father figure, since her parents' untimely death.

"Hi you two," Sam yelled back, opening the back door for them. She was delighted to see that Luthias came along too this time, in the form of a man. Ever since her recent abduction, she'd been delighted to see him, in either form. Her mind recalled Kieron's statement about having a good friend who may someday help her. It was so true. Samantha had learned to appreciate Kieron's friends, knowing they were all valuable assets to her, if she ever needed them. She ran to him, hugging him tightly, while Kieron looked on with a smile. He owed Luthias big time, and now considered him one of his closest friends.

"We'll be in the study," Kieron told them, as he, Niall and Luthias headed toward the hall. "Just yell if you need anything."

Sam nodded, sitting down at the table with her friend. There were always the last minute things to discuss.

Before they left, Kieron flipped on the outside sensor light next to the kitchen window, then checked all the doors and windows to be sure they were closed and securely locked.

Finally, he blew Sam a kiss, and joined the others in the study.

The two girls sat in the kitchen drinking tea, swapping girl talk, and discussing tomorrow. They passed the time laughing and joking about what life would be like for a woman in the 17th century.

"Be sure to make a list for me," Brianna reminded her, "I want to be able to experience everything, just as you did. Remember to jot down the good and the not so good," she giggled.

"Oh I will," Sam promised, as she took her hand and squeezed it. She was her best friend now, more like a sister when she thought of it. Who else would believe all the crazy, insane stuff she told her? If only she were able to come along too, Sam thought sadly.

"Before you know it, we'll be back," yet deep in her heart, she feared she'd never see the 21st century again.

Time went by, neither noticed the late hour. Both were busy mapping out how Sam's trip through time would proceed. Something in the corner of the room caught Brianna's eye. She turned to find Luthias, trotting into the kitchen at a rapid pace. Strange, she thought. He's now in feline form, and seems to be in a hurry.

"What's up with Luthias?" she asked, giving Sam a strange look. "He seems to be in a hurry to get in here."

"Or get out of there," Sam smirked. "Perhaps he's tired of hearing about time travel." The cat stopped for a split second, gazing at both girls.

"That's odd, Brianna noted, "it's almost as if he's telling us something."

Sam put her glass down. "Had enough?" she grinned, as the cat suddenly sprawled out against the back door.

"That's odd," she said, looking over at the feline. "He never leaves Niall's side. I wonder what happened."

"Do you think they even noticed?"

"Are you kidding? Those two don't miss a thing, I mean nothing. There must have been a reason. Let me go see what's going on."

As Sam stood up from the table, the outside sensor light suddenly clicked on. She frowned, looking toward the door. "Now what," she sighed. The cat was immediately on his feet, green eyes fixed on the backdoor.

"What the heck is that?" Brianna shrieked, watching a mist materialize just outside the kitchen window.

"No!" Sam screamed as she watched the mist slowly take on the form of a man. "God, it's him!"

Merlin stood silently with that same cruel smile, staring at her through the glass.

"Kieron!" she screamed in terror. "Kieron hurry!"

As if on cue, the cat sprang to the window, scratching at the glass and hissing wildly. Its eyes changed to a dark iridescent green, and it let out several threatening growls and hisses. The sorcerer just laughed, taunting the large black cat, totally unaware of its identity.

Then, in an instant, he changed. Luthias shifted into a large sleek warrior, much the size and form of Kieron, with long black hair, black leather pants, and a thick leather belt around his waist. He pulled the dagger from his belt. With one powerful crash, he broke through the door, tackling the unsuspecting sorcerer, and knocking him to the ground.

"Luthias!" he yelled, suddenly recognizing him. "I thought I finished you off centuries ago." He was still in black, but this time his clothes were definitely medieval.

"Obviously not," the fierce warrior growled as he pressed the silver dagger against his neck. "Give me one reason why I shouldn't cut your head off right here and now. It would give me the greatest pleasure, kind of a payback."

"It wasn't me who cursed you, Luthias, but another," he sneered arrogantly.

"I don't care," he spit, "it's all the same to me. The satisfaction will be mine anyway."

He held the dirk tightly, piercing a small section of the sorcerer's skin. Black blood began to drip down his neck, as Merlin's eyes filled with terror.

In a flash, Kieron and Niall were there, placing themselves protectively in front of the two girls.

"No Luthias, let him go," Niall yelled. "He must not die in this manner!" Merlin's death alone would be of little help to Sam.

"Why are you here, dark one?" Kieron growled. "It's not yet your hour."

He fixed his evil stare on Kieron. "We will meet again, Son of Light, on other soil." His eyes were filled with contempt.

"It can't be soon enough for me," Kieron spit.

"Don't speak to him now, brother," Niall advised. "He can't harm her while she's within your house."

Kieron nodded in understanding. The many spells he'd placed around his home effectively kept any evil from entering.

After one last chilling smile at Sam, Merlin disappeared into the darkness of the night.

As suddenly as he changed into a man, Luthias was once more a cat, which proceeded to sit and clean its paws, as if they had been dirtied somehow.

"He grows more brazen each second," Niall said, as he looked outside where the sorcerer had been. "I believe he already knows of our plans to return."

"Good!" Kieron continued to growl, "I can't wait to cut his head off and hand it to Duncan!"

Niall began to roar in laughter. "They'll celebrate until the next moon!"

Kieron looked at the girls. "Are you okay?"

"I think so," Brianna said, finally releasing Sam's hand. "I just never believed in that kind of stuff, but I certainly do now!" She was visibly shaking.

Niall was at her side immediately. "I'll never let any harm come to you," he told her.

She smiled at the bravery shown by this feeble old man. Such a sweet old soul, she wished he could be with her forever. Somehow, she knew he'd always be there to protect her. "Thank you professor, that's very sweet."

Sam looked over at Niall. "What exactly did he mean by it wasn't he who cursed Luthias?"

A trace of a smile started as he recalled the day. "Luthias is a very dear friend of mine, who saved my hide from an embarrassing situation quite a long time ago," he explained with a good degree of embarrassment.

"What do you mean?" Brianna asked.

Niall began to turn red. "I'd rather not say," he muttered sheepishly.

Kieron couldn't hold his laughter in any longer. "Seems the good professor decided to sow his oats in the wrong field, and was caught!" he roared.

"Really, Kieron," Sam scowled, "that wasn't necessary at all."

"It happened a long time ago," Niall blushed.

"Before you met your wife?" Brianna asked, shocking everyone.

Niall turned serious. "Oh, quite definitely lass, ages before her time. I was never unfaithful to her, not once in fifty years of marriage. It's against my Oath as a Keeper. I firmly believe that a husband should remain faithful to the end, doing all that's needed to keep his mate happy. I did my role well."

"Indeed you did," Kieron stated, clamping his shoulder. "You never wavered from being a faithful husband, right to the very end." His voice held deep conviction.

"Such chivalry," Brianna sighed whimsically.

Niall gave her a strange look, one filled with definite hidden meaning. It was a look she could not yet understand.

"Chivalry is *not* dead lass."

"So what happened to Luthias?" Sam asked.

"Cursed by another powerful witch," Niall informed her.

* * *

It was now near midnight, and Kieron thought it best if they called it a night.

"What about that door?" Sam scowled. "We can't just leave it like that for the night."

Kieron looked over at the smashed, broken remains of the door. "Never said I was going to." Before she could utter another complaint, the kitchen door was as good as new.

"I just love how you do that!" Sam marveled as she looked at the new door. It was exactly the same as it had been before the sudden encounter between the two nemeses.

"You were always a bit better at that than me," Niall admitted. "Well, time to rest up till tomorrow morn," he said, getting up to help tidy the table.

"Don't be making me look bad, brother," Kieron joked.

"Can I watch?" Brianna asked eagerly, referring to tomorrow's leap in time. She was beginning to think of Kieron as her big brother.

After mulling it over a few seconds, he said, "I guess there's nothing wrong if you do, as long as there's no one else around. This isn't exactly something I want others to see. What do you think?" he asked, glancing over at Niall.

He shrugged. "Seems harmless, as long as there's no other witnesses."

CHAPTER SIXTEEN

Niall unlocked the door to his Land Rover, waiting for Brianna to say her good byes, then drove her back to the house where she once lived with her parents. Luthias waited patiently in the back seat. As he dropped her off, he made it a point to remind her to be ready at 7:30 a.m. sharp.

"Don't worry about me," she said, smiling up into his old eyes. "I'll be up and ready on time, probably won't be able to sleep a wink from nerves alone!"

He walked her to the safety of her front door.

"Thanks so much for seeing me safely home," she told him, as she slipped the key in her door. "It still seems kind of strange, coming home to an empty house now that my parents are gone.

He smiled down at her. "Don't worry lass, I feel very soon you'll meet the man you've been waiting for. Just give it a little more time." She nodded her head, and waved goodnight. Niall saw the sadness and deep loneliness in those eyes.

Niall McInnis had been a widower for some years now, and often contemplated quitting his wrinkled old man's guise, to return to his own youthful appearance.

He too, was getting tired of living without his soul mate. Although he loved to teach in the university, it didn't fill that hole in his life caused by his wife's tragic death.

Niall had always loved Brianna, and now that she was a lovely young woman, couldn't ignore the attraction he felt toward her. Throughout the years, he watched over her, from a newborn until she had finally blossomed into a lovely young woman. Always admiring her from a distance, but staying very close to her family.

He had befriended her father Donald, years ago, when the two met during a Highland Festival in Glenfinnan. They had much in common, and soon became close friends.

Her soul spoke to him from before her birth, when her mother still carried her in the womb. Niall stayed married and faithful to his wife until her death, being the noble knight he was, and honoring his Oath of Purity. But his heart was eternally sealed to another, his soul mate, this small baby who he watched grow throughout the years, until the time to claim her was right. Now, it was time for that change.

Brianna was approximately five and a half feet tall, and petite in build, like Sam. Their resemblance to each other was sometimes very uncanny. Her hair was a chestnut brown, and she wore it cut short in many feathered layers, attractively complementing her petite face. Her eyes were a stunning bluish green, which turned a deeper shade of green when angered. He found her absolutely alluring as a grown woman. He would be kidding himself if he said he never thought of returning to his youth and claiming her for his own.

Niall had always felt sorry for her since her parents' unfortunate car accident, a few years ago. It had been a very trying time for the young woman, without brothers or sisters there to guide and protect her. He had taken on the task of guardian, in their place. It irked him enormously when he saw how the young men at the university watched her lustfully.

Unfortunately, in his present guise, he was unable to say or do anything, without giving himself away. Loneliness sucks, he thought as he drove back home through the dark streets. Well, he decided with a grin, it's time for a change.

Samantha and Kieron spent that night and early morning in lustful satisfaction. He endeavored to show Sam the debts of his love, in many various ways. Their lovemaking was most important to him that night. Who knew what tomorrow would bring? If anything went wrong, he wanted Sam to be assured of his true feelings for her. He knew that in a few hours, her world would be turned upside down. His only hope was she would be able to do what was necessary.

It was already 8 a.m. when the doorbell rang outside Kieron's small home. He was up and dressed, having used the shower much earlier, as Sam slept. Fresh aroma of coffee filled the kitchen, as he opened the door for Niall, trailed by Luthias and a very sleepy eyed Brianna.

"Good Morning," Kieron greeted them with a grin.

He stepped over to the coffee pot, and began to pour them both a cup.

"Oh please don't give me any of that toxic substance!" Niall laughed. "Are you trying to kill me before we even begin?"

Kieron grinned, throwing a box of tea bags at him. "I'll put the kettle on, it'll only take a second. Have a seat," he said cheerfully, as he pulled a pitcher of fresh cream from the fridge. Looking at Luthias he said, "I know you're not a coffee lover, is a glass of milk okay?"

"I would much prefer cream," he stated seductively, glancing at Brianna."

Niall laughed. "Watch it Luthias, I *am* her guardian,"

"Of course," he smiled, "until someone else comes along."

He gave the shifter a wink. "That may happen sooner than you think. Until then, hands off!"

Luthias just grinned, took his glass of milk, and headed toward the library.

"He loves to read the old tomes," Niall told her.

Keion put his cup down. "He wrote many of the ancient manuscripts himself, if I'm not mistaken, didn't he?"

"Indeed," Niall agreed "Some are still in libraries around the world, but unfortunately, most burned during the great fire at the Library of Alexandria. It was a terrible tragedy for all mankind. Seems the story goes that Julius Caesar and his men burned it down in retribution against the lovely Cleopatra, but in reality it was because of Luthias."

"What?" Brianna gasped. "Why on earth would they do such a thing, then blame Luthias?"

Kieron began to laugh. "Male pride, is the best way to put it, I guess. You see, Luthias had such a well-known reputation as a skillful lover, it put Caesar to shame. It was a vengeful attack on our friend, and nothing else."

The two recalled the fateful day the world's largest house of ancient records was destroyed by Caesar and his men.

"Fool" Kieron added. "He blamed a country and a people for his own masculine short comings."

"Well brother, seems you're in a good mood this fine morning," Niall said, as he watched Kieron gulp down his second mug. "I'll never understand how one can drink that stuff black," he frowned. "As for me, nothing beats a good cup of Scottish tea."

Kieron put the empty cup down on the table, then glanced over at Brianna. She had become strangely quiet since their arrival. "Are you okay, lass?" He studied her intently for a few seconds.

"I'm fine. Sorry, I guess this is just still too unreal for me to believe. Are you sure Sam will be alright?" She toyed with her cup, then looked up to Kieron for some kind of reassurance.

"Don't worry Brianna," he smiled. "Her safety is my utmost priority."

Sam was up, showered and dressed as she headed down the hall toward the kitchen. On her way to the kitchen, she passed the library, where she found Luthias, lost in a book. He was sitting comfortably in Kieron's chair, sipping from his glass of milk.

"Madainn mhath," he said. His grin was definitely sexual in nature, his eyes filled with scorching lust.

"You too," she answered. "You'd better stay right there, or you'll definitely end up one dead cat."

"Your every wish is my command," he replied with a sly grin. She heard his soft laughter, as she continued down the hall.

"I just passed Luthias," she told Niall. "He was busy with his head in one of Kieron's books."

"Oh he'll be busy for hours now," he grinned. "Reading is one of his favorite pastimes. Kieron has many of his favorites here."

Brianna rolled her eyes and threw up her hands. "I'd never believe it," she quipped. "Both good looks and brains!"

"Oh yeah," Sam replied, glancing timidly at Kieron. "He looked pretty good to me."

Kieron immediately caught the drift of the conversation. He stood up, blocking the doorway, "Perhaps it's best to leave Luthias alone as he reads, he doesn't like many distractions."

"He *is* the distraction!" Brianna blurted out. "Are you quite sure he doesn't want to go along with yo?"

"No lass," Niall said. "He much prefers this century, for the moment. He's happy to housesit for Kieron, until they return."

Kieron gave Sam a wink, pulling her close to him. "Tha gaol agam ort," he told her . . . "I love you," as he began to plant kisses up and down her neck.

Niall spoke up immediately. "Come now, you two young things, it's morning now, and no time for that kind of stuff."

"Did you sleep well?" he asked Sam, eyes filled with mischief.

"Once I finally got a chance to close my eyes!"

She turned to Brianna. "Kieron wasn't much for sleeping last night."

The professor began to cough, almost spilling his tea.

"Oh, sorry professor, I guess that was a little uncalled for in front of you," she apologized.

Kieron looked up with a grin. "I do believe the good professor has sown enough wild oats in his day." He snickered, as he looked directly at the old man with the wrinkled face and hands.

"Please Kieron," Niall said sheepishly, "let's not bring that up now, there are still a few things which need to be done. We need to begin now, the sun is already climbing."

"You're right," Kieron agreed, looking out at the sky.

"Where does one go to do this kind of thing?" Brianna asked nervously.

"We must go up to the castle grounds," Kieron told her, "the portal is there."

The four spent the next half hour hastily reviewing their plans, and finishing up any last minute business. Niall left the kitchen to check up on a few things in one of Kieron's old astronomy books. He wanted to be sure of the exact time of day the portal would be most accessible. Although they'd done this many times in the past, this time was different. Samantha was going along with them on their trip back through time, and he wanted to be completely sure that nothing went wrong. Although he would miss Brianna terribly while they were gone, Niall was glad she would be staying at home, free from any atom splitting difficulties.

"Professor, are you just about ready?" Kieron called out.

"Do you ever remember a time when I wasn't?" he heard the old man yell from the hall. He turned to find his old friend limping down the hallway with a heavy stack of books in his arms, as Brianna watched from the kitchen.

"Here, let me help you with those," she said, reaching for a few.

"No lass," he told her, "I can handle them."

"I'm sure you can, old man," Kieron said jokingly. He glanced over at Samantha, who was trying to hide a smile.

Niall put the stack on the table. "There are just a few things I wanted you to be aware of, before we leave," he said, rubbing his left shoulder, obviously in a lot of pain. Brianna couldn't help but be concerned. "Are you sure you'll be okay for time travel?" she asked.

"I'm sure that's just what he needs," Kieron teased, giving the professor a mocking smile.

"Oh, don't worry about me lass," Niall told her, "I'll be better than ever, especially when I get back to the seventeenth century." He shot Kieron a knowing smile, and Brianna wondered what she was missing.

Luthias was instantly there, ready to wish them a good trip. He hugged his brothers, then kissed Sam's hand.

"If you ever want to come over and do some reading," Niall said, "I'm sure Kieron won't mind at all."

Luthias began to grin, a slow smile filled with promise. "I'd enjoy the company," he purred seductively.

Kieron laughed as he reached for his keys. "You *will* behave, won't you Luthias?"

"He most definitely will," Niall intervened. "I've already read him the riot act." He turned to look at Brianna. "You must be firm with him lass, he tends to want his own way at times."

"Sounds like a plan to me," Sam laughed, despite Kieron's sharp scowl.

"Is he always this attentive to every woman he meets?" Brianna asked, as they walked toward the car.

"Aye!" the two men answered simultaneously.

The four climbed into Kieron's car. Sam nervously peered out her window, as he continued up the old road leading to the castle. It was now littered with machinery, drills, and other pieces of heavy equipment.

Brianna sat silently in the back seat during the trip. Kieron hoped she didn't start to cry. That's the last thing he needed, a crying female. Sam had managed to stay strong, and he hoped Brianna would too.

The professor took her hand, hoping to sooth her rattled nerves. "It'll will be alright lass, please don't worry. We'll be back very soon," he said, looking deep into Brianna's eyes.

At first she thought she saw something different in the old man's eyes. Something she couldn't quite name, or understand. Then it was gone. How very kind he is, she thought, dismissing the whole thing. I'll really miss him terribly while they're gone.

Kieron pulled the car over to the side of the road and parked it. He reached around to the back seat and threw Brianna the keys. "Take good care of it while I'm gone," he told her, "and no boyfriends," he smiled mischievously.

Niall immediately spoke up. "They'll be no boys driving or sitting in this car with her. I'll make sure they become very ill, if they even try," he laughed, but his eyes were dead serious. Brianna sat there, wondering what prompted his remark.

"We'd best be hurrying," Kieron told them, looking to the morning sky. It was amazingly clear, with just a few low lying rain clouds. Good, he thought, one less thing to go wrong.

The sun was nearly directly above them.

"We have ten more minutes before it's noon, and the sun's rays hit the astral sphere," Kieron informed them as the small group hurried up the hill to the north wall.

Brianna remained baffled at how he could tell time without a watch.

"I don't own a watch," he told her. "There's no reason for one, it's easier to just read the heavenly bodies," he stated casually.

In just a few moments they reached the north wall, where the giant stained glass sphere was heating up in the late morning sun. Every piece of glass was beautifully illuminated from the sun's direct rays, a magnificent sight.

One by one, each took their turn saying goodbye to Brianna. By this time, she was in tears.

Niall was last. He hugged her tightly, and kissed her forehead. "Don't worry lass, *I will return for you*," he promised, gazing deep into her eyes.

She tried hard to keep from crying. He was all she had, and although he was up in age, she'd miss him terribly.

Kieron grabbed Sam's hand and led her directly in front of the large crimson center stone. He positioned her so she was standing directly in front of the crystal. She felt the strange heat generating from it, hitting her back. It seemed to tingle as it radiated onto her body. It felt revitalizing, and she began to anticipate what she'd soon be going through. Sam remembered Kieron telling her the color red increases the strength and force of the earth's magnetic energy, necessary for the vortex to open.

Niall stood directly to her left. The two men began to chant in unison, strange sounding words which had been used throughout the centuries for this exact purpose. Sam briefly turned to Brianna giving her a final thumbs up, and a smile. In seconds, her dearest friend would be gone, centuries away from being born.

Brianna watched from several yards away, where she was told to stand for her protection. Wiping her tears, she waved her final good bye.

Suddenly, there was a loud sizzling noise, then an even louder crack that reverberated around the entire castle grounds. The sky was filled with a dense swirling fog like substance. A spinning vortex opened directly above them. The swirling noise was almost deafening. Large bolts of electricity shot down toward them from the opening in the sky above. The next second they were gone!

Brianna just stood there in shock. What she'd just seen defied logic. They were actually gone. She stared at the spot where just a few seconds ago, her closest friends said their good byes. Now, there was nothing. She had witnessed time travel for the first time. It had been both an exhilarating and terrifying event, one she'd never speak of. A single tear trickled down her face. She immediately felt a loneliness never before experienced. They would return, he had promised her.

CHAPTER SEVENTEEN

Aberdeenshire, Scotland 1610

"Ouch!" Samantha yelled, as her body hit the hard ground. She landed on her butt, only a few yards away from Kieron, who was tossed from the vortex mere seconds before her.

"Are you ok?" he asked, getting up and walking over to where she sat.

"I guess so," she said, checking her arms and legs for any injuries. She looked around at the scenery. He'd done what he'd promised. She was now in a time totally foreign to her.

"So this is the 17th century," she muttered, noticing the absolutely beautiful gardens where they landed. "Not bad so far."

"Aye," he said as he took her hand and helped her up, "but it seems we're missing someone."

"I'm up here, and I seem to be stuck," a male voice came from directly above them.

Sam squinted as she looked up into the giant oak. Sure enough, Niall was tangled up in several thick branches.

Kieron broke into a fit of unstoppable laughter, while Sam remained more polite.

"Do you need my dirk?" he was able to ask between bouts of hysteria.

"Don't think so." He jumped down after untangling himself from a large branch, the front of his shirt almost completely torn off.

Kieron fell back onto the grass and roared in laughter.

Sam's mouth dropped, as she gazed at this gorgeous stranger standing in front of her. Gone were the wrinkles, silver grey hair, and heavy bifocals. Gone was his limp and slumping shoulders. What she saw was a sexy, strong young man, in his late twenties.

Bright, intelligent blue eyes replaced older cloudy ones. Long golden brown hair hung loosely around his broad shoulders, and down his rippled torso. He grabbed what was left of his shirt, and ripped it off, showing off a beautifully toned body. He was perfectly sculpted, just like Kieron, and there was no doubt in her mind that he was just as powerful.

"Professor?" she asked with a good bit of confusion.

"Time for a change," he smiled proudly.

Sam stared in disbelief. She couldn't believe what she was looking at. This man was young enough to be the professor's son, and there was absolutely no resemblance.

Well, what do you think?" he asked, grinning ear to ear.

"Is that really you?" Sam gasped with saucer sized eyes. "God, what a change, but, what happened? I don't mean to sound rude, but what *did* happen?"

Niall shot her one of his sexy smiles. "I got tired of being an old man."

"So, is this another illusion?" she asked, not being able to tear her eyes from his his rock hard chest, and finely tuned biceps.

"No lass, it's no illusion. The old man was the illusion, this is me, Niall McInnis, and I too am a Keeper of the Light." He held out his left palm, proudly showing her the symbol of the sun. A thick golden cuff adorned his left bicep, etched with strange symbols.

"How beautiful," she said, admiring its sparkle under the direct sun. "Must be very special."

"It is lass, my wife gave it to me, many years ago.

"Your wife?" she asked impulsively. She remembered that his wife had died a few years ago.

"Not that one," Kieron said, stepping over to her. "His soul mate."

Now she was really confused.

Niall laughed. The sound of his young voice, and complete happiness touched her heart. "I will explain the whole thing to you at a later date," he promised.

God, he was beautiful too, she thought.

Kieron stepped over and possessively pulled her close to him. "Don't be making his head any bigger than it is."

"Hey," Niall said, "a little flattery can't hurt, after all, it's probably been at least forty years since any young woman even took a second look. All for the love of teaching."

"Wow!" she gushed looking up at the two warriors. They were devastatingly gorgeous, and her poor brain was on overload. For some reason, her mind shot back to Brianna. Oh girl, you'd love this!

Kieron smiled at his friend. "I'm sure glad you decided it's time for a change. Who would I have told Duncan and Angus the old man was?" That set them off on another bout of laughter.

They had landed in a section of Rosestone's gardens. It was a densely grown area surrounded with lush flowers, and exotic bushes located on the top of a plateau which overlooked the sea. The waves crashed dangerously below.

Niall looked at the proximity of the water. "You certainly judged that distance correctly," he laughed. "A little to the south, and we'd be swimming right now."

Kieron laughed, and took Sam's hand. "Come Sam, there's something I want you to see." They took several steps to a small clearing between the fruit trees. Sam sucked in her breath when she saw the view.

Rosestone stood tall and majestic before her, illuminated by the sun's golden rays. It was a spectacular sight, an archaeological treasure.

Absolutely breathtaking, it commanded your immediate attention. Not some crumbling ruin where mothers told their kids not to play, but a real castle. Her castle.

"Well, what do you think of your inheritance now?" Kieron teased.

The sky was clear blue, and the whole scene reminded her of a beautiful picture, done by one of the masters.

Sam looked up at her castle in awe. "I can hardly believe it's true!" she sighed. "That's got to be the most regal sight in the entire world. I've never seen anything so beautiful."

Kieron smiled in agreement. "Aye, she is a beauty."

"Was it worth the trip, lass?" Niall asked with a wink.

"Most definitely!" The three stood in silent admiration for several seconds, each lost in his own private thoughts.

Kieron began to point out different parts of the castle. It stood five stories high, over eighty feet tall, and had been skillfully constructed from large blocks of magnificent red

Scottish sandstone. The stone from which it was built had a pinkish tinge, giving the castle a magical touch. Niall explained that the color came from the high content of iron within the stone. Lovely rounded turrets added to its beauty. A sight to take anyone's breath away.

The only way to gain entrance into the grand fortress was a small stone bridge, cut deep into the rock along the jagged cliffs of the mountain, overlooking the sea. It was a steep descent, and could prove quite deadly if not traveled by skilled horsemen.

Graceful battlements ran along the parapet, where guards stood watch over the bailey and shore below. The walls were approximately eight feet thick, and encircled the entire castle. All in all, it had been magnificently constructed, showing most definite signs of advanced engineering, considering the date.

A lovely two story arched chapel was attached to the great hall by a long vaulted stone tunnel. Niall explained that many of the newly appointed knights held several special rituals there. They often gathered in an underground Chamber of Knowledge to perfect themselves in ancient wisdom. "They are among the finest of men," he said proudly.

She turned to Kieron. "Will you bring me down there someday? I'd love to see it. I was always interested in that kind of thing.

"Most definitely," Kieron smiled, "you'll see that and a lot more, whatever your heart desires."

"Deeper underground in the castle's lower levels, the Hall of Records is kept. It's very closely guarded. Much of the births and deaths of people who've lived in Rosestone throughout the centuries are shelved there. Also a very rare collection of tomes written by the first Celtic druids dealing with ancient wisdom."

"Really?" she asked in amazement. "What kind of things, and how are they preserved from time?"

Niall laughed at her persistent curiosity. "For now, it will suffice to say a few spells keep them free from dangerous toxins in the atmosphere."

"I'll be sure to take you there soon," Kieron said, "I know you'll enjoy it."

The castle gatehouse was two stories high. Kieron explained how the ground floor contained most of the guard rooms. The second floor was the guard headquarters, where most of the weapons were stored.

In the back of the castle, where they landed, was a perfectly manicured garden, with bushes and hedges which had been shaped to magnificent designs. Sam noticed one which formed a Celtic eternity sign, like the stunning piece of marble Kieron had given her.

A fountain stood in the center of the magnificent gardens, with water gracefully cascading down over each tier. It was a magnificent sight, and brought her thoughts back to her own time, and the fountain she'd planned to construct there. Strange, she thought, it was exactly the same.

The front door was massive, made from solid oak.

On the wall, was the Royal Crest of the MacClaire Clan. Beautifully crafted stone benches graced the entranceway, and brightly colored flowers were everywhere.

Kieron pointed out the large stable, buttery and kitchen. It was enormous, and had everything, including a loving family whom she was about to meet.

Two tall men on horseback rode across to where they stood. Sam felt as though she was watching a movie. She could hear the men yelling out to them, as they neared. "Kieron! Niall! Welcome home brothers!"

Kieron turned, taking her hand in his. "Sam, you're about to meet your family."

Sam held her breath as the two rode up. They brought two extra horses along with them.

Duncan leaped off his huge black stallion and scooped her up in his arms. She held onto him for dear life.

Angus, his brother, was overjoyed to see them. He immediately ran to Kieron and Niall, hugging each firmly. "It's good to have you back," he said, brown eyes misting over with emotion. "My senses told me you'd be coming back soon, but it was Duncan who confirmed it.

Angus was a tall, muscular man somewhere in his mid-forties, who greatly resembled his brother. His hair was long and very dark, now sprinkled with grey. He had Duncan's features with deep blue eyes, and a broad sculpted body. Like Duncan, he wore a claymore strapped across his back. Just one look at him, and one could tell he was both efficient and highly skilled with the blade.

After a few heartwarming moments, Duncan took Sam by the hand and stepped over to the other two. "Failte, welcome brothers. It's been too long," he said, hugging each one. "Did the vortex treat you well?" he asked comically, eyeing the white powder like substance on their clothes.

"Aye, it went without a hitch, except for Niall, who fancied landing in that tall oak rather than the conventional manner," Kieron joked. "At least he dumped that old man guise."

"Old man?"

"Aye," Niall grinned, "it's been my favorite for the last several decades, easier to teach with."

Duncan started to laugh. "And the lasses?"

Kieron chimed in. "What lasses?"

"That will all change when we return," Niall told them confidently. "I have a plan."

"Danu protect us!" Angus roared, and once again they all joined in hearty laughter.

This is family, Sam thought happily. I suddenly feel I've been away for a very long time, too long. Although she encountered no problems with the vortex, she was now physically exhausted, and very hungry. Travel through the vortex had been draining for her. Her head still felt a little fuzzy.

"Samantha," Angus said softly, as he pulled her into his arms. "Time has been good to you, lass," he smiled looking down at his niece. "We've sorely missed you, welcome home."

Her spirits lifted instantly, feeling welcomed and loved. It must have been heartbreaking she thought, to have been banished from this wonderful place because of a life threatening curse. Her resolve and defiance to stop this dark sorcerer was even stronger now. How dare he force me from my home and family she thought, gaining emotional strength by the moment.

"Thank you," she told him and kissed his cheek.

For a while, the group just stood there chatting and catching up on things. It reminded Sam of any other family reunion. People with loved ones they hadn't seen in perhaps years, except in this family, it was centuries.

"We have a wee problem," Duncan informed them as they readied the horses to return. "Angus and I have spent many a night discussing this. Do you think it's wisebringing her directly back to the castle? He will be waiting, in one form or another."

Kieron shot him a questioning look. "Why not? She's under the protection of four warriors. I doubt whether he'd be insane enough to try anything now. Anyway, Niall and I have researched every book written in antiquity concerning the curse. We've discovered we must find the famed Amulet of Avalon, worn by Dermott MacClaire."

"Dermott MacClaire?" Angus was surprised to hear that name. "He died several hundred years ago. I've no knowledge of where he was interred."

"That's the problem," Niall added, "I thought the Hall of Records might be a good place to start, since there are many recordings of births and deaths housed there. Hopefully we'll get lucky. It's certainly worth the chance."

"Perhaps," Duncan said, "yet I know from personal experience that Rosestone is filled with many other hidden halls and chambers, some have been sealed off from antiquity, for various reasons. It could be anywhere."

"We'll find it," Kieron stated confidently He glanced over at Sam. "I have no doubt."

Niall looked off into the distance. "Well, it would appear we have our work laid out nicely for us. It'll prove a difficult chore, to say the least."

Duncan turned to the others. "You already know you'll have our complete cooperation in whatever it takes. I won't let him win this time."

"I've never heard of this Amulet of Avalon," Angus told them. "What exactly is it, and what's its function?"

"We'll tell you everything once safely inside the castle," Kieron informed them. "I don't want to keep Sam outside too long right now. He's very cunning, and one never knows what weapon he'll use next, supernatural or other."

"Good idea," Duncan said, mounting his black stallion. "We'll discuss this plan of yours at length. Do you still ride lass?" he asked, turning to Sam. He watched her eye the large animal.

"A little, but not that well. I haven't been riding for a very long time."

"You'll ride with me," Kieron stated emphatically taking her hand and helping her onto one of the stallions. He climbed up behind her, and took the reins. The horse bobbed its head as if to welcome them.

Next, Niall mounted. "Ah, I've missed this," he said longingly as he ran his hand through the stallion's fine mane. "It's the only way to travel."

"There's nothing wrong with that Land Rover, if I remember correctly," Kieron told him. "It's a fine machine."

"Fine it is," he joked, "but it'll never win over the feeling of mounting a grand stallion, like this.

CHAPTER EIGHTEEN

21st Century

Brianna sat in a large, overstuffed chair, enjoying a tall mug of hot chocolate topped with a healthy dose of whipped cream. Comfort food, she reasoned, since she felt so lonely and miserable. She tried to get involved with the paperback she bought that afternoon, but the love scenes only made her more lonely and miserable. Her life was falling apart now since her dearest friends vanished into thin air before her eyes. It all seemed so meaningless and hopeless.

Putting the book down, and pushing off the soft throw covering her legs, she sat up and stared out the window. Looking out into the night sky, she wondered where they were now. Life continues she thought sadly, as she watched people come and go, to work, shopping or whatever. It was the usual rhythm of life, but not for her. It had only been days since they left, but their absence was like a gaping hole in her heart. How did the time leap go for them? Did they arrive as a trio, was anyone missing, or worse yet, hurt? Her mind was filled with thousands of unanswered questions. These heavy thoughts plagued her constantly since that day when they said their goodbyes. Everything would go as planned. They had told her so.

The following day, Brianna tried to occupy her mind with the stacks of paperwork and phone calls on her desk at work. The law firm was exceptionally busy that morning, and she tried to concentrate on things in the office. It was totally futile, she needed to see them again, all of them.

She occasionally drove Kieron's car up to the castle site after working hours, and sat down on the ground where she saw them last. It seemed to somehow help.

One afternoon in particular, she was more depressed than usual. She told her boss she was feeling ill, he let her leave a few hours early. She smiled when remembering the comment the professor told her about no boys in the car. Honestly, it couldn't happen even if I wanted it, she thought dismally as she headed up the old rocky trail which led to the castle.

Brianna was desperate to find, as she put it, a *real* man. One that she knew she could depend on right or wrong. At times she felt there was someone especially for her, out there somewhere. She certainly wished he would hurry up. The grass was growing under her feet. Get over it girl, she said as she continued the conversation with herself, those kind of men aren't around anymore. Sam was lucky enough to catch the last one.

She remembered Luthias, minding Kieron's house while they were away. Whew! I bet he could make me forget life for a while. Not quite ready for that, she let the idea go. Somehow she didn't want to get heavily evolved with a shape shifter. Let's see what Kieron can bring home she thought, remembering his promise.

The old dirt road was now cluttered with pieces of heavy equipment and machinery, since Kieron told the workers to stop until he returned. The weather wasn't the greatest. Thick dark clouds were forming, with the promise of rain.

She pulled his car close to the building for security. This way, she had a quick escape, if need be. After all, she was alone, and after hearing Sam's tales of horror she was taking no chances.

Brianna wasn't easily scared, she tried to remain open minded and logical about things. She had come to accept much since meeting Sam, especially after being abruptly introduced to time travel, and seeing three adults disappear into thin air! Today she braved it all, just to be there at the place where they left her world. It somehow gave her a false sense of comfort.

The wind seemed to be picking up, as she sat doodling in the dirt, her heart heavy with sadness. Much to her surprise she began to cry. Silly girl, she thought, pulling a Kleenex form her purse. Why am I crying like this, it won't be forever, yet she had her doubts. She recalled what the professor told her. "*I will return for you.*" She knew he meant it, and that was enough to boost her spirits.

After a while the skies grew darker as it began to get late, she knew she should leave. The sound of waves crashing angrily on the rocks below were beginning to spoof her. She sat there on the ground, fishing in her large bag for Kieron's keys, when she swore she heard her name! It was slightly muffled, as if someone was calling to her from another room, or time? The voice was definitely male, yet she didn't recognize it. Immediately she jumped up, expecting to see someone she knew come around the corner. There was no one. Again, the muffled echo.

Her stubborn side kicked in, as she took several deep breaths and attempted to calm herself. So what if I heard my name, she thought. There must be some totally logic explanation . . . right?

Determined not to be frightened away, she ventured further to the rear of the castle, and sat on the bench where Sam had first seen her father, several weeks ago. Never before had she felt so totally at home, yet so home sick. Just a few more minutes, she told herself, curling her fingers firmly around a bottle of mace.

As Brianna sat there enjoying the strange peaceful feeling of being near the castle, she took in the barren, overgrown castle grounds. Now, she could understand just how overwhelmed Sam must have felt seeing Rosestone for the first time. It was such an undertaking. So much work.

Her eyes were drawn toward the huge trunk of an ancient oak next to her. She remembered her school days, and learning about the ancient druids. Oak trees were very symbolic and sacred to them. Something had been etched into the thick trunk long ago, but it was impossible to read from where she sat.

Curiosity eventually got the better of her. She stood and took two steps closer to the old weathered oak, to read what someone had apparently thought enough of to carve. Bending down close, she traced the carving with her finger, then jumped back in shock.

Before her eyes was an ancient carving which read, "Brianna." The fact that it was her name began to scare her. It was way too much of a chance happening. She had to leave, and now. Sam had apparently never seen it. Brianna was sure she would have mentioned it, if she had. Who and why was her name there? Was it simply a mere coincidence?

Remembering what had happened to Sam, she bolted for the car. Once safely inside, she locked the doors, then took a deep breath. There was no one around, and she was going home. For some reason, she thought of the old professor. It seemed he was always there for her throughout her life at times of danger. How she wished he was there now.

Starting the car, she took one final look. Still no one. She threw the car into reverse, and left the castle grounds immediately. Lonely and sad, she recalled his last words. "I will return for you."

CHAPTER NINETEEN

17th century

Samantha was beginning her adventure in the 17th century. She, Kieron and Niall followed the others across the rocky trail up to the castle's main gate. They headed to the stable, where they quickly dismounted, and gave the fine animals over to the teenage stable boy.

"Welcome Lords," he addressed them, directing his gaze to Samantha. His eyes slowly swept over her body from head to toe. Kieron quickly noticed the heated passion in the young man's eyes.

"I wonder what he thinks about my clothes?" she laughed as they left the stable. She had left the twenty first century dressed in snug faded jeans and a pink cotton tee. They clung to her petite figure, showing off her feminine curves.

"I can tell you exactly what he's thinking," Kieron said gruffly. "A young boy of sixteen. His hormones are running wild. At least he's got enough sense not to act on it."

"Aye," Niall laughed. "He savors his next hot meal, and values his head!"

"Ian is a good worker," Duncan interceded, "and I'm quite happy with he and his family. They're all employed here at

Rosestone, have been for years. I'm sure the smile was purely innocent."

"You are indeed growing old Duncan," Niall pointed out. "It's good that your daughter has a husband who doesn't miss a thing."

"She will be changing into a gown immediately," Kieron said sternly, looking directly at Sam with his "end of discussion" look.

"Aye sir," Sam said mockingly. "And just what was wrong with my clothes?"

"Nothing," Kieron grinned, "in the twenty first century. Here the women all wear gowns, and so will you. Sam, we don't want to attract attention from the wrong one, it's not time yet."

"Don't worry," she smiled up at him lovingly, "I understand."

They left the stable and traveled down a beautiful grayish blue stone walk. The large octagon shaped stones interlocked with each other, forming a unique design. The walkway was edged with strange tall flowers, which gave off a lovely fragrance. Again, she was keenly aware of the same vibrations that she felt in her century. She stopped, looking up at Kieron. "Electromagnetic energy?" she grinned proudly.

Niall turned with a smile. "She's a quick learner, Kieron."

At the main gate Kieron and Niall were greeted by several hired guards, some of which were good friends of theirs. They too were large burly men, picked by Duncan himself to stand guard outside the castle's main entrance. Judging by their size, they were not men that one would choose to pick a fight with. Each one was tall, with massive biceps, and rock hard chests, definitely necessary if there was an altercation at the main entrance to the castle.

Wow, Sam thought wickedly as she was gradually introduced to each one. The women in my time would love this!

With his arm protectively around her shoulders, Duncan introduced Sam to each man, so they would be sure to know she was the lord's daughter. As she stepped up to each, greeting them pleasantly, one stood out.

He was a tall, ruggedly handsome guard with long dark hair, who seemed especially interested in her. He lewdly and blatantly took in her perfect, curvy figure. Sam was repulsed by the conspicuous act of disrespect, but said nothing. If I were back in my time, she thought, I'd cut you to ribbons, mister.

Oddly enough, neither Duncan nor anyone else had picked up on the rude gesture. She found it impossible that Kieron had missed it. It just wasn't his nature.

Totally ignoring the man, she continued with the others, giving each a pleasant "hello," then followed Duncan and Angus through the main door and into the Great Hall.

Kieron hesitated just long enough for them to disappear, then spun around on his boot and stalked up to the man.

"Blackguard, what is your name?" he demanded harshly as he pinned him firmly against the iron gate with his rock hard body. The guard glared back at him with hatred and contempt.

"Callum," he told him in a low growl filled with sarcasm.

Kieron grabbed the shirt around his neck and pulled his face close. "Tell me Callum, are you an intelligent man?" he asked menacingly. There was no reply. He stared deeply into his dark eyes, and placed his left palm on his throat. Immediately, the man screamed out in agony. Kieron removed his hand, leaving the mark of the sun on his neck. The sickening smell of burnt flesh quickly filled the surrounding air.

"If you ever look at her again for whatever reason, I promise you I will turn you to ashes instantly." The man's eyes dilated in terror as he grabbed his throat in pain.

"Let this be a warning to you, and anyone else who wishes to cross me." He turned and looked at the others. There was total silence.

"I am capable of killing you at any time," Kieron threatened, "I need not be there. The woman is mine, and mine alone. Do you understand?"

Callum nodded his head, clutching his throat as he choked and gasped for air.

He turned to the guard next to him. "Go and get this fool water, before his throat burns," then nonchalantly followed the others into the Great Hall.

"A wee problem?" Niall grinned as he waited just outside the main door.

"Not at all," Kieron smiled, "just a slight misunderstanding."

Niall placed his arm around Kieron's shoulder and began to laugh. "I wondered if you saw him."

The Great Hall was a massive room, with a high loft ceiling. The walls were painted in a soft gold. Lush red velvet drapes covered the tall beveled, diamond cut panes of glass.

Large torches along the wall lit the interior, illuminating the wall art which had been skillfully done by master painters. Stone basins used for washing were located near the entrance, and several luxurious fur carpets were strewn over the floor.

Pages and servants scurried about, placing silver platters of food on the long trestle tables. In the center of the back wall, a giant hearth burned brightly, adding a special sense of warmth to the large room. Pleasant fragrances of sweet smelling herbs such as lavender, rose petals and fennel filled the air.

Large family portraits were proudly hung along the tall walls for all to admire. They showed a long history of Rosestone's past lords, dating back from the castle's original construction around 1000 A.D., up to the present day of 1610, with the final portrait of Lord Duncan MacClaire, and his wife Lady Kathleen.

Kieron smiled with nostalgia as he recalled the previous ancestors who had once inhabited Rosestone, generations ago. All noble people, he reminisced, except for the dark Vikings who battled fiercely for her possession.

There were also banners in the clan's colors of indigo and gold, and many diversified and beautiful clan targes.

The lord's table was centered at the end of the hall. The lord and his lady, and any other members of nobility or guests of the lord were seated there also.

On the wall directly behind, hung an enormous silk tapestry of the Hunt, woven in intense, vivid hues. It was a masterpiece, depicting Lord Duncan himself accompanied by his brother Angus, and several clan members, as they followed large wolfhounds caught up in the chase for wild boar. An impressive sight, hung high in a place of honor for guests of the castle to admire.

Maids and pages were busy bringing heavy platters of food to the tables. An exquisite feast of roast pork was placed on each table, for the enjoyment of both clan members and guests. Platters of boiled vegetables, and plenty of cheese and freshly baked bread were also placed along the long tables for their enjoyment. The scene was one of happiness, as family members and welcomed visitors filed up to Duncan's table to meet the new arrivals. A perfect welcoming party.

"I've someone who's been waiting impatiently to meet you," Duncan said with a warm smile.

Sam looked at the beautiful youthful woman with long auburn hair and bright green eyes. She was stunningly lovely. Unsure of what to do, she glanced over at Kieron, who nodded his head in encouragement.

"Mother?" she whispered nervously.

"Samantha!" Katie cried out, as she jumped up from the table and grabbed her, hugging her close to her heart. "You've come back to us!"

It was a bittersweet moment, for all to see. Katie MacClaire's heart swelled with joy at having her only remaining daughter back home with them once again.

Her sister had already taken ill, and died several years ago at this point in time. Duncan had been quick to send Samantha off soon afterward, in Kieron's powerful protection. The two eventually married.

Tears fell as Sam held her mother close. Despite all previous doubts and disillusions, somewhere in Sam's heart she knew this was home. She would definitely miss her family back in Boston, but if she had to, she would be happy to remain here with Kieron. It would be a hard decision to make, but despite the obvious hardships and disadvantages for someone from the 21st century, she knew this was where she wanted to be.

Once again, pain and disappointment clenched at her heart as Brianna came to mind. She thought of her, patiently waiting, sometime in the future.

After a period of tears and hugs, the large clan finally settled down to enjoy the feast which had been prepared especially for them.

The dinner was out of a dream. Sam sat between her parents, with Kieron and Niall across the table. Angus and his wife, Morna sat next to them.

Sam chattered happily, answering a barrage of questions about the twenty first century. She suddenly found herself at a loss for words, as the endless line of well-wishers filed up to the table to greet her.

"Don't worry love," Kieron said, blue eyes filled with concern at her frustration, "you'll get to know everyone very well in due time."

She smiled and gulped done a healthy mouthful of wine to ease her nerves. It was smooth and delicious, not at all what she'd expected from that time period.

As the evening quietly rolled on and the hall finally emptied out, Kieron started to question Duncan about the guard outside.

"Tell me what you know about this blackguard Callum, who stands guard out front," he asked causally.

"Callum?" Duncan replied, giving it thought. "He's a new hire, just a week ago."

"Who hired the man?" he asked in a chilling tone.

"I believe it was Tearlach's call. He's now the captain of our guard, and a fair and decent man. He'd been down in the village, scouting around for more able bodied men. We've had need of more, lately. He returned a few days later with several strong men. They all seemed genuine and willing to work for weekly coin. Is there a problem, brother? If so, tell me and he'll be dismissed immediately"

"I think it's best if you watch him closely," Niall added from across the table. He seems to have a strange attraction to your daughter."

Duncan tensed, as Niall proceeded to explain what had happened earlier.

Kieron broke in, eyes twinkling. "He and I have an understanding," he told Duncan as he attempted to smother a laugh.

Angus looked over with a look of amusement. "Is he still alive?" he asked, trying to keep his laughter at bay.

"Somewhat," he replied. "He carries the mark of Light on his throat."

Duncan finally relaxed a bit, knowing the situation would not occur twice. "Then he won't pose any more of a threat to us, I imagine," he smiled, pleased at Kieron's solution to the problem.

"I'm very sure he will behave himself," Kieron added, "but I'm wondering why he's here. Somehow I get the idea that steady pay may not be all he's after," he said, glancing over at Samantha.

Suddenly, all eyes turned toward Sam, who was trying hard to enjoy her first night's dinner at Rosestone. She instantly chilled recalling the rude, obnoxious guard.

Kieron noticed her expression, and reached across the table taking her hand in his. "Don't worry love, you aren't alone."

"Do you think it's him?"

"It's a puzzle, lass," Duncan told her. "We know he'll appear, yet in what form and when are yet unknown." He turned to look at his wife, who had been strangely quiet throughout the entire evening.

"It's a well-known fact he'll return to try and claim her, one way or the other," Katie said briskly. "Kieron, you've told us that you and Niall had worked something out. May I ask what it is, since it's my daughter too, which we're talking about," she said coolly, casting Duncan an icy glance.

"Just saying he'll eventually return isn't enough," she continued, making direct eye contact with her husband. "I need to know what exactly you're going to do about it, or else I will be forced to take matters into my own hands."

Ouch! Kieron thought, you could cut the tension here with a knife.

Niall coughed nervously, feeling he was suddenly in the middle of a simmering clam feud.

Sam began to notice the difference toward women in this century. They were basically powerless, unless married to a wealthy, powerful man. Feeling sorry for her mother, she got up and kissed Katie's cheek.

"Don't worry about it," she told her soothingly, trying to alleviate some of the obvious tension. "I'll clue you in on everything, later."

Katie smiled up at her. "Thanks, dear. That would be most appreciated. You'll soon find that women's opinions aren't as highly valued as they are in our time, if at all," she said sarcastically. She glared at her husband, feeling that she'd been left out of the entire situation, most assuredly because she was a woman.

Life was difficult in the 17th century, for the slim, attractive wife of Duncan MacClaire. She had accidentally been drawn back in time while vacationing near the castle ruins, during the late 1990's. Her attraction to the sexy lord of Rosestone had been immediate, and undeniable. The two fell madly in love, and married. Life was good, until a dark sorcerer entered their world, killing their oldest daughter, then causing Samantha to be sent away from her home, for her own protection.

Although in her heart she knew it wasn't Duncan's fault, their marriage had never been the same. It was often said behind closed doors, that the Lady of Rosestone would gladly return to her time, if at all possible. Duncan had heard those whispers, and it broke his heart. It was common knowledge throughout the castle that Katie was very unhappy. Duncan was desperate to fix things, and change her mind.

The evening rolled on uneventfully. Kieron advised they wait until after dinner, then find safety behind closed doors and away from prying eyes, to explain things to Katie.

Dinner was slowly wrapping up, when Ciaran, one of Duncan's trusted guards, burst into the room obviously quite distressed. He headed straight toward Duncan. Kieron and Niall pulled their blades, ready if necessary.

"My lord," he said, flustered and out of breath,

"Someone has opened the stable door and let the horses out!"

"What!" Duncan roared, jumping up from his chair and reaching for his dirk.

"Aye, lord," he answered nervously.

"Can't you just round them up, and drive them back inside?" Kieron asked calmly. It seemed the logical answer.

"Nay Lord Kieron, they have been purposely driven away. There is not one left in sight."

"Tell me Ciaran," Niall asked, "was Callum standing on guard tonight when it happened?"

The flustered man thought briefly. "Aye, Sir Niall, he was. But I haven't seen him in perhaps an hour."

Niall glanced over at Kieron, locking eyes. Ciaran was a member of the clan, and Duncan trusted him completely. He had, on several occasions, saved his life.

"Call the captain, I wish to speak with him," Duncan ordered briskly.

"Immediately," Ciaran said, then obediently hurried from the room.

"Perhaps it would be safer to put Sam and Katie somewhere more secure," Kieron offered.

Duncan turned and faced his wife. "My love, would you and Samantha please retreat up to the solar for the time being? I don't know who is to blame here, but I want no chances taken with either of your lives."

"Of course, my lord," Katie said sarcastically. Turning to Sam who was already on her feet and ready to bolt, she said, "Come love, let's go up to the solar where we'll be safe. Let the men do the fighting." Duncan felt the sting of her comment.

On their way up the steps, Katie turned and looked at her daughter. "Can you still defend yourself if need be?"

Sam grinned at her mother, "Oh, aye," she laughed. "I'm murder with the dirk, and can handle the heavy claymore if needed. Kieron taught me well."

Katie smiled proudly. "I can see you still have a lot of me in your personality. I'm honored. We'll barricade ourselves in your father's solar. There's a lot of weapons up there," she smiled confidently.

While Duncan and the others remained at the table, Ciaran burst into the hall a second time. This time he was white as snow, and visibly shaking. Duncan automatically sprang to his feet.

"What's wrong man?" he asked, wondering how much worse the situation would become.

"It's Tearlach, lord. He's in the barn, throat's been cut," he said hysterically.

Duncan bolted for the front door, when Kieron and Niall both grabbed an arm, holding him back.

"No Duncan!" Kieron yelled. "Can't you see, that's exactly what he wants? He'll kill you when you least expect it. Stay in here, there's more safety in numbers."

It took several seconds, but Duncan eventually calmed, seeing their logic. "Tearlach was a good man, I will avenge his death," he stated emphatically.

"Aye, you definitely will brother, but not like this," Kieron advised, as he and Niall coaxed him back to the table.

Sam and her mother scurried up the stairs, and into the solar. All the time Sam kept her father's silver dirk, which she had brought with her through the vortex, hidden snugly in her clothes. Unfortunately she thought, things are moving right along. She had hoped for at least several days of peace before the action started.

"He knows I'm here," she told her mother nervously.

Katie nodded. "Are you well prepared?"

"Yes," she replied without hesitation. "I am."

The door to the solar was made from thick solid oak, the name MacClaire skillfully engraved in the center. Katie opened the heavy door, revealing a lovely round room, with several tall windows. Large wood trestles ran horizontally across the ceiling, supporting the sloping roof, and giving the room depth and character. The walls were painted a soothing off white.

There was a large hearth to the side, grey stone inlay encircling the circumference. All in all, it was the perfect getaway when the lord of the castle wished to escape his subjects, Sam thought comically. Her mother slid the double bolted lock across the door, to insure their safety.

A very large portrait of Duncan and his wife on their wedding day graced the center wall.

"Oh," Sam gushed, "this is just beautiful," as she stepped over to admire it.

"Yes," Katie said softly, "those were better days." It was the first the two women had the chance to speak frankly, in private.

Sam stepped closer to her mother, taking her hand. "Do you love him?" she asked quietly. There was a second of silence, and Sam feared the worst.

"Yes, Sam, I love him with all my heart. It's just that here in this century, things are not the same. I'm sure that you, of all people, can understand."

"Unfortunately, women have not yet been elevated to the point they were when I lived in the 1990's," she reminisced.

"Oh, I can definitely understand," Sam chimed in. "My friend kept begging me to bring her with us through the time vortex, so she could find a good man here."

Katie smiled and shook her head. "She would most definitely find herself a good man, but whether or not she would want to stay here with him is quite a different story." They both broke out in laughter at the truth of the statement.

"Just how did you end up here?" Sam asked curiously.

Katie took her hand as they sat down on a long, beautifully cushioned window seat. Soft furs were scattered over the wide wood beam floors.

"Well dear, it's a long story, but I'll give you the short version," she joked. "I was vacationing in Scotland by myself, still very young, only twenty. Something about this country seemed to call to me, literally," she laughed.

"What do you mean?" Sam asked, totally intrigued with the story.

"Well, I had made arrangements to stay at a B&B here while on vacation. It was something I'd always wanted to do. The problem was that it was haunted! Anyway, to make a long story short, it was your father and his druid abilities calling to me, over time itself. He wanted me here with him in the 17th

century. I eventually went snooping in a part of the structure that hadn't been excavated as yet, and basically fell over a special type of scrying crystal left there for centuries. Being the curious one, I picked it up. As soon as I touched it, well, the rest is history."

Sam stared at her for the longest time. How she admired this strong and very courageous woman, her mother.

"I'm so glad you did," she said softly. "That's a fantastic story!

"Time travel is something that wasn't ever understood in my time," she told Sam.

"Oh, I know," Sam added. "I thought Kieron was flat out crazy when he told me I had to return to the 17th century in order to kill the sorcerer."

Her mother looked at her for several minutes. "Yes Sam," she said with determination, "and kill him you will."

Katie started a fire in the stone hearth, giving the room a warm homey kind of feeling. Long red velvet curtains graced the windows, and white candles flickered everywhere.

"I really like this room," Sam said as she stepped to the window and looked down on the bailey, then further to the dark blue waters of the sea. It was a breathtaking view, with waves crashing on the reefs below. She watched the guards change on the hour, as they patrolled the outer gate. It was black outside now, and the burning torches below created a beautiful stark difference against the blackness of the night.

Suddenly, Sam thought she saw a small group of bright lights coming up from the water. They seemed to surface, then disappear into the night sky. "What on earth?" she blurted out.

Katie looked at her and smiled knowingly. "You've seen them, haven't you?" she said, stepping over to the window.

"What in the world were those things?" Sam asked in surprise. "You've seen them before?"

"Sometimes," Katie smiled. "It's a type of paranormal activity that occurs occasionally. That's all I know."

Sam's mouth dropped. "Paranormal activity? What are you talking about? Have you told Duncan this?"

Katie took her hand. "Of course I have Sam, but you'll soon discover that women, especially ones from another time, don't get answers that easily. He told me that it's been happening for decades, and that I shouldn't worry about it."

"That's ridiculous!" Sam told her. "I'll ask Kieron later, I know he'll tell me the truth."

Katie just smiled. "That's exactly what I thought, Sam." The two women continued to talk, getting to know each other, and bonding as mother-daughter. All the while, Sam kept the silver dirk close to her heart.

A sudden loud knock at the door shattered the mellow mood. "Sam it's Kieron. Please open."

Sam looked at her mother in hesitation, something was different, and she could sense it. She gave her mother a troubled look. "Do you think it's okay?"

"Are you absolutely sure it's him?" Katie replied. "You are your father's daughter," she told her proudly. "You have inherited his druid capabilities, use them. They can't be erased or altered by the fabric of time."

Sam looked startled, then understood. "Alright," she whispered softly, "I will." She closed her eyes, concentrating on who or what was on the other side of the thick oak door.

"No!" she cried out defiantly, being thrown backward by the sheer force of power lurking beyond the door.

Katie ran to her, helping her up from the floor.

"It's him!" she gasped, as her mother motioned her to stay still.

Just at that moment, they heard voices in the hall, and men running up the staircase toward the solar. "It's Duncan," Katie said as she fumbled with the two metal bars. The men rushed into the room. Kieron grabbed Sam instantly, holding her tightly against his body. "He was here, wasn't he?" he said, clutching her in a death grip.

"Kieron, please. I can hardly breathe," she joked as she struggled to free herself.

"Sorry love," he started to apologize, "I was so afraid that maybe . . ."

"No Kieron," Katie made a point of interrupting, "she is fine. She used her druid capabilities for the first time. It was very successful, I might add."

"Thank God" he whispered.

"Lord Duncan," a tall brawny man gripping a broadsword, yelled up the steps.

"Aye," Duncan replied, ready to hear more bad luck.

"There is no sign of Callum as yet, but there are a score of men out searching. We will search until dawn if need be."

Niall snorted in sarcasm. "It'll take more than a score of men, if our suspicions are right."

Kieron nodded in agreement. "It's a waste of time."

CHAPTER TWENTY

The small group left the solar, returning to the Great Hall, and eventually to their prospective chambers for the night. There were only a few hours remaining before sunrise, and the unknown dangers of a new day.

After climbing a large marble staircase, Kieron led Sam down a stone hallway, on their way to the bedchamber which was to be theirs. As they walked along, Sam took in all the beautifully carved alcoves, as well as many intricately woven tapestries. Some were very old, the oldest being particularly troublesome to her.

"What's this about?" she asked, stopping abruptly to stare. It showed several people who were a combination of human and animal or bird formations.

"Collectively, it shows the many shape shifters which once occupied these lands, thousands of years ago. There were many different species here at one point, some which modern day humans have no knowledge of."

"You're kidding," she said, studying the different animals which seemed to be existing peacefully with mankind. "You mean like Luthias?"

"Somewhat," he smiled

"Where did they come from, and what finally happened to them?" She was filled with questions, and Kieron did his best to accurately answer each one. He took her hand and redirected her back down the hall.

"Many came from other worlds, where other types of species exist, quite different from those in your world. Most were probably trying to escape, and got lucky enough to cross over the border undetected. Some are just a product of interbreeding between humans and various animals, or reptiles."

"Interbreeding!" she gasped in disgust and horror. "Who on earth would do such a horrible thing?"

Kieron looked at her for a moment, then said. "It's not done on your earth."

Now she was really scared. "What do you mean, Kieron?"

They're the products of many vile experiments done in other realms, or dimensions. Some are the result of experiments gone wrong. Merlin himself has openly admitted that he controls all of these poor misfits, as he does other dark spirits."

"Ugh, shape shifters," she whispered low. That gave her something else to brood about. She tried to push it from her mind, for the rest of the night.

The entire castle was absolutely delightful. Sam tried hard to make mental notes for Brianna, as promised. "It's like a fairy tale come true!" she later told Kieron.

"Oh lass," he sighed, rolling his eyes in disgust. "Please don't speak of the Fae tonight. I've had enough trouble for one night, without experiencing their cunning games." He squeezed her hand gently, and gave her a quick kiss.

After a short walk down the dimly lit stone corridor, they arrived at the bed chamber especially designated for them.

"Wow!" she said as Kieron opened the door, and she got her first glimpse.

"Well," he smiled, "what do you think?"

The extra-large bedchamber was done in different shades of lavender and rose, with long velvet drapes to coordinate.

"It's my favorite color!" she said, looking around the lovely chamber. Kieron just smiled, as though he had known that for a very long time. This room also had a white stone hearth, which was already burning brightly, filling the spacious room with the soothing sent of heather.

"Someone really put a lot of thought into this room," she said, then saw the sly grin on his face. "It was you, wasn't it?" she said, seeing his satisfied expression.

Kieron tried his hardest not to laugh, but in the end it was too much. "Aye love, it was me."

Sam stepped over to the tall windows, and pushed aside the thick velvet curtain. Blackness surrounded the immediate castle, but further down was the bright lights of torches burning in the nearby village. Nothing but blackness, not one light was to be seen.

"No lights," she murmured as she stared out into the night.

"Sam," he said as he stepped near to her, pulling her into his arms, "What did you expect? This is the 17th century. No traffic out there yet, and we still have to wait awhile for the light bulb," he smiled, playfully nibbling on her ear.

Sam tried to retain her composure as he kissed a trail under her chin and around her neck. "There's moonlight," she said, looking up to the beautiful round light in the night sky. "Somehow it seems much brighter here."

"It is much brighter. It's due to the lack of artificial lights which dull the moon and star light in your century."

"Hmm," she said, trying to concentrate on what she wanted to say, not what he was doing. "It sounds so funny, *my century.*

"Are you sorry you came?"

"No! Never, I would never have wanted to miss such beauty. To think I'm standing here in Rosestone during the 17th century, well, it's just hard to believe."

"1610 to be exact," he teased.

"You know, I'm kind of sad that Brianna couldn't have come, just to see all this beauty for herself. She would have loved every second of it," she said sadly, wondering what her friend was doing now.

"Ah, Brianna. She hasn't been born yet, lass," Kieron told her, as he slowly began to tug at her gown.

"Yes, I know. It's just hard for me to absorb all this. I'm sure she would have found a good husband here. You know, someone who would really love her, and stand by and defend her right or wrong."

"A knight?" he laughed, as his fingers unbuttoned the back of her gown. Sam was finding it very difficult to concentrate.

"Don't worry about Brianna," he whispered softly. She'll be getting just such a knight, who will fulfill her wildest dreams, and much more."

Sam quickly pulled away from him. "Really? Who is it Kieron, tell me!" she asked filled with happiness for her friend, then in a flash she understood. "Niall! It's Niall, isn't it!"

"Aye, the old professor, she is his soul mate, from long ago. He told me he knew it since her birth, but was already married to another. Being a very noble man, he patiently waited until his wife passed on. He's now done with his guise as an old man, what you see now is the real person. When we return, he'll claim her as his own, his soul mate and wife."

"Oh how wonderful!" she gushed, eyes sparkling with joy for her best friend. "That is so wonderful! It's going to be great seeing her reaction," she said, as he pushed her down on the soft feather filled mattress.

Their first night together in 1610 would be one Sam would never forget, in any century. Kieron was tireless, and their lovemaking lasted to the early hours the following morning.

* * *

Morning came quickly with the constant possibility of new threats. Many were gathering to break their fast in the great hall. The castle was waking up, and preparing for another day. Pages were busy scurrying about from the kitchen to the tables, with foods for the morning meal. The delightful smell of freshly baked bread filled the air.

One pretty young maid had been eyeing Kieron since his arrival. She placed a large platter of assorted cheeses down in front of him, giving him a sweet enticing smile. She made it a point to tug the bodice of her gown down, causing her full breasts to all but overflow.

"Is there aught else I may do for you, Lord Kieron?" she smiled flirtatiously. Niall choked at the clear insinuation.

Kieron took a piece of cheese from the platter, giving her one of his gorgeous sexy grins, as Niall held his laughter. "No, thank you," he told her politely, sending her away from the table blushing, and with crushed hopes.

"It's a good thing Sam isn't here to see that," Niall joked.

"What?" he said innocently. "It was just an innocent thank you," he replied with a sheepish grin. "I have no need of another woman."

"Brother, I haven't seen you this happy in a very long time," Niall told him. "Samantha has done wonders for you," he smiled, noting Kieron's contentment since he'd met Sam.

"She has. She is my soul mate," he told him with a sense of long awaited peace, "there can be no other, ever. Was it the same for you and Brianna? Come on, tell me about it. Your wife has been dead a long time now."

"Aye," Niall said quietly.

"When did you first know? You've known her since she was a wee babe," Kieron pushed.

"I've known her since she was still a babe in her mother's womb. Do you remember when you told me that Sam's soul spoke to you?"

Kieron nodded immediately.

"Well, it was the same for Brianna. I knew she was my mate from the start, but unfortunately I had already married another in error. My wife was a good and loving woman, as you know, but she was not my soul mate. I decided to be a good man, and honor the rules of our code. I waited until the day she passed from this life to the next. I was never once unfaithful to her," he said solemnly.

Kieron was touched at his friend's nobility and honor toward his late wife. "I'm proud to have you as my warrior brother," he told him, putting his hand on Niall's broad shoulder.

Kieron shot him a grin. "So, does she have any idea?

"What, as an old man who can hardly walk or see? That's not exactly how one goes about wooing a maiden. No brother, I will return to her as myself, and then make known to her that I am indeed quite capable of fulfilling my duties as her husband!" The men began to laugh loudly, getting strange looks from several curious maids working across the room.

Hot tea, sweet cream and pitchers of fresh fruit juices were brought to the table. A platter of sliced smoked ham was available, to tempt the hungry.

Samantha had gone to greet her mother before coming to breakfast. This gave the men an opportunity to speak frankly without disturbing her. She was beginning to suffer from a new and very unique problem.

"At first, she was afraid she was hallucinating," Kieron explained. "She was alone in the library, reading up on Norse mythology, when suddenly these strange unknown people appeared in front of her, talking and going on about their business, as if she wasn't there at all. Understandably, she was scared to death. She told me she stayed perfectly still, then slowly began to realize they couldn't see her. They're somehow from another dimension."

Niall frowned. "It sounds like she may have been experiencing visions from the past. She's apparently highly susceptible to the enormous energy waves given off here at Rosestone. It seems to be magnifying, drawing in the energy from past experiences which happened within the castle walls."

Duncan nodded in agreement. "There are many who believe that the energy lines on which this castle has been built, allows supernatural forces to become more powerful, and unfortunately may attract dark magick. What exactly has she been seeing?" he asked, as he began to fill his plate.

"She says they're like strange scenes of everyday life going on here, within the castle," Kieron told him. "She doesn't recognize any of the people, and told me it's similar to watching different parts of a movie play out, over and over. Almost like seeing ghosts but they can't see her. It's giving her a good case of the creeps."

"Poor lass," Duncan said. "It *would* frighten her since she hasn't experienced anything like it before."

"Aye," Kieron agreed. "Do you think Merlin has anything to do with this phenomenon?"

Niall rubbed his chin, looking out over the rolling fields. He could already sense the growing irritation in his friend, from the mere mention of Merlin.

"It's hard to say," Niall said, "but I find it strange she didn't suffer from this in her own time."

Angus walked into the great hall, pulling out a chair next to them. "Madainn mhath," he told them cheerfully. "Is there something amiss?" he asked, looking around the table.

Niall wished him a good morning in return, then explained what had been happening to Sam, in explicit detail. Angus listened to the entire story.

"It's been said over the centuries that the original builder of this castle was a very powerful druid, with capabilities which have been long lost over the ages," Angus told them. "It's even whispered that he was involved with dark magick, and performed unnatural and sinister things with the great mystical energy surges from the ley lines."

Niall came to his defense. "I have often heard that he was a good man, but had been framed. Dermott MacClaire was not what the sinister realm wants us to believe. He did none of the evil atrocities that he was accused of. He was a good and righteous man, and the first Keeper of the Light, making him our brother."

"Aye, so much is true. What has that to do with Sam?" Kieron asked.

"Well, Sam is apparently very susceptible to this power. She is attracting things that happened years ago," Angus answered.

Kieron listened intently, picking up a mug of hot black tea. "If she can attract that power," he said, "it could be very dangerous for her, she could be able to attract other things as well."

"Right," Niall noted, as he watched Sam and Katie enter the room.

Katie had let Sam pick several of her gowns to wear while she was here with them. Luckily, they were exactly the same size. Sam had chosen a beautiful dark green gown, cut low at the bodice, a little too low for her liking. Her gleaming red hair hung loosely around her shoulders, and her green eyes sparkled.

"What a beautiful sight," Duncan smiled as he kissed his wife's hand and hugged Sam affectionately.

Kieron instantly stood up, pulling Sam in for a quick kiss, and seating her protectively next to him. "You look lovely this morning," he told her, then whispered in her ear.

She quickly turned a bright red, causing an instant outbreak of laughter among the men at the table.

An older maid carrying a tray of freshly baked bread came to Katie's side, asking if there was anything else she may need. Katie smiled at the woman, and informed her all was fine, hopefully alleviating any fears.

As they began to eat, Kieron told the women what they had been discussing.

"Is it just the past that you're are able to see lass?" Angus asked, as Sam began to cut a piece of roast ham.

She glanced over at him, "What do you mean?"

"Have you been able to see any visions of the future?"

Sam thought for a brief moment. "No, not that I'm aware of, but I am getting frequent visions of a very tall, handsome man, a warrior."

Kieron frowned. "What does this warrior look like, Sam?"

"Well, not like any man I've ever seen. His hair is very red and long, and he wears it in long braids with gold adornments attached to the braids. His clothes are much different from yours. He has beautiful green eyes, and he can see me. He stares straight at me in my visions, smiling, and pointing to a strange beautiful necklace that he wears around his neck. Then he vanishes. It's always the same in my visions."

"Dermott MacClaire," Niall said immediately. He's been dead for over 600 years, yet somehow he is able to communicate with her."

"Sounds like he's telling her something," Duncan added.

"Aye, I believe so. He's the keeper of the Amulet of Avalon, the one single item which has the power to kill the dark threat forever."

Duncan faced his daughter. "Can you tell us something of the surroundings, what do you see in these visions?"

Sam thought for a long minute before answering. "I'm not really sure, but it looks like he is surrounded by grey cement."

The men stared at each other in confusion. Then finally Niall spoke up. "Sam, is he laying down?"

Kieron looked over with a scowl.

"His place of internment," he explained.

"Of course," Kieron agreed.

"No, he's standing, and is very tall. Might be close to almost seven feet."

Kieron looked at Duncan. "What about those old sealed passageways that you spoke of?"

"There's several that have been sealed for centuries before my birth," Duncan told him. "Several rumors were circulating about them, but no one knows if they're true."

"Any about Dermott MacClaire?" Kieron asked immediately.

"No, but it's always good to go down under the castle's belly, and have a good look.

"Good idea," Kieron agreed. "We'll go there early tomorrow morn. Hopefully we may discover something."

Sam was intrigued at the frequent visions she was having of this very tall, handsome warrior with long braided red hair. She decided to go on a witch-hunt herself, while Kieron and the others left for the nearby town to acquire land on the eastern shore of the castle. It had been recently up for sale, due to the clan lord suffering a fatal blow during battle outside Scotland.

Sam knew only too well that neither Kieron nor her father would ever allow her to go snooping around in the underground catacombs and ancient passages deep below the castle. Yet, she had no fears, almost as if she already knew this fierce warrior from centuries ago.

After finishing breakfast with her mother, Sam kissed Kieron and her father good bye, she would see them later that day. She told her mother she'd see her in the afternoon, using the excuse she needed to "spend some time putting my new wardrobe together."

Always excellent at color coordinating, Sam was thrilled to get many, almost new gowns from Katie. She wanted to spend some time "arranging her closet."

Katie understood, and left her alone for the remainder of the morning.

After kissing her mother's cheek, she walked toward the large marble staircase, as though she was going up to her room. After watching her mother vanish to the kitchen to speak with the maids about the afternoon meal, she quickly darted from the hall, and scurried around the corner to the secret door where her father and Kieron had disappeared yesterday. Once again, checking to be sure she wasn't seen, she opened the door, and quickly descended down the old stone steps into the lower passageway.

This long hallway was supposedly secret to all who lived at Rosestone, except for her father, husband, and his closest friends. She watched them disappear down the stairs late yesterday afternoon, not knowing why. Now, she was compelled by some strange force to follow their footsteps and do some exploring of her own.

Sam approached the door, and saw the lock. Afraid that it wouldn't open, she pushed gently. To her surprise, it swung open. She dashed down the steps, and into the pale light thrown off from the moonstones which hung from the wall. Sam didn't know where she was going, but followed this incredible urge to continue down the passageway to wherever it took her.

After several long moments, the construction of the hallway seemed to change. It became narrower, and took a sudden turn in another direction. She noticed the walls were made from another stone now, not the beautiful red sandstone that she loved so much, but a stone resembling rocks of a deep grey color. She realized she had probably entered the original section of the hall.

Strange, she thought, as the feeling continued to pull her along. She felt no fear, just this undeniable desire to follow. Then, after a few more seconds, the feeling ended. She stood there looking around, totally baffled.

As she looked around the passageway, she noticed strange designs carved out in relief fashion on wall plaques, in front of her. Strange creatures, somehow slightly familiar, were carved there, two headed dragons, strange reptilian birds with long talons and hideous lizard like creatures with scales, were everywhere. Suddenly, it hit her. They were the creatures from her nightmares, the very ones which also tried to attack her on the castle grounds several times. "What the hell?" she whispered, half afraid to stay another second.

She traced the horrible depictions with her fingers, then suddenly it happened. As she touched one panel in particular, an invisible door appeared, opening in front of her very eyes.

My God, she thought, what have I done? She knew she should leave this place immediately, then saw the tall warrior in another vision. He was smiling, beckoning her to enter. No longer possessing a will of her own, Sam slipped through the doorway, which ceased to exist after her entrance. She felt trapped, almost on the verge of hysterics, when she saw it close.

There, directly in front of her, was a very long, dark grey sarcophagus. It appeared to be made of a granite, or something similar. Sam stepped closer to get a better look. What was this, she wondered, as she touched the smooth, cool stone? There was a crest on the wall directly above it. It read, "*Here within lies the body of Dermott MacClaire, First Keeper of Light*"

She leaned down to blow off dust which covered the top. A large angel had been etched into the hard stone. It was incredibly beautiful. Sam gasped when she finally realized what she'd found.

My God, she realized, the crypt of Dermott MacClaire the original builder and designer of Rosestone! The thought was mind blowing. Everyone was searching for this very thing, and here it was, Sam alone, had found it.

It's as if I was supposed to find it, she thought. Could there possibly be any remains left of this great warrior, after 600 years? More important, would she find the long fabled Amulet of Avalon, which was the only thing powerful enough to kill Merlin forever?

Sam tried to leave, but couldn't. Her mind was telling her one thing, open the top of the crypt. Mindlessly, she obeyed. Her hands pushed, and finally slid the cover to the side. After another push, the lid fell off, falling onto the dirt floor. She gasped as she stared down into it.

It was empty! There were no remains, not even ancient dust, or bone fragments. Nothing, and no amulet. What happened to him? Was this all for nothing, and what of the curse?

"Looking for something?" a smooth, friendly, very thick Scottish accent asked. Sam screamed, and spun around to find the tall warrior of her visions standing directly behind her, smiling.

"Hush lass, you'll wake the dead themselves," he laughed. His smile was friendly, sincere. Her mouth dropped in shock, as she realized who she was looking at.

"Samantha MacClaire," he said bowing, "thank you for coming."

"How is this possible?" she asked, obviously quite stunned. "They all thought you were dead."

"Dead?" he joked, "do I look that bad?"

Her eyes were immediately drawn to the gorgeous sparkling amulet around his neck. It threw off brilliant sparks of golden light. Then she noticed his left hand. There, on his palm, was the same mark of the sun that Kieron and Niall had, except this one was noticeably larger, and glowing.

Impossible. Was he truly the first Keeper, as they had said? If so, she knew he would never harm her, for he was indeed an angel like the rest.

He answered all her unspoken questions, before she asked. "I am Dermott MacClaire, your ancient ancestor, and I've been waiting for you. Aye, I am the first Keeper of Light, much like your husband and his warrior brother, Niall."

He gave off enormous amounts of energy, and his entire being seemed to shimmer. He was different from Kieron and Niall. Much more powerful, if that was possible. His high intelligence was visible in his bright blue eyes, which seemed to see through to her very soul. What things he must be capable of, she thought.

"They said you did terrible things down here, is that true?" she dared to ask. Sam knew no Keeper would do anything evil which wasn't warranted.

"What do *you* think?" he challenged.

"No, you didn't," she said with conviction. "No Keeper would."

He gave her a warm smile, showing her approval. "Kieron is a good man, I see he taught you well. That's good. This menace which stalks you is ageless, but I will not allow it to take this castle, nor will I ever permit this marriage to take place. You, Samantha MacClaire, are already married to one of mine, and that can never be changed throughout any fabric of time. This timeless evil will be eliminated by me, with your help."

He smiled, stepping closer. She relaxed, knowing he would never harm her.

"Centuries ago, I walked the hallowed halls of this castle, a castle designed for peace, and angelic harmony. He threatened to take the castle I spent years in perfecting, and give it over to his dark, lawless followers. It's a place of sanctity, a hallowed place where the many pure angelic forces hover and like to think of as home. Have you not heard them singing at times Sam, perhaps in the gardens, or throughout the long halls? This was their home, until these vicious, heartless dark spirits, embodied as Vikings came to conquer and ravish my holy domain." Sam found herself clinging on his every word.

"Six hundred years ago, Merlin gained huge power by seducing these dark Vikings to his dimension. When they finally discovered they were trapped in that dismal place, they began to do his bidding, for a chance to escape. Merlin desired Rosestone, and tried various ways to gain it for his own. One way was to marry into the title of lord, through one of the MacClaire daughters. Duncan refused, and so the oldest daughter was cursed. In fear of her life, he sent the younger daughter from the castle, to live with a powerful knight. Sound familiar?" he grinned.

Merlin knows only too well, that the only way left is to marry you, and produce a child. This child would be an abomination to God, even though you are his mother. That is his unholy, selfish plan for you. There's just one thing wrong, I have returned, with your help Sam, just as it was prophesied 600 years ago."

She stood there speechless.

"Samantha, you alone were prophesized to find me. By the way, what's the date now?" he asked comically.

They were all wrong about him, she realized. He was no murderer, or horrid monster. Sam developed an immediate liking to him.

"1610" she told him, with an amused grin. "Bye the way, everyone's looking for that amulet. It's supposed to be the only way to kill the dark one who's stalking me, except for my father's dagger."

"Ah, that it is Sam. The dagger will certainly come in handy. I will kill this darkness for you. It will be my pleasure, lass. It's the least I can do for another relative," he grinned.

"Bet you never thought you had an angel in the family, did you Sam?" he joked again. "And you are my direct descendent." Do you know why he wants you so, Sam? Is it okay if I call you Sam?" he smiled down at her.

"Sure" she laughed. She was actually laughing! Having a pleasant conversation with an angel, who was ageless and most powerful, and she was laughing!

"It's because you have eternal angelic blood flowing through your veins. You are eternal, like we are."

Her mouth dropped in complete shock.

"I guess it's quite a surprise, huh? Hope I didn't scare you too much," he chuckled softly.

Sam needed a second to compose herself. "Are you telling me that I will never die?" she asked, as she braced herself against the cold stone wall.

"That's it, lass," he winked. "You have the eternal blood of the Keepers in you. Not everyone in your ancient linage does. I never quite figured out how that thing works with humans, seems to jump and skip entire generations, but trust me Sam, you are immortal. Such will also be true with your two sons."

Two sons! Now she was really feeling a little faint.

"Aye lass, you and Kieron, who is a fine Keeper, might I add, will be the very proud parents of two fine boys, immortal as you and he are. They are destined to become great in their own time."

"God," she gasped. "It's so hard to believe. Does Kieron know?"

"Not yet," he told her. "It's funny how things play out sometimes. I'm sure he'll be delighted to find out. If you would like, I will visit him, and tell him for you."

"Oh please do, he'll never believe me," she begged.

"Consider it done, lass" he smiled. "Now, as far as the amulet goes. I will be with you in your time of need, never fear. We are clan, and clans back up each other, right? I think it comes out to something like this . . . you are my great-granddaughter times 600 years, or something. Oh my, do I look that old?" he asked humorously.

"Anyway, it matters naught. I am here now to assist you in killing Merlin. I have waited 600 years to have special assistance from you alone, Sam. You should feel proud. Together, we will kill this dark evil, which has plagued this earth since the beginning of time, and you will regain your rightful place as heir to my magnificent castle."

She suddenly loved this ancient relative, who gave her such wonderful news and knowledge. He was her special angelic backup, and she could do no wrong.

"You must leave for now, but remember, I'll come to visit with you often. We'll discuss our plans with Kieron and the others. These holy grounds need to be cleansed," he winked again.

"Where did you come from?" she asked him. He once again smiled down at her. It was a patient, loving smile, one of total acceptance.

"I've been in the realm where Kieron was born. Another magical dimension, where only the angelic can exist. The mere mortals who've inhabited my castle think I'm dead. I come and go at will, Sam. You too, have full rights to this place whenever you will it, once your prime directive, so to speak, has been completed. Go now, your family will be searching for you. Bring my deepest regards to Kieron, I will visit with him soon."

With that he snapped his fingers, and the invisible door once again appeared, opening on its own. He suddenly disappeared. Samantha MacClaire walked back out to the hall, a new being, filled with hope and peace.

CHAPTER TWENTY ONE

The next day was quiet and uneventful. Katie and Sam enjoyed swapping stories from their times, and Katie helped Sam to understand the huge amount of work necessary in running a castle. All the time, Sam relived the meeting she had with her great grandfather of ages past.

"I'm sure it will be wonderful when you're finished," Katie told her wistfully. "If only I could be there with you," she trailed off sadly.

Although she had only been there a few days, Sam was already bonding tightly with her mother. She knew that going back would be hard, but it was now starting to become unthinkable. She would miss her family back in Boston. And then there was Brianna. What was she doing now? Sam knew she was patiently waiting. Her heart broke to think of never returning.

Kieron noted her somber mood, and knew she was becoming reluctant about returning to her own century. "Don't worry love. I fear you're feeling sad about who you've left behind. I've been waiting for the perfect time to tell you this, perhaps this is the time. You can visit with them anytime, and still live here with us."

She turned and gave him a strange look. "Forever?"

"Aye, forever. Once you've traveled back in time, you will never die, Sam. It's one of the fringe benefits, so to speak."

Kieron sat quietly, awaiting her reaction, but Sam was silent.

"Did you hear me lass, you will be immortal."

Again, he waited. Again, nothing.

"Sam, what's wrong with you?" he said, beginning to worry that she may be ailing.

She turned, and looked up at him with peace and deep serenity. "I'm already immortal," she said softly.

He looked down at her, thoughts that she may have lost her mind filled his brain. "What do you mean Sam, are you feeling ill?"

"No, I'm fine, never better," she smiled. He looked at her closely, there was something different about her. No fear, or hesitation about anything. She was totally at peace with the world.

"Sam, what are you talking about?"

"I finally met Dermott MacClaire, and he told me I'm immortal, and of angelic blood like you."

Kieron almost fell over. "Dermott MacClaire!! You *met* him! Are you daft, lass?"

"No, she's quite sane, and very beautiful. Excellent taste, Kieron," a voice came from the shadowy corner of the room. Dermott stepped into the light, showing Kieron who he was.

Kieron dropped to his knees immediately, lowering his head. "Forgive me, Master" he whispered.

Dermott laughed. "Get up Keeper. You have pleased me greatly. Anyway, I don't like talking to the floor," he laughed.

Kieron stood immediately, but kept his eyes lowered.

"It's alright son, you may look at me."

Kieron's eyes beheld one of the most powerful angels in the heavens. God's right hand man, so to speak.

"What have I done to deserve such a visit?" Kieron whispered.

Dermott laughed. "Well, I actually came to talk with my granddaughter, but I do have a thing or two to tell you. What she said is true, she is my descendent, and quite a beauty, too. I expect you to take excellent care of her."

Kieron choked. "Always, Master."

"She and I had a lengthy discussion the other day. I'm quite sure she'll tell you about it anon. She is of my bloodline Kieron, angelic blood runs through her veins too. That's why he wants her. He thinks that by mating with her and producing a child, he will gain rights to this castle."

Kieron didn't dare glance over at Sam. He could feel her pride. He stood ramrod straight, and listened.

"I explained how this is a holy domain for angelic beings, and nothing else!" he said angrily. I will assist her when she does battle with this nemesis. I owe her much, as she found me despite their evil plans to camouflage and spell the walls. She was able to see through, where others have not. She listened to my thoughts, and *obeyed*. For that she will be eternally blessed. Now, I am once again free to walk my castle as prophesied six hundred years ago."

"Tell him about the babies!" she said anxiously.

Kieron was shocked at the way she spoke to this supreme angel, with such familiarly and ease. Again, he choked. "Babies?" he whispered.

"Aye son, your wife will have two sons, twins, sometime in the future. They too will be immortals, and a source of greatest pride to you both, although one will be a bit headstrong," he laughed.

His smile heated Sam's soul. She loved him dearly.

"That is enough for now. I'll return to plan again with you soon." Dermott stepped over and kissed Sam's hand, winked at her, then vanished.

Kieron stood speechless. He was lost in shock. One of the highest angels came to *his wife*!

"Well," Sam said, giggling as she looked at his expression. "What do you think?"

There was no reply.

"Come on Kieron, he's gone now, you can talk to me. Remember, you have to be extra nice to me, since he's my very old grandfather," she beamed.

Kieron turned to her with a stunned expression. "I don't know what to say to you. When did all this happen?"

"The other day. I went snooping in the underground passage that I saw you and Duncan use. I felt drawn, in some odd way. I had to follow. I walked as far as I could, then the feeling stopped. There was an invisible door at a certain part of the older passageway. I guess that someone long ago tried to keep it secret. Spelled, I presume."

"What older part?" Kieron asked, clearly baffled.

"The part where the stone on the walls changed from sandstone to granite."

He looked at her like she grew a second head. "There is no such part," he told her flatly.

"Kieron, I was there, I saw it."

He stood there thinking. "Perhaps it too, was invisible, and meant to be seen by only you. So, please continue, I'm very curious to know how you met him."

"Well, I stopped when I couldn't feel the pull any further. There were several plaques of stone on the wall at one point. They showed terrible demons, dragons and horrible birds."

"Like the ones in your nightmares?"

"Yes, it seems like they are held in place there, perhaps held under his great control."

"No doubt," he replied.

"Anyway, I pushed on a certain part of the wall by mistake, and suddenly an invisible door opened. Kieron, it was never there to begin with. I saw a vision of him, telling me to enter. Then, I saw this long grey sarcophagus, and thought maybe the amulet was still inside. I pushed it open, but it was empty. That's when he spoke to me."

"That's almost unbelievable," Kieron answered, "But I saw him now. I never knew you had the blood of Keepers in your veins. No wonder I love you so," he said, pulling her near.

"Yeah, and how about those two sons?" she gleamed, joyfully.

"It's truly a wonder. Guess we'll have to get busy, won't we?" he whispered with a mischievous gleam in his eyes.

"Do you regret marrying now?" she asked hesitantly.

"No, love of my life. I will never stop loving you and have absolutely no regrets," he whispered as he held her close to her heart. Several minutes went by as they held each other tightly. Sam's happiness was enormous. She would be with her hero forever.

* * *

The next few days were happy ones, filled with meeting all the inhabitants of the castle. Sam and her mother were by now inseparable. They toured the castle, Sam taking mental notes on how things should be, for when she returned. All the time, Kieron or Niall followed protectively behind.

Duncan had noticed how close the two women had become lately. Although he was overjoyed, he knew it would be difficult when it came time to return.

The cheerful days at Rosestone rolled by uneventfully. Callum hadn't been seen again since that fateful evening. All the while, Sam kept her father's dirk hidden close to her heart, remembering what her great grandfather had told her.

Finally, with much help from her father, Sam managed to convince Kieron there was no need to wander aimlessly around behind them. It was tough, but he finally ceded that the grounds were well protected, and as long as they stayed within the castle limits, no harm would come to them.

"You must give her some breathing room," Duncan laughed. "There are several guards walking the boundary lines, night and day. They report to me immediately if there is something wrong. Give her this short time with her mother."

Kieron thought for a second, then agreed. Still it bothered him not being able to see her.

"Macho overbearing protector." He grinned as he recalled the many times she'd called him those words when they were still in the 21st century. Perhaps Duncan was right, she needed breathing room.

One lazy afternoon Sam and Katie wandered down the beautiful flower path behind the castle. The path finally ended at the breathtaking stain glass window that Sam had admired so much before her time leap. It appeared even lovelier now, with its vivid colors shining brightly in the morning sun.

"Isn't that a beautiful piece of art?" her mother said, shielding her eyes from the sun.

"Yes," Sam told her, "it definitely is. I admired it often. Kieron told me it's called an astral sphere." They paused briefly to take in the breathtaking sight. The day was perfect, filled with lots of bright golden sunlight.

As they wandered aimlessly down the garden path, discussing men and the latest gossip in the castle, two men on horseback appeared from nowhere, riding up the path to where they were standing. Katie didn't recognize either, and assumed they were some of her husband's new hires.

"Madainn mhath," the younger man said, addressing Katie with a polite nod of his head, and a pleasant smile. The other sat quietly, obsessed with Sam.

Sam began to get a very bad feeling about these two unknown riders, and turned to her mother, who was apparently just as stunned to see two men on horseback trampling over everything in her flower garden. No employee at Rosestone would have ever done such a thing. The gardens were revered as being the greatest in Scotland. Immediately, they sensed something was very wrong.

"What is it?" Katie questioned the first rider.

"I've been instructed to bring you both back to the Great Hall," he answered immediately.

"Instructed by whom?" Sam shot back asked brazenly, not believing a word he said.

"By Lord Duncan. There is trouble there, and he fears for you and milady."

Sam looked over at her mother. "Don't go, there's something wrong here. Kieron would never, ever have another man bring me back to him. It isn't his nature."

"You are so very right, lass," the second man smirked cruelly, as they both jumped down and ran toward the women.

"Run!" Sam yelled, but it was too late. Katie was already struggling with the younger man.

"Don't struggle so, milady. We mean you no harm. It's that one we're after," he said, looking at Sam with an icy grin.

Sam turned to run, then heard her mother scream. Her assailant hit her in the back of the head with a blunt object, knocking her unconscious, and carelessly tossed her body to the side of the road.

"We won't be needing her," he said, as he spit on the ground where she lay bleeding.

"No!" Sam screamed wildly, turning toward the two men. "My father will kill you for that, and it won't be pretty!"

Before she realized it, a third man jumped out from behind several thick pines, locking her in a steely hold.

"Callum!" she gasped in surprise, as he roughly pushed her toward his horse.

"Did you miss me?" he smirked. "I was counting the days until I got my hands on your body. This will be a fitting surprise for Kieron, your immortal, ever protecting lover," he laughed cynically. "He's so good at protecting you, let's see what he thinks about this."

She looked up at him with hatred. "What did he ever do to you?"

He laughed, a chilling terrifying sound. "I want to thank him properly for giving me this mark." He tilted his head up, displaying the mark of Light which had been burnt into the flesh on his neck.

She grinned. "Yeah, well you're lucky you're even alive," she snapped. "He should have wasted you while he could. Now you'll face certain agony," she shot back bravely.

"Bitch!" he said. "Tonight you'll not be returning to Rosestone, or your lover, but to someone else," he taunted.

One of the men pulled out a piece of cloth, ripping it in half, and advanced toward her. "Sorry lass, but we can't have you see where we're taking you," he grinned

Sam fought him valiantly, but it was no use. They were too strong for her. She stopped and stared into his eyes. "You will burn in agony."

The man slipped the folded cloth over her eyes, and tied it firmly, then threw her over his shoulder and draped her across the horse, climbing up behind her. "We'll see about that," he snorted arrogantly.

They started to leave, when a tall man with long red hair stepped out from the bushes, blocking their path. He seemed to shimmer in the sunlight. "You have two choices," he told them. His eyes glowed and made them dizzy just looking at him. "You may release her immediately, and flee my castle forever, or be burned to cinders. It's said I am a barbaric man, who performed many tortures. Shall we see if that's true?" He wore no weapon, no sword and displayed no dirk.

They looked at him and scoffed. "What manner of fool would confront three armed men?"

He looked into their eyes, "Dermott MacClaire."

The two men looked at each other in sudden horror. His name was legendary, even among the dark side, and they'd heard of his many atrocities.

"Give me the woman," he commanded. The one holding Sam pressed his horse near, as Dermott retrieved the blindfolded Sam. He untied her scarf.

With a sudden, "Good day lord," they turned their horses, and took off down the path at record speed.

"Are you alright lass?" he asked.

"I think so," she answered, rubbing her head. "Katie!" she suddenly remembered. "Hurry! They hit her head, and left her to die!"

"Do not fash over it, child," he told her softly. "She is being cared for as we speak."

He whistled, and a tall majestic white stallion suddenly appeared from nowhere. He helped her up, then mounted, turning the horse to return to the castle. "They play a dangerous game," he told her as they rode. "Kieron will be most upset."

* * *

Kieron paced irritably. "It's soon gloaming, and they're still not back," he roared, as Duncan came downstairs from the solar.

"Relax," Niall told him, "we'll go and get the women ourselves. They're probably having too much fun gossiping about the latest affairs going on between the maids and the stable hands."

CHAPTER TWENTY TWO

Kieron was already at the door, halfway down the steps, when he stopped dead in his tracks. His face turned white, and his features drew taunt. "Duncan, now!" he yelled. Duncan was there immediately. One of the guards was carrying a slumped, unconscious woman in his arms. Her limp body hanging loosely, as the guard guided his horse over to the front gate. Several others ran up to him, clearly alarmed. She looked dead.

"Katie!" Duncan roared, as he flew down the steps and over to the sorrowful, tense guard. He looked at the caked blood on her face.

"Katie, my love, answer me! What happened to her!" he demanded from the poor innocent rider. His rage mounted by the second.

"Lord, I was patrolling the far side of the garden, when I noticed her lying on the ground at the edge of the road. There was no one else around. I saw the fresh blood on her head, and feared she was dead. I quickly brought her to you." Katie's battered, bloody face was now beginning to show severe bruising.

"Where's Sam?" Kieron demanded.

"I don't know. There was no one else there, although I did find several footprints and signs of more than one horse."

Kieron's anger raged as he watched Duncan gently take Katie from the guard. "He's found a way to get to her," he spat, and took off toward the stable.

Niall looked down at Katie, then over to Duncan. His heart broke for him, and he worried about Katie's recovery. It seemed tragedy was becoming all too frequent lately.

"She's alive," Duncan told him, as relief filled his heart. "Hurry and find my daughter, for I fear the worst."

Niall nodded. "We'll find her, this I promise you," then left for the stable to join Kieron.

"Maids!" Duncan bellowed, as he carried his wife up the three steps leading into the Great Hall. Immediately several terror struck women ran out to see what the problem was, each looking down at Katie with shock and disbelief.

"Go prepare my wife's bed, and fetch her night shift. Prepare a basin with some warm water also. I need to wash this blood and dirt from her before I change her into something more comfortable," he instructed them.

"Shall I call Fiona?" the older maid asked.

"Aye, have her meet me in my chamber, tell her it's urgent."

They obeyed immediately, all except one. Bridget was his wife's favorite. Duncan looked up and saw her tears, then understood.

"What happened to her?" Fresh tears rolled down her tender young face.

He spoke to her gently, "I have yet to find out, child. Do not fash over it, she is strong and will recover, and then I'll know the facts."

"Aye, Lord," Bridget replied obediently, and went to join the others.

Kieron and Niall tore out of the stable, heading straight to the lower bank when they saw Dermott's white stallion. He saw Sam sitting in front of him, seemingly unharmed.

"My God!" Kieron yelled, "he found her."

Dermott smiled at them as he brought his stallion up close to Kieron's. "She is untouched," he told him calmly.

Sam jumped to Kieron's embrace, then turned to face Dermott. "How can I ever thank you," she said with a smile. "I don't know what I would have done without your help."

"It's nothing lass, you are clan. I won't permit harm to befall you. Take her home to safety, Kieron. I will visit with you again anon."

"Immediately Master," Kieron replied.

Niall bent his head low, in respect.

"You have been a faithful son, Niall. I will reward you with one wish. Think on it carefully, for it will be the only one."

Niall was humbled. "My eternal thanks. I'll do as you say."

Dermott winked at Sam, as was his habit, then he and the beautiful white stallion vanished into thin air.

"Are you harmed, Sam?" he asked, sweeping over her body with his eyes.

"No, just damn scared. They hit Katie, and threw her to the side of the road! They thought she was dead! Where is she now?"

Kieron saw the tears forming in her eyes. "Don't worry Sam, she's back at the castle. One of the guards making rounds found her lying by the edge of the path. He immediately scooped her up and brought her home in time, before it was too late. She's unconscious, but I think she'll pull through."

"Ohh," Sam moaned, touching her head.

"What is it, love?" he asked, studying her closely, "Are you in pain?"

"I don't like to complain, but I'm feeling kind of sick right now."

"She most likely needs rest from the ordeal," Niall advised.

"Then rest it will be," Kieron smiled, as they turned their horses and headed back to Rosestone.

* * *

"So, what's it to be?" Kieron teased, as they arrived back at the castle.

"I don't really know," he shrugged, "think I'm still in shock. I'll have to think on it. Perhaps I'd ask for Brianna to be permitted to come here and be my soul mate forever."

"How precious!" Sam said, fighting off a splitting headache, "that would be wonderful! I do hope you make that your wish."

"Can't really think of anything I'd like more," he smiled warmly. "I've been alone too long."

* * *

"It's my fault," he told Niall later that evening, as they stood near the spot Sam was abducted.

"Ridiculous, Kieron. How could you have known?" he said, trying to lend some support to his troubled friend.

Kieron quickly dismounted, kneeling down in the dirt to examine the prints. "I can see two sets of foot prints."

After a minute, Niall found another set of footprints nearer to the trees. "Looks like one of them hid behind the pines, waiting. It appears that whoever they were, they put some thought into their plan. There are large prints of a man here, then it looks like something had been dragged in the dirt."

"Sam," Kieron said immediately, fists clenching and fire raging in those awesome eyes.

"Appears they were ambushed as they walked," Niall continued. "She must have put up a good fight. Three men against two wee unarmed women. What kind of man picks on defenseless women?" he bellowed.

"Perhaps it wasn't a man at all," Kieron answered. "I'll make him pay in the worst possible way. It's fortunate for them Dermott gave them the choice to prove the traitorous lies about him were all false."

"Seems a shame," Niall said, shaking his head. "I would have much rather killed them immediately. Well, I feel our paths will meet again, then brother, we will have our shot at revenge."

*   *   *

"Everyone expected them to be safe walking the castle grounds," Duncan said as they hurried to check on Katie's condition.

"Their safety should have been secured as long as they didn't stray from that area," Niall added.

"But they didn't," Kieron stated flatly. "That place is far from those limits."

Niall paused. "And no one crossed over from the other side, or they would have been seen. Which means?" He looked at Kieron with dreaded realization.

"Which means," Kieron finished, "that they are in hiding here, somewhere on the castle grounds."

A sudden thought swept through Niall's mind. "The underground caverns."

"I believe so," Kieron agreed. "It's the only place he could have been all this time, without us being aware of it."

"I doubt they were just innocent hands from Duncan's recent hire. Those men are being paid a fine amount of coin weekly for their duties at the castle. I doubt very much that any would want to become involved with the lord's wife, or daughter," Niall added. "It would be an instant death sentence. They'd be flat out crazy."

"These two were most assuredly demons, using the guise of human men. They are quite intelligent, and as you already know, can change their forms to whatever their master requires."

"Shape shifters," Niall said suspiciously.

Duncan looked up at them. Callum also?"

Niall nodded. "Oh, I'm quite sure that bastard was one of them."

Katie lay unconscious on her bed, surrounded by her husband, Angus, his wife, and several maids.

Duncan removed her gown in private, then gently bathed her bruised body, removing the caked on blood and dirt from her face and neck. He asked assistance from Bridget in helping him change her into a fresh shift, and placed a cool cloth on her forehead. Fiona, the castle's healer was summoned immediately, to check for any broken bones.

There had been no changes in her condition for the last three hours, and despite Fiona's encouragement that she would soon recover, Duncan continued his bedside vigil.

It was soon meal time in the great hall. The clan members, and any guests of Rosestone, were now gathering for their evening meal. Family members who had been helping Duncan with his wife, now left her bedchamber.

"Duncan, come down and eat something, you'll need your strength for later when the bastards are found," Angus told him. He was worried, his brother hadn't left her side for a moment since her arrival. "I'll sit here for you while you get something to fill your stomach."

He shook his head somberly. "Nay, I can't eat a thing until I see her fully recovered, and discover who these sons of bitches are who would attack innocent lasses."

As they spoke, Kieron and Niall quietly entered. "How is she?" Kieron whispered, as he stepped over to Katie's bedside.

"There's been no real change," he said, "but Fiona says she has no breaks, and should soon be fine."

Kieron suddenly tensed at the mention of Fiona.

Niall followed him to the bedside. "Bastards!" he said in a low whisper. "I still can't believe a man could do this to a wee innocent woman."

Duncan turned his attention to Kieron. "How's my daughter?" he asked nervously.

"There's no injuries. She was just a bit shaken, but now appears fine, and is currently asleep."

"Thank God," he smiled. "I was so worried that . . ."

"No brother, she's fine, just a little shaken up. She needs a good sleep."

"Dermott MacClaire rescued her," Niall added proudly.

Duncan's eyes lit up instantly. "Amazing! I must thank personally. He saved her life."

Duncan was both heartbroken and guilt ridden at his only remaining child's misfortune.

"She knew the dangers when we came, Duncan," Kieron told him. "She was willing to risk those dangers to kill this timeless abomination. Sam knows what must be done, and carries your silver dirk at all times, ready to accomplish it."

"Now she has the protection of her ancestral grandfather," Duncan smiled. He stood, threw his arms around Kieron and wept. "I can't express my immense humility and thanks to him. I have been truly blessed with this child."

"She's certainly the apple of his eye!" Niall joked, lending some lightness to the immediate situation.

* * *

"Why are you crying, Duncan?" a soft voice came from behind. He spun around and looked down at Katie, lying there smiling at them. Her face was severely bruised, but her smile radiant at being home again.

"Katie!" He bent down and very gently gathered her in his arms. "Thank God, I was so worried. How are you feeling?" he said, cradling her gently.

"A little sore," she told him, touching the back of her head.

"It's best to leave that alone," Duncan advised, "Fiona said it will heal completely in time."

Again, Kieron scowled at the mention of the old healer's name.

Katie's memory suddenly kicked in. "Sam!" she yelled, "They've taken her!"

"Relax Katie, she's fine," Kieron reassured her. "She's untouched, and sleeping in her bed. There's no need for tears. What we need now is for you to tell us exactly what happened, so we can find them."

Katie nodded slowly, as Duncan caressed her head and shoulders. She finally calmed, and was able to talk with out crying. "We didn't leave the boundary, Duncan," she said as if asking forgiveness.

"I know you didn't, love," Duncan said soothingly. "Try to tell us everything, start at the beginning," he prompted calmly, trying his best to hide the rage he felt.

"Sam and I were walking along the pathway, below the west wing. We were laughing about some silly gossip I'd heard, when suddenly two unknown men on horseback came out of nowhere. One told me that you had sent for us, and they were told to return us to the great hall immediately."

Kieron's rage was evident, as he forced himself to remain calm for everyone's sake. A show of major fury would benefit no one.

"He said there was some kind of trouble there," Katie continued.

"What!" Duncan bellowed. "I would ask two unknown men to bring you back!"

"Calm yourself brother," Niall said softly, placing his hand on Duncan's shoulder. "Let her finish this. We must learn everything if we're to be successful."

Katie took a few seconds to recover from her husband's loud outburst, then continued. "That's what Sam said. She told me it was a trick, and not to go. Kieron, you would have been very proud of your wife," she said, wiping her tears.

"She was very brazen, told him he was nothing but a liar. She told him that you would never, ever send another man to bring her back to you."

Kieron's temper was dangerously close to the breaking point. "She's correct," he said glancing at Duncan, "I would have no one but myself or one of my brothers bring her back. I *am* very proud of her, Katie."

She covered her eyes and cried for several seconds.

Duncan attempted to console her, but Niall held him back.

"She must free herself from the experience. This is her way, let her go, Duncan."

They waited patiently, then encouraged her to continue.

"Ok, I'm alright now, sorry."

After taking a second to compose herself, Katie took a deep breath and continued. "After Sam confronted her assailant, he actually agreed with what she said. He laughed smugly as he stalked toward her, then pulled out a piece of cloth from his saddlebag, and wrapped it around her eyes, so she'd have no idea where they were bringing her. Before they took her away, she told him face to face that he would burn in agony. They had already hit me, and tossed me to the ground. They thought I was unconscious, but I heard the whole thing, then passed out soon after they left."

Kieron was beyond consolation. He balled his large fist and slammed it into the wall, causing the wall to crack from the fierce blow. His body shook with an unearthly rage, a powerful heat radiated from his body.

"When I find them, no one will stop me," he hissed in a deadly tone.

"Nor will they try to, brother," Niall added.

"Duncan, a word with you in private, please," Kieron said, trying to control the anger in his voice. He kissed Katie on the hand, and left the room.

Duncan kissed his wife, and stepped outside, leaving Angus standing guard over her.

"We believe Merlin may be in hiding somewhere in the subterranean caverns, deep below the castle's north wing. If no one ventured onto Rosestone's grounds, the only other place they could go undetected would be the caverns, or somewhere in the underground passageways."

Duncan thought for a moment. "Aye. I believe you're correct, that would be the only other place."

"Wait . . . there is one other place," Kieron remembered, "yet to tell you the truth, I don't understand how she found it."

Niall flashed him a strange look.

"When Sam ventured down into that passageway, she said she followed it until it became part of the original castle, and the walls were different. They were constructed from another type of rock, grey in color."

Niall looked up at him. "We were just down there the other day, I saw no such change in color or formation in the walls."

"Yes, but Sam did. Somehow everything changed at a certain point in that passageway."

Duncan glanced toward the two men. "Is it possible that that it had been spelled, or someone erected a false wall to make one think it ended there, when in fact, it didn't?"

Several seconds passed, as they considered the possibility

"The idea is indeed intriguing," Niall said, "but then why was Sam able to see it?"

"Because she was supposed to," Kieron stated with conviction. "She alone was to follow the passageway to its natural ending, in order to find the mausoleum where the crypt of Dermott MacClaire was interred, 600 years ago."

"But he never died to begin with," Duncan added.

"Correct," Niall added, "he only made it look like he died. A Keeper is an angelic being, incapable of both telling a lie, and dying."

"Would make sense," Kieron agreed, "especially since he told her it had been prophesized that one of his ancestors would stumble onto his place of rest, and recall his spirit from another realm, at the appointed time."

Duncan looked at the two men. "Sam has often asked if I've ever heard angels singing here. Have you?"

Kieron and Niall both smiled in unison. "Of course," they answered. "We hear them each morning, when the sun first rises, in the afternoon when it is full strength, and during sunset, when its majestic power slips from this world."

Duncan stood silently, awed by this part of his castle's history he had no knowledge of.

"And Sam?" he asked.

"She's asked at different times of the day, if I've ever heard people singing," Kieron admitted. "She's heard it too, but I didn't as yet realize angelic blood runs through her veins, and gave her no answer."

"Is there another way of getting to where Sam saw the original walls?" Kieron asked.

Duncan nodded." I believe so. There's a long forgotten passageway which leads in that direction. It passes the Chamber of Knowledge. The knights used it in case of an assault on the castle, among other things, in years gone by."

"How very convenient," Kieron smiled. "Do many here in Rosestone know about this passageway?

Duncan shook his head. "I doubt it. Perhaps the past lords, and a few select knights, that's all. It was frequented mainly by the new knights who held their secret orientations there. They kept it strictly secret, to protect the castle's integrity if there should ever be a full scale assault.

Kieron smiled. "Can you take me there, now?"

"Most definitely."

They left Angus to stand guard at Katie's bedside.

Samantha was still sleeping soundly, with a trusted guard of Kieron's choice at her door, so the men felt free to explore. The three descended to the bowels of the castle, headed for the ancient room where many wonders were stored.

CHAPTER TWENTY THREE

Duncan led them to the rear of the castle, through a small door near the kitchen. A special lock kept the curious from entering.

Niall smiled, as Duncan pushed on a designated area. The lock opened magically, permitting the men to enter. They carefully descended the narrow stone stair, placing their feet in the worn indentations of thick stone steps, formed from footsteps hundreds of years before them.

The passageway was mysteriously illuminated by strange bluish globes, attached to the sandstone walls. They cast an eerie glow throughout the hall. Niall stopped to examine one.

"Moonstones," Duncan told him. "Legend says they were mined from the earth where the castle was constructed. They never grow dark."

"Strange," Kieron noted, as he fingered the softly glowing stone.

They continued down a long, narrow tunnel. "Does this lead to the same spot?" Niall asked.

"Aye, it will bring you to the area where Sam said the old building could be seen."

"Quite convenient for a quick escape," Kieron smiled.

Niall was fascinated with the depictions of old pagan deities, craved into the sandstone along the walls. "It seems someone enjoyed a touch of demons," he joked, as his finger traced the ancient carvings.

"Many dark Vikings reputedly put their art work on these walls," Duncan told them. "They're most likely creatures from the realm of bondage where Merlin holds them hostage. I've heard the fiercest creature in his domain is a dragon named Odious."

Kieron glanced at Niall. "Feel like burning some giant dragon wings?"

"I've often heard from other Keepers that many of Merlin's favorites were given a special place of honor," Niall told them. "At least they have their immortality on these ancient walls. I doubt they were so fortunate when they fell from grace with that moron!"

"Fools," Kieron added with a grin. The group laughed at the thought of the ageless wizard believing all would stoop to his power.

"There are so many hunting for him, I'm surprised someone hasn't already knocked him off," Duncan joked.

"Be assured many have already tried, just haven't been that lucky as yet," Niall said, as they moved down the passageway, deeper under the castle's foundation.

Suddenly Duncan made a sharp right turn, and they came nose to nose with a strangely decorated brass door, covered with ancient Celtic symbols and letters. A line of runes etched the perimeter of the beautiful door, coming together at a six point star depression where a handle would have been. Three glowing moonstones, much brighter than the others, were perfectly aligned above the door.

"Spelled?" Niall asked, looking at the strange star shaped indentation.

"Actually, it opens by special key," Duncan replied, reaching above the moonstones and retrieving a star shape piece of metal. Niall and Kieron watched in fascination as Duncan fit the piece of metal snuggly within its indentation.

"A perfect fit," Niall marveled.

The door slowly swung open, emitting a bright glow from within. The men followed Duncan inside, stepping aside as he closed the heavy door behind him.

Kieron and Niall surveyed the chamber in amazement. It was a large room, rectangular in shape. The walls were covered with a strange sand like material which glowed brilliantly like bits of sparkling gold.

Niall stepped over to touch a wall. "Crushed gold," he said, trailing his finger along the rough surface.

"Correct. It allows the room temperature to stay at a constant sixty two degrees," Duncan explained.

Several pedestals stood at various locations around the room. Each one held a vibrant, colored stone. Some were glowing, others pulsated, while others emitted brilliant flashes of light from deep within.

"Amazing," Kieron whispered reverently, as he stepped closer to the stones. "The fabled Stones of Wisdom. And to think they've been housed below us all these years,"

"Indeed," Niall agreed, "I thought they were just a myth, never thought they actually existed."

Duncan stepped over and carefully picked one up.

It was a deep green, with a vibrant emerald glow coming from deep within its core. "The Gerick Stone," he told them, "It's rumored this magical stone has the power to cause instant madness to those who stare into it for long periods of time."

"Please but it back," Niall joked. "I need my senses to woo my mate when I return."

"I think she'll be interested in more than just your brains," Kieron said, trying to hold in a laugh.

Niall shot him a sheepish glance. "Let's hope so," he grinned.

"I believe there is one here you may be especially interested in," Duncan told them, as he stepped over to the corner pedestal. A smaller, cobalt stone was pulsating, shooting off different shades of brilliant blue into the air.

"This is a very special stone, one which reminds me of my own soul mate," he said quietly.

Niall looked over at him with surprise. "Katie?" he asked.

"Aye, it's my favorite. I owe all of my happiness to it, for it's this very stone which pulled my Katie back in time to me. I immediately took it from her hands when the vortex deposited her on my library floor," he laughed.

Kieron was intrigued. "How did that happen?"

"She was on vacation during the 1990's, came to Scotland to see the ruins of various castles. Fortunately for me, one was Rosestone. Being curious in nature, she entered a section which was off limits, and found this magnificent stone. The moment it touched her skin, she was whisked back in time . . . to me."

"Sounds romantic," Niall said with a smile. "I never knew the story behind your romance with Katie."

"Aye, romantic it was, until he cast his dark shadow on these hallowed grounds," he growled. "After my oldest daughter died, it was never the same between us."

"What about that one," Kieron asked, stepping over to a lovely golden yellow sphere. It glowed like the sun itself, and emitted a warmth that could be felt across the room. Kieron felt a clear attraction to its beauty.

"They call it The Keeper's Stone," Duncan explained. I've heard it was found, or perhaps brought, to our world by the very first Keeper of Light, Dermott MacClaire, millennia ago," Duncan said.

"Really?" Niall smiled. "We'll have to extend our thanks."

"We'll probably see him again, soon," Kieron joked.

"He and my wife are inseparable now."

"That's truly unbelievable," Niall said.

"It warms my heart and soul," Duncan told them.

A silver bowl caught their eye. It was filled with a sparkling crimson powder, which shimmered and glowed.

Niall eyed it curiously. "And this," he asked as he reached out to touch the fine powder.

"Don't touch it!" Duncan yelled out. Niall stopped short, pulling his hand back from the bowl, and glanced over at Duncan.

"It's a poisonous inhalant," he said, stepping closer.

"Poisonous?" Niall repeated eyes twinkling.

"It's rumored that those who breathe in this finely ground powder will die immediately," Duncan explained. "Their blood will freeze up in their body within seconds."

Kieron flashed them a dazzling smile. "Are you thinking the same as I?" he said, staring down at the powder.

"Aye brother," Niall replied. Then, turning to Duncan, "Where's it from?"

"Unknown," Duncan answered, shrugging his shoulders. "It's been here since long before I was born."

"I doubt it's from this world," Niall added.

"What are the chances of killing him with this?" Kieron asked, as he stared down into the bowl.

"That's a good question," Duncan replied. "I don't recall the last time it was used. Probably the early years, perhaps as far back as the early first century."

"If I recall correctly," Kieron said, "the ancient Celtic Druids used something like this during the first Roman invasion. It certainly worked well," he laughed, remembering the scene.

"Aye, I remember," Niall laughed, "they ran like frightened rabbits! Perhaps we should take a small sample along with us. You just never know who will be needing a good dose."

They watched as Duncan carefully poured a handful of the shimmering powder into a small glass flask, handing it to Niall. "That should do it," he grinned.

The men left the chamber, following it down the dimly lit hall to its natural end. All the while keeping a watchful eye on the stone formation in the wall. Soon they came to a section where the wall did indeed change in color and type. The sandstone suddenly switched to a dark grey stone, much larger in size. Taking note, they continued down the narrow passage.

Suddenly they heard a low rumble which gradually increased in volume. Kieron gave Niall a cautious look. A seven foot dragon appeared from nowhere. It screamed, hissed, and spit bright scorching flames from its mouth. Bright green iridescent scales covered the length of its entire body, and it glared down at the men with fiery red eyes,

"Must be Odious," Niall said casually, as he tried to figure out which part of the wall it came from. He noticed the inscription carved in the stone near them. "Few enter into this realm, even fewer leave."

"Competition?" Kieron joked.

"Doubt it," Niall grinned.

"Feel like doing that dragon wing thing we spoke of earlier?" Kieron asked with an evil grin.

"I was hoping you'd ask," Niall smiled, as he lifted his left hand and blasted the giant dragon to a pile of smoldering ashes.

Duncan smiled. "Guess he'll have to get a new inscription."

"I believe so. More like . . . Enter whoever feels like it," Niall said, bordering on laughter.

"You could have used that special powder on Odious," Duncan told them.

Niall shook his head. "Too much work."

"So where exactly is the door, or portal, or whatever it is that gets you in," Kieron asked, as he touched the different stones on the wall. Suddenly, his hand disappeared through a section of the wall.

"Guess you found it," Niall said, examining the wall for himself.

"Different," Kieron noted, stepping through to the other side, with Niall immediately behind him. In a matter of seconds, the three men found themselves inside a small limestone cavern. It was filled with stalactites hanging from the ceiling, which had slowly built up over years from deposits of sea water seeping through the cave's roof.

"The King's Cave," Duncan whispered, looking at the different petroglyphs which had been carved into the wall. They showed various monstrous creatures.

"Hmm, someone had a vivid imagination," Kieron noted.

"Doesn't this cave sit directly under the rocky reef in back of the castle?" Niall asked.

"Directly under the posterior foundation. It seems to have quite a reputation also. I remember when Angus and I were kids, and wanting to come down here to play. Da threatened us with a week in our rooms if we even tried it," Duncan laughed. "There were rumors of monsters coming out from this cave, half animal and half human."

"Ancient shape shifters from other dimensions." Kieron guessed.

Duncan nodded.

"I have a good hunch that many of the creatures which are after Sam, came from here instead of hiding on our hallowed grounds," Niall added. "Those grounds have been blessed so frequently that I doubt any could survive there very long."

"True," Kieron added, "and even if they did manage to survive the many of blessings, they'd be easy prey for the angelic hordes which still frequent Rosestone."

"Such a perfect ending," Niall smiled.

"So this is under the original castle," Kieron noted, taking in the odd limestone pillar formations which had supported the castle for thousands of years. "God knows how many demons crept ashore through here."

"True," Duncan told them. "If you follow through the caverns themselves, you'll eventually come out in front, several yards from the front of the castle."

Satisfied with knowing where the passageway led, they quickly returned to the upper level.

*　　*　　*

Duncan returned to his wife, who was now surprisingly alert, and wanted to get out of bed. After a brief fight with Fiona, Katie stood up and put on her robe.

"Isn't it best if you remain in bed for a while?" Duncan asked affectionately.

"No, I feel much better now," she said, looking out to the rough sea. "Where have you been?"

"We went down to the bowels of the castle, to see if there was any clue as to where Merlin has been hiding out. Tell me Katie, have you ever heard singing here?"

"Singing? No Duncan, never," she told him, waiting for an explanation. There was none.

"Why do you ask?"

"No reason in particular, just wondered." he said.

"You mean, singing like your daughter hears?"

Duncan turned in shock.

"Yes, I know about it," she admitted. "She told me about it the other night, when she visited me with her great grandfather, Dermott MacClaire."

"He came to you?" he asked. "Well, what did you think?"

"I say we are extremely lucky to be blessed by such an angelic daughter," she beamed.

Duncan pulled her into his arms. "It would have never happened without you, love," he sighed as he kissed her tenderly.

He held her tight, placing his big hand gently under her chin. "Katie, I now things haven't been the same since our daughter's death. I swear to you, I'll not let the same thing happen again." They held each other close for many minutes, trying desperately to rekindle a love which was quickly fading.

"Lord Kieron, she's gone!" a frantic voice rang out through the great hall. It was Hamus, who had been assigned the task of standing guard over Sam's bedchamber as she slept.

"What!" Kieron bellowed, with a voice that shook the rafters. "What do you mean, gone!" he yelled, as he headed for their chamber.

"I was standing guard as you ordered, when I heard muffled cries from within. I asked if there was something wrong, but there was no reply. I ran in the room immediately, blade ready, but she was gone. I don't know how he did it, I was awake the entire time, and saw nothing. Forgive me, Lord," he begged, as he dropped to his knees awaiting Kieron's wrath.

Kieron's fierce expression softened as he saw the expression of terror on his friend's face. "Get up, Hamus," he said quietly, as he put his hand on the burly man's shoulder. "Your heart is pure, and you would have died for her, I can see it in your soul. I thank you for your honest and faithful attempt to protect her. There are forces at work here which are beyond your control."

Hamus rose and hugged his lifelong friend. "I am forever at your disposal, Lord," he told him with tears in his eyes. "I have failed her."

"You can be of great assistance to me by heading up a group of men to go with us, we'll be leaving momentarily." Hamus saw the face of death in Kieron's vengeful eyes. He obeyed immediately.

After several minutes of chaos, the small group of men assembled in the hall. There was much to discuss about how this plan was to be effectively pulled off.

The King' Cave was basically undiscovered ground to most of the castle inhabitants, that is except Katie. Unknown to all but Bridget, her faithful maid, Katie had once braved the cave to rescue a poor fawn which had been chased into hiding by a ravenous wild boar.

She had sworn Bridget to secrecy, and never mentioned it to anyone, especially her husband. Duncan would have been wild with worry, if he ever found out. She'd managed to keep this from him for several months.

Now, Katie MacClaire would keep another secret from him. She would brave the dangerous cavern herself, armed only with her husband's dirk and pure rage, for this dark force who had taken her only remaining child. A mother's love, she thought spitefully. I'll show you what it means.

After much planning, the group of men were ready to start out on their search for Rosetone's only remaining daughter.

Quietly, as the men prepared to leave, Katie dressed, and slipped on a black hooded cloak. She had taken one of Duncan's other daggers, slipping it snugly in the inner pocket of her gown, and crept from the room.

Once in the hall, Katie headed for the kitchen in the rear of the castle. She took the back servant's stair to alleviate being seen, desperately hoping there were no maids or servants around yet to cause her trouble. The men had already left, and the castle was quiet for the night. It was only 2 A.M. and the morning shift wasn't due for another two hours.

The room was dark, except for two torches on the entry way wall, which burned continuously. Katie made her way past the large sink and cooking oven, where embers from the last meal still glowed. Heavy cauldrons hung over the sink from an iron rack.

As she crept through the dark room, she hit the end of a metal pot with her elbow, causing it to plummet to the stone floor with a loud crash. She instantly stopped, holding her breath.

One of the many castle hounds began to bark, but after a few seconds returned to its bed.

Whew, that was close, she told herself. If even one servant were to see her, it would be reported immediately to the lord the next day, and Duncan would basically keep her on lock down, she smiled to herself.

When she reached the door to the outside courtyard, she saw the usual two guards on patrol. They had stopped just outside, chatting and laughing for a few seconds. It seemed like an eternity, but finally they moved on to the southern walls of the castle.

Katie fumbled with the heavy iron bars until they were released. Opening the door, she carefully looked around the courtyard for any guards, then disappeared into the blackness of night.

She was now free to attempt her final obstacle, getting in and out of the stable without creating a disturbance. There were always two or more guards around the stable, especially since that night when Callum had let all of the horses go free. Since then, Duncan and Angus bought several horses from a neighboring clan who were all too willing to receive good coin for a few stallions.

Mounting her own personal stallion, she effortlessly rode out of the stable, heading left toward the entrance to the cave.

CHAPTER TWENTY FOUR

21st Century

Brianna tossed and turned in her bed, having another all too frequent nightmare. She saw Sam, bound and gagged in a place Brianna couldn't describe. It was dark, except for a few torches. Sam was unable to move or speak, just sat motionless as if waiting for something, or someone. The scene was terrifying.

She saw what looked like sand, covering the floor. Sam was staring straight at her, as if she could see her in the nightmare. An inherent druid ability from years ago?

"What the hell does it mean?" she yelled in frustration. What was she to do? It was only a nightmare, or was it? She felt totally helpless and very frustrated.

"I can't help them with anything," she cried to herself in the lonely darkness of her bedroom.

Sitting there alone in the dark, her mind began to wander. She thought of the professor, and how he had always been there to help her after the tragedy which claimed both her parents.

"Whenever you have need of me, just think of me and call my name, I will hear you."

He frequently told her that while she was a small child, and into her teen age years. Of course, she hadn't believed him, but smiled and said okay, anyway.

"What if?" she thought? "It couldn't hurt. The worst that could happen is nothing at all," she said out loud in the dark. Lonely and desperate for help, she closed her eyes and concentrated on his warm wrinkled face.

"Help me professor," she whispered into the darkness. "You said you could always hear me, no matter how far.

I guess this is really far," she said, as a tear rolled down her face. She refused to give up.

"Sam is in terrible trouble, but I don't know where. There is sand and water all around her, and she is bound and gagged. Please, help her. She needs you!" she finished in a low whisper. Her cheeks were wet from tears, but somehow she felt better.

She had done all she could to help. He always told her that he would hear her in times of trouble. Could he have possibly meant it? Although it seemed totally impossible, she took the chance. What could she lose? Sam was definitely worth the try.

As she wiped the tears from her face, she noticed a thin white mist beginning to take form in the air directly across from her. Brianna jumped back in terror. What was it? It slowly took on the form of a human face. A gorgeously sexy young man's face. Bright blue eyes, one day's growth of beard, and long light brown hair. He looked straight at her and smiled. She felt a warmth radiating from that smile, and in some strange way, felt close to him. Who in the world could he be? Was she really losing it?

They locked eyes for several seconds, then he was gone. Never uttered a word, just gave her a warm reassuring smile.

"That's it," Brianna said. "Now I know I've lost it for sure. Seeing sexy young men's faces in my bedroom? Don't I wish!"

The humor of it made her laugh. "Well whoever he was, I sure feel better."

After reliving the event a hundred times, she felt relaxed, crawled back into bed and slept peacefully.

* * *

17th Century

Duncan went to the solar to kiss his wife before he left. The rest were ready to leave, and he wanted to see her once more before they left the castle. He slowly opened the door to their bedchamber, only to find an empty bed.

"She's gone!" he yelled, loud enough to wake the slumbering castle.

"What do you mean, gone?" Angus asked, looking around the room.

"There's her shift, she had it on when she went to bed," he said, picking up the thin nightgown from the chair. Stepping over to the clothes wardrobe, he noticed that her cloak was missing also.

"She's gone Angus, and I fear I know where. I told her about the cave, and how we suspect that Sam is being held there. I bet that head strong woman has slipped out during the night. She'll get herself killed trying to save Sam by herself."

Niall and Kieron showed up at his door. "What happened?" Kieron asked, looking around the room.

"It's Katie," Angus said, "She must have slipped out sometime in the night."

"I think she's headed toward the caverns," Duncan said, searching in his dresser drawer for his dirk. "It's gone! The fool woman took my dirk, and left to get Sam alone. She'll be killed!"

They headed downstairs to talk to any servants who might have seen her leave. "No, Lord," they each replied to his questioning.

Just then the head entered the Hall, carrying a basket of baked bread, and surveying the room for the coming meal. Duncan pulled him aside. "Have you by chance seen her Ladyship early this morning?"

The steward looked at him strangely at first, then shook his head. "No Lord. I have only just started in the kitchen one hour ago."

"Have you seen anything out of the ordinary happen since your start?" Kieron asked.

The steward was beginning to get nervous, wondering why he was being questioned. "No, Sir Kieron." He hesitated for a few seconds. "I did notice that the back door was unlocked somehow. I thought it strange, because I checked it myself last night before retiring. I asked one of the guards leaving night shift it he knew of anything amiss, but he told me no."

Duncan turned to Kieron, "I wonder how much of a lead she has?"

"Hard to say," he shrugged, "depends on when she left, and the route she took. The high road that hugs the sharp cliffs is quicker, but much more dangerous, especially at night."

"And we weren't blessed with a full moon, which doesn't help," Duncan added. "The path would be dark, and slick with sea mist."

They turned to leave the hall when Niall pulled Kieron aside. "I felt Brianna call to me in the wee hours this morning, while I slept. She was crying and quite upset. Said she saw Sam bound and gagged in a nightmare."

Kieron was stunned. "Does this happen between you two often?"

"Never. But I've always told her since childhood that she only has to call to me in times of danger and I will hear her. She never has, don't think she ever believed me."

"I can understand her being upset at such a dream," Kieron said. "Did she see anything else, like where she was?" he asked anxiously.

"She said the place was dark, and the floor was covered with sand and water."

Angus's eyes immediately brightened. "The caves," he said. "They've been there from the earth's beginning. It must be there."

Duncan nodded. "Seems you're right. We just returned from the Chamber of Wisdom. There's indeed a back way into the caverns from that passageway."

"It would make more sense to split up," Kieron told them. "Niall and I will take the front, while you two block the rear. This way no one can escape."

Angus nodded in agreement. "Excellent plan. This time he'll be out numbered."

Duncan and Angus returned to the underground passageway.

Niall and Kieron left the great hall, running to the stable. The two headed up the mountain slope to the steep rugged cliffs above the sea. To their left, close to the castle's back walls, was a sheer drop of perhaps one hundred feet, straight down to the ocean and rock littered beach. It held a fatal reminder for those unfortunate enough to lose their way at night.

CHAPTER TWENTY FIVE

Katie neared the small entrance of the subterranean cave. In her early days at Rosestone, she heard many disturbing rumors of ancient rituals which took place there.

Fiona, the castle's healer, told her that dark magick had been performed there during the initial construction of Rosestone, sometime around the early 1300's. Rosestone had always been considered hallowed ground, especially to the Keepers. These immortal Lords of Light had pledged themselves to keep dark magick from the castle's grounds. Their sudden involvement had eliminated most of the dark spirits, banishing the remaining to another realm.

In minutes Katie arrived at the mouth of the cave. It was almost indistinguishable, completely covered with moss and rambling growth, with the sea's raging waves crashed disturbingly near. Only someone with previous knowledge would ever know of its existence.

Slowing her stallion to a stop, she checked the grounds for any signs of danger. There were none. They have her inside, she thought, I can feel it.

Katie forced herself to control her mounting anger. How dare this entity take her children, she thought furiously.

Checking to be sure the dirk was still in place, she silently slid down from the horse, tying it firmly to a nearby tree trunk. The wind was starting to pick up, dark clouds covering the moonless sky.

Slowly, but with steely determination, she began to enter the cave. There was no noise, not a sound. Was she too late? Her heart beat wildly.

"Sam, it's me," she thought as she directed her mind to that of her daughter's. She desperately hoped that Sam's inherited senses would pick up her presence.

"Can you hear me?" she thought. Nothing. "Use your Druid senses," she continued. Still nothing. Just then a bright thought flashed through her mind . . . "Hurry!"

Katie was terrified. What was happening to her daughter? Pure rage engulfed her. Without a sound, Katie rushed along the winding natural tunnel of sand and rock.

The walls of the narrow tunnel were made up of limestone, only a few torches illuminated the area. Sand was everywhere, as she tried to smother the urge to cough from lack of fresh air. The growing trickle of water silently flowed in from the incoming tide.

She finally arrived at the point where the tunnel opened into a large cavern. The area was dark, with the exception of a few torches shoved deep in the sand. It took a few seconds for her eyes to adjust to the dimness of the cave. Then she saw her.

Sam sat on the ground, hands and feet bound, and a rag stuffed in her mouth. She sat silently, staring straight ahead. There was absolutely no recognition in her haunting eyes. She was either drugged, or under some spell. The sight was infuriating, and more than Katie could take.

She looked around the area of space, but saw nothing but stalagmites. It was just the two of them in a dark, watery grave.

"Sam!" she cried out, running straight toward her, but Sam continued to stare straight ahead, eyes glazed, totally unaware that Katie was even there.

"Do you know me?" she whispered, bending close to her face. Her pupils were dilated, eyes fixed and expressionless.

"I believe she doesn't feel like talking just now," a deep male voice said from behind.

Katie jumped with fear, then spun around. The sorcerer stood tall, wrapped in an indigo cloak. His grin was threatening and dangerous. She was instantly aware of who she was looking at.

"Aye milady, it's I, Merlin. So nice of you to come for your daughter. Sorry, she won't be leaving with you," he taunted as he pulled open his hood, showing long black hair, deep blue eyes, and a surprisingly handsome face. He appeared to be about thirty five, and the flowing cloak did little to conceal a perfectly toned body.

"You see, Samantha and I have made a pack, haven't we love." Sam sat motionless, eyes staring directly ahead as if watching someone.

"No!" Katie broke in defiantly. "She *never* made a pack with you. Don't lie to me. I remember how my husband banished you from our grounds that day. She was sent away from Rosestone under Kieron's protection. They were married, and that's something you can never change!"

"Ah, such defiance" he smirked. "The women of your century are much to be admired. They know what they want, and are obviously not afraid to go after it. So refreshing from 17th century women," he grinned, eyeing her lustfully. "Won't your wonderful husband be missing you, out here all by yourself?" he whispered, as he stalked toward her.

Katie pulled the dirk from her skirt, pointing the sharp blade directly at him. "Stay exactly where you are, don't take one more step, or I'll . . ."

"You'll what, milady?" he mocked, as he continued his advance. The dirk suddenly flew from her hand, hitting the limestone wall and landing in the water six feet from where she stood.

The entire time Sam sat motionless, as if in communication, eyes fixed on something unseen and powerful which waited in the dark shadows.

Katie's rage was quickly turning to fear. Without the dirk, she was easy prey for this ageless wizard. Just as he was about to seize her, a strong voice bellowed from behind.

"Is it always your habit to play with innocent women, dark one?"

Merlin spun around, too obsessed with Katie to notice Kieron standing behind him, claymore in hand, a merciless expression on his face.

"We meet again, Son of Light. What do you want with me?" he glared as he watched Niall step up to Kieron's side.

"I do believe you're mistaken, Merlin," Niall said sarcastically. "The woman belongs to Kieron, and is his rightful wife, according to sacred rite." His grin was mocking, anticipating.

"It matters not what he believes, brother," Kieron said calmly. "She is mine."

"What is your intention?" Merlin asked, as he eyed the deadly blade. Kieron remained silent.

"Remember how it must play out," Niall whispered, referring to Duncan's silver dirk.

Kieron nodded his head, eyes glued on Merlin.

Sam remained motionless, as if drugged. "What have you done to her?" Kieron demanded harshly.

"Nothing permanent," he smirked. "Just a wee spell. She is unharmed. I can see you're not ready to honor our agreement either."

"There is no agreement," Kieron spit.

"Let them go!" a deep voice came from the rear of the cavern, "they've done nothing to deserve your wrath."

Merlin spun around, clearly shocked at the sight of two MacClaires standing there, blades ready. He smiled mockingly and bowed low.

"Ah," he grinned sarcastically, "I see you've let all your dogs out to play this time. Very well, as you wish."

Katie stepped over to pick up the dirk from the shallow water.

"Leave it!" Merlin ordered sternly.

She looked to Duncan. "Outside now," he told her. With a final glace of hatred, she slipped past the men, and ran from the cave, into the night.

Suddenly, Sam began to move, twisting and kicking at the ropes in an effort to free herself.

"Kieron!" she managed to scream through the rag gagging her.

"No," Kieron told her. "Remain quiet for now." It was a command. She instantly went still.

Merlin laughed. "Ever the obedient one I see. It's quite unfortunate for you that she and I will be joined as one in a few days."

"It will *never* happen, sorcerer," Kieron spat back in a deadly tone. His eyes ablaze with fire from deep within.

"Cut her free," he demanded, raising his palm at him.

"Think twice, Son of Light. She'll remain spelled, even if I'm ashes. Will you take her like this your entire life? Only I can break this enchantment," he stated arrogantly.

"Break this spell immediately," Kieron said once more, stepping closer.

Merlin thought several minutes, then smiled back at him. "No. She will remain spelled as retribution to you. I think it only fitting that you take her back like this," he smiled cruelly, "after all, you want her so badly. Then he thought for several seconds.

"I will once again venture into your hallowed castle, proclaiming what is mine on the next full moon," he gloated brazenly.

"On that night, she will become one with me at the Ring of Brodgar, washing away any prior thoughts of you or her family inside the mystical circle of stones. Never again will she be belong to you. I will then proclaim myself Lord of Rosestone."

"I think not," Niall yelled, suddenly holding the flask of deadly powder in his hand. He instantly threw it into the sorcerer's face. Merlin shrieked in horror as he recognized the shimmering substance, then fell silently to the muddy cave floor.

Suddenly, a glowing light stepped out from the shadows. "Well done, Keeper," the mighty angel smiled.

"It's good that you restrained yourself, his death alone will not help Sam." He turned to look at Samantha, still bound and gagged, her gaze locked on his every move.

Stepping over to her, he snapped his fingers, and the spell was instantly broken. "Rise, child," he smiled gently, taking her hand, and helping her up from the dirt and mud. She raced into his arms, and hugged him fiercely.

"I knew you would come," she smiled up into his rugged, intelligent face.

"I will always be near," he smiled, then vanished into thin air.

Kieron and Niall were stunned. "He is always around her," Kieron said, filled with deep humility.

"Sam love, how do you feel? Did he injure you at all?" Kieron asked as soon as they were clear of the cave.

"No, he didn't hurt me. Just threatened to kill you."

Niall broke out in laughter. "I'd wait a lifetime to see that."

Kieron pulled her close. "I'm alright," she told him softly, "just very tired, and scared. Why was I in that place, wherever it was?"

Kieron kissed her forehead gently, but avoided her question, boosting her up onto his horse. "I'll explain everything to you after you're safely back home. You probably won't remember most of it, but that's of little importance right now."

"Are you ready, brother?" Niall yelled through the rain, as he prepared to steer his horse down the dangerous pass.

"Ready," Kieron replied. He wrapped his strong arms around her waist, holding her securely in the saddle. The sea crashed below with loud, thunderous waves.

Sam quickly fell asleep once the horse started the downhill ride across the uneven wet terrain. Kieron covered her head with a small blanket, to help shield her from the pouring rain. It pelted against them as they continued, and he was glad she was asleep.

Kieron's mind went back to the cave, and the threat he made. He would never give her up, so bring it on sorcerer, he though cunningly. He long awaited Merlin's demise.

Sam was fast asleep, slumped against Kieron's warm chest when they arrived at the stable. Niall quickly dismounted, taking Sam from Kieron's arms. She was so innocent, Niall thought as he stared down on her sleeping face. He knew Merlin was playing a very dangerous game, and that Kieron had no intention of losing.

The castle was beginning to come alive with the bustle of activity, as it did early each morning. Servants and maids scurrying around performing their everyday tasks. Guards swiftly changed shifts, and the stable hands preparing their routine for the day.

Kieron slipped down from his horse, handing the fine animal over to the competent stable groom. After taking the sleeping Sam from Niall, they walked together back into the great hall, to Duncan, Angus and a very worried Katie.

"What happened in there? Is she alright?" Katie asked as she ran over to see her daughter.

"She's fine. Just needs rest for now. Niall will explain everything to you. For now, I just want to put her to bed, and be sure all is well," Kieron told them.

Fiona was instantly at his side, as if somehow knowing what had happened. "How is she?" she asked.

He eyed her suspiciously. "She'll be fine after a good night's sleep," hugging Sam close to his body. There was something about her that he distrusted.

"Shall I come and care for her?" the old women asked. She seemed too eager, in his opinion.

He stopped, looking deep into her eyes. "No, I don't think your services will be necessary," he informed her politely, and continued up the stairs.

Niall watched the scene from the table where he sat with the others. "Fiona," he called out, as she began to hobble toward the kitchen.

"Aye," she quickly replied.

"Come sit with us and tell me exactly what you know about that cave, and the foundations of this castle."

The wrinkled old woman obeyed instantly, slowly making her way over to the lord's table with obvious difficulty. She stood next to Niall.

"Please sit with us, it's alright," Duncan said, as he pulled over a chair. He understood her reluctance to sit at their table.

"Thank you, how may I be of service?"

"My wife tells me you know quite a bit about what happened down there during the early days of the castle."

Fiona looked around nervously. What were they up to?

Katie smiled and took her wrinkled hand. "Don't be afraid Fiona, no harm will come to you. You are helping us greatly. Tell them what you told about me about the human sacrifices."

"Human sacrifices?" Duncan bellowed. He lowered his voice realizing he was probably causing more damage by frightening the old woman.

"Forgive me, Fiona. It's just that I'm slightly surprised to hear that." He gave her a reassuring smile.

"Please go on," he told her, reminding himself to try and stay calm no matter what he heard, or she may decide to leave. She wrung her deformed arthritic hands for several seconds, then looked up at his kind face.

"Will I be punished for doing this?" He could hear the hesitation and fear in her voice.

"No, I give you my word. She finally began to relax.

"Maid," Katie called out to a nearby table maid, "please bring a pitcher of hot tea," hoping that it might help her relax. It was vitally important that they learned all they could about Merlin and what happened in those caverns long ago.

By this time, Kieron had come back downstairs.

"How is she?" Katie asked immediately.

"Don't worry, she's fine, sound asleep," he said. "I guess the rocking from the ride helped sooth her nerves."

Katie sighed in relief. "Perhaps I'll go check on her a little later."

Although he strongly disagreed with what Katie had done by going to the cave alone, he greatly admired her love and dedication to her daughter.

"Brother, you've returned just in time," Niall grinned.

"We're about to hear Fiona's story of what took place in the caverns, years ago."

Kieron eyed the old woman suspiciously. "I'd definitely enjoy hearing that."

Fiona began her story cautiously, surrounded by the MacClaires. She tried to correctly recount what she had been told as a child.

A maid soon came to the table with a pitcher of hot black tea, and gave her a mug. She placed a small jar of honey, and pitcher of sweat cream next to it.

Fiona wrapped her thin deformed fingers around the warm mug, and drew it to her mouth, savoring the warmth. The heat from the tea seemed to calm her nerves, and help with the pain. Slowly, she sipped the hot brew, and began to recant her story.

"It's a story I don't usually tell others, except for my own clan members," she confessed with embarrassment.

"We are all one clan here, Fiona," Duncan said reassuringly, as he placed a gentle hand on her thin shoulder. "You need not worry."

"Of course, Lord." She felt somewhat less fearful as she looked at Duncan's gentle expression.

"You see, I was just a wee child when I first heard the stories, or perhaps I should say, rumors, about the subterranean cave and passageways under this castle. My Seanmhathair, or grandmother, would sit in the kitchen with the others in the evening, when all the servant's chores were done. The old ones would swap stories with their friends. They spoke of Dermott MacClaire, and the dark Vikings. They said he would allow the dark ones to come to our realm unhindered. It wasn't fair, but then there was no one strong enough to stop them," glancing cautiously at Niall and Kieron.

"Some say he made horrible sacrifices to a strange God, Odin, far beneath the castle's foundation. He allowed monstrosities to come to Rosestone, and run the land unchecked. They would kidnap clan members and kill them in brutal uncivilized ways, offering them up as sacrifices."

Kieron could feel the rage surging in his body. He knew that Dermott MacClaire was innocent, and this old hag was lying. Just the thought of innocents being subjected to the foul trickery of the dark Vikings made him want to explode with fury. Their God was nothing more than a barbaric fool, as Kieron himself had told him face to face, many times.

"Easy, brother," Niall said as he felt his irritation grow.

"We will soon have our moment."

"I remember Dermott's name being whispered in private behind closed doors, several times," she continued. "They said he'd cursed the ground the castle was built on in a special ritual held down in the caverns, and after that the crops stopped growing, and cows and poultry would stop eating and die." She stopped, glancing over at the others.

"I do remember one old woman telling the group that it was always Merlin's intention to be lord here at Rosestone, but he could only accomplish that if he married into the MacClaire bloodline. He would then be free to rule the castle, and the underground, which is what he's wanted for thousands of years. But he had to wait until a daughter was born into the family."

Kieron glanced over at Duncan, "That's where Sam comes in."

"I guess that's what he planned to do when he tried to seduce the older sister, if you don't take offense at me bringing it up, Lord."

"Of course not," Duncan said, as he waved his hand for her to continue.

"My people always claimed to have 'the sight', you know, able to see certain things which others couldn't.

I guess it's passed on through the generations. When I was naught but a small child, I went down to the caverns with my younger cousin. She wanted to see if it was true."

"What did you see down there?" Duncan asked, intrigued with the old healer's story. She was quiet for a moment, recalling the scene.

"I saw the people of the past, and Dermott MacClaire. It scared me so that I ran out, and never returned. May I take my leave now, Lord?"

"Of course Fiona, any thank you. We never meant to upset you."

The woman left the hall with great difficulty. Niall looked at Kieron with a smug grin. They didn't buy it for a second.

"All lies," Kieron said arrogantly.

"Undoubtedly," Niall quickly agreed. "I will never believe he did such things. She is covering for the sorcerer."

"That must be what Sam's experiencing," Kieron told them, as he recalled the sudden unexplained visions that she was having since her arrival at Rosestone.

"It seems to be something passed on from generation to the next," Duncan said. "I'm really surprised that it's affected her, since she is so far removed from that time period."

"Well, now we know why he's after Sam. She is the only daughter left, and one who carries angelic blood in her veins," Angus said as he got up to leave.

"And one he'll never get," Kieron growled.

The days were passing rapidly. Soon there would be a new moon, and the sorcerer would expect his reward.

"Do you think we should tell her what happened?" Duncan asked one morning, as he and Kieron walked back from the bailey. It had become their routine, over the last few days, to engage in a one hour bout of swordplay each morning, to hone their skills. They never knew when it would be challenged.

"I don't know," Kieron said as he sheathed the sword on his hip. "She's asked me repeatedly about what happened down there. I never went into detail, didn't want to terrorize the lass."

"I see," Duncan said, stopping to greet two guards who were about to start their rounds. "Then she doesn't have any idea what he's planning."

"Fortunately not," Kieron told him. "I wanted to speak with you about Fiona."

Duncan could tell by his expression that something bothered him. "Is there a problem, Kieron?" he asked, as they greeted several more guards, and slowly headed back to the hall.

"I'm not sure, but something about her tells me there's more to her than meets the eye. How long has she been employed here?"

Duncan sighed and looked across the fields. "I guess she's been at Rosestone all her life. Her family has always been employed here, never had a problem with any. Tell me brother, what is it that fashes you?"

Kieron stopped short and faced him. "I can't quite put a finger on it, but I'm troubled about how hard she's trying to get close to Sam. Even the other night, she insisted on going to our chamber to care for her."

Duncan's brow wrinkled with thought. "And you feel there's something wrong with her behavior?"

"Not her behavior, her. I think Fiona is a demon, more so, I think her entire clan may be tied to Merlin in some fashion."

Duncan's expression was one of pure shock. "Demon? Are you sure Kieron?"

"I've cast my senses several times," Kieron told him, walking up the steep ramp from the bailey to the castle entrance. "Especially the other night, when she sat next to me with her story.

"And what did your senses tell you?"

"They tell me she's dark. I know it sounds crazy, for the woman portrays a loving gentle healer. But I fear her knowledge of healing springs from other, more sinister knowledge. She knows too much about what went on down there. Any other woman would have been terrorized at just the thought of going down there. She also has quite a vast knowledge of the dark Vikings, if you've noticed."

Duncan looked as if he'd seen a ghost. "Have you discussed this with any of the others?"

"Just Niall. He feels the same. That's why he called her away from us that evening, and over to the table. He wanted to see her up close. He thought it best if I discussed it with you."

"Demon," Duncan repeated. "And all this time she's been gathering information for him?"

Kieron nodded, "It would seem logical. I for one question that limp, and those arthritic hands," he said mockingly. "It's almost like she's trying to divert our attention."

Duncan stood thinking for several minutes. "Shall we tell Sam?"

"I'll let her know about my hunch," Kieron told him, as they passed a score of armed men who were preparing their horses.

"It's best she's aware of it, just in case."

Duncan nodded in agreement, as they entered the hall.

CHAPTER TWENTY SIX

Sam was keenly aware that something was going on. No one would tell her what had happened in the cave that morning, and Kieron had up to now, been very tight lipped.

After a long sumptuous dinner, they bid all a good evening, and headed up to their chamber. "Why did you leave the rest so soon?" she asked with a trace of irritation. He pulled her into their cozy room, with sweet smelling peat already burning in the hearth.

"Why do you think?" he answered suggestively, pinning her small frame against the inside of the door. He had a stressful day, and was more than ready to have her satisfy his urgent needs.

"Absolutely not!" she railed at him, slipping out from under his arms. She positioned herself in the middle of the room, arms folded and glared at him in absolute defiance.

"Do you and the rest of your family think you can keep secrets from me, and I will just go along with it?"

He looked at her cautiously, waiting for her to pick up something to throw at him. He'd already learned back in her time, not to 'push her buttons,' as she put it.

"Calm down, lass. I intend to tell you everything tonight."

"You did like hell!" she continued, becoming more and more angered by the second. He positioned himself in the corner, away from things which may suddenly fly through the air at him.

"Such fury," he laughed, as she heaved her shoe at him. He caught it instantly, and placed it on the floor next to him.

"Well, are you about to throw the other one at your husband, or would you rather calm down and listen to me?" She stopped and looked at him with a strange expression.

"Were you really going to explain everything to me? Or was that just a line to get what you want?"

He gave her a lustful glance. "Is that all it takes?" he grinned, ready for another object to fly in his direction.

She surprised him by sitting down on their bed and staring at him. "Kieron, I want you to be truthful with me. I expect no less, and would be the same with you. This is the core of our relationship," she told him with heart wrenching honesty.

Kieron felt the guilt rise up in him, she was right. He should have told her from the very first morning. He slipped his arm around her shoulders and pulled her close.

"Forgive me, Sam," he whispered low, kissing her gently. "What I have to tell you may be difficult for you to hear. That's the only reason I haven't explained what happened to you that morning. I would do anything to keep from causing you pain." His eyes told her the truth.

Sam looked down at the floor, "Katie, and the others?"

He nodded slowly. "They have all been honoring my request that you not know until I felt it's time." He looked deep into her beautiful green eyes.

"So you think now is the time?" she asked as she searched his face for the answer. He took her hand in his, placing it over his heart. "Yes Sam, it's time."

Kieron spent most of the evening recounting every morbid detail of what had occurred that morning in the cave.

Sam sat back, listening. It was as if she were reading one of those fictional novels, and it was happening to someone else. "Was my mother harmed?" she eventually asked. The realization of what could have occurred finally hit home. Her brain was still in a fog, trying to shrug off the remains of the spell.

"No, but she's quite fortunate that we got there when we did. I believe he was about to have his way with her, also."

Sam was furious. "That bastard," she yelled. "He gets whatever he wants, and no one stops him. No wonder she had enough, and decided to take things into her own hands!"

Kieron smiled at her fierce determination. He greatly admired her love for her mother, but she must understand that willful, headstrong behavior mustn't happen again, it would only result in terrible tragedy.

"She was very wrong Sam, and quite lucky we came when we did. He has no use for her, she could be eliminated very easily."

The chilling thought cut through to the bone. Her loving mother. She could have very easily been killed, for nothing. She'd never be strong enough to fight him off.

"You're right. She should have never left here alone. I guess Duncan was pretty upset, huh?"

Kieron began to laugh. "To put it lightly! Niall and I were starting to wonder if perhaps she was safer in Merlin's hands! He was worried to death, and quite angry to boot."

"So, how many more days are left until the new moon?"

He looked over at her sadly. "Two. Don't worry Sam," he told her, pulling her close, "we'll work this thing out somehow. I have no intention of letting him have you. You are mine. Period."

He took her in his arms, and kissed her. "Promise me that you'll never do anything so thoughtless, Sam. I would go insane if I didn't have you here with me."

"Never," she promised.

This night was just for them, and they would use each second of it to prove their love to each other. Kieron knew the clock was ticking the moments down. Merlin would not take his joy.

It was nearly midnight, as Niall, Duncan and Angus sat discussing things downstairs. The tension in the hall was thick enough to cut. Everyone in the castle was now well aware of what was to happen in just a few short days. œ

Several of the guards who had just finished the evening watch filed in, laughing and ready to wind down for the night. They came over and greeted Duncan in respect. Most in the castle were sleeping, and the great hall was very quiet.

Hamus stepped to Duncan's side. "I would have a word with you in private, Lord."

Niall and Angus looked up at him. The guards obliged him and left the table, kidding and joking about their evening as they made their way to the end of the Hall. A young maid awaited them with several tankards of ale.

"What is it Hamus?" Duncan asked. "You may speak freely here, in front of my brothers. Come, sit with us and speak your mind," he said, pointing to a nearby chair.

"Thank you."

"Is something amiss?" Angus asked, noting his behavior.

"I don't know. I usually don't watch what the women do as a rule, but for some reason I felt I should tell you this."

"Tell him what?" Niall asked, with a trace of irritation. He wondered what kind of nonsense involving women couldn't wait until the morning. This better be good, he thought, watching Duncan's reaction.

"As I was finishing my watch around the castle's lower walls, I saw Fiona run into the back woods. I called to her, but she just stopped and looked at me with a strange stare, then continued into the forest. It was the look she gave me, as if to warn me of something. I felt that was very unnatural for someone with her years, alone at this hour."

"Perhaps it's just my imagination, but it seemed very unnatural. I even questioned Craig, who walked rounds with me tonight. He said it was quite odd, and suggested that I inform you, anyway."

Niall's face filled with concern. "Kieron was right. He's been saying all along that there's something very wrong about that old crone, soothsayer or not. He feels that she may be a traitor, running to Merlin with whatever is said here."

Duncan sighed, then nodded. "He told me so, earlier this morning in the bailey. It was difficult for me to believe at first. I should have picked up on it myself, but I never really paid that much attention to her. Her family has been here for years. Guess I just took her for granted to do her job."

Angus took another sip of ale, swallowing it slowly.

"It would make sense. She's always been such an odd bird, but I must say that I never would have thought of her as one of his."

Duncan was silent, then turned to Hamus. "Do you remember at what point she ran off?"

"Aye Lord."

"Could you take me there?" he asked, getting up from his chair.

Hamus looked surprised. "Are you going there now? It's almost midnight, and might prove quite dangerous."

Duncan disregarded the warning. "Niall, go wake Kieron. He will most assuredly want to come along. And take care not to wake Samantha."

Niall proceeded up the steps to Kieron's chamber. At the first knock, Kieron was at the door. Immediately he knew it was Niall. He turned to see if Sam was still asleep. Luckily, she was sleeping soundly.

"What's wrong?" he whispered.

"There's been a lengthy conversation downstairs. Hamus claims he saw Fiona run into the night while he and Craig were doing their rounds. He said she was acting very strange, and wouldn't answer when he called out to her. A few of us are going out to have a look. Duncan asked if you'd come along too."

"Immediately, I'll dress and come right down." He closed the door softly, then glanced over at Sam. She slept soundly. He quickly dressed without a sound, then strapped on the thick leather belt which held his blade and headed toward the door.

Sam . . . should he wake her? He thought twice, then decided not to. He was counting on her sleeping until the morning. Kieron knew only too well that if she were to wake during the night and found he was gone, she would be furious. He stood there for several seconds waging a mental battle, then blew her a kiss, and silently left the room.

The others were waiting outside at the gate. "It's high time I learn if Fiona is telling me truth," Duncan told the others, as they waited for Kieron. "I never thought her anything but a crippled old healer. Now I will see for myself."

"What are your thoughts?" he asked Kieron, after they greeted the guards, and slipped through the main gate.

"I'd like to find out what the old cailleach is really up to," he told them. "My senses tell me she is nothing but an imposter."

"I'm beginning to think you're right," he said, as the group followed Hamus.

He led them across the jagged cliffs to a densely overgrown area of trees and bushes. "This is the spot," he told Duncan, pointing toward the ground. There seemed nothing unusual about the area.

"What's on the other side?" Kieron asked, as he began to work his way through the bush.

"Not much of anything. It used to be an old druid burial grown in ancient times. I remember my father telling us that on certain days of the year, strange things would happen there. Bright lights and strange loud noises could be seen through the bushes and trees."

"Portal," Niall grinned, looking around. "Do you remember exactly which days of the year that would have been?"

Hamus thought, scratching his head. "I'm not exactly certain of this," he said, "but I do know that it happened sometime in the late fall and early spring."

"Samhain and Beltane," Kieron said. "It's a time portal probably not used in centuries."

"So why is Fiona running off to an abandoned time portal which isn't being used anymore?" Angus asked.

"Because it *is* being used, by Merlin," he explained. "If my hunch is correct, Fiona is most likely one of them, returning to them with information on Rosestone. That's why we've never seen anything strange on the castle grounds. They're using this portal instead."

"But if it's so old, and not being used that often, what's powering it?" Angus asked curiously.

"There are a few other ways which one could use for time travel, the mind being one," Niall answered.

"How?" Angus asked again, always hungry to learn more.

Kieron smiled. "Your Chamber of Knowledge holds many ancient secrets, one being various ways a body can transcend from one plain to others."

"Pure mental energy," he continued. "Invisible lines of magical power harnessed from the earth, mixed with human thought waves. Combined together, at a certain time of day at the right location, is capable of opening a time portal. It's been one of the preferred methods of time travel as far back as I know. There are also other options, such as the Cobalt stone, which brought Katie back in time."

"Most interesting," Angus said. "That explains the strange lights and sounds coming from the area at certain times of the year."

"Well, Beltane would definitely explain the bright lights. I'd bet it was only in ancient times that they used it. Probably Samhain, Beltane and the Solstices. Now, he most likely uses it whenever he wants," Niall said.

"Correct," Kieron added. "A two dimensional portal to and from Rosestone. How very convenient."

"Hamus, you say you watched her run into the night. Did you see her return?" Duncan asked.

"No, we watched the spot several minutes, but nothing else happened."

"Sounds like she's back on their plane for now," Duncan reasoned, as he studied the dirt from the old site. Rocks and small pebbles were scattered all around, as if being thrown by some strong force.

"Look," Kieron said as he crouched down and touched the grass. "It's been burnt, and quite recently I'd wager." Large rocks formed a perfect circular formation, the ground inside almost pure white in color.

"There's been recent activity here," he told the others, as he stepped inside the circle of rocks. "The soil has been oxidized to almost pure sand," he explained, letting the crystallized sand like material run through his fingers. "It's warm even now."

"It's been scorched by the many times the vortex has heated up," Niall added.

"When do you think she'll return?" Hamus asked nervously. Now that he knew Fiona was a demon, he most certainly wanted no part of being near her.

Niall smiled. "It's hard to say." He understood Hamus was trying hard to remain courageous, and respected him for it.

"We might as well return," Kieron said, looking around the grassy field, "there's not much use in us remaining here. Now that we know she's dark, it may help us in our decisions about Sam."

The others agreed, and Hamus was more than happy to head back home.

The night was quiet, a soft breeze moved through the trees. In the distant hills an occasional wolf howled for his mate. Kieron wondered what else was happening in those hills, and who else was using that vortex.

CHAPTER TWENTY SEVEN

"You should refuse him, Kieron. At least that way he can't have her," Angus stated flatly, as they made their way through the tall grass back to the hall.

Kieron turned to him, anger evident in his eyes. "That's what we've planned. He has the power to spell her once again, but he must be present to accomplish it. I would gladly incinerate him now, if that would help, but the curse on Rosestone would still remain."

"Correct," Niall added, "it's Sam herself who must do the act. That's what the ancient texts tell us."

Duncan looked over at him, "Does she still have my dirk with her?"

"Always," Kieron replied. "Either in her gown, or strapped to her leg. I make sure of that. Sam is very intelligent, she will not be caught off guard," he told him proudly.

Dawn was slowly breaking on the Scottish Highlands, and Kieron prayed to his God that Sam was still asleep. They took a few minutes to greet the three guards posted at the front gate.

"Out seeing the sights this fine night?" one joked as he watched the men return from the field.

Duncan smiled, "Something like that, I guess," he told them and walked inside.

The great hall was all but empty. Two older maids sat in the corner next to the blazing hearth. They were deeply involved with their knitting, and didn't see Duncan come in. Upon seeing him, they immediately jumped to their feet with surprise.

"Be seated," he told the women. "It's been a very long night, and I'm going to sleep."

"Oidhche mhath," he told each, wishing them a good night, as he climbed the steps to the solar.

With that, the women turned to Angus and Niall, who thanked them and told them the same.

Kieron walked silently through the hall to his chamber, praying Sam would still be asleep. He was tired, and certainly didn't feel like arguing with her over something foolish. Women from her century were so very different from Highland lasses of this century, he thought as he reached their room. In the 17th century, women would receive a good thrashing for disobeying their husbands. Sam, instead would heave every item in the room at him, he laughed quietly. So different, so precious.

He opened the door, and found his sweet, precious wife sitting up in bed, arms folded, and a scowl on her face. Well, he thought, so much for dreaming.

"You're awake my love," he said, as he attempted to sooth her. "Have you been up for long?" Kieron felt like he was doing battle. She was fuming, eyes throwing daggers at his very heart.

"Where have you been?" she demanded, accusingly.

Realizing that coddling her was useless, he decided to get to the truth. "Alright Sam, I'll tell you the truth. You know I am bound by it, although I must admit, at times a good lie would suffice," he said with a wicked smile.

He unbuckled his belt, placed the blade in the corner, and stood in the middle of the room, wondering what exactly she was so mad at.

Sam was not amused. "I don't want a lie, I want the truth."

"And that's exactly what you'll get," he answered sharply, not being in a frame of mind for her foolishness.

She could see that he was in no mood for arguing. No longer the complacent lover, trying to banish her every fear, but a very serious warrior. She instantly calmed, fearing that it might be something she really didn't want to hear.

Kieron stepped over to her, and sat down on the bed. He made no attempt to kiss or touch her at all. He was tired, and wanted no games.

Something was definitely wrong here, she could feel it in his behavior. In fact, it began to frighten her.

"I was asleep at your side, when Niall came to the room several hours ago."

She looked up at him, about to open her mouth. He put his hand up for her to stay silent. She sensed a sudden chill.

"Please let me continue. What I have to tell you is very important. I'll answer all of your questions afterward."

She relaxed, and scampered back against the soft, fluffy pillows to get more comfortable. He patiently waited for her to get settled.

"He told me that Hamus had seen Fiona run into the darkness last night, and refused to answer when he called out to her. Your father and the others found it very strange behavior, so decided to follow her tracks and see where she went. They wanted me to come along, so I quickly dressed and left you sleeping."

She gave him a look of remorse.

"I purposely didn't wake you. Sam, this was very important and I didn't want to waste time arguing with you, do you understand?"

Her eyes filled with regret, ashamed of her childish behavior. Her ridiculous fears that he was with another woman quickly vanished.

"Yes, please go on," she told him meekly.

"Hamus led us to the area where she disappeared. We continued, and found an old burial ground, used by the druids of old. Sam, it's an ancient portal, one which I'm very sure was used for travel to and from Rosestone during the early years." He looked over at her, waiting for a reaction.

"It's a time portal?" she said. "But why would Fiona have any interest in that? She's just an old healer."

"Think about it Sam," he continued. "She claims to be a healer, but she's been trying to get close to you since we've arrived. I don't for one second believe that limp, or guise of an old woman."

Sam gasped as reality hit like a brick. "Demon," she said, looking over at him in disbelief.

"Exactly. That's why she wants to be close to you. I don't trust her, and I want you to stay away from her at all times. If you need her for any reason, you'll call me instead, understand? Whatever you need, I am definitely up to it," he laughed, taking her hand in his. "Are you still mad?"

She lowered her head, ashamed of herself. "No, I'm not mad Kieron, and I apologize for my childish behavior. I was just upset at something really stupid."

He pulled her into his arms. "No Sam," he whispered, "I wasn't with another woman."

Sam pulled away suddenly, looking up into his eyes. "You said you never read people's minds, except in times of need."

"That's right, and this is definitely one of those," he grinned. "I didn't want to live in fear of something else hitting me in my back," he joked.

He caressed her face lovingly, "There is no one else Sam, never will be."

* * *

The following morning, Duncan called a clan meeting.

He wanted all to meet with him regarding what plans needed to be made. The days had quickly rolled by, and only one night remained before the new moon. It was vitally important that everyone was in agreement with what was to be done.

They slowly filed in. Katie called for refreshments. The maids quickly brought what she requested, plus sweet rolls, various fruits and jams. The atmosphere was one of heavy anticipation, and seemed to affect everyone.

"Well, have you made up your mind yet, Kieron?" Angus asked, as he and Morna sat down. He was totally against the idea of bringing Sam to the Stones of Brodgar, even if Kieron had no intentions of leaving her there.

"Brodgar is not an option," Duncan stated stiffly, as he looked at his wife. The two had spoken about it previously in private. Katie was beside herself with worry, and Duncan had assured her that Sam would remain safe, and out of Merlin's reach.

"Well, Kieron, what do you and Sam have to say? You told us you've been discussing your plans for a few days now. Tell us your ideas," he said, giving his daughter a gentle smile.

Kieron began. "It's our joint decision to remain here at Rosestone. If he wants her that badly enough, he'll have to come through me," he told them firmly.

"Aye," Angus agreed. "That's more like it. After all, we aren't young babes, terrified at the slightest threat. He's cursed this castle and its people before, took a sweet innocent girl from her prime, and now wants to claim Samantha for his own. Never! I personally will stand in front of him before he ever puts hands on her," he snarled.

Duncan smiled in admiration. His brother and wife had no children of their own, and they loved Samantha as their own.

"You Niall, we haven't heard your thoughts as yet," Duncan asked. Niall put down his mug, and stood next to Kieron. "I am a Keeper of the Light, along with my warrior brother. It's my responsibility to keep slime like him away from the earth and its inhabitants. I can understand why my brother didn't kill him instantly in the cavern that night. The spell he placed on Sam would have remained, forever. That much is true. In order for him to spell her once again as he's threatened, he must be physically present."

"I've talked at length with Kieron and Sam, and I say we remain here, at Rosestone, and wait. He'll definitely come. At that time, we'll finish him off."

"Then what, Niall? Are you saying we should fight the sorcerer here, on our doorstep?" Angus asked, temper heating up.

"Easy Angus," Kieron said calmly. "Sam and I have decided that since he now says he wants her for his wife, we should demand a proper Christian wedding here, at Rosestone's Chapel. Why would he disagree? That will be our time to act."

"That's where I come in," Sam smiled proudly. "He claims he wants me so he can proclaim himself the real Lord of Rosestone. That, of course, is totally ridiculous." She glanced over at Duncan. "I came into this century for one reason, but find myself wanting to stay for many," she smiled tenderly at her family. "I will convince him to marry me immediately, in the chapel. I can see no reason why he shouldn't, since I'm agreeing to go through with this."

An eerie silence filled the hall. It was the sudden realization that evil would once again enter Rosestone, and trespass on her hallowed grounds. The thought made Duncan and Katie sick, and enraged Niall and Kieron.

"I for one, don't like the idea of that menace stepping foot anywhere near this castle," Angus growled. "He shouldn't be allowed to desecrate her scared grounds!"

After a moment of thought, he calmed. "Then what?" he asked.

"Then," Niall continued, "When the priest asks them to repeat the sacred vows of marriage, Sam will be close enough to do what needs to be done. Only she can break the curse, in the manner prophesied by the ancient text."

"Aye," added Duncan. "Seems only fitting that he should die here, in our chapel."

Angus shot him a defiant glance. "Brother, have you lost your mind? I know you and Katie haven't forgotten the grief he brought the last time he came. What of Dermott MacClaire? What role does he play in this?" His anger and frustration were mounting.

"That remains to be seen," Kieron said calmly. "He has promised her his help when the time is right. We have no right to question him. I know my wife, she has full confidence in him."

"He *will* be with me," Sam told them all with a calm certainty. "He promised."

"Are you afraid, Sam?" Katie asked with motherly concern.

She shook her head. "Not at all. He needs that dirk deep in his heart, and I for one can think of a no better wedding gift," she grinned. "After all, I'm getting kind of tired carrying it around with me." The hall was suddenly filled with the joyful sound of laughter.

Kieron pulled her close and kissed her. "You make me proud, lass," he told her, trailing his thumb along the edge of her cheek. "There could be no other woman for me in all of eternity."

"Excellent plan," Duncan said, as he got up and kissed his daughter. "You are Kieron's beloved wife, and my precious, irreplaceable daughter. You honor all of us with your selflessness and bravery."

Sam noticed the unshed tears in his eyes, and the ones rolling down her mother's face.

"So then, is everyone in agreement with this decision?" Duncan asked, searching each for some complaint.

"Aye," they said in unison.

"So be it, we'll start preparations for his arrival immediately," he said. "I for one, will be happy to be done with him."

"I'm sure he'll be rather upset when he sees his reception," Niall snickered.

"Good," Kieron spit. "Why stop at just one? I plan on giving him several reasons to be upset."

"I too, brother. It's only fitting," Niall added, blue eyes dancing with mischief, "after all, it's his big day."

"A toast," Angus shouted standing at the table. "To Samantha, Rosestone's beloved daughter." He looked over to

Sam, who was sitting under Kieron's overly protective presence. Angus loved her dearly, as the daughter he never had. He too, was prone to being overprotective when it came to her safety. Kieron smiled in appreciation.

"You'd better notify the priest, and explain all the morbid details to him," Kieron advised. "I'm sure he won't be expecting that kind of drama in his chapel."

"Indeed," Niall grinned, "we certainly don't want the good priest fainting when he sees our plans for the new bridegroom." The others chimed in with laughter.

"He'll never get to that point," Kieron growled. "Sam will put an end to his dark work here once and for all. Then, she will claim what is rightfully hers by birth."

"At last," Duncan sighed, glancing proudly at his daughter.

"He said he wanted to marry at midnight?" Sam asked in disgust.

"Aye love," Kieron smiled, "and so he shall, a nuptial that Rosestone will never forget.

* * *

The castle was in a state of emergency. Each person performed his or her job, as directed by Duncan, in preparation for the worst. He doubled the men stationed on guard along the walls as the time drew near, so that no one would be caught off guard alone or defenseless.

Even the maids, servants and pages did their work in twos, as they went about their daily chores and responsibilities. Each inhabitant at Rosestone was aware of the terrible tragedy which happened to Samantha's older sister, and were only too aware of the of the castle's curse.

Duncan decided to find the castle's chaplain, and explain what would be happening. He wanted no unnecessary problems to interfere with their plan. He set out to the chapel, entering the vaulted stone hall through its entrance at the great hall.

The hallway was made from beautiful blue stone, forming strange, yet lovely Celtic designs along the walls and floor. The windows were long and narrow, to keep the occasional intruder out. Made from several sections of stained glass, each window displayed a different scene from Rosestone's past, done in vibrant colors.

Throughout the centuries, the past lords had insisted the scenes remained pagan, keeping Christianity limited to the chapel itself. Several bright torches illuminated the way, as Duncan hurried down the hallway.

Arriving at the main sanctuary, he found the chaplain seated in one of the farthest pews. He seemed deeply engrossed in a thick manuscript, which rested on his lap. Duncan immediately noticed it was not a Christian Bible.

"Greetings, Father," he told him, as the man looked up, obviously unaware he had a visitor. He started to stand, but Duncan put up his hand, stopping him.

"Please, stay seated," he told him kindly. "I've come to discuss an issue of grave importance," he said, sitting next to the priest.

Duncan was well versed in the book which rested on the old priest's lap. It was the Book of Driesis, a pagan bible from antiquity, filled with dark prophesies and sinister spells. He found it very strange that this man would read such material in a Christian Chapel. "Father, what prompts you to read from a book which clearly denies the Christ?"

Caught off guard, the priest closed it quickly, offering Duncan the lame excuse that he picked it up by mistake.

Not buying it, Duncan said, "I'm very surprised that you, of all men, would even permit such a thing in your presence."

The priest's face turned a deep crimson. "How may I help you, Duncan?" he stammered, clearly being caught off guard.

Not being of the Christian faith, Duncan was mindful to act with the utmost respect in front of the main altar. Christianity was a leading religion in Scotland, and Duncan wanted to assure all who lived at Rosestone they were welcome to practice their faith whenever, without repercussions. He quickly got down to business, explaining the plan to the older priest.

"Father, I do hope you understand, I know this kind of thing would be most likely against your beliefs," he politely explained. "Please understand that I have no other choice." He attempted to explain the upcoming situation to him. "It must be done in this manner."

The chaplain looked at him coolly. "Murder of any kind will not be tolerated in the house of God," he told him sternly.

Duncan let out a heavy sigh, not wanting to add arguing with a priest, to the list of his current problems. "You will obey me in this one request, Father," he said sternly, leaving him no room to argue. His nerves were already frayed, and he refused to take anymore, especially from a man of the cloth.

Niall suddenly entered the chapel. He greeted them with his usual friendly smile. One look at Duncan's frustrated face, and he knew something was wrong.

"Problems?" he asked, glancing at the priest.

"Unfortunately, it seems our dear priest has a problem with our plans," Duncan explained.

Niall eyed the priest suspiciously. "Is there a particular reason why you won't comply with his orders?" he asked, trying to ignore what his senses were starting to tell him.

"It's for a very important reason, or Duncan would never ask such a disrespectful thing in your house of worship." As he saw it, the priest had no room to argue, and was forced to do what was asked of him.

He looked at Niall defiantly. "No, I absolutely will not allow such an atrocity in here!"

Niall caught him glancing down at his left hand.

"What is that you have on your palm, my son?" he asked nervously.

Niall grinned, suddenly understanding what caused the priest's bout of nerves. A grin slowly spread across his handsome face. "I am a Keeper of the Light."

The priest paled, and began to fidget nervously. Niall looked deep into his eyes, scanning him with his senses.

"Why would that make one who follows the Christ nervous? We are here to protect the innocent and fight demons, there is nothing to fear for a man of God."

He attempted to bolt for the door, but Niall's sudden grip on his arm was too strong.

"Perhaps because you are a demon!" he growled, holding up his left palm toward the imposter.

"Get back!" he warned Duncan, who jumped in time to see a flash of purest white light shoot from Niall's palm, hitting the demon directly over its heart. It screamed out in agony, then immediately turned to a pile of hot black ashes at Niall's feet.

Duncan looked down at the smoldering ashes. "How did you know?" he asked. "He's been a priest here with us for generations."

Niall smiled, as he kicked the ashes with his boot. "You mean an impostor, most likely running to Merlin with every little bit of information. What man of Christ would refuse to have a dark sorcerer killed?"

At that point Kieron walked into the chapel hall. "Problems?" he grinned in amusement, noticing the dark ashes. "I can see my brother has indulged himself in his favorite form of entertainment," he laughed, throwing his arm around Niall's broad shoulders in satisfaction.

"A mere disagreement," Niall confessed innocently with a grin. "Our good priest refused to comply with Duncan's requests, which I found quite odd for a follower of their God."

"Demon," Kieron muttered, as he looked down at the black ashes. "A dead giveaway," he laughed. "No pun intended."

"When I arrived in the chapel, I found him reading intently from the Book of Driesis," Duncan explained.

"I always thought that was kept in a special place in the Hall of Records, heavily spelled to prevent it from being stolen?" Kieron said. "After all, it's not exactly something that Christians would enjoy reading."

"Could he have obtained a copy?" Niall asked pensively.

"Doubt it, more like he was able to remove the spell long enough to get the information he needed, then return it, spelling it once again. A demon doing Merlin's bidding," he said in disgust, spitting on the smoldering ashes.

The three left the chapel, and started walking back through the vaulted passageway.

"How long will it take to bring another priest from the village?" Kieron asked, as he admired the lovely Celtic adornments on the blue stone walls.

"I can arrange for one to be brought up this evening. Shall I explain certain things to him first?" Duncan asked, with the trace of a smile.

"I'd say not. We're getting too many imposters as of late. Let's save it as a surprise," Niall grinned.

"Good. Then a surprise it will be. I hope this one's younger."

"Why's that?" Duncan asked, with a puzzled expression.

"Better for his heart when the action starts."

CHAPTER TWENTY EIGHT

Sam spent most of the remaining time with her mother. It was a beautiful day, sunny with no clouds. They chose to remain together on this, the last day before the new moon.

Any other time, they would have walked in the fragrant gardens, or strolled along the high cliffs overlooking the beautiful North Sea. But today was different, and the men were taking no chances with their safety.

Kieron and Duncan requested as politely as possible, for them to remain indoors, in lieu of the impending danger. They climbed to the solar, deciding to remain there the rest of the afternoon. They were now more like very close sisters, rather than mother and daughter. Sam greatly enjoyed hearing Katie's stories about when she too lived in Boston, before her time leap.

"Can you believe that!" Sam laughed. "What are the chances of us both living in Boston at the same time!"

"I know," Katie laughed, "you would have been a very small child when I went on my fatal vacation."

"Who would have thought?" Sam laughed at the irony of the situation.

They talked and laughed for hours. Katie asked the maid to bring them biscuits and tea. Sam longed for the usual comfort foods she enjoyed in the 21st century.

"What I wouldn't do for a chocolate bar right now," she said longingly.

"And I often crave potato chips in the worst way," Katie laughed.

"Oh Yeah," Sam agreed. Which kind?"

"It's got to be the salt and vinegar ones, I could eat a whole bag at one sitting!" Katie admitted with a grin.

"Me too! I love them."

The two sat quietly for a moment, gazing into the distance, reminiscing about their homes and what they gave up.

All at once they heard a terrible crash, like glass shattering. The women looked at each other in fear, each hoping they were wrong. Sam started to go for the door, but Katie grabbed her arm, holding her back. "No Sam, you don't know what's happening down there. Kieron and your father know where we are, and they would want us to stay put."

Sam paused in thought, "Yeah, I guess you're right. They can pretty much handle anything, we would just get in the way."

"Exactly," Katie assured her. "Just relax, they'll come up when they're able. We'll just have to wait it out for the moment."

"It sounded like windows crashing," Sam said nervously.

Katie hugged her daughter tightly, in a motherly embrace. "Be strong Sam. I know you're up to this, whenever it comes. Remember that Kieron and your father will be close at hand," she said as she squeezed her tightly.

"I just wish I could do it in your place," she sobbed.

How dare he! Her heart broke at the sight of Katie's sweet face, now covered by tears of worry and anguish.

"Please don't cry," she pleaded. "I'll be okay, I swear it."

Her entire body was suddenly overcome with hatred. From nowhere came a deep urge to kill this darkness that was coming to destroy her new wonderful world.

"*I will end this now.*"

She stood up and faced her mother. A calmness she never experienced flowed throughout her body, as if someone suddenly flipped a switch. Her green eyes clear and focused, she smiled calmly at her mother. "This is my time," she said, and opened the door.

21st Century

It was a busier than usual day at Tiller &Wagner Law Firm. Brianna's incoming tray was on overload, even though she had been working diligently for the last few weeks. She was flooded with a longing to know something about her dearest friends, who'd vanished one month to the day.

"Does time pass as fast there as here?" she found herself muttering out loud, as Brad Tiller approached her desk.

"Is there something wrong Brianna?" he asked politely.

"I certainly don't mean to invade your personal space," he said, "but I've noticed that you seem to be, well, let's say somewhat distracted during the last few weeks. I just wondered if there may be something I can help you with."

Brianna was mortified. Was it that obvious? She was speechless, caught off guard.

"Oh, well I guess I've just been a little stressed out over some personal things," she explained, hoping he would take that as an answer, and leave.

"I see," he said, glancing down at the stack of untouched files littering her desk. Okay, you're going to tell me to straighten up or I'll be terminated, she thought somberly.

"Not that it's any of my business, you understand," he continued, "but there are things that one can take now, you know, to help you get more focused."

Lawyers, she thought, always dancing around the subject, and worrying about being so politically correct.

She looked up at him. "Antidepressants?" she said, never wavering in eye contact. He became more flustered than a small boy caught stealing a candy bar.

"Yes, well something like that," he stammered, clearly embarrassed. "I just wanted you to know that I'm friends with a great doctor, if you're at all interested."

Deciding it was time to leave, he gave her a brief smile, and walked back into his office.

Thank God! I bet he thinks I need a shrink! I suppose he'll bill me for the advice, too. Professor McInnis was right, they're just a bunch of blood thirsty sharks. Professor McInnis . . . she trailed off in thought. How she missed that sweet old man. Somehow he'd always managed to be at her side, through the many bad and difficult times since her parent's death.

Oh God, she thought, here comes another crying jag. Grabbing a handful of Kleenex from her desk, she headed for the Ladies Room, hoping no one would notice. At least there, she could cry in private, without prying eyes.

After fifteen minutes, Brianna was back at her desk, working feverously on her laptop. She looked none the worse, and felt much better. Thank goodness I've brought my makeup case, and all my other girlie accessories, she giggled to herself. She had made it a habit to tuck eye drops in her make up case, for cases such as this. It was suddenly becoming a habit.

I can do this, she thought with fierce determination, as she plugged along back at her desk. I won't give him reason to fire me. He probably uses that shrink himself, she laughed. Mr. Type A personality. It's a good thing I didn't tell him about my dream, or that gorgeous face that appeared in my bedroom, she chuckled. He would have definitely had me committed on the spot!

The day slowly moved on, and Brianna was occupied with different clients, each needing specific information, and having a million questions to answer.

Throughout the day, her mind kept going back to that tree, and the name carved in it . . . . Brianna. Something about it gave her the chills. She tried her best to forget it.

"Hey Brianna!" a friendly voice called out. "Long time no see." She peered up over her computer, to find an old boyfriend who she hadn't seen in over a year.

"Sean Elliot," she smiled, as she looked up into that familiar handsome face. "I thought you had moved to London, at least that's what you told me the last I saw you."

He was as cute as she remembered, tall with bright red hair that had a certain natural curl to it. His eyes were dark green, they reminded her of Sam's. She swiftly checked out his ring finger. Nothing. "Hmm" she thought at the prospect.

"Well, I did move down there for a few months with my company," he explained, "but last month they started relocating, so here I am."

He was a very attractive twenty six year old, originally from Inverness, but moved to Edinburgh when his job transferred there a few years ago. They had dated for a while, but nothing serious. Brianna knew he was the type to be married to his job, wherever it took him. Although she was attracted to him, he just wasn't the one she'd been looking for.

"So, what are you doing here?" she asked, worried that Mr. Tiller would see she wasn't working, with those eyes in the back of his head.

"I had to drop a package off to be mailed next door, and I thought I'd look you up. I didn't know if you were still working here," he smiled brightly.

"Unfortunately," she whispered, afraid to be heard by the others.

Sean laughed. "How about some dinner after?" he asked, with an impish smile. "That is, if you're not involved. It would be nice to catch up on things."

She understood his meaning immediately.

"No, I'm not married, or involved with anyone right now, and yes, I'd love to have dinner later," she smiled sweetly. Maybe this day would end better that it started, she hoped.

"Are you at the same place?" he asked, taking a pen from her desk and pulling a card from his jacket pocket.

"Yes," she smiled, "same place." She felt a little ashamed even saying it, almost like she should have moved on by now.

"Good, give me your number again."

She quietly gave him her cell number, glancing around the office at the sweet smiles of understanding on the older women's faces.

What was wrong with her, anyway? Here was a smart, handsome guy, who wanted to take her out . . . again! The problem was, she wasn't at all that excited.

"When do you get off?" he asked, ready to have a nice enjoyable evening with a good friend.

"I leave at five," she said softly, praying that none of the lawyers were watching this go down.

"Well, I better get back to work, you know how they are about wasting company time," she smiled nervously.

"Oh yeah," he joked, "I can certainly relate to that. I'll call you at home after five," he grinned, as he pulled out his keys and walked over to the car.

Just as sweet as when I dated him, she thought.

What have I gotten myself into, she thought, checking the hall for any suspicious lawyers. Sure, he's a nice guy, and I know this would be perfect for me right now, but . . . it just didn't feel right. Something had changed, yet he was as charming as ever.

It certainly wasn't that she had a million gorgeous men knocking down her door. Beggars can't be choosers, she mumbled to herself. I guess it's better than sitting home crying for people I may never even see again.

CHAPTER TWENTY NINE

17th Century

Sam opened the door to the solar and stood at the top of the stairs, ready for whatever fate threw her way. She wasn't prepared for what she saw when she reached the great hall. All the lovely stained glass windows had been blown out, as if some terrible wind from hell had arrived at the castle.

Servants and maids were running wildly, dashing around the hall, carefully gathering up large shards of slivered glass and debris, before darkness fell.

"What happened?" Sam yelled, as she stopped a maid who was carrying large pieces of glass in a basket. The howling wind was nearly deafening.

"I don't know," she attempted to yell over the deafening howl, "there was a sudden loud crack, then all the windows blew out. It seemed to shake the castle to its very foundation. We were preparing for the evening meal. It was terrible!" she said, clearly shaken and white as snow. Not wanting to rattle the poor woman any further, she let her go. She hurried off with glass in hand, to help the others as they attempted to clear the hall.

Sam spotted one of the older male servants who was attempting to direct some kind of clean up, in the corner by the main door. Her mother once mentioned he had always been one of the Duncan's favorites. Apparently, his clan and the MacClaires had been very close while Duncan and Angus were small boys. They'd spent much time playing together, as young children.

"Alistair," she yelled out, over the howling wind, "where are the men?" An eerie fear began to fill her heart.

"Just a moment," he yelled, as he gathered five pages together and pointed out where to start gathering the large pieces of broken glass.

He hurried over to her, carefully weaving through the piles of glass, shattered iron and debris. "They ran out front, to see what was happening."

"Kieron and Niall too?" she yelled through the raging wind.

"Aye, I heard Lord Kieron mention a "portal" or something of that nature. I know it makes no sense."

"Portal," she murmured to herself. "Oh, it definitely makes a lot of sense. Thanks," she yelled, as she bolted for the door.

He grabbed her firmly by the arm as she ran past. "Please forgive me, but I know that Lord Duncan would not want me to let you go out there. It's way too dangerous."

Sam stopped, giving him a gentle smile. "I totally understand, Alistair. You are only doing your job, as I'm quite sure he would have wanted, and I do appreciate your loyal devotion to him. There's no offense taken," she told him as he relaxed his hold, and let her go.

"But you must understand that I'm not a 17th century woman anymore, and won't stay put in here while my loved ones may be in danger. Plus, I'm not very good at taking orders, either," she grinned.

The man smiled down at her. "I've heard as much from your father," he grinned. "Please take care, Samantha," he told her as he helped her with the door. She dashed out into the unknown, just as Merlin had planned.

"Sam, no!" her mother yelled frantically as she watched her daughter leave the castle alone, but it was too late. Once outside the thick door, Sam was immediately seized by a pair of steely arms.

"Let me go!" she screamed defiantly, as she tried to free herself. The man was much too strong. He dragged her off to the side of the castle wall, then released some of the grip he had on her.

She craned her neck, to see who this fool was. Didn't he know that he would be killed as soon as Kieron found out?

"Callum!" she choked, staring into a pair of lustful eyes.

"Aye," he grinned lewdly. "Did you think I'd give up so easily?"

"Let me go immediately!" she raged. "Kieron will kill you the second he sees you, and this time they'll be no stopping him."

"Don't worry. I doubt he'll be in the picture this time," he smiled. His expression was filled with hatred.

"What do you mean?" she snapped. "You can't kill him, he's immortal."

Callum laughed cynically. "Little fool. You're so in love with your hero that you aren't thinking clearly. He doesn't have to be dead to fit in with our plan." His smirk was irritating, and Sam wanted to put her fist in his face, hopefully taking out a few of his perfect teeth.

"What do you mean?" she demanded. "Where is he? I have the sneaky feeling you've something to do with what's just happened, don't you?" she snapped fiercely.

"Such courage," he said "It's truly a shame I can't have you for my own. It would be so satisfying to teach you your place," he growled.

"And *you* are a dead man," she told him smugly.

"Aye, lass that I am, and there's nothing that your lover or his friends can do to harm me." His laugh was terrifying, and seemed to steal any warmth there was from the night.

"I wouldn't count on that," she threatened. For a split second, she saw a look of sheer terror spread across his face, as if acknowledging a terrible threat.

"He won't be coming to save you this time. Unfortunately, they've been detoured, so to speak," he smiled sinisterly.

"The portal, you intentionally did something to that portal, didn't you?" she shot back at him.

Callum gave her a calculated smile. "You are a quick learner, love. Too bad Kieron won't have you by his side as a life mate. You'd prove to be quite a lovely little asset," he told her, as he looked down at her with dark, soulless eyes.

"You're a liar!" she screamed. "Kieron will kill you just because he can, and you won't be able to stop him!" sh sneered, spitting in his face. "You're nothing but a lying soulless fool!"

He glared at her with contempt and pulled his dirk, preparing the fatal blow.

Somewhere in the night, a ferocious blood curdling growl, which shook the very ground Rosestone was built on, could be heard. It was unlike any creature on planet earth. Callum wondered if he spoke too soon.

Immediately, he was thrown several yards in the air, landing on a giant jagged rock. Sam could see the sharp edge protruding out through his heart. He hissed and yelled, issuing a string of unknown words, then went still. Her mouth flew open, staring at the gruesome sight.

Dermott MacClaire materialized from nowhere, a bright welcoming smile on his ruggedly handsome face. Long red braids blowing in the wind. He looked over at the still form. "Guess he's out of words," he laughed. "Are you alright, Sam?"

I think so," she said, trying to stand. He immediately reached down, and helped her to her feet.

"How did you know where I was?"

"I see all things, especially that which is unjustly done to my great granddaughter," he smiled. "I won't allow anyone to ever harm you Sam. You will always have my special protection."

Sam knew she was protected by one of the most powerful angelic beings in heaven . . . her great grandfather. They walked off into the night, grandfather and granddaughter, separated by 600 years.

* * *

"Sam, Sam, please answer me!" Katie screamed into the howling night. She was desperate to find her daughter, and feared the worst. She tore out of the castle, heading toward the dark fields below. Guards were running everywhere, trying their best to secure the castle and discover the cause of the violent blast. She ran down the garden's edge, her long hair whipping her face from the windy gusts. "Sam, where are you? Answer me!" she continued to scream frantically.

To the left, Katie saw a glowing light off in the distance. Something about it was frightening, almost supernatural. Golden sparks were shooting out from the center, and she could hear a strange whirling noise.

"Sam!" she tried to yell over the noise, but to no avail.

"Katie!" Duncan screamed through the bushes, "get back inside, *now*!" He ran up the side of the hill, with Kieron, Angus and Niall at his heels.

"Get in Katie!" he screamed into the wind. "Obey me on this!" She heard his warning, and turned in a panic to return to the castle. A huge gust of wind slammed into her, knocking her on her back. She was suddenly paralyzed, unable to move arms or legs.

"Duncan!" she screamed, as she watched him and the others run to where she lie, helpless in the night.

Out from nowhere, above her in the night air, a shimmering mist began to take form. She laid there helpless, unable to do anything but watch it. It took the form of a hideous reptilian bird, with long talons and a sharp jagged beak. It was covered with long grey scales, and shrieked in delight as it saw her helplessly struggling below.

Before she realized it, Kieron was there at her side, his mighty hand opened and directed toward the ghastly creature.

"Burn!" he commanded, as a bright beam of pure white energy shot from his left palm, hitting the creature. It screamed a second of agony, then turned to dark ashes, littering the green terrain below.

Duncan arrived a few seconds after, crouching down to cradle his wife. "What happened?" he yelled to Kieron.

"The demons have been let free to cross the portal," Kieron yelled. Most likely Merlin's doing."

"Oh I'm quite sure Merlin had a good deal to do with it," Niall agreed.

"Duncan, I can't move!" Katie screamed frantically.

He turned to Kieron with pleading eyes. "Can you help her?"

Kieron nodded. "It's an energy draining spell cast by these demons, so they can prey on humans without a struggle."

"Oh God!" Katie sobbed.

"Duncan, you must not touch her," he yelled. "None of your life force must mix with hers, or it won't work." Duncan nodded his head in agreement, as Niall took his arm and gently guided him away from Katie's life force bubble.

Kieron stretched out his left hand above Katie's body. Immediately, she moved her arms and legs, sobbing in relief.

Duncan hugged him, then ran to her, scooping her up in his arms and carrying her up the rocky path to the front gate.

"Where's Sam?" Kieron asked, as soon as they were safely inside.

"She's gone," she cried. "She went out to help you. Alistair tried to stop her, but she refused to listen. She said you might need help," she sobbed into Duncan's chest.

Kieron punched the wooden table, cracking it in two. "He's got her!" he seethed. "Tomorrow is the new moon, and this was his way of throwing us off guard." He kicked an iron bucket across the room with his boot.

"Well, looks like he's not going to play by the rules," Niall said. "Perhaps we should do the same." His eyes twinkled with deadly anticipation.

"Aye," Kieron answered, "it's time to pull out all the stops." He turned, and stalked toward the chapel.

CHAPTER THIRTY

Dermott led Sam to the front of the Chapel. "He'll be waiting but have no fear, *I* am watching over you. This is your time, let nothing stand in your way."

She hugged him tightly, then took a deep breath and advanced toward the door. I will do this right, she told herself.

Suddenly she saw him. The cunning sorcerer was waiting, as if he knew she'd be there. She turned for a final look of confidence from Dermott, but he was gone, vanished into the night air. She was alone to fulfill her destiny. His words lingering in her head. "I am watching over you."

Merlin was an unusually attractive man. Dark eyes filled with sexual promise, and a smile which would captivate every woman he met. If one didn't know better, she thought, a woman could find herself in a lot of trouble. Like me, she thought ironically, as she pushed the windblown hair from her face.

"Sorry for the dramatic entrance," he smirked, "but I really don't have any more patience with your immortal boyfriend."

She looked up at him, trying to keep a cool façade.

"I see that your ancestor had his way with my henchman," he growled.

"He only got what he deserved," she said bravely. "It should have happened a long time ago."

"You must have really pissed him off," he smiled arrogantly. "He gets a little short tempered at times, you know. What did you do?"

"I spit in his face," she said coolly.

Merlin smiled, "So, you're feeling courageous tonight," he said sarcastically. "We'll see how long that lasts. Are you ready?"

"This wasn't part of our bargain, and you know it," she shot back with surprising calmness.

"Really?" he joked. "Is it that I came a little early, or perhaps that I was slightly dramatic," he grinned. "Doesn't matter, we'll soon have a new moon, so why wait?"

Sam took a deep breath. They were counting on her to make everything right again, and she would, no matter what it took.

"You owe me an apology," she demanded sharply.

He looked over at her in amazement. "You're serious, aren't you?"

"You're damn right I am." She was defiant, suddenly filled with fearless rage. Sam stood perfectly still, as the wind howled around her, hoping to God that her plan would work.

He was quiet for several minutes, as if contemplating his next move. "What is it I must do to win your forgiveness?" he taunted, as the indigo cloak whipping in the wind.

"If we're to be truly married, then I insist on doing it here in Rosestone's Chapel." She held her breath and waited. He looked at her as if she had truly lost her mind.

"The chapel?" he balked. "Absurd! Why should I grant such a boon, when I pay no reverence to your God? It will be in the Circle of Brodgar, as agreed."

"I *never* agreed to such a thing. It's you who's crazy!" she shot back. Sam was walking a tightrope, and she knew it. She really had nothing to use as leverage. He paused for an instant, then smiled at her lustfully.

"Very well," he laughed, "we'll make another bargain."

Oh God, she thought, this better be good. I can't afford to screw it up.

"What kind of bargain?"

"I'll agree to the marriage taking place in the chapel, if you promise you'll be totally obedient to my every desire on our wedding night. I don't want to fight over what's my right," he said, raking his eyes lustfully over her small frame.

She almost got sick, there and then. The idea of vomiting in his face was even quite appealing at the moment. It was all she could do to keep up the charade, and play her part. Please Kieron, come soon, she silently prayed.

"Of course I will," she lied. "If you play your part, then you can be assured I will play mine, perfectly."

Merlin grinned in satisfaction. "Very well, let us proceed."

Sam could feel panic fill her chest, threatening to choke her. It wasn't time yet! No one would be there, and there still was no priest. It was becoming crystal clear that Sam would do this alone.

Where was Dermott MacClaire? He'd sworn to be at her side at this minute. She knew in her heart, he wouldn't forsake her. She had to hope for the best, and trust in him.

"I haven't had time to change, and my face is a mess," she pleaded for time.

"It's fine," he said coldly. She hated him fiercely, and it only helped to strengthen her resolve.

Go ahead Sam, give him what he truly deserves, a voice whispered in her mind. Katie? She thought, recalling her words. Yes, I will, she smiled confidently, as she prepared herself for what she was about to do.

21st century

Brianna thought about her date with Sean. She would enjoy the evening, she told herself. He was a perfect hunk, one that any girl would jump at. Polite and handsome, yet something was wrong. There was something missing, but she couldn't figure out what it was. "What's wrong with me?"

They spoke on the phone earlier, deciding on where to go for dinner that evening.

"How about Italian?" he asked cheerfully.

"Sure, that's great."

"Good, I'll be over at six, if that's alright with you. I know you've had a trying day, and I don't want to rush you."

So sweet, she thought. She decided to give him a second chance, after all, he was a great guy and just what she needed right now. Or was he?

After a quick shower, she opened her closet, deciding what to wear. She thumbed through her clothes absent mindedly, her thoughts far away.

Once again, that gorgeous face came into her mind. Who is he, she wondered, and why do I keep seeing him? I could sure go for a stay at home date with him, she smiled wickedly. Just the thought itself made her body heat up.

Well, you'd better get over it girl, cause he's not coming to your door, she thought sadly.

Brianna slipped on the new pink dress she bought two days ago, and grabbed her heels. I really don't want to hurt him, she thought, checking her make up for the third time. I'll do my best.

Her thoughts went back to Sam, and what advice she'd give. Somehow, that made things even worse.

At six sharp, Sean was at her door. "Hi," he said cheerfully, "you look lovely."

Brianna was flattered, but felt anything but lovely. She had cried for an hour just after arriving home, and spent the next thirty minutes with wet tea bags over her eyes to help with the swelling and redness.

"Thank you," she replied politely, as she locked her front door on the way out. This was going to be an interesting evening.

17th century

Kieron knew where she'd be if all went according to their plan. "She'll try to persuade him to go to the chapel," he told Duncan.

"That is if she can get him to change his mind without too much of a struggle," Duncan reminded him.

"Don't worry, it's not over yet. Sam can be very persuasive if need be. I'm putting my faith in her. Remember, she wants him dead as much as we do."

They started down the passageway leading to the chapel. "We must be careful not to alert him. He's extremely sensitive to any life force, and I don't want to ruin her plan," Kieron cautioned.

They stopped abruptly. Kieron heard the sound of voices arguing. Sam was . . . . yelling at someone? He couldn't believe his ears, and quickly motioned for the others to stay quiet.

"There's someone else there," Niall whispered,

"Someone very powerful."

"We don't even have a priest yet!" she yelled. "How can we possibly get married?"

Just then, Kieron saw Dermott MacClaire, standing quietly in the shadows. He didn't say a word, but smiled in recognition.

"He's here!" Kieron whispered in excitement. "Somehow I knew he'd wouldn't fail her."

Even in the dark shadow of night, they could see the powerful glow from his body, something only seen by other angelic beings.

Niall grinned. "She hasn't seen him yet," he whispered, "but I'm very sure he has a mind-blowing plan for the dark sorcerer. After all, he's been a thorn in his side from day one."

"I said we could perform the ceremony here, "Merlin argued. "I didn't say we needed one of your so called priests. We'll say our own vows, just as we would in the circle of Brodgar," he growled. "I grow tired of this foolish game."

Merlin turned suddenly. "What have you done?" he growled, "this room has suddenly become unbearably warm." He began to survey the chapel for the source of heat. "What childish game are you playing now?"

Sam was at a loss for words, not being able to feel any change in temperature. "I don't know what you're talking about," she shot back. Kieron smiled at her defiance and bravery.

Then she saw them, her heart filled with hope. She knew not to draw attention to them, or Merlin would instantly whisk her away. Filled with a new determination, she continued the game.

"I feel no change in temperature," she told him sharply. "It must be in your mind."

From nowhere, a small fire started at his feet. He stamped it out angrily. "How did you do that?" he demanded.

She was stunned at the sight of the fire. She still hadn't seen her great ancestor lurking in the shadows, and had no clue what was happening.

"I have no idea what happened. You're the famed wizard, you figure it out!" she said with contempt. He flicked his wrist, and the fire ceased.

"Arrogant bitch!" he hissed, then rose his hand to strike her. Instead of striking Sam, his arm suddenly froze in midair. He cursed and swore a million oaths, but it remained in place.

Sam began to laugh, she had no clue what was happening, but was unable to repress her laughter.

"Having a small problem?" she smirked, as Kieron tried his best not to roar in hysterics. A second later, his arm was once again free.

Merlin shot her a look of absolute contempt. "You will pay dearly for that move."

Not if I can help it, she thought. She remembered all the times they'd rehearsed this scene. She would not fail.

Sam took his cold hand, shivered, and led him up to the altar. "Just say whatever sounds right to you," she encouraged, almost gagging at the thought.

"Good," he sneered as he looked at the burning votive candles. "I never did believe in your God."

I'm counting on him, Sam thought. She prayed for forgiveness from that same God, silently asking him for his help with what she was about to do.

"I insist we say them in old Gaelic," he told her.

"I don't know Gaelic, so that's impossible," she shot back. She really couldn't care less what language he wanted, she just wanted to get on with it. Afraid to even glance Kieron's way, she continued the charade

Sam wanted to kill him then and there, but knew the importance of timing. She could feel the coolness of her father's dagger against her heart, giving her needed courage. Any minute now . . .

"Hurry up!" he snapped. "This is your game. Say whatever the hell you want to, then we'll be done with this waste of time," he mocked. "And make sure you mean it."

Sam smiled cruelly. "Of course I'll mean it . . . every word. Then I'll be all yours, and will never utter Kieron's name again."

The chapel was dimly lit. Just three torches burned on the walls, with several red glass votive candles at the foot of the main altar.

She was so close now, and wanted to be sure he didn't change his mind, and drag her away to the Stones which he valued so highly.

Merlin started to speak, words she didn't understand. How ridiculous, she thought. He could be saying anything. Why do I even care? Suddenly he stopped, and turned to look at her. "It's your turn," he told her with an icy stare.

Please God, guide me through this, she thought as she took a deep breath. She turned to face the altar. Her hands were shaking, and her mouth was suddenly very dry.

Kieron and the others waited in the dark hall, anticipating the next move. Good girl, you're almost there, he thought nervously. They stood silently, awaiting Dermott's move.

Sam began, trying desperately to keep her voice even and strong. A quick glance at Kieron earned her a warm, encouraging smile. His pride in her was evident.

"I, Samantha McKinley, do promise to do what's right for you at all times."

"And you will do whatever I ask," he added, smugly.

Kieron burned with a hatred he didn't know he possessed. You're doing fine Sam, he thought, we're almost there. Somehow she sensed his strength and support.

"Yes," she said with firm conviction. "I will most definitely do whatever's good for you, most of all, this . . . ." In a flash of movement, she reached into the bodice of her gown, pulling out Duncan's silver dirk, and aimed it at his heart, when the dirk suddenly flew across the room, hitting the stone wall.

"I had a feeling you'd try something like that," he sneered.

Her heart sank, it was over, and she had lost her only chance to kill this timeless evil.

"Now we go to Brodgar, and do it right."

CHAPTER THIRTY ONE

"I think not," a deep voice came from the shadows, clearly taking the sorcerer by surprise.

Merlin spun around. "Who's there?" he said, suddenly aware of an immense threat.

Dermott stepped from the shadows, into the light. His body shining with the light of a thousand suns.

"Tis I, Dermott MacClaire, come to settle this matter once and for all."

The sorcerer's mouth dropped, as he once again gazed at this powerful angel. "MacClaire," he said in shock. "I thought you were gone ages ago."

Dermott smiled cruelly. "No, evil one. Just awaiting my day to reclaim what's rightfully mine."

Merlin sneered. "You will *never* claim this castle for your own. I will join with this woman, and the castle will become rightfully mine at last."

"Wrong," Dermott said coolly, "she will never be yours. She's married to one of my own, and that can never be changed, in all eternity."

"He no longer wants her," Merlin smiled smugly. "He freely released her from any marriage bonds, and gave her to me."

"Never!" another booming voice rang out, as Kieron stepped from the shadows. "I'll kill you myself before that happens."

"And if I choose to take her to Brodgar right now, you can't stop me."

"But you cannot," Dermott smiled, "my powers are far superior to yours."

Merlin tried to seize Sam, but was immediately stopped from behind by a dirk pushed firmly against his throat. "Give me a reason," Niall said coolly.

"Seems you aren't too well liked around here," Dermott chuckled. "How could you possibly want to claim a castle where the inhabitants hate you so?"

Merlin laughed. "They can be trained, taught submission."

"I doubt that very much," Dermott grinned. "Angels are quite fussy about who they like, and they're not very good at submission."

At that second, the dirk Sam held was lifted off the floor, and appeared in the air before her. "You know what to do, lass," Dermott told her with a smile.

Sam was ready, she needed no further encouragement. She grasped the dirk from midair, holding it firmly in her small hand. A look of sheer terror covered the sorcerer's face.

Dermott winked at her. "Go ahead and recite your wedding vows."

With a smile that lit up her entire face, she began. "I, Samantha MacClaire, do hereby pronounce my everlasting union to the angel Kieron, as long as God lets me live." She drew back her fist, and thrust the dagger deep into Merlin's black heart.

"Bitch!" he hissed viciously. "Did you think it would be that easy?", then pulled the dirk from his heart.

"Actually, I didn't," Dermott laughed, holding the sparkling amulet in his hand. I just wanted a little drama before I finished you off, once and for all. I happen to have this little trinket that will finish the job nicely. Step aside, lass."

She quickly moved away. Merlin's face filled with horror seeing the pulsating treasure. "It doesn't end here," he said, letting out a chilling laugh.

"I think it does," Dermott mocked. He lifted his hand, and pointed the jewel at Merlin.

A burst of radiant light, brighter than the sun, shot across the room, knocking the sorcerer to the ground. They watched as he burst into flames, shrieking loudly. A strong force sent the glass encased votive candles flying everywhere. They crashed as they flew across the room, and landed on the stone floor, sending small pieces of glass everywhere.

Kieron and the others were at her side immediately, shielding her face from the flying glass, and pulling her from the evolving danger.

"Keep her free of his life force!" Dermott yelled, as they watched dark energy explode everywhere inside the chapel.

Kieron grabbed her, dragging her to the far side of the chapel. Suddenly, a beam of pure black energy burst from Merlin's body, as he immediately decomposed on the hallowed stone floor.

A suffocating stench spread throughout the room, forcing Sam to cover her nose and mouth. The force of the energy shot upward through the air, blowing a hole in the chapel's roof.

Large wooden ceiling beams cracked and fell to the ground, as they were violently torn from the roof. They could see a dark vortex open in the sky immediately above, and Sam felt a foreboding sense of despair and hopelessness as she looked into it.

With a loud sucking sound, it absorbed every speck of black energy, until it was totally gone. Kieron tried to cover her eyes from the awful scene, but she refused to hide. "I want to see the end for myself," she told him firmly, drinking up each second of the morbid sight. After the vortex closed, the small group stood silent for several seconds.

A swarm of angels appeared from nowhere, covering the vortex, as if to close it for eternity. They swirled through the sky, graceful feathered wings completely covering where the vortex existed. Dermot smiled in satisfaction, as the angels stopped midair, bowing slightly in his direction.

"It's over Sam," Kieron whispered.

"I don't think we'll be seeing him again," Duncan smiled down at his daughter. "You did what you set out to, and I'm so proud of you." He pulled her from Kieron's arms, and kissed her tenderly.

"So am I," Dermott said, hugging her and holding her close. "We did it, lass, just as we planned."

"That'll teach him," Niall grinned, hugging her tightly.

She was strong and selfless, and just ended the curse which hovered over the majestic castle for over 500 years. Her castle now, and forever.

They stood there together, silently watching the destruction of the darkest sorcerer in history. Kieron held Sam tightly, half afraid to let her go. Just the very thought of how close he'd come to losing her forever was like a knife in his own heart.

"I think we should leave this place, at least for now," Niall suggested, as he looked around the battle strewn chapel. Something was wrong. There was still a slight trace of black smoke, lingering in the air in front of the center altar. He eyed it cautiously.

"I believe you're right about that," Dermott said as he surveyed the room for any further dangers.

A quiet evening breeze coming through the gaping hole, silently blew the remaining black ashes across the chapel's floor. The nauseating smell of burnt flesh permeated the air, as Sam covered her nose with Kieron's handkerchief.

She looked up through the hole in the ceiling, as if thinking of something. "Sam?" Kieron smiled, watching her stare into the sky.

"So that's what happened to it," she said, as if suddenly fitting a puzzle together.

"That's how what happened?"

"The roof," she grinned. "I always wondered what happened to the top of this chapel, when I first saw it in my century."

Niall laughed as he studied the gapping, jagged hole. "Well, it could have been worse," he joked. "At least we still have the walls.

"Perhaps it's best if you take her out from this place now," Dermott told Kieron, eyeing a trace of residue smoke. His tone left no room for arguments.

Niall took a few steps and carefully picked up the silver dirk from the floor where it landed.

"I believe this is yours," he told Duncan.

Duncan wiped it clean with an old cloth, and started to put it into his boot, when Dermott stopped him. "I'd be careful with that blade," he said, "You might want to wash it well before putting it close to your skin."

"Aye," Kieron added, "and I think a few spells wouldn't hurt either. You may want to burn that cloth too." Duncan caught his grave expression, this was no joke.

"You take Sam and Duncan back to the Hall, I feel it's best to give this space a few Celtic blessings, just to be sure," Dermott said, as he suspiciously eyed the trace of smoke which seemed reluctant to be blown away with the breeze.

He turned to Niall. "Are you up to it?" he grinned.

His expression was filled with meaning, and Sam began to wonder where all this could lead.

"Honored" Niall replied.

Sam clung tightly to Kieron's arm, as they turned back thru the passageway. "What's going on?" she asked him with a troubled look. "He's worried about something, I know it. And why is Dermott staying with him?"

"It's nothing Sam," Kieron reassured her. "You know Niall, he's your typical obsessive compulsive personality. Everything must be done to one hundred percent perfection. He's very thorough with this kind of thing. It's just the way he's wired," he joked, but Sam still had her doubts. He tightened his grip on her, and hoped she would eventually forget all this in time, without any permanent psychological scars.

Just as they reached the great hall, they heard Niall's thunderous yell. Kieron instantly pushed her into Duncan arms. "Get her out of here *now*, and don't leave her side for any reason, do you understand?"

Duncan nodded, grabbed his daughter, and hurried down the hallway.

"No, Kieron don't go!" she screamed frantically, but he was already gone.

Katie flew up to them, hugging her daughter tightly. "Sam!" she cried, "Are you alright?" An ocean of tears poured down Sam's face.

Katie looked up at her daughter. "It's over Sam," she whispered soothingly.

Sam looked up at her mother, "Kieron went back to help Niall and Dermott," she sobbed in anguish.

"Help them what?" Katie asked, glancing at her husband.

Just as Duncan started to explain, a loud blast came from the north end of the castle, exactly where the chapel was located.

Duncan stood up, ready to bolt, but then remembered his promise. He sat down, with Sam tightly wedged between he and his wife. He knew Dermott's strength, and that Kieron would never leave a brother warrior, no matter what.

Several guards tore out of the hall toward the chapel. Duncan sat with an arm around both Katie and Sam, hugging them close, as he waited impatiently for some word.

After what seemed like an eternity, Hamus ran in, searching the hall for Duncan. His face was pale, and he was visibly shaken.

"Lord!" he cried, running toward their table.

"What is it, man? What's happened?" Duncan roared as he stood up.

"It's the chapel, it's *gone*!"

CHAPTER THIRTY TWO

21st Century

Sean opened the passenger door for Brianna, then got into the driver's seat of his Jeep. After making sure the seat belts were secure, he started the engine and they took off down the street, onto the busy highway.

"Nice car Sean," she said, trying to create some conversation.

"Thanks, "he smiled. "I made reservations at Angelo's," he told her, as he pulled off the busy main drag and onto a smaller side street. It was a very popular Italian Restaurant, which maintained a strict reservation only policy.

He turned his Jeep into the back parking lot, and managed to find an empty spot.

"Thank goodness we weren't five minutes later," he smiled, as he backed the Jeep in. They walked in the front door, and were greeted by the friendly maître d'.

"Right this way, Mr. Elliott," he said politely, as he led them through the busy dining room to a cozy table.

"Is this okay?" Sean asked politely, pulling out the chair.

"It's perfect," Brianna told him. She admired the lovely curtains, and romantic glowing candles. A small vase of fresh roses graced each table, adding to the romantic feel of the restaurant. What a perfect spot to unwind!

Another waiter brought them menus. Sean selected Chianti from the wine list. As he was handing the list back to the waiter, she noticed his left palm. It had the very same mark of the sun that Kieron and the professor had. That's way too much of a coincidence, she thought. Was she hallucinating from fatigue? She stared at him, unable to think of anything to say.

"Is there something wrong, lass?" he asked, seeing her sudden change.

Brianna looked him in the eye. "You're a Keeper."

He smiled at her inquisitive nature. "Aye, I tried to keep it hidden last time. Very good, Brianna. I didn't think you'd notice that quickly. Niall and Kieron have done an excellent job," he smiled.

Her mouth dropped at the mention of their names. "How do you know about them?"

"Don't be afraid," he said, skirting around the question. "I've come on behalf of a very dear friend, who is quite concerned about you right now." His eyes were filled with deep compassion, and she knew he was telling the truth.

"A friend? What are you talking about Sean?" she asked suspiciously. He raised his glass, sampling the wine.

"I hope you're not upset with me, put I figured this may be the only way to get your attention for the evening," he said with a guilty grin.

"Well you've sure got it now," she answered. "So please tell me what the heck is going on, and who you're talking about."

Her temper was starting to boil. Sean grinned, handing her a glass of wine. "Okay Brianna, have a drink," he said,

"And promise to let me explain everything before you start shooting questions."

She nodded, picking up her glass and quickly gulped down several mouthfuls.

"Easy lass," he laughed.

"Don't worry about me," she said emptying her glass, "I can drink you under the table."

Sean burst into laughter, appreciating her frankness. "Aye," he smiled, refilling her glass. "I've no doubt of that."

Brianna started to laugh.

"That's more like it," he said, flashing his brilliant smile. She was pleasantly relaxed now, thanks to two glasses of Chianti. The waiter left, leaving them to talk.

"Okay Sean, let's hear it," she smiled, in a flirtatious manner.

I must remember she belongs to my dear friend, he quickly told himself.

"Well, now you know who I am," he started, testing the waters.

"I guess I finally do."

"One of our dearest mutual friends has been very worried about you, here alone since he and the others traveled back to the 17th century."

She was speechless. "You know about that, too?" she asked.

He shot her a sexy grin. "Aye, Brianna, I know. I also know that they miss you terribly, especially Sam, who has just gone through a most trying experience."

She put her glass down immediately. "Is that what happened to me the other night? I knew something terrible was happening, when I saw her bound and gagged somewhere full of sand and water."

"But she is no longer there," he explained with bright intelligent eyes. "They're safe now, free from the curse."

"She did it!" Brianna yelled out, attracting the attention of almost every person in the restaurant.

"Shh," he grinned, "do you want them to throw us out?"

She stopped immediately, trying to control her enthusiasm. "You can *see* what they're doing?"

"Not just see them, I can go there and speak with them, much the same as I'm talking with you right now."

Is he crazy, she began to wonder? She looked down at her empty glass. "There's a problem, isn't there. That's why you brought me here. Okay, out with it, Sean."

Silence.

Her heart instantly filled with dread. "You came to tell me they're not coming back, didn't you."

He looked into her troubled eyes. "No, Brianna, they're not."

Her heart shattered into a million pieces. She wanted to die, right then and there.

"But wait, there's more." He reached across the table and took her hand. "Please don't cry so, I was never very good with crying women," he joked, trying to lighten her mood.

She grabbed the napkin and dabbed at her eyes. "What else could there possibly be, they've left me here all alone, and promised they wouldn't, *he* promised."

Sean squeezed her hand reassuringly. "That's exactly why I brought you here. They want you there with them."

Her head flew up immediately. "What? What did you just say?"

"Aye lass, they miss you terribly, but in the time they've spent there, they've made a collective decision to stay."

"All of them?" she hesitated, recalling his promise to her. A terrible loneliness began to fill her soul. They left her, her worst fear had come true.

She looked at Sean with complete and total heartbreak. "Well, I guess I can understand, after all, she has Kieron there with her."

"It's not just Kieron, it's her whole family, your family too."

She looked over at him like her grew another head. "*My family?* How is it my family Sean, that's ridiculous?"

"No Brianna, it's not."

Her face paled, as she tried to make some sense of the conversation. The waiter came and quickly took their orders, then returned to the kitchen. Tonight, Angelo's was busier than usual.

"I don't understand what you're telling me, and it's beginning to scare me."

He took both her hands in his. "I'm not trying to scare you lass, just tell you the truth. You are Samantha's sister."

"What? That's impossible," she said, beginning to pale. "I just met her a few months ago. She's from America, quite far from where I was born."

"That's correct," he said with a gentle smile. "Sometimes the Highest Power works in strange ways, understood only to himself. We aren't to question how it will be when he feels a soul, or in this case two souls, are ready to return for another incarnation. That handsome face you've been seeing?" he chuckled, "that's no other than your loving professor, one of my warrior brothers."

"Now I know you're crazy! That's completely impossible Sean, how could you even say that? That man has to be at least seventy, and I've known him all my life."

"Exactly," Sean laughed out loud. "Oh, he would be flattered. I think you should add another 10,000 years at least. That's been Niall's disguise of choice while he's been in Edinburgh. Don't kid yourself. He's an immortal, Brianna, like the rest of us, and he's waiting for you, right now as we speak."

She was completely and totally taken off guard. "I can't believe all this. Are you sure you aren't lying to me?"

He looked down at her, eyes shining. "I'm bound by the oath I took as a Keeper of the Light, and am incapable of telling a lie."

"Like Kieron?"

"Aye lass, the very same thing."

"Was that really the professor?" she asked anxiously, beginning to focus on the breathtaking thought.

Sean laughed, "Of course, that's the real Niall. Do you think he fits the bill?"

"Oh God, does he ever! He's just gorgeous!"

Brianna realized what she just said, and was ashamed. "That was rude of me, I should know better. I never meant to hurt you," she told him with heartfelt sadness. He only laughed even harder.

"He is my brother, Brianna, and you are his soul mate. He told Kieron and I last night, when we met together in a place outside your time. He's been granted a special wish, so to speak, by someone very special. Niall wants you there with him, and asked me to talk to you, since he is unable to return at this time. That's why I contacted you to begin with."

She felt relieved already.

"What is your answer, lass?"

She gave him a dazzling smile. "When do we leave!" she blurted out, her eyes aglow with happiness at last.

The waiter rolled their dinner over on a serving cart. "Bring the food back," she instructed the baffled waiter, "we're leaving."

She grabbed her bag and stood up, ready to walk. The man looked at her, clearly stunned, then turned to Sean.

"Is there something wrong, sir?" he asked nervously.

"No, everything's fine," he told him reassuringly. "We just realized we have somewhere to go."

"Here," he said, handing him several bills. "Sorry about the inconvenience, have a nice evening." They turned, and hurried out.

"Is there anything you'd like to do before we leave?" he asked, as he maneuvered the Jeep through the evening traffic.

"No, I'm ready right now, just as I am," she grinned.

"Are you sure?" he persisted. "What about your job, and the lawyers? Should you tell them?"

She was touched by his concern. "No, serves them right," she said, with a definite gleam in her eyes. "Let them try to figure it out themselves, after all, they're the brainy ones."

Sean smiled in admiration. "Lucky Niall," he said, as he shot her a sexy grin.

"What about you?" she asked, as they drove along the highway. "Is there someone special in your life?"

"Funny you should ask," he grinned. "I've been at Rosestone quite a bit lately, talking with Duncan and Angus before Sam arrived. I spotted a cute little maid who seems to have captured my heart."

"Oh Sean!" she yelled, "I'm so glad for you. Does she know you're interested?"

"I'm not sure yet. I've been pretty busy lately, you know, 'on assignment' so to speak. But when we return, I'll make very sure she understands my intentions," he grinned.

"She's a very lucky lady," Brianna said, as she took a good look at him. He was sweetness and bravery, all tossed into one charming man. She was sure that whoever this young woman was, she would be very happy with such a fine catch. She smiled even more, remembering the sexy face of her own personal warrior, patiently awaiting her. Could she be any luckier? One more obstacle to conquer, and all would be fine . . . the time vortex.

"There's one last stop I can't forget to make before we return, or I'll be dead meat!"

She gave him a surprised look, with no clue of what he meant.

"Luthias," he told her with a huge grin. "I can't forget to pick him up, he's chosen to return with us."

"We're bringing back a cat, through the vortex?" she asked nervously. "Can that be done?"

"No," he told her, "we're bringing back a man. Niall wanted to know if he wished to return with us, now that all of us will be back in the 17th century."

She looked at him with a huge grin, "And you've already asked him?"

"Certainly, before I picked you up. He's bringing a few texts from Kieron's library with him."

They drove to Kieron's house, parking the Jeep in the driveway. Brianna thought the house looked lonely and sad, until she saw Luthias step out the front door, texts in hand, and emerald eyes fixed directly on her.

"Greetings," he said, with a huge grin. As usual he wore no shirt or shoes, just jeans hugging his hips, lower than needed.

"Are you ready, brother?" Sean laughed, as he opened the door, letting Luthias hop in the back seat.

As they drove off headed for the castle, she turned to speak to him.

"Traveling light today," she said, implying his lack of clothing. Black hair hung to his trim waist, his eyes glowing seductively. He stared back at her in the most unnerving way, almost controlling her mind.

"Are you a Keeper, too?" she asked innocently, suddenly finding herself unable to think straight.

"Heavens No!" Sean's laughter rang out from the front seat. "We Keepers must take a strict Oath of Truth and Purity."

"I am no Keeper," Luthias purred as he looked into her eyes. "My art is one of pure seduction," he boasted.

Brianna instantly turned scarlet, and looked away.

Sean was enjoying a second bout of laughter, as he drove up the road to the castle. "Just be careful who you practice this art with," he warned. "I doubt Kieron or Niall have any intentions of sharing."

"You are a very beautiful woman," she heard him tell her softly, almost a whisper, beckoning her to face him again. She was instantly on fire, erotic chills running down her spine. What was happening to her?

"I could teach you a thousand things about your body you never knew," he continued in that odd, sexy accent. She dare not even look at his beautiful face, but instead decided to concentrate on Niall, her soul mate, who was waiting for her.

"If you should tire of your soul mate . . . be sure that I can satisfy your most intimate desires."

Would he ever shut up? She was doing her best to forget that he was sitting back there, but it was useless. There was something very different about him, he seemed to have control over her thoughts. She blushed at the scope of erotic ideas suddenly flashing through her mind.

Sean intervened, "Luthias, there will be many beautiful young women at Rosestone. I'm sure you'll find the right one," he told him, coming to her rescue.

"Indeed," came that sexy accent again, "and I will have them all," he smiled with a hefty degree of self-confidence.

"Will you stay at Rosestone?" she asked Sean, trying desperately to ignore that heat coming from the back seat.

He pulled onto the dirt road, passing all of the parked machinery. "Aye, I believe my time here in your century is over. I want to be with my brothers once again."

He pulled the Jeep up to the north wall, and parked it. "Too bad I have no one to leave the car to," he joked. He placed the keys on the driver's seat after they all climbed out, and closed the door. "I'm sure the police will have it by tomorrow."

They walked to the spot where the others disappeared, Luthias at her side, sending her molten hot glances with those gorgeous emerald green eyes.

"Are you sure about all this?" Sean asked casually. "It'll be a big change, you know."

She rolled her eyes, then laughed. "If there's one thing I really need, it's a big change," she said, avoiding Luthias altogether.

Sean led them around the corner. She could hear the sea crashing on the cliffs below.

"This isn't the spot they left from," she noted, looking where they were now standing.

"I know," he said reassuringly, "but that's not the only way to open the vortex. Kieron used it because it's easier at noon, but this will work just as well, even without the strength of the sun. Are you ready?" he asked as he took her hand.

Brianna nodded. She had never been more ready for anything in her young life. Luthias took her other hand in a strong grasp, and she prayed the vortex would soon open.

"It's your last time to change your mind," he grinned.

"I want this, Sean, with all my heart. Do you think he'll know we're coming?" she asked nervously.

"He awaits you," Luthias told her smoothly, silky black hair blowing in the night breeze. God! He was gorgeous!

Sean roared in laughter. "Most definitely! If I know Niall, he'll be standing there waiting for us, and you best not be holding his hand when we arrive," he teased, looking over at Luthias.

Brianna's heart pounded in her chest, her fears vanishing at the thought of Niall waiting for her, her own warrior.

"Hold onto my hand tightly, and don't let go, no matter what," he instructed. She nodded obediently, as he began to chant.

Suddenly, a loud crack was heard directly above them, then a sizzling sound, like electricity. Brianna saw the bright vortex once again appear directly above them. It slowly began to crackle and swirl, then opened. The next second they were gone.

CHAPTER THIRTY THREE

17th century

Smack! Brianna landed on her back, in the lush green grass of the southwestern side of the castle. Luthias was on the ground close beside her, with a very promiscuous grin. It took her a few seconds to catch her breath, then attempt to sit up, deliberately ignoring him. Her hands and feet tingled a bit, but she otherwise felt great. Well, that wasn't as bad as I had expected, she thought.

"At least you got within good range," she heard a deep male voice laugh.

"Aye, much better than the tree Kieron told me you landed in," Sean's voice teased.

"Up with you Luthias, this one is mine!" the same voice told him. Luthias automatically jumped to his feet, giving Niall a huge hug. "Your woman is beautiful" he told him.

Brianna sat up slowly, only to find her handsome warrior at her side, welcoming her in a strong embrace.

"You have that correct Luthias, *my* woman."

"Careful Niall," Sean joked, "you'll kill her with those arms!"

"Professor?" she said, once he let her breathe again.

"No lass, the professor is gone forever. I am Niall, your intended husband, and soul mate," he told her lovingly. "That is, if you'll have me."

Brianna thought her heart would burst from happiness.

"Absolutely!" she managed to say, while being crushed by rock hard biceps. "The sooner the better!"

He smiled down at her, blue eyes filled with love.

"Welcome home Brianna," he said as he released her. "I've missed you." Tears of joy ran down her face, as Niall brushed them aside with his hand.

Sean watched with pride. Another warrior brother soon to be married off, he thought proudly.

Niall turned to him, face aglow. "Thank you for bringing her safely home to me." He held Brianna tightly in his arms once more, and listened to Sean explain what had been happening in the 21st century.

"We'd better hurry back. If I know Kieron and Sam, they're waiting anxiously," Niall told them, as he helped to steady the somewhat shaky Brianna.

"I can always carry you," he offered with a sly smile. She looked up into his ruggedly handsome face. One day's growth of beard, firm jaw line, beautiful blue eyes. His long golden brown hair hung almost to his waist, and she stared at the gleaming golden armband on his left bicep.

"Look familiar?" he asked her softly, as he kissed her neck. For some crazy reason it did seem remotely familiar, but Niall said no more, just held her tightly. He was beautiful, and so gentle. Never in her young life did she ever expect to win such a prize.

"I think I'll be okay, once I take a few steps," she smiled confidently.

"Oh Please!" Sean kidded, "If you pick her up, we'll never see her for the rest of the day!" he laughed, turning toward the castle.

It was then he noticed the gaping hole where the chapel had once stood.

"What the hell happened, Niall?"

"A slight misunderstanding," Niall smirked.

"I'll say, what started it?" Sean asked, still amazed at the huge hole.

"Oh you missed the good part. Kieron and I watched as Sam and Dermott put an end to the sorcerer. They were magnificent!"

"She killed him by herself?" Brianna asked in awe.

"Aye, with the help of her great grandfather," Niall smiled.

Sean looked over at him like he was truly nuts. "Great grandfather?"

"Aye, Dermott MacClaire"

Sean stopped dead, as if he'd seen a ghost. "You mean the original?"

"The very same. He's awaiting our return now, so we best hurry."

"How is that possible, he's been dead for over six hundred years?"

"A long story," Niall laughed, "I'll bring you up to speed later."

"Why didn't he come here with you? Sean asked.

"He's glued to Sam's hip," Niall laughed, "never leaves her side. He's very protective."

"I bet Kieron loves that," he chuckled.

"Actually, he's quite proud. We watched cautiously from the far side of the chapel, as Sam and the sorcerer began to recite their vows."

Brianna looked at him, shock in her eyes. "Vows!" she gasped.

"But she knew what she was doing. At the exact moment she was to pledge her undying love to the demon, she pulled out her father's dirk, and gave him that instead," he boasted proudly. "Then Dermott took over. It was great! A majestic scene, only one problem, he refused to leave."

Sean started to grin . . . "This should be interesting."

"That it was. Kieron quickly led Sam and her father out of the chapel, free from harm's way. I stayed behind with Dermott, eyeing a suspicious dark trace of life form, which continued to hover in the air. We had a hunch, and it proved correct."

"So you had to show him the way out, so to speak," Sean grinned.

"Aye, but he wasn't seeing things my way, so I was forced to blast him back to his own kind the hard way, by blowing up the chapel."

Sean fell to the grass roaring with laughter. "That was perfect!" he howled.

"Are you guys always so dramatic?" Brianna asked, as she watched the other two roar in laughter. Luthias actually joined in, quite proud of their actions.

"Sometimes," Sean grinned, "it's more fun that way." He put his hand on Niall's broad shoulder, "Excellent move," he smiled proudly, "let the demons that hate him decide what to do with him now."

They hugged each other again, then all four headed off toward the castle and their future, Niall's arm firmly wrapped around his future bride.

That evening was a feast which was rivaled by none other in recorded history. Rosestone was once again alive and thriving.

A noble family, once destroyed by a dark curse and separated by time, was finally reunited. Happiness and joy now resided where there was once only grieving parents. Given the chance, no one ever wanted to return to the future, if possible. They were all too happy where they were, where they belonged.

Luthias had the time of his life, being introduced to every woman in Rosestone, by none other than Kieron. He was quite anxious to get him involved with as many eligible young women as possible, and away from Sam.

The years that followed were happy ones. The MacClaire Clan grew with new members, and the castle itself prospered. Now, each morning Samantha and Brianna wake to the melodious sound of angels singing. The beautiful sound fills the air three times a day, as Kieron, Niall, Sean, and of course Dermott enjoy what had been taken from them so long ago . . . *Rosestone Castle.*

The end, of the beginning.

EPILOGUE

The following days were happy ones for the members of the MacClaire Clan.

Dermott MacClaire decided to stay in his castle, to watch and protect this new generation, and offer guidance.

Brianna and Niall quickly married in a grand ceremony in Rosestone's lush gardens. She wanted no part of the new chapel which was now under construction.

Luthias pursued his calling, to entice and seduce every willing female living in or around the castle.

Sean Elliot quickly popped the question to Bridget, Katie's maid, and will be married soon.

And Sam and Kieron became proud parents of twin boys, Dermott and Cormac, who grew in strength and wisdom to continue the magical MacClaire legacy . . . . as something very evil watched intently from another dimension.

NOTE FROM THE AUTHOR

I do hope you've enjoyed Ancient Echoes. It's the first in a series of time travel adventures about this wonderful and unique family, the MacClaires. Please join them in the second of the series, Highland Guardian. I hope you enjoy that, as well.

I'd love to hear your thoughts or comments. Please contact me on my website, barbaramonahanbooks.com. I look forward to your feedback!

Printed in the USA
CPSIA information can be obtained
at www.ICGtesting.com
LVHW040923070424
776683LV00028B/162

9 781463 474331